HUNDREDS OF YEARS TO REFORM A RAKE

*His touch
pulled her
irresistibly
across
the mists
of time*

LAURIE BROWN

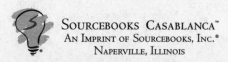

SOURCEBOOKS CASABLANCA™
AN IMPRINT OF SOURCEBOOKS, INC.®
NAPERVILLE, ILLINOIS

Published by Sourcebooks Casablanca, an imprint of Sourcebooks, Inc.
P.O. Box 4410, Naperville, Illinois 60567-4410
(630) 961-3900
FAX: (630) 961-2168
www.sourcebooks.com
ISBN-13: 978-1-4022-1013-6
ISBN-10: 1-4022-1013-2

Library of Congress Cataloging-in-Publication Data

Brown, Laurie
  Hundreds of Years to Reform a Rake / Laurie Brown.
    p. cm.
  ISBN-13: 978-1-4022-1013-6
  ISBN-10: 1-4022-1013-2
  1. Parapsychologists—Fiction. 2. Time travel—Fiction. 3. Ghosts—
Fiction. I. Title.

PS3602.R72227H86 2007
813'.6—dc22
                                                    2007025429

Printed and bound in Canada
WC 10   9   8   7   6   5   4   3   2   1

To my dear friend Mary Micheff,

Thank you for the tremendous gift of your help and encouragement, and most of all for your friendship. This book would not have been possible without you.

Acknowledgments

I owe a debt of gratitude to those who have helped in the process of writing this book. A special thank you goes out:

To editor Deb Werksman for choosing this manuscript, which is not the same old, same old romance.

To agent Lucienne Diver for believing in this story and in my writing.

To my friends: Mary Micheff for helping with everything, Jeanne Anderson for generously reading pages and offering invaluable input, Martha Powers and Debbie Macomber for sharing expertise, advice, and a whole lot of laughs during the Shop and Plot Weekend.

To all of my coworkers at the Poplar Creek Public Library District, especially Patricia Hogan, Darly Doyle, and Sue Haisan, for being understanding and supportive.

To the fabulous writers of the Chicago-North Chapter of RWA for unfailing enthusiasm and insightful critiques.

And last, but definitely not least, to my family: Jared, his wife Laurie, and the kids for arranging visits around a crazy writing schedule; Adam for pitching in; and to my husband Brit, who is my real life hero and the wind beneath my wings.

One

NO EVIDENCE OF PARANORMAL ACTIVITY. Josie Drummond keyed the final notes on her Castle Waite investigation into her computer. She wished things had been different. Poor Ms. Thornton had been so positive Josie would certify the existence of a ghost. *Discontinued monitors at,* she glanced at her watch, *three twenty-five.*

As her hand touched the off switch, the sound monitor sputtered to life with a burst of static. Hopes rising, she turned up the volume instead. Two of the maids chatted as they entered the great hall. Again Josie reached to turn the monitor off but hesitated when she heard her own name mentioned.

"Miss Drummond is leaving after tea?"

Josie checked her voice printout and identified Emma, a recently hired maid.

"And it should have been sooner, to my mind. With that ghostbuster still here, we'll have to set for three." Vivian's whining voice was easily recognizable.

Josie hated the term *ghostbuster*. To those who

took her work seriously, she was a paranormal researcher. But eavesdroppers should expect to hear nothing good about themselves. This wasn't the first time she'd been called that name, or worse.

"Being as it's Thursday, we'll have to drag everything into the library," Vivian continued. "Never mind that it's extra work for me. No one ever thinks of that."

"I thought the swells always took tea in their drawing rooms. Three? Is someone else coming?"

"Mind you, I'm not one to gossip, but I might as well be the one to tell you. Amelia Thornton is crazy as a loon. Every Thursday, she entertains the ghost of Deverell Thornton, and *she* says Lord Waite prefers *his* tea in the library."

"You mean him?" Emma squeaked.

Josie pictured the plump maid pointing to the life-sized portrait that scowled down from the landing of the grand stairway. He was posed casually despite his formal evening clothes; one elbow on the mantle, a nearly empty brandy snifter close by, and a thin cigar dangling from his long elegant fingers. His snowy neckwear was tied in an elaborate knot as if he were about to leave for dinner at his club or for a romantic assignation at the opera. Yet his gray eyes held no merriment or anticipation. His gaze seemed to mock the pretense of posing, to challenge the artist to be unflattering, to dare the observer to look into his tainted soul. A shiver shook Josie's shoulders, an echo of the jolt that had ricocheted down her spine at her first confrontation with his saturnine countenance.

"The ninth Lord Waite, famous for his wicked parties and his lavish generosity to his mistresses, had been killed in a duel after thirty-seven years of debauched living," Vivian said, her tone that of a tour guide. "There are those..." she continued, her voice dropping to a conspiratorial whisper, "who claim to have seen his ghost riding to the hounds or striding through the gallery."

"Really?" Emma whispered, her tone revealing rapt attention.

Josie turned up the volume another notch. She hoped for details of a recent sighting, names, dates. Maybe the servants knew more than they'd been willing to share with an outsider.

"I say crazy Amelia is in the library alone," Vivian said in a superior tone. "Everyone knows a ghost doesn't take tea."

The women moved out of range. Josie had set up monitors only where sightings of the ghost had been reported: the great hall, the library, the drawing room, and the gallery. Listening to conversations was her least favorite part of the job. Next year, if she got the Burkes-Sheetz Grant for Scientific Research, affectionately known as the BS Grant, she'd buy a new computer that filtered out identified voice patterns. For now, her company, Paranormal Certification, operated on a shoestring budget.

She unplugged the equipment, packed the instruments in their padded cases, and piled them by the door with her luggage. She'd pick up the monitors on her way out. Looking around to be sure she hadn't forgotten anything, she realized she'd miss the quaint blue and white bedroom with the old-fashioned poster bed, ruffled-skirted dressing table, and comfortable chaise next to the fireplace.

Finishing the Castle Waite job early left her with two unexpectedly free weeks. A call to her office in Chicago brought more unwelcome news. Her next appointment had canceled. Now with five vacant weeks, she really should visit her mother, but then she would have to listen to the *"your body clock is ticking"* speech. At age thirty, Josie didn't need reminders.

Since breaking up with Richard eleven months, three weeks, and four days ago, she'd totally immersed herself in her work. Maybe she'd paint her apartment as she'd been meaning to do for nearly a year. Or purchase some artwork for the still bare walls. Slipcover the old couch that came with the furnished space. One unappealing plan after another occupied her until teatime.

Josie dreaded the interview with Lady Amelia Thornton because she still hadn't come up with a gentle way to dash the hopes of the sweet, apple-cheeked woman who had made her so welcome in her ancestral home for the past three weeks. At precisely four o'clock Josie presented herself at the open library door. The afternoon sun sparkled through the leaded glass of the mullioned window, dispelling the gloom of the dark wood paneling and weighty books.

Her hostess motioned her to a Queen Anne chair covered in deep green damask and seated herself on the matching sofa. Amelia wore a light gray cashmere sweater with a single strand of pearls, an over-the-knee tweed skirt, and sensible shoes, the outfit that comprised the afternoon uniform of every country gentlewoman past the age of sixty.

"Beautiful day today for September," Lady Amelia said as she poured tea from a pot shaped like a country cottage. She handed Josie a delicate china cup decorated with pale pink rosebuds. "Did you get out to enjoy the weather?"

"No, I didn't." Josie breathed an inward sigh of relief, but her reprieve was short-lived.

"I hate to seem in a rush, but do you give me the certificate verifying our ghost now, or should I expect it in the post?"

"Actually, I..." Josie hesitated. Quite against her natural inclination to maintain a professional distance, she'd become fond of the eccentric older woman, even if her conversational leaps were sometimes difficult to follow.

Amelia added a dollop of cream to her cup and settled back into the overstuffed sofa with a wiggle of her shoulders. "I ran into Ruth Simms this morning at the Altar Committee meeting. I told you about her, didn't I? She owns Twixton Manor, across the river, and she said she's made enough money from her guests to put on an entire new roof."

Josie knew Amelia planned to open her home to tourists to bolster her sagging financial situation and pay for the much-needed repairs to the aging castle. "No, but..."

"Of course, her ghost plays the harpsichord. They say it's Mina Cracklebury. The Cracklebury girls were known to put themselves forward. No relation to the Simms who bought the manor in 1897; came up in trade you know, and the Crackleburys were long gone by then. Did I tell you this castle has been in my family since the first stone bailey was built in 1273?"

"Yes. That was in the history I requested." Amelia hadn't sent the usual dry report of building dates and styles, but a rollicking saga of knights and their ladies, intrepid explorers, and dashing heroes. That was probably one reason why Josie was disappointed at failing to find evidence. However, she wasn't one to put off unpleasant tasks in the hope they'd fade away. "About your ghost…"

"I can't imagine Deverell playing the pianoforte for guests. Why, I don't even know if he can play, but surely the ghost of an earl will have more draw than a baron's daughter. This would be so much easier if he were…well, accommodating is not a word I would use to describe him." Amelia paused to sip her tea. "I'm rather anxious to get started. That nice young man from the National Trust said the south wing needs immediate work to prevent a total collapse."

"I know this is important to you." Josie wished she'd found something, anything to substantiate a ghostly presence. "Unfortunately, I can't issue a certificate. I found no scientific evidence to support your claim. You have a delightful home. I'm sure guests will come."

"But I've seen the ghost, talked to him." Amelia blinked. Her tight gray curls bounced as she shook her head in denial.

"I'm sorry. I monitored nothing out of the ordinary."

"Maybe you looked in the wrong place at the wrong time. You could stay longer, try something else." Amelia leaned forward and touched Josie's arm as if the action would hold her there.

"I checked for sound, temperature, and air movement in every room you named." Josie's passive sensors even covered the full electromagnetic spectrum from infrared to gamma and x-rays. There was no ghost at Castle Waite. "I'm sorry."

Amelia looked away, but not before Josie noticed the glisten of tears.

Josie couldn't totally rob the woman of the small comfort her delusion seemed to give her. "Maybe he appears only to you." She knew it was a sop, but what harm would it do?

Amelia sniffed and straightened her shoulders. "That won't do me any good in the tourist market. One must have a gimmick to be successful on the scale I need to restore this castle."

Josie stood. She was trying to think of some consolation, some way to close the assignment on a positive note, when a sphere of opalescent light near the fireplace mantle caught her attention. Chimes tinkled as if a breeze teased unseen bells to life. The ball of mesmerizing light lengthened to a column within which tracings of bright blue electricity and ribbons of rainbows swirled and twisted around each other, faster and tighter. Goose bumps rose on Josie's arms.

A clap of sound as sharp as a gunshot startled her. Then the unearthly light coalesced into the figure of a tall handsome man. Dressed in a navy blue coat, snowy white shirt with a stand-up collar and elaborately knotted cravat, buff trousers, and knee-high black boots, he looked nearly as solid as if he'd walked through the door in the usual way. When he stepped forward, the last bit of the shimmering light clung to him like an aura.

She recognized the dark visage, black hair, and deep-seated gray eyes from his portrait. She recognized Deverell Thornton, ninth Earl of Waite, and ghost of the castle, before Amelia triumphantly introduced him.

Virile is the word that came to her mind, and she'd never used that term to describe a man before.

Josie's legs buckled, and she plopped back into her chair, her gaping mouth clacking shut. She'd built her career on the supernatural. She'd photographed misty apparitions and recorded eerie wailing with equal aplomb. But never had she confronted a fully materialized ghost. Could this really be happening? She shrank farther into the cushioned chair and stared at the oh-my-god, honest-to-goodness apparition.

Deverell was unperturbed by her rudeness. He'd meant the flash and flourish of his entrance to shock her, to impress her. After sitting in his favorite high-backed leather chair, he accepted a cup of tea and allowed Amelia to chastise him for not making himself known earlier so Josie's gadgets could detect him.

"Now we can proceed," Amelia said. "I think we should begin with an advertisement in the *Travel Times*. Tastefully done, of course." Her usual buoyant spirits apparently restored, she popped a tiny cucumber sandwich into her mouth.

"Tasteful advertisement is an oxymoron." Deverell set his cup on the table with deliberate care. "I fear you misunderstood my purpose in advising you to hire Miss Drummond."

Indeed, he had intended she should. The very idea of strangers tromping through his home, gawking at his belongings for the price of a night's lodging, was absurd. A member of his family reduced to the status of innkeeper; he shuddered at the thought.

Perhaps he was partly to blame. He should have noticed the deteriorating condition of the castle. However, financial matters were so tedious, and it wasn't his nature to worry about shillings and pence. Now the situation had reached a crisis, forcing drastic measures.

"I never intended for her to certify my existence," Deverell enunciated. He spoke to Amelia, but he did not want either woman to miss his meaning. "My apologies for misleading both of you as to my purpose, however I deemed the small ruse necessary. This family's finances began to decline after a gypsy seer fleeced my gullible mother by holding expensive séances in a futile attempt to recover a lost family treasure." He purposely left out the other reason his mother had paid the gypsy the bulk of her fortune.

"Your mother was quite avant-garde. Even though Swedenborg's books had been around for more than fifty years, spiritualism did not become all the rage until the Victorian era." Amelia shook her head. "Back to the point, I can't see that séances held nearly two hundred years ago are relevant."

"I am simply providing a bit of background for the benefit of our guest," he nodded toward Josie, who still stared at him with wide eyes, "And in so doing, the resolution of the current problem becomes obvious. If you want to kill a snake, you do not cut off its tail, you cut off its head."

"I don't see—"

"The solution is simple. Miss Drummond will accompany me backward in time to 1815 to unmask the charlatan who stole your inheritance."

"Time travel?" Josie asked, her voice a raspy whisper. "That's impossible."

"While not effortless, it is possible."

"It's the stuff of science fiction. Books that—"

His quelling look halted her explanation. "There is nothing wrong with my memory." Despite a few gaps that he'd rather not explain, he was not unaware of the world. "Jules Verne published *From the Earth to the Moon* in 1866, speculative fiction of the most imaginative sort...until your countrymen actually went there." He turned to Amelia. "Your grandfather was much enamored of H.G. Wells's work when he was a boy, but I always—"

"That's different." Josie jumped up from her chair. "Science—real science—deals with facts. Quantum theory proves time distortion is possible only if one travels faster than the speed of light, which is physically impossible."

Deverell also stood as good manners decreed he should. He was not surprised by her reaction. He did not expect a scientist to believe easily. But he had researched her career quite thoroughly before choosing her. Possessed of quick intellect, she'd written several articles on techniques of detection that revealed that she was not only logical and precise but also open to innovation. He schooled his expression to one of blasé disinterest that he had used so successfully when holding a winning hand at the gaming tables. In truth, it mattered not in the least whether she believed; it mattered only that she agree to help him.

She appealed to Amelia for support. "You can't seriously think he..."

Amelia looked to Deverell. "When you go back, will you confront Sir Albert? Perhaps he knows where the jewels are?"

"Bah!" Deverell's mouth twisted with a sour taste at the very thing that had obsessed his mother and caused her to fall prey to every charlatan who claimed a dubious connection to the afterlife. "The emeralds are a myth perpetuated by fools and believed by the foolish. I, Madame, am neither."

"Who is Sir Albert?" Josie blurted out.

Deverell wished Amelia hadn't mentioned that despicable old pirate, but now that she had, he must offer some sort of explanation. "Albert was the ghost of the castle prior to me."

Josie put her fingers to her temples and pressed. "Two of them?" she muttered. Her equipment had detected nothing!

"Please pay attention. I find repeating myself quite

tedious. Albert was here prior to me, and he is not relevant to my plan. Now as to the matter of your role..."

She shook her head. "You're crazy. Your plan is crazy. And I'd be crazy to listen to any more of this...this...nonsense." She turned and went to the door.

Over the years Deverell had refined the skills of a simple poltergeist to a fine art. With no more effort than a flick of his fingers, he caused the door to shut and the lock to click into place. She was his best hope for success, and he could not let her walk away before she'd had a chance to fully consider his offer. Surely she would come to her senses. He allowed Josie a few minutes to struggle with the door and with herself. His inquiries had led him to believe that she would embrace an opportunity for unusual research, but the behavior of modern women was difficult to predict. Particularly, that of modern American women.

Josie stared at the immovable door. Somehow she knew that Deverell was responsible. How dare he presume to keep her prisoner? She tugged on the doorknob with both hands. That ghost was a menace. Ghost? Damn.

Of course she'd always hoped to find definitive evidence of a ghostly phenomenon. As a paranormal investigator she should have been prepared for the unexpected. So what had she done in the face of the overwhelming experience of coming face-to-face with a fully materialized ghost? Had she reached for the digital camera in her purse? Tape recorder? Any device?

No. She had tried to leave.

She let her head fall forward, banging it on the ornate carved wood, but even pain couldn't stave off the hot blush of embarrassment that had been the bane of her red-headed existence. Where was her professionalism? Her scientific detachment?

"All I ask is that you hear me out," Deverell said.

She took a deep breath and released it slowly to the count of ten. Panic attack under control and outwardly composed, she returned to her chair and took out her camera. Since none of her scientific instruments had previously detected his presence, she held slim hope that the small camera would, but she had to try.

"May I?" she asked him.

After she was seated he also returned to his chair. "Yes, however," he hesitated at the flash then continued, "I doubt you'll be satisfied with the results."

The tiny screen displayed an empty chair. She adjusted the settings. "Say cheese." Again nothing. On the fifth try she got a hazy spot that could easily be a reflection of the fading sunlight. With a muttered curse she dropped the useless piece of equipment back into her purse.

"Shall I continue?" Lord Waite asked as if her rash exhibition hadn't taken place. Josie nodded, then picked up her cup of lukewarm tea, concentrating on keeping her cup from rattling against its saucer.

"I have determined that the best time for you to be present for a séance will be at one of my mother's frequent summer house parties. In order to act the part of a guest, certain training will be required. Amelia and I will tutor you in manners, decorum, and dress. I have written instructions." He handed Amelia some folded papers. "I am allowing one week for this course of study."

"That's insufficient," Amelia argued, leafing through four pages of precisely spaced, flamboyant handwriting. "Young women spent years learning what you expect Josie to absorb in days."

"One week will be sufficient. Miss Drummond's letter of introduction will place her as the long-lost, great-niece of the Duke of Landemere. Society always welcomes excellent breeding. As the heiress to a significant legacy, any *faux pas* will be tolerated as an eccentricity. In fact, from an American, less than perfect behavior will be expected."

Josie bristled at the insult. "I thought the essence of good manners was not to offend," she said with mock innocence. Satisfied at their twin expressions of chagrin, Josie changed the subject. "Other than the obvious flaw in your grand plan, that being the whole time travel thing, won't the Duke object to a surprise relative?"

Deverell had quickly masked his contrite expression with one of bored indifference. "Luckily, his grace was in his dotage and quite the recluse. Never left his estate. Never had any visitors. Perfect for my purpose."

"How accommodating of dear Uncle Landy," Josie said with an oh-so-sweet smile. Although Deverell had dropped the ugly American theme, his superior attitude kept her on the defensive. She didn't like lying, and she told him so.

"A certain shading of the truth is necessary." He heaved a dramatic sigh. "If it makes you feel better, you are, in fact, related to Landemere on your mother's side through his sister who married an American before the Colonial War. Satisfied? Now may I proceed?"

He was crazy, and obnoxious, but Josie couldn't deny her curiosity or her attraction to him. He was, hands down, the most interesting man she'd met in...ever. She nodded.

"I will be there to smooth over any difficulties. Once at the house party, you will observe the séance and expose the fraud. I'll bring you back to the present, and the problem of finances will have been solved at the source. Simple and straightforward." Deverell sat back as if he expected applause for his brilliant scheme.

Amelia complied. "What a marvelous idea."

Josie tuned out the gushing praise and sorted through the facts. She firmly believed that any attempt at time travel would fail. Obviously, Deverell wasn't up to date on physics. But, if she agreed to play along with his plan, she'd have seven full days to question the ghost about his existence. Think of the value to her research. This was the opportunity of a lifetime. She'd get the BS Grant for sure. On the other hand, she'd also have to spend a week with the overbearing, devastatingly handsome Lord Waite.

"Why do you need me?" she asked. "You said you would be there. Why don't you do it yourself?"

Deverell nodded, a tacit acknowledgment that her question was intelligent and appropriate, something he seemed to have difficulty admitting aloud.

"Naturally I first considered accomplishing this myself. However, since I was alive at the time, if I were to appear fully materialized, I could offer my mother advice only as myself. Guidance I'm quite sure she would ignore."

Deverell forestalled Amelia's argument with an elegant swipe of his hand. "I have no illusions about my mother's opinion of my rakehell, misspent life." He pulled on the cuffs of his jacket. "The other option, disguising myself and attending the séance as a ghost, would only prove the gypsy seer's proclaimed ability."

Josie nodded her acceptance of his explanation.

"I know the seer was a charlatan," he said.

Her experience supported his belief. If a ghost could be produced on demand, her job would be much easier. "Why me?" she asked again.

Deverell cleared his throat. "I do not have the expertise necessary to determine how the seer produced her apparitions," he mumbled his confession quickly, without looking at Josie.

That was probably as close as he'd get to admitting he needed her. Josie suppressed her smile with the same effort Deverell had undoubtedly exerted to swallow his pride.

"I accept your offer," she said.

Deverell smiled.

"On one condition."

His quick grin faded.

"Of course, you'll be paid," Amelia said. She squinted and bit her bottom lip as if calculating the balance in her checkbook. "This is a bit beyond the terms of your contract."

Josie fought the irrational desire to make him smile again, fought the warmth his seductive grin had started inside her. She had a sneaking feeling the phrasing of her condition would prove important, and she wanted to cover all her bases.

"My contract stands, as I had originally expected to spend another week or so here. If you still wish to proceed despite the certainty of failure..."

※   ※   ※   ※

Deverell tilted his head and motioned with his elegant hand for her to continue.

"I'd like your word that you'll answer all of my questions about your existence to the full extent of your knowledge." Josie had felt confident with her request when he clamped his jaw so tight that a muscle in his neck throbbed, but her fleeting elation changed into uncertainty when he visibly relaxed.

"I accept," he said with another devastating smile.

What had she left out? Why did she feel like the kid with the short half of the candy bar?

"With one condition of my own," he added.

Uh oh. What could he want? Josie held her breath.

"You will not monitor my every movement with your infernal gadgets."

"My *scientific instruments* will provide important material for future analysis and reference. That material is the only reason I agreed to your scheme."

"Let me assure you that I am capable of expending the appropriate amount of negative energy to erase any recordings you may make. However, I am asking for your word that it will not be necessary."

Josie crossed her arms. "I'm a scientist by inclination and education. I cannot change my nature on your whim."

Deverell's laugh sounded more like a bark. "Hardly a whim. Dodging your monitors has proven a bothersome restriction. As to your inclinations, you will gain much in the form of empirical knowledge. No recordings. However, I will concede so far as to allow you to record your observations the old-fashioned way. You may take notes. That is my condition."

Josie was tempted to argue. Here was the perfect excuse to call off the whole deal. If she did walk away, would she always regret the missed opportunity? Maybe. Probably. Definitely. She agreed before common sense made her change her mind.

"Excellent!" Deverell said. "We shall begin immediately." With a flick of his wrist, he caused two books to fly off the library shelf and into his grasp. He held the volumes out toward Josie.

"How did you do that?" she asked.

"What?"

"Make those books jump into your hand?"

"Did I?" he answered, looking from the books to the shelf. "I wasn't aware...."

His expression reminded her of a boy caught near a broken window with a baseball bat in his hand. Josie wasn't buying the innocent act. "You agreed to answer my questions. Going back on your word already?"

"Certainly not. A gentleman's word is not to be doubted."

She gave him a stare that said *I'm waiting.* Deverell's lips twitched as if to subdue a smile.

"Don't you have documented instances of a poltergeist moving objects?" he asked.

"Of course," she said. "But I want to know *how* you do it."

Deverell shrugged. "I've never thought about it one way or the other. In the future, I will endeavor to pay closer attention to my actions so I can keep to the letter of our agreement," he said, presenting the books again.

Realizing that was all the answer she was going to get for now, Josie leaned forward and took the heavy volumes, careful not to touch his hand in the transfer. She wouldn't exactly admit she was afraid of physical contact with the ghost, but she justified her precaution as scientific prudence. When she peeked up at him, he gave her a knowing grin.

"Can you read my mind?" she asked, voicing a sudden fear and trying to remember all her earlier thoughts.

"I'm a ghost," Deverell said. "Not some sort of common psychic entertainer. I cannot read minds, nor would I want to if I could."

Josie sighed in relief.

"In my day I was deemed an exceptional card player. A reputation founded less on luck than on my ability to read nuances of behavior in my opponents and bet accordingly. Your thoughts are, at times, quite obvious."

"Then it's a good thing I'm not a gambler."

"Oh, but I think you are. You're still here, aren't you?"

Desperate to change the subject to anything other than herself, Josie dropped her gaze to the books in her hands, *The Honours of the Table* and *A System of Etiquette*, both from 1804. She looked at him with her eyebrows raised. "A little light reading before dinner?"

Deverell either missed her sarcasm or chose to ignore it.

"Those volumes will give you the basics. Because total immersion is the quickest method of learning, we will recreate as nearly as possible the conditions of my mother's house party." He paused and then said, "You will live for the next week as if in the year 1815."

Josie found his habit of making statements as if they were royal pronouncements particularly annoying.

"What about the servants?"

Amelia's voice startled Josie. She'd practically forgotten that the older woman was in the same room. Josie peeked guiltily at the ghost and caught him glancing back in much the same manner.

"Won't all this seem strange?" Amelia continued, stacking the used dishes onto a tray. "What am I supposed to tell them?"

Josie laughed at the shocked look on Deverell's face. He'd obviously never considered it necessary to explain his actions to servants. However, he quickly recovered his composure.

"You might tell them that your inn will have a

Regency theme and that this is a practice run."

He said *inn* with a derisive curl of his upper lip. He must have practiced that look in the mirror to scare off dogs and salesmen. What about scaring off curious paranormal researchers? Josie shivered, hoping he'd never turn that sneer on her.

Deverell rose and assumed a position on the right side of the fireplace where he'd first appeared. He propped one elbow on the mantle in a pose similar to that of his portrait. Had the artist chosen that particular stance because it was his usual preference? Or had Deverell copied the portrait because it showed his physique to advantage?

Particularly tall for a man of his time, Josie figured him at just a shade under six feet. More than enough for her, at five foot two, to have to stretch her head back to look him in the eye when they both were standing. Because she was seated, her neck ached with the effort, and she dropped her gaze. A modern man would probably consider the high collar and lavish cravat too feminine to be worn by a man. On Deverell, the froth of linen and lace served to highlight the masculinity of his slightly aquiline nose, high cheekbones, and strong jaw. His cutaway coat accented his broad shoulders, an embroidered silk vest fit snugly across his flat stomach, and his closely tailored breeches left little to her imagination. A warmth that started deep within her threatened to erupt in a hot blush, and she forced herself to look at the fancy buckles at his knees.

"Or you can say Miss Drummond is tempting

your ghost...to appear," Deverell said with a wide smile that caused a deep dimple to wink momentarily in one cheek.

He was talking about the explanation to the servants, wasn't he? Josie sat up straighter. "I'd rather you didn't put words in my mouth," she said to him.

Deverell tipped his head back and looked down his nose at her. "If you thought the ploy would work, would you use it?"

Josie had to admit she would.

"Then I am simply saving the time it would take to manipulate the conversation so you would make the suggestion yourself."

"Your logic is lacking. I...I might not respond as you expect." Josie's argument sounded weak, even to herself. With disgust she realized that her usually dependable brain went fuzzy when he smiled at her. When was the last time a man had made her stutter over her words? But he wasn't a man. He was a ghost. If she was getting this goggle-eyed over a bona fide specter, handsome or not, she needed to get out more often.

"Manifestation uses energy," he said, breaking into her self-chastisement.

She focused on his words and tried not to let his deep intoxicating voice distract her.

Two

"MANIFESTATION USES ENERGY AND I DO not have an unlimited supply. By my calculations I can spend only a few hours a day in this form without depleting my reserves," he continued. "I see no point in wasting precious time pacifying servants or applying verbal balm to your outraged sensibilities."

His insulting attack was a bucket of cold water to her senses, but the information he'd inadvertently disclosed caused her to duck her head to hide a satisfied grin. Already her agreement to cooperate was yielding valuable material. A ghost had a definable and limited amount of energy that he could choose how to expend.

"In that case, I agree with you," Josie said. She made a mental note to start keeping a journal. She didn't want to forget any tidbit of information that could prove valuable later.

"Well, I don't agree," Amelia said. "Neither of you seems to understand how difficult it is to keep decent servants." She stood and straightened her sweater over the waist of her tweed skirt. "I'll call a staff meeting and use both explanations, the Regency theme for the inn, and Josie setting bait for the ghost." She looked meaningfully at Deverell. "This scheme had better work, because I'll probably have to pay them extra."

Deverell, who had also risen, said, "I've arranged for several trunks to be in the attic. They contain appropriate wardrobes for you and Miss Drummond, uniforms for the house staff, and livery for the butler and coachman."

Amelia blinked. "We don't have a butler or coachman."

"You do now. I used that ugly object you call a telephone to contact an employment service and engaged them to begin work tomorrow."

"But I don't own a coach."

"You do now. Your new coachman will find it buried under several layers of junk in the stable. I transported it here from an earlier time when it won't be missed. The coach needs some spit and polish, but it will do quite nicely."

Amelia reached one hand out to grab the jamb of the unopened door and put her other hand to her heart. Fearing for the older woman's health, Josie rushed to her side. Amelia, seeming to gather her strength, faced the ghost.

"I suppose you *transported* horses, too," Amelia said with only a faint quaver in her voice.

"Nonsense," Deverell said, leaning forward and propping his elbows on the back of a leather chair. "Live animals are more difficult to move than inanimate objects. I purchased horses."

"How?" Josie asked but he either didn't hear her or simply ignored her question.

"Also two saddle mounts. Not the best blood, but adequate." He straightened and slapped his thigh. "I have missed riding since you disbanded the stable."

"Do you know what it costs to feed a horse?" Amelia cried, her voice rising.

"How did you purchase the horses?" Josie asked again.

Amelia put her hands on her hips. "Yes, where did you get the money? Horses cost more than a few odd pounds. Did you *transport* that, too?"

"That would be robbery!" He straightened to his full height and assumed a haughty mien. "I am not a thief."

"Then, where did you get the money?" Forget the horses for the moment. Where does a ghost get money if he needs it?

"I have not spent the last two hundred years under a rock."

"That doesn't answer the question," Amelia said.

His expression remained impassive, but the tips of his ears turned crimson. "Perhaps we should discuss family finances at a later time," he said with a slight tilt of his head toward Josie.

"You're the one who decided to make her a part of your scheme," Amelia argued. "She might as well know all the details."

After a moment of strained silence, Deverell nodded. "Very well. I obtained a credit card in your name, Amelia. Did you realize a person can order practically anything delivered without ever leaving home?" He examined his fingernails. "Quite handy."

Amelia closed her eyes. "You'd better hope the séances are real, and Josie helps the gypsy recover Sir Robert's emeralds. We'll need a treasure just to cover the bills."

He took Amelia's hands in his. "Please trust me," he whispered. "I promise everything will turn out right."

Josie was glad she wasn't in the other woman's shoes. It would be hard to deny the pleading look in his eyes, hard to deny him anything. She looked away. The unscrupulous ghost would use any means to achieve his ends. She'd do well to remember that.

Josie knew the exact instant Amelia succumbed to Deverell's blatant charm because the woman relaxed and smiled.

"In for a penny, in for a pound. If the family Waite is going down, at least we'll do it in grand style."

Deverell bowed gallantly and kissed Amelia's hand.

"I'll meet with the staff right away. We'll dress for dinner, of course. The dressing gong will sound at seven o'clock," she explained to Josie. "The next tone will be the signal to assemble in the hall." Amelia opened the door, now mysteriously unlocked, muttering a list of things to do. "Fetch the trunks. Polish the silver. Candles! We must have candles."

Josie turned to follow. She didn't want to be alone with Deverell. She admitted that she was in over her head. Admitted the crazy, charming, insufferably arrogant and handsome ghost was more than she could handle. Why didn't she wise up and leave? If she was as smart as she thought she was, she would run screaming from the room and never look back.

Yet she hesitated. She'd already learned so much. He could manipulate the physical world, moving things at will. He could transfer things across space and time. Or that's what he'd said. He'd used the word "transport." Something about something from an earlier time? Drat. She wasn't sure, and a blown opportunity wasn't likely to repeat itself for her benefit.

She'd answered her own question. She couldn't leave. A chance like this would never come again. The key to surviving the experience would be to focus on her research. Determined to appear calm, she straightened her shoulders and assumed what she hoped was an intelligent expression. When she turned to face Deverell, he'd disappeared.

"Just look at all these lovely clothes," Emma said, dancing around Josie's bedroom with a pink tulle dress held against her new serviceable gray uniform. The maid had taken to the role-playing with enthusiasm. "It's like when I used to dress-up in me Mum's old party togs."

Josie eyed the pile of clothes on the high four-poster bed with less appreciation. The trunk of Regency style clothes had been delivered to the same bedroom she'd occupied for the past three weeks. Determined to do whatever it took to proceed with her research, she'd allowed her already packed suitcases to be moved into storage, along with all of her equipment.

However, Josie had refused to give up her carry-on bag that held essential twenty-first century products. Not even for the chance to interview a ghost was she willing to give up her toothbrush, deodorant, or Lancôme tinted moisturizer. After a quick bath in the old-fashioned claw-footed tub, she'd wrapped herself in a red silk dressing gown while Emma searched for an appropriate dinner outfit.

Pulling a paisley shawl from the trunk, Emma draped it over one shoulder. She wiggled, and the gold fringe danced in response. "Don't you just love fringe," she cooed.

Even though Josie's personal taste ran to tailored suits and crisp cotton shirts, she didn't want to dampen Emma's excitement. "It's lovely," she said with a weak smile.

"I'll get all this put away as soon as we get you dressed," Emma said. She threw the shawl on top of the growing pile of fabric on the bed and stuck her head back into the large trunk. "There must be knickers or pantaloons of some sort in here."

Kneeling on the floor, surrounded by pasteboard boxes over-flowing with tissue paper, gloves, hats and handkerchiefs, the bright-eyed maid looked like a child on Christmas morning.

"You'll need these," Emma said, tossing leather slippers to Josie one at a time.

Laughing, Josie caught a shoe in each hand. With reverent care, Emma unwrapped and laid out a pair of white stockings made of the sheerest silk. While Josie smoothed on the knee-high stockings and tied the red ribbon garters, Emma scrambled to answer the knock at the door.

"You two seem to be having a good time," Amelia said as she breezed into the bedroom, looking regal in a bronze watered silk dress trimmed at the hem with a black Greek key design. The Empire style slimmed her hips, and the matching turban, adorned with a tall feather fastened over her forehead with a brooch, gave the flattering illusion of additional height.

"This is so much fun," Emma said, making a place for Amelia by clearing assorted articles off the remaining chair and dumping them back into the trunk.

Amelia sat gingerly on the edge of the seat, arranging her new gown with loving pats and tugs. "Vivian complained the whole time about the extra work," she said, wrinkling her nose.

"Then Emma should be your maid," Josie said to Amelia.

"Can't," the maid interrupted. "Vivian has seniority. If I was to be put above her, that upset applecart would spill sour grapes for sure." She picked up a blue dress with a satisfied grunt and turned, stopping suddenly. "Sorry, milady," she said with a bob of her head and credible curtsey. "Didn't mean to discuss downstairs politics in front of your guest."

Amelia nodded. "Actually Josie needs to learn about this type of situation if she is going to...going to continue her research into the daily life of our ghost," she finished blandly.

Emma hugged the dress to her breasts, her eyes wide. "Do you really think he'll appear?"

"Hopefully not right now," Amelia said. "Josie is hardly dressed to receive visitors."

Emma seemed to catch the not so subtle hint. She returned to the bed and sorted through the mounds of material. Under Amelia's direction, the maid selected a chemise and handed it to Josie.

Josie examined what had passed for underwear in a previous century, sort of a short nightgown with a drawstring neckline and tiny puffed sleeves. She stepped behind the dressing screen. The soft material of the chemise caressed her skin as she shimmied it on, but the matter of the ghost preyed upon her mind.

He'd mentioned his materialized state. Logically that meant he also had a dematerialized state. Could he be in this very room? Surely a gentleman wouldn't peek at a woman's bath, but it wouldn't hurt to lay down a few ground rules the next time she saw him, such as, he should let her know if he was in the room, even if he didn't materialize. He couldn't object to that. Satisfied with her reasoning, Josie stepped back into the room and reached for the blue silk gown Emma held.

"No, no, no," Amelia said. "First the corset, then the underdress, then the overdress."

Josie crossed her arms. "You can't expect me to wear a corset," she said even though Emma was already scrambling to retrieve the named items.

"Every proper woman wore a corset, whether she needed it or not," Amelia said with a nod toward Josie's slim physique. "It won't be so bad. Just don't take any deep breaths."

Emma approached, turning the corset over and around, the strings flipping and dangling every which way. "How does this contraption work? Does it lace up or down?"

"It doesn't matter," Josie said. "Besides, didn't I read somewhere that Regency women had discarded the corset and even dampened their gowns to achieve the natural look."

"That was a French custom. A few daring englishwomen tried it in London, but contrary to popular belief, it wasn't the custom at country estates," Amelia explained. "Why anyone would believe an otherwise sane woman would wear a wet dress in a drafty old castle is beyond me."

"Yet that same supposedly sane woman voluntarily wore a torture device," Josie said.

"The corset was an accepted fact of life," Amelia said.

"How do you know so much about these clothes?" Josie asked. "And the manners? I understand Deverell lived that life, but you're, I mean, you're not..."

"Not that old?" Amelia asked with a chuckle. "Well, not quite."

"I'm sorry. I didn't mean to offend."

Amelia patted Josie's shoulder. "You haven't, dear. In fact I taught history at University for so long, the rumor was that I recalled many of the events from personal experience." She chuckled again. "I admit that knowing Deverell contributed to my fascination with the Regency period. He and Jane Austen. Have you seen the fashion displays at the Albert and Victoria Museum? Absolutely fabulous. The costume curator is a former student of mine."

Josie nodded, shook her head, and nodded in turns, and as usual had difficulty keeping up with Amelia's quick changes of topic.

"You could give it a try, and if it's too uncomfortable, take it off," Emma suggested, holding out the corset.

Unable to refute the maid's simple logic, Josie capitulated. She stepped forward with her arms raised. While Emma tightened the laces, Josie looked down and observed with surprise the phenomenon of instant cleavage. She'd never had cleavage before. Was this why women had put up with corsets for so many centuries? Okay, it wasn't unbearable if the laces were loosened a little.

After donning the blue silk gown, Josie looked in the cheval mirror. The low-cut bodice bared her shoulders and the tops of her breasts, now nicely rounded by the pressure of the corset. From the dark blue ribbon under her bust, the deep azure silk fell in smooth lines to where the sky blue undergown peeked out just above her ankles. Would Deverell find her attractive? Josie chased the thought out of her brain. These clothes were only the trappings necessary to continue her real research project, questioning the ghost. However, it didn't hurt her self-confidence to confront him looking her best.

"You look like a princess," Emma said, making a deep curtsey. "And here's your crown." She reverently presented a turban made of matching blue silk.

Josie stepped back. "I don't wear hats."

"But it goes with the outfit," Emma sputtered.

"I can't wear that...that thing," Josie said, staring at

the ornate concoction of silk, feathers, and ribbons. Hats made her claustrophobic, panicky. She didn't want to explain that particular neurosis and its antecedents in the riding accident that had left her in a body cast and her head in traction for most of the year she was thirteen. "My head sweats," she explained.

"Horses sweat, men perspire, ladies glow," Amelia said, chastising Josie's word selection.

"With that on my head, I'd glow like a neon sign in the rain." The determined arbiter of Regency fashion didn't relent. Josie tried another tack. "Hats give me a headache."

"Well, unmarried women were not required to wear a cap indoors during the day. However in the evening, in order to be proper, you must wear something on your head." Amelia took the turban, and yanked off the ribbons and the white egret feathers. She found a needle and thread in a side drawer of the dressing table, fashioned the bits and pieces into a hair ornament, and attached her creation to a comb. "We can sweep one side of your hair back and anchor it with this."

After all Amelia's work and the destruction of the original hat, Josie felt obligated to cooperate. When she again stood in front of the mirror, she had to agree with the other women. The hair ornament was just the touch her outfit needed. Josie moved her head from side to side. The fancy comb didn't restrict her freedom and therefore didn't cause any claustrophobic panic.

Emma helped Josie pull on long gloves that reached above her elbows and fastened the tiny pearl buttons at her wrists. Then the maid held up the fringed shawl. Josie eyed the large red and pink peonies in the pattern and shook her head. "I never wear those colors. Not with my hair."

"Nonsense," Amelia said. "This will perk up your complexion." She nodded to Emma who then draped the shawl over Josie's shoulders.

Josie turned to the mirror and, to her surprise, saw that the color did flatter her. She rubbed the luxurious fabric.

"Wool challis," Amelia said. "Quite handy in a castle where drafts seem to come from nowhere." Another nod to Emma produced a flat box. "And now for a touch of elegance." She revealed a magnificent necklace of luminescent pearls accented by tiny diamonds. Also nestled in the back velvet lining were the matching bracelet and earrings. "We call this parure the Young Queen's Pearls because they were a wedding gift from Victoria to my great-great-grandmother, who was one of her ladies-in-waiting."

Josie stepped back. "I couldn't..."

"Of course you can. I'm only lending them for the evening, not giving them to you."

"But what if something happens to them?"

Amelia clucked her tongue. "Don't be such a Nervous Nellie. Sometimes you just have to relax and enjoy the moment." She fastened the necklace around Josie's neck and stepped back to admire her handiwork. "Lovely."

Emma added the bracelet and earrings and handed Josie a beaded reticule and a fan painted with violets.

"I do believe we're ready."

Josie jammed a small notebook and stub of a pencil next to the lacy handkerchief and tiny vial of smelling salts in the reticule dangling from her wrist. The assembly gong sounded, the signal to begin round two with the ghost. Deverell would be waiting for her—for them—at the bottom of the grand staircase.

Deverell paced the wide foyer, unseen and unheard by the servants in the dining room. As he'd predicted, Amelia's fear of revolt was unfounded. The servants appeared invigorated by the change in routine, except for one whiner. He entertained the notion of a quick materialization to scare the drudge witless, but he dismissed it as unworthy. Bad enough that, in his concern for Amelia, he'd eaves-dropped on servants. He suppressed a shudder.

The toll for his years of inattention to his duty was not pleasant, but then what else could he expect of a penance? Today he had taken the initial step to rectify the financial situation in a manner that would free him again to concentrate on his assigned task. Tonight would be the first test for Miss Drummond. Could she learn everything she would need to know in time? Would she honor her agreement when she learned the truth?

No, he refused to think about that just yet.

He tugged on the sleeve of his impeccably tai-lored evening coat. Although dematerialized, he retained a sense of himself, knowledge of his being. For the first time, he wondered why. He had always accepted his existence without questioning it. If he needed something, he concentrated his thoughts, and it appeared or happened or whatever. Over the years he had learned a few limitations and many shortcuts to conserve his energy. Yet he had never thought about why or how, until now. Until Josie and her insatiable curiosity.

Deverell shook his head. She would be disappointed. He had no answers to far-reaching metaphysical questions on the meaning of life. How soon would she realize that she had made a bad bargain? Surely he knew something she would find interesting. He could stretch out his small store of facts. Requiring Josie to ask specific questions would delay the inevitable, as would limiting their time together. Unexpectedly, the latter held little appeal.

Waiting for a desirable dinner partner made him feel like an eager young buck, and he had not experienced anticipation in many years. That wasn't good. This wasn't a social event, and he certainly was not a young man. He had best remember that, regardless of how she made him feel.

He materialized when Josie appeared at the top of the grand stairway, and he quickly realized that his resolution to limit their time together would be easier made than kept. He'd known that the fashions of his time would suit her petite figure and gamine, impish haircut. The blue of her dress accented her eyes and complimented her auburn curls. She was an original. At least that's what they'd called a singularly beautiful woman when he was alive.

Suddenly Deverell felt the weight of his years,

his eternal burden. He could damn the curse of his existence, but he would never let Josie know the agony she caused him.

"Don't look at your feet," he growled up at her, his voice louder than he'd intended.

Josie let out a squeak of surprise and, missing a step, tripped on the hem of her gown. She grabbed for the banister, but her beaded reticule caught in the fringe of her shawl, shortening her reach. She couldn't grasp the railing.

Josie had only a vision of herself landing in an undignified heap on the marble floor. There went her plan of making it through the evening with cool scientific detachment. Dropping her fan, she twisted her body and groped for the banister with her right hand. She windmilled her other arm in the air as she tried to regain her balance and free herself from the demonic shawl that had gained a life of its own. She heard a woman scream, but she didn't know whether it was she herself or Amelia.

Suddenly she felt strong hands on her waist, lifting her back to the top step. She looked downstairs, but Deverell had disappeared. The servants rushed out of the dining room. Amelia quickly made up a story about a furry rodent to cover the shriek, but Josie paid little attention. She sensed Deverell's presence beside her.

"You're welcome," he whispered in her ear.

His deep husky voice sent a tremor down her spine.

"Don't do that," she hissed from behind the cover of her hand.

"Don't what? Don't rescue you from falling?"

She dismissed her racing heartbeat as the after-effect of fear. He'd scared her, nearly killed her, and now, he was trying to make her feel guilty for not being grateful.

"I heard a man," Vivian said from the bottom of the stairway. She planted her fists on her ample hips. "He yelled, *Don't cook a poor meat*. I heard it clearly." She peered around the foyer, as if someone might be hiding in the suit of armor or preparing to jump out of the large Chinese urn.

Amelia managed a lilting laugh that sounded only slightly forced. "You must be mistaken," she said as she descended the stairs with regal grace. "Why would anyone say something so silly?"

"I know what I heard," Vivian said, raising her chin to a mutinous angle.

"If you've been nipping at the sherry..." Amelia let the implied warning linger in the tense air.

Vivian drew a deep breath as if to continue the argument, then merely harrumphed loudly before stomping back to the dining room.

When they reached the bottom of the stairs, Amelia motioned Josie into the library with a conspiratorial air.

"That was a close one," the older woman sighed as she closed the door to the library and leaned against it, her hand over her heart. "For a minute there I thought Vivian had caught him." Amelia walked to an elaborate cabinet and removed a crystal decanter. "Speaking of sherry, I believe I'll have a nip. Josie?"

"No, thank you. I don't understand. The servants know there's a ghost."

"They don't think he's real," Amelia explained. "Oh, they repeat the stories over a pint at the pub, but I've learned from experience that servants will accept working for an eccentric, but employment in a real haunted house is a different kettle of fish altogether."

"But they know I'm here to certify the ghost's existence."

"Pish-tosh. Most of them think you're humoring me for the sake of your fee. A few think you're crazy, too. If they don't actually see or hear him, they can choose not to believe in him."

Josie rubbed her temples. In front of the servants, she should pretend to be humoring a crazy old lady. In reality, the ghost would be teaching her etiquette so he could take her back in time to attend a séance and debunk a gypsy seer. Oh, yeah. She understood. Perfectly.

"What she means..." Deverell said, suddenly appearing, seated in one of the leather chairs.

"Don't do that!" Josie said.

"So you said earlier. I am unclear as to your meaning."

Was Deverell being purposely obtuse in order to irritate her? Josie refused to let him see he'd succeeded. "I mean don't materialize without some sort of warning. Amelia may be used to you popping in and out, but I'm not."

Deverell leaned back and regarded her with a grin. "What do you suggest? Shall I rattle some chains or rap three times on the ceiling?"

Josie rewarded his teasing with a quelling look. "I was thinking more along the lines of moaning in eternal pain," she said with a false, sweet smile.

"Nonsense. Both of you," Amelia said, breaking the tension. "That will scare the servants. You'll have to come up with something silent." Her expectant gaze fell on Josie.

Struggling to come up with an idea, Josie cleared her throat. "Well, earlier, I sort of felt a tingle of awareness at Deverell's presence." Josie couldn't, didn't want to, look at the ghost as she tried to explain. "If he could project that, it should provide enough warning so he won't startle me into falling down the stairs at least."

"Do you mean like this," he said, stretching out his hand as if he expected her to take it.

Josie felt a connection to him, felt a warm curl of response to his magnetism, felt the need to grasp his hand and draw him closer. Instead, she pushed herself away, instinctively holding up her hands in front of her as a shield. "No," she said, shaking her head. Her voice didn't quiver like her insides, but she knew a plea for mercy was in her eyes.

Deverell nodded as if he understood and agreed to comply with her unspoken request.

"I'm sure you'll think of something," Amelia said, cheerful as ever and apparently oblivious to the tension in the room. "Dinner is nearly ready, and we should begin your lessons."

Josie wasn't sure how much of this lecture she'd remember. Her head was still spinning, but she dutifully opened her notebook.

Three

"BEFORE THE BUTLER ANNOUNCES DINNER," Amelia said, her tone revealing her experience as a history teacher, "the hostess matches up the dinner partners. She provides introductions, if necessary, and she often suggests a topic of conversation of mutual interest."

"Josie will not be called upon to act as hostess," Deverell interjected.

"Of course not, dear. But she should have an appreciation of the magnitude of your mother's responsibilities." When he offered no further argument, she continued. "The hostess lines up the guests for the promenade into the dining room in order of precedence."

Josie made a note to relocate the table of precedence in the book she'd glanced at earlier. She was comfortable in the role of student and was confident she would excel and maybe even surprise Deverell.

Besides, she hadn't been raised in a barn. She knew which fork to use. They wouldn't have to tell her not to drink from the finger bowl.

"The host leads the procession with the highest-ranking woman on his arm. The hostess is last in line, escorted by the highest-ranking man. All the other pairs of guests range in between with any extra unescorted guests left to follow behind. Of course the goal is to have an even number of male and female guests so as to have everyone paired with a dinner partner of the opposite sex."

"Top to bottom, bottom to top," Josie said. "I've got it."

Deverell snorted and rolled his eyes.

Amelia giggled. "That would pair the second highest female with the lowest male. Hardly appropriate. Perhaps it would help to envision them at the table." She borrowed Josie's pen and paper and drew a diagram. "Fourteen was considered the ideal number to seat at a table. The highest-ranking woman is to the right of the host, the second-highest woman on his left. The highest-ranking man is to the left of the hostess, the second-highest man on her right. That puts the third man to the left of the second woman, making them partners. The third woman sits to the right of the second man, making them partners."

"I see a pattern," Josie said as Amelia drew little boxes for chairs and labeled them. "Sort of like giving each rank a number that corresponds to a particular chair."

"If only it were that easy. Suppose the third woman is married to the second man. They can't be seated next to each other. The point of going out to dinner is to converse with someone other than your spouse."

Deverell leaned forward. "Add to that, who sat next to whom at your last dinner party, and who was paired with whom by some other hostess the previous evening."

"Then there are likes and dislikes," Amelia said. "And personalities. You wouldn't partner an avid bluestocking..."

"I would not invite an avid bluestocking," he said.

"... with Deverell," Amelia finished, as if he hadn't interrupted her. "A guest would never say anything rude to upset the hostess, but a reputation can be shattered."

"I remember a particular incident," Deverell said with a wicked grin. "I can't recall her name, but a duchess was seated next to a man she absolutely loathed. When the table turned, requiring her to speak to him, she recited the multiplication tables rather than cause a scene. She vowed never to attend another dinner party given by that hostess."

"Oh, dear. I do hope it wasn't your mother," Amelia said.

Deverell laughed. "No. Mother had a plethora of poor relatives with decent titles who lived nearby and who could spout inane dinner chatter at the drop of a fork. Fortunately for her, they also had enormous appetites and were always eager to fill out a table of fourteen on short notice."

Josie scribbled furiously. "Wait a minute." She held up one finger while she flipped back through her notebook pages. "You said something about a table I didn't understand."

"You don't know what the multiplication tables are?" Deverell asked with mock horror.

Josie spared him a quick, scathing glance as she flipped through her notes. "Here it is. You said *when the table turned*. What's that?" She had a fleeting image of a dining room table built like a lazy Susan. Conversational spin the bottle.

"When a hostess speaks to the man on her left, each female guest speaks to the man on her left," Amelia said. "The hostess turns the table by speaking to the man on her right. Each woman follows her lead and speaks to the man on her right."

Josie liked her own explanation better. At least it sounded like more fun. She shook her head and returned to drawing and redrawing lines on Amelia's diagram. This was harder than it appeared. A Regency hostess must have felt as if her social standing depended on putting together a jigsaw puzzle blindfolded and wearing heavy work gloves.

Josie tossed the notebook onto the table. She hadn't figured out the first problem with the married couple, never mind the feuding duchess. It hurt to admit defeat. Especially since her intellect was the one area of her life where she'd always felt confident. She folded her arms and slumped back in the seat. "I'll never get this."

Deverell raised one eyebrow. "Giving up already?"

Josie wanted to stick her tongue out at him.

"Don't be discouraged, dear. As Deverell said, you'll never need to act as hostess. Truly, you'll do just fine. Simply pay attention to Deverell's mother and follow her lead."

Amelia's sympathetic tone and expression only deepened Josie's depression.

Deverell sat back with an insincere smile. "I quote your President Roosevelt, 'If you can't run with the big dogs, stay on the porch.'"

Drat his superior attitude. How Josie would love to take him down a peg or two. "I do believe the correct quote is 'If you can't stand the heat, stay out of the kitchen,'" she said.

"Other than wordage, is there a difference?"

The man didn't know when to stop. He was asking for a set down. Josie sat up straighter and assumed a nonchalant pose. "Are you claiming the difference between right and wrong is simply a choice of words? Is accuracy a matter of semantics?"

"I see that modern women, just like the women of my time, take a man's words and twist them to their liking."

Josie knew she had won the first point in this round when Deverell had been reduced to gender bashing to form a response. He nodded his acknowledgment of her triumphant smile.

Pushing aside a dangerous glow of pleasure, Josie reminded herself of her reasons for cooperating with the ghost in the first place. She'd already wasted half the evening.

Lost in her thoughts, she followed Amelia into the dining room. Josie realized that Deverell had maneuvered her into taking up the gauntlet, manipulated her into accepting his challenge.

One point for Deverell in round two. Although he was unseen, she knew he was near. Just as she knew he wore a triumphant grin. She nodded graciously in recognition of his point. The score was now tied, but the evening was still young.

"As you can see, dining *à la Russe* was the style," Amelia said as they entered the dining room and were seated across from each other near the head of the table.

The footman, in actuality the gardener's nephew George, who had been pressed into service and who had received a crash course in his new duties, nervously placed the napkins in the ladies' laps and served the soup and wine.

"I think we can dispense with the usual practice of the footmen standing in attendance in case a dinner guest should need anything." Amelia dismissed George with a reminder that she would ring the bell when she was ready for him to return.

George backed out, his oh-so-serious expression spoiled by a last minute grab to keep his white wig in place.

Josie breathed silent thanks that she wouldn't have yet another witness to her first efforts using the awkward-looking two-pronged forks and huge spoons. No wonder the napkins were so large.

"All the dishes are on the table when the guests enter the dining room. What we would consider a complete meal from soup to nuts was presented simultaneously, savory and sweet together. This course would then be followed by two or more removes, so called because every dish, and even the tablecloth, was removed and replaced by fresh linen and more dishes."

"There are a lot of dishes," Josie said, looking down the long table that would comfortably seat a football team. Every square inch of the center was filled with a compote, tureen, salver, server, tray, or dish of some sort.

Amelia laughed. "Tonight they're empty, placed on the table only for effect. At a gala party there would be so many dishes and huge elaborate centerpieces that you could hardly see the people seated across the table. Of course that wouldn't have been a problem then because it was considered rude to speak across the board."

Deverell appeared, but Josie had no chance to comment on his sudden materialization because Amelia immediately welcomed him.

"Please accept my apologies. I was unforgivably remiss earlier in not mentioning how ravishing you both look," he said with a graceful bow. "A stunning tribute to womanhood."

Amelia thanked him for the lavish compliment. Josie tipped her head graciously, unable to trust her voice. She gripped her hands tightly together in her lap and fought the glow his words ignited within her. "So, tell me, Lord Waite, exactly when, and how, did you realize you were dead?"

Amelia gasped. "Really, dear. Deverell's demise is hardly an appropriate topic. In the Regency, conversation was considered an art form, and masters of witty repartee were desirable guests."

"And double *entrendres*, the more risqué the better, were also appreciated," Deverell added with a chuckle.

Amelia appeared to ignore him. "Guests came to the table prepared to discuss several matters of general interest to those present. Topics might range from the weather..."

"Unimaginative," Deverell interjected with a dismissive gesture.

"To the latest acceptable literature...."

He stifled a fake yawn.

"To the progress of the war with Napoleon," Amelia finished.

"I didn't mean to offend," Josie said, "but ghosts are one of the few subjects we have in common."

"We have your lessons. There is much for you to learn." Amelia demonstrated how a woman exposed her hands for eating without removing her long gloves. She undid the tiny pearl buttons, slid her hand free, and tucked the fingers of the glove under the material at the back of her wrist.

Josie mimicked her mentor's actions with considerably less dexterity and grace. She frowned at the misshapen lumps and pushed and poked at the excess material, but it would not lie flat and smooth the way Amelia's did. Practice was obviously necessary.

"I am not offended by Miss Drummond's curiosity," Deverell said, stopping by the sideboard to pour himself a drink before finding his chair at the head of the table on Amelia's left. "I have, after all, pledged to answer her questions to the best of my knowledge."

Josie could only wonder why he found his own comment amusing. "I see you drink. Do you eat solid food?" she asked, indicating the plate set at his place.

"I can, if I am fully materialized and wish to do so. There are only a few dishes worth the effort. I do enjoy my tea and my brandy," he said, raising the snifter in salute.

"What about…" Josie stopped herself. She didn't want to cause Amelia to faint by asking him about going to the bathroom.

"Not necessary."

Deverell answered her unasked question as if he had read it in the tell-the-whole-world-what-I'm-thinking blush she'd always hated.

"When I return to my normal dematerialized state, anything I have ingested dissipates."

Josie could tell from the twinkle in his eye that he enjoyed putting her on the spot. Yet she couldn't think of a witty comeback when he smiled that devastating grin. Her insides performed gymnastic flips that would have earned tens from an Olympic judge.

"As to my demise…"

"Deverell! This is not…"

"It's quite all right, Amelia. You wouldn't have me go back on my word as a gentleman, would you?"

She shook her head.

"Perhaps later," Josie suggested in deference to Amelia's pained expression.

"No sense putting it off. My memory of the incident is a bit fuzzy, but to the best of my recollection I had the misfortune to have my pistol misfire during a duel. The affronted husband defending his wife's honor aimed for my…leg, and he managed to plant a bullet directly in my heart. Wingate always was a dreadful shot."

"You don't seem bitter."

"It happened a very long time ago. Oh, I railed at the perceived injustice at first. After all, I had never touched his wife, much to her dismay. My particular code of ethics, lax though it may have been, did not include tupping the wives of my friends."

Amelia choked and coughed to hide a little moan of dismay.

Josie was not fooled by Amelia's cover-up or by Deverell's attempt to shock. "Quite noble of you, I'm sure."

"Dining lasted several hours and was considered an entertainment as well as a meal, thus the elaborate presentations," Amelia said.

Deverell continued speaking as if he hadn't heard Josie's caustic comment or Amelia's feeble attempt at changing the subject. "I would have laughed at his challenge and settled the matter over a glass at the club, but poor Wingate challenged me in the midst of a crowded ballroom. I was forced to defend my honor, if not that of a lady love."

"You sound more sorry for him than for losing your own life."

"He was the one shackled to a philandering wife. I had always rather expected to come to a bad end, and I suppose being shot was no worse and probably better than I deserved. There was only an instant of burning pain, and then I seemed to view the entire debacle as if floating above the field in a balloon." He snapped his fingers. "Then blackness."

"No beckoning light?"

"Nothing but stifling, unrelenting blackness. A void. Emptiness. Even the fires of hell would have provided a welcome diversion. Believe me, if there had been any sort of light, I would have gone toward it out of sheer boredom."

Though Deverell seemed almost flippant in his manner, Josie saw something else deep in his eyes. Regret? Disappointment? Her throat tightened. Maybe this wasn't such a good topic of conversation. Maybe she didn't need to know about his death. After all, it was his current existence that interested her. "How did you get here?"

Amelia made a little moaning sound, and Josie glanced over to catch her unusually pale hostess removing the old-fashioned smelling salts from her reticule.

Josie immediately changed the subject. "I find the possibility of eating dessert with the meal quite appealing," she said.

Of the same mind, Deverell spoke at the same time. "When dining *à la Russe* you simply serve yourself from the dishes within your reach."

Amelia sneezed and seemed to gather herself. After blinking a few times, she resumed her history lecture as if she'd not been interrupted by her unruly student. "Women took extremely small portions. Not only were large lumps of food on the plate considered vulgar, but certain foods were deemed inappropriate for a delicate constitution. They spent much of the evening with their hands in their laps."

"Must make it hard to pass the potatoes," Josie muttered under her breath.

"Dishes were not passed from hand to hand as in a boarding house," Deverell interjected with a curl of his lip.

"What if I want something beyond my reach?" Josie asked. She regretted her phrasing when Deverell raised an eyebrow.

"A man might offer a choice morsel of something within his reach to the woman seated next to him," Amelia said.

"That was considered a signal of preference. Miss Drummond will have no need to allow such intimacies," Deverell said.

"She certainly can if she wants to."

"As my mother's guest, her reputation must be above reproach."

"It will hardly be considered improper for her to accept a tidbit of food."

"Guys," Josie said, waving her hands to get their attention. "There's no need to talk about me as if I weren't here."

Amelia apologized to Josie immediately. "I suppose discussing the fine points of etiquette is counterproductive when you have so much to learn."

"There should be no argument," Deverell said. "I am the expert."

"From what I hear, you're more familiar with the improprieties of the time," Josie said, her sweet tone hiding none of her defense of Amelia.

Deverell raised his glass in response. "One must know where the line is drawn in order to cross it."

If the man had traced a thick black line on the tablecloth with a felt tip pen, it couldn't have been more obvious that he had just challenged her to step up to the mark and defend herself. Did she dare? There were few things in this world that scared her, and a chauvinistic buffoon was not one of them.

"Then again," she said with a nod to acknowledge her entrance as a contestant in the latest battle of wits, "the boundaries constantly change. One can easily be left so far behind the times that he is no longer in the same ball game, much less the correct ball park."

"Oh dear. I never did understand sports metaphors," Amelia said with a sigh. "Unless, of course, they referred to riding or hunting."

"Fox hunting is more than a sport," Deverell argued. "It is indicative of a lifestyle. A reminder of accepted behavior patterns this century would do well to readopt as standards."

"Such as viewing women as chattel? Such as the old double standard?" Josie cautioned herself to remain calm. She would lose this argument by default if she let her temper fly out of control.

"Morals were upheld."

"Ah, yes. How could I have misconstrued rampant syphilis, the white slavery trade, and open opium addiction to be immoral behavior?"

"Oh me, oh my." Amelia flipped her fan open and worked it rapidly in front of her face. "Did you attend the Impressionist Exhibition at the Royal Gallery in London last month?"

"I refer to the best of society as a model, while you bring up the dregs as representative of the whole," Deverell said.

"Oh, yes." Josie nodded thoughtfully. "Among the aristocracy those terrible things surely never happened. Perhaps I should have mentioned the blind eye turned to mistresses, wife beating, and the sexual harassment of domestic help." Josie batted her eyelashes and smiled directly into Deverell's scowl.

"That sort of thing was much rarer than Gothic novels portray. One needed only repair to Covent Garden or walk down Haymarket Street to realize that the baser needs could be satisfied outside the home."

"Our seniors group from the church went up for the day. Ruth Simms and I quite enjoyed the exhibit," Amelia said, her voice an agitated squeak. "Though she appreciates Monet better than I."

"Imperfect performance in striving for a goal does not lessen the value of the goal," Deverell said, lounging back in his chair. He swirled the brandy in his glass and inhaled the fragrance before taking a sip.

His casual air did not fool Josie. The strength of an argument wasn't dependent on the volume of the speaker—in fact the opposite was often the case. This was a tactic on his part to goad her anger. She wouldn't let him manipulate her. She took several deep breaths.

"I suppose it's terrible to admit, but I think Monet's landscapes look like toxic swamps," Amelia said, rambling on about her visit to London. "I prefer Renoir and Degas, especially the portraits."

"Speaking of the best a society has to offer," Josie said when Amelia paused for a breath. "I think today's woman is much better off than women in your day. She can choose a career and choose her husband. Independence is a great equalizer, though I admit, we still have a ways to go."

"It is difficult for me to understand why a woman would choose the uncertainty of supporting herself over being put on a pedestal and cosseted."

"Statues belong on pedestals," Josie countered, "decorative and concerned only with the limited area they're allowed."

"We saw some lovely sculptures at the gallery. In fact, Castle Waite has always enjoyed a reputation for our fine garden statuary," Amelia said, with a pleading look at Josie.

"A woman raised on a pedestal would not see it as limiting; she should see it as her proper place, the natural order of things," Deverell pronounced with the certainty of the righteous.

"Now you're making the assumption that all women are either near-sighted or unintelligent," Josie replied. Amelia cleared her throat and Josie spared her an apologetic smile before turning back to face Deverell. "I'm sure even the women of your time noticed the disparity in the freedoms allowed men and those denied women."

"I never heard my mother or any other women I knew complain."

"Perhaps they feared the consequences of rocking the old pedestal, of risking a fall from grace. Or, perhaps you never bothered to listen." Josie knew she had hit home when her comment caused a muscle in Deverell's jaw to twitch.

Amelia rose from her seat, and Deverell also stood. Josie followed suit, placing her napkin unfolded on the table in the manner of her hostess.

"During the remove," Amelia said, her voice raised a notch in volume. "The guests might mingle, but each remained partnered with her dinner companion as they moved around the dining room. This took a bit of skill to dodge the servants bringing in mountains of food without seeming to notice them at all."

"I'll use this break to excuse myself to the lady's room," Josie whispered to Amelia.

"That's fine dear. I must mention that in the past it was considered very rude to leave the dining room for any reason until the hostess signaled for the ladies to depart."

"But..."

"A convenience chair was provided in the corner. Behind a screen, of course, for the discreet use of any guest needing the necessary," Amelia explained in a rush, obviously distressed by the need to discuss the subject. She rang the tiny bell by her plate.

"A chamber pot in the dining room? You call *that* a desirable lifestyle?" Josie asked, turning to Deverell.

He had disappeared as the servants began resetting the table for the second course.

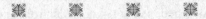

Josie propped her feet on the chaise and folded the ends of the silk kimono over her legs. The nearby fireplace provided welcome warmth in the chill of the late September evening. As she scanned the two etiquette books again, she had to admit that they made more sense after she had experienced the formal dinner earlier that evening.

Deverell had not returned to the table after the first remove, and she and Amelia had been able to concentrate on the task at hand. Josie blamed the flatness of the conversation on the dull subject matter. She refused to admit that the spark had gone out of the evening when Deverell had left.

Josie skipped through the order of precedence, past royalty and the assorted archbishops. She would never need to know that part. Imagine Josephine Drummond meeting mad King George or the Archbishop of Canterbury. She reminded herself that she wouldn't actually *need* any of it because the time travel wasn't going to work, but she did want Amelia to think her lessons were effective.

Josie read the list aloud one more time in her usual method of committing lists to memory. "Dukes, marquises, earls..." She interrupted herself to respond to the knock on the door. Emma must be returning for the tray of hot cocoa and biscuits. "Come in. Earls, viscounts, barons..."

Deverell sauntered into her room. "Ranked among themselves by date of creation in the following order: English, Scottish, of Great Britain, Irish..."

Josie sat up straighter and tucked the edges of her kimono closer together across the embroidered yolk of her nightgown. Not that she was indecent by any stretch of the imagination. She'd been in public places wearing much less than the floor length, long sleeved, cotton granny gown. Perhaps the candlelight made the atmosphere seem intimate. Or maybe the cozy fire. Whatever it was, she was suddenly conscious of her nakedness under the voluminous nightgown. And obnoxious Lord Waite was the last man...make that ghost...the last being...she wanted to be cozy with. She tucked the kimono around her knees.

"How in the world am I supposed to know the order of their creation?" Josie slammed the book shut and placed it on the table.

"Didn't Amelia include a copy of Debrett or Burke's?"

Josie waved toward the stack of books on the dressing table. "Isn't an earl an earl regardless?"

Deverell raised one eyebrow and tilted his head back to look down his nose at her. "A ninth generation title is more prestigious than a recently awarded one. It also makes a difference if the earl in question is the eldest son of a marquise or the younger son of a duke."

"As a modern American, I find the whole business of precedence nit-picking and tedious."

"I was under the impression that Americans had their own version, senators before congressmen, governors before mayors, that sort of thing."

Josie knew she was on unstable ground for another argument. That American titles were earned rather than inherited would hold little consequence with this man. Better to try another tactic.

"Why are you here?" Josie realized too late that her words sounded rude so she softened their effect with a smile. Since Deverell had remained standing, and she was uneasy with him looming above her, she waved an invitation for him to take the other chair by the fireplace.

Deverell shrugged and draped himself in the chair before responding. "I saw the light under your door."

Josie remained silent to encourage him to continue. He smiled at her as if he recognized the negotiator's trick he had used so effectively earlier. His slow grin caused one deep dimple to crater his cheek. Tingling goose bumps sped along her extremities.

"I wanted to apologize for leaving without an explanation."

"If an apology is due, it belongs to Amelia."

Deverell nodded. "A small bouquet of flowers will arrive in the morning." He shook his head and chuckled with self-depreciation. "Once started, I seem to have succumbed quite readily to the convenience of the telephone and credit card."

Josie resisted the urge to comment on his flagrant use of someone else's credit card. Amelia would be thrilled to receive the flowers, even if she wound up paying for them herself.

That was the problem with elaborate rituals of manners. Were sincere feelings expressed, or was it simply obeisance by rote? If someone felt required to send flowers, did the flowers still convey any meaning? For Amelia's sake, she wanted to believe his actions were motivated by true contrition.

Since he seemed to be feeling magnanimous, now was certainly a good time to continue her interrogation. "You mentioned earlier that you are aware of modern times...."

"Only in a general sense as pertains to the world at large. My concern has been this castle, so I've been aware of the lives of this family."

Josie aped his raised eyebrow and he chuckled in response.

"You are correct, of course. I've paid little enough attention to the family's affairs, or Amelia wouldn't be in this predicament. I have spent most of my time trying to read every book in the library."

Josie pictured the large library with its massive floor-to-ceiling shelves and appreciated the enormity of the task. Even an enthusiastic reader would have material for at least two hundred years. She recalled the matched sets of leather-bound classics, though in truth the shelves that were filled with her favorite romance novels were more enticing. "An admirable goal," she said.

"Humph," Deverell snorted. "An onerous, Sisyphean task. My curse was to be born into a family of readers and book collectors. Amelia brings home bags of paperbacks from the church rummage sale. If the south wing collapses, it will be from the weight of the crates of books stored there. I loathe reading. Too solitary. Too inactive."

"Then why do you do it?"

Deverell raised one hand and, with the flick of his wrist, produced his signature snifter of brandy. Did he use it as a prop to convey a relaxed attitude? His long, tapered fingers curled around the globe of glass, caressing the curves absently as he gazed into the fire.

"Never seems to taste right," he mused. "Even fully materialized, I cannot generate the body heat required to warm the brandy properly."

Without thinking, Josie reached for his brandy snifter. Silently she cupped the glass in two hands, gently, slowly, swirling the liquid for several minutes before handing it back.

He breathed the aroma and took a healthy swallow, his eyes closing in an expression of intense pleasure. "Thank you."

The simple heart-felt words meant more than any elaborate phrases. She knew instinctively that he could have easily called any number of flowery speeches into use. A warm glow spread through her stomach as if she had sipped from the snifter herself.

"If you dislike reading, why are you trying to read through the library?" she asked, as much to get her mind back on a safe topic as to satisfy her curiosity.

"Because I must complete the task in order to be free of my obligation."

Josie waited, not comprehending his meaning.

Deverell rose to pace the small chamber. "When I died, I chose to redeem my worthless life by assuming the guardianship of this castle. Rather than a specific time span, my term will last until I complete a task designed to improve my character. Then, another guardian can take my place and I will move onward."

Josie shook her head, still not understanding.

"The task assigned to me by the former guardian is to read every book in the castle library." Deverell faced her, his gray eyes stormy. "It was a trick. A fancy lure hiding a barbed hook. The old reprobate's idea of a grand joke. And I never knew I'd been caught until the hook was well set, and I was left floundering like a fish in the bottom of a boat."

Josie watched Deverell as she shifted around and groped blindly for her notebook and pen. She let it fall open to any old page, not taking her attention off Deverell. "Who tricked you?"

The ghost shoved one hand through his hair. One black lock fell back across his forehead leaving him looking...approachable. He sat in the chair again, leaning forward with his elbows on his thighs and his hands clasped between his knees.

"Earlier this evening you mentioned the ghost of Sir Robert...." Josie's voice trailed off in uncertainty as he stared at her notebook and poised pen.

"Now I know how bacteria feel under a microscope." Deverell conjured up another brandy and held it out to Josie to warm. "If you please."

She balanced the notebook on her lap, then cupped the snifter in her palms. "We can talk off the record, so to speak, if you prefer. We can simply chat as friends." She handed him the glass.

Deverell leaned back in his chair, crossing his legs and pushing the wayward lock of hair back off his forehead before downing half the contents of the glass. "Interesting concept, a woman friend. Can't say the idea has ever occurred to me."

"Amelia is your friend."

"She is my great-niece several times over. I watched her grow up. You, Miss Drummond, have been here precisely twenty days, and we met a mere seven hours ago. We are virtually strangers." Deverell did not flinch at his deliberate shading of the truth.

He had researched her quite thoroughly. She had a weak spot for the underdog and a fondness for old black and white films, and she was attracted to totally unsuitable men because they did not present any threat of emotional entanglement. Deverell probably knew her better than she knew herself. "You are not here for companionship, but rather for your professional expertise."

Josie stiffened at his rebuff. He knew he had hurt her, but it had been necessary. As the elder party...Hah! There was an understatement. The mantle of responsibility was his. He must confine their relationship to that of teacher and student.

"I shall bid you good evening." Deverell rose and hesitated until she nodded.

He stopped with his hand on the doorknob. He would not allow himself to turn around to see whether the tears that had glistened in her eyes had fallen down her cheeks. Still, with his back to her, he offered her the explanation she sought.

"Sir Robert was the former ghost of the castle. After completing his task of counting every stone in the castle, not an easy job because the family was forever building and rebuilding one part of the castle or another, Sir Robert recruited me to take his place. He cleverly set a task that would insure the family a guardian through eternity."

Josie called his name. Deverell hesitated, but forced himself to remain facing the door.

"If you go back in time, won't you meet Sir Robert again?"

"Egad, I hope not. It might prove difficult to kill a man who had already been dead for five hundred years, and I would surely want to murder him."

Deverell could not resist turning at the sound of her laughter. Josie sat cross-legged on the chaise, the edges of her kimono tucked under her toes, the ever present notebook open in her lap. She looked even younger than her years, somehow more vulnerable, as she gazed at him with sparkling eyes.

He raised one eyebrow in query.

"I didn't mean to laugh," she said, stifling another giggle with her fingertips. "It's just that you sounded so macho, as if you wanted to challenge him to a duel with pistols at dawn, or to run him through with your sword. You may be dead, but you're still a man."

Deverell didn't bother to open the door, but walked straight through the oak panel. Josie had verbalized the very crux of his dilemma. She was an intelligent woman, a perceptive, beautiful, vibrantly alive woman.

And he was still a man, even if he was a ghost.

Four

"Ouch," Josie said. She dropped her embroidery hoop and stuck her finger in her mouth.

"You don't want to get any blood on your sampler," Amelia said as she pulled a handkerchief from her sleeve with the flair of a magician. "Here."

Josie shook her head at the proffered item, not wanting to stain the delicate lace-trimmed square...though Amelia seemed to have more than enough of them. She had one tucked into every pocket, one in each sleeve, and tons more stashed about the house.

"You didn't tell me needlework was dangerous," Josie mumbled. Or tedious. Or boring. She picked up the hoop that had fallen to the floor and eyed the uneven stitches with a frown. She was not accustomed to new things being difficult for her to learn. In three hours she'd managed a wobbly J and a lopsided O. She seriously considered shortening her nickname.

"Sewing was an important part of every Regency gentlewoman's day. Even if she had only a few spare minutes, she picked up her thimble and thread. She carried a bit of work with her when she made social calls. The ladies did not just do decorative needlework. They made clothes for themselves and their family."

"What about tailors and dressmakers."

"In the country a seamstress would visit seasonally with prints of the latest fashions, and she might spend several weeks in residence while sewing new dresses. The women of the family made their own aprons, caps, underclothes, nightwear, shirts for the men, and outfits for the children. Girls started sewing items for their trousseau at quite a young age. Then there was the making and mending of all the household linens, and of clothes for the poor."

Josie groaned.

"Of course we won't be going over how to do all that."

"My sore fingers thank you."

"Since you've worked so diligently I'll let you in on a little secret. We have a special treat later today," Amelia said.

"Really?" Josie managed an interested smile. "At breakfast you surprised me with your friend who gave that...amazing lecture on the language of the fan." And an hour of practice.

Josie laid her embroidery hoop on the table and stood up, stretching, as she walked to the large parlor window that faced the gardens. Although sheets of cold rain obscured the view, she fought the urge to go out for a walk. She wasn't used to so much inactivity. "Such an ugly gray day."

Amelia came up beside her. "All this history is not really your cup of tea is it? I miss his lively presence, too."

"That's not at all what I meant," Josie lied. It wasn't as if she would ever actually need any of the useless information. If learning outdated skills was the price she had to pay to further her research, then she would make the best of it. "What's on the schedule next?" she asked brightly.

Amelia gave her an understanding look and then began to pack the sewing things back into their tapestry-covered box. "Two former colleagues of mine promised to come out this afternoon. Ian Smythe collects music from the Regency and Victorian periods, and his wife Cecily did her postgrad work on dance through history. Quite interesting. Her theory is that major changes in popular dances directly predate radical social change rather than reflecting it. She just received a generous government endowment to continue her studies."

A grant to study dancing? Josie couldn't think of anything to say.

"Smile, my dear. This will be fun."

Josie could hardly wait. And where was Lord Waite? Did he intend to uphold his end of the bargain?

"Dancing well was considered an essential accomplishment for both men and women," Cecily Smythe said as she arranged armless chairs in a line. "As being among the few opportunities to socialize with members of the opposite sex, balls, assemblies, and dance parties were widely popular."

Josie would have preferred helping Ian Smythe set up his portable keyboard and other sound equipment in the corner, but she stayed in place and wondered how Cecily managed to speak without moving her lips.

"The Regency was a period of transition in dance," Cecily continued. "The stately minuet was still danced at court until 1820 and at balls given by the more conservative of the aristocracy. Most assemblies and balls were filled with the lively country dance, Scotch reel, and the somewhat more subdued cotillion. A couple stood up for a set, two dances, which could last half an hour."

Although Amelia appeared fascinated by Cecily's droning lecture, the afternoon stretched long before Josie.

"I wish we had a few more people to set up a proper line," Cecily said.

Josie wished for someone, anyone, even Deverell to appease the tedium.

Amelia left and returned in a matter of moments.

The sounds of a synthesized harpsichord filled the air just as the others who had been drafted to participate arrived. Cecily arranged everyone in two lines facing each other, Ian, George the footman, and four of the chairs on one side, and the women on the other. Amelia curtseyed gracefully to her partner George. Josie and a giggling Emma followed suit facing their wooden partners.

"I've named my chair Raoul," Josie whispered to Emma.

"Mine is Colin," the maid replied, giving a flirty wave of her fingers in its direction.

Cook smiled tolerantly, but Vivian folded her arms and stared up at the ceiling.

Cecily took her position at the end. "We are lined up for the longways country dance. There are also circle formations. This type of dance can be performed by six couples or by more than six hundred couples, the only limitation being the size of the hall."

"Or the endurance of the dancers."

Josie heard Deverell's voice, but when she looked around he was nowhere to be seen. And no one else appeared to have heard anything out of the ordinary.

Cecily did look to her left down the row of women, but she simply signaled for them to straighten up the line before continuing her lecture. "In its simplest form, the dance is rather like Follow the Leader."

"I always preferred a game of cards," Deverell said, his disembodied voice causing goose bumps on Josie's arms.

"The first couple executes a series of moves; then the other couples repeat them. Then the first dancers go to the ends of their respective lines, and the second couple presents their series of moves.

This continues until the first couple returns to the starting position. If the lines were long, this could take up to an hour."

"Reason enough to avoid dancing with someone you do not fancy."

This time when he spoke, Josie saw him. Only faintly, rather like an unfocused photo seen through frosted glass, but that deep smoky voice could belong to no other. Yet no one else noticed him seated on the chair directly opposite her.

Josie squinted, trying to see him more clearly. Knowing what distress his sudden appearance in front of the servants, not to mention in front of her friends, would cause Amelia, she whispered, "What are you doing here? Go away."

"Beg your pardon?" Cecily stepped forward and looked directly at Josie.

"Are you speaking to me?" Deverell asked.

Josie ignored him and spoke to Cecily. "Sorry. My foot fell asleep." She shook her leg for emphasis. "Please continue."

Deverell stood and stepped toward her. "You *were* speaking to me. That's strange."

Very strange, since no one else seemed to see or hear him. Either that, or they were ignoring him, a strategy Josie decided to adopt because the other alternative brought up questions she wasn't ready to ask...or answer.

"Can you see me? How many fingers am I holding up?"

With some effort she refrained from looking in his direction.

"Josie has a valid point," Cecily continued. "This system left many of the participants idle when they wanted to be dancing. The next evolution came when a series of moves became fixed and could therefore be learned in advance and danced by everyone at the same time. But enough of my chatter. Ian and I will demonstrate a move, and then we'll all do it together."

Josie learned how to *single*, *double* and *cross-over*, *chassé,* do a *gip*, and do a *mad robin*. And Deverell became more difficult to ignore as he chose to take the role of her partner and personal dancing master. His presence become clearer and clearer, at least to her, until she saw him distinctly with only a bit of shiny aura around the edges. Almost like a full body halo. But he was no angel. His caustic comments became increasing difficult to let pass without a response.

"Step lightly. You're dancing, not stomping grapes."

"Graceful arm movements. Not like you're chopping wood."

"The floor is even and smooth. There is no need to look at your feet."

"Don't slump. Good posture must be maintained at all times."

"Dainty steps. This is not a gallop."

"Enough!"

"What?" Emma asked.

Josie realized she'd spoken aloud and had to cover her *faux pas.* "I was just telling Raoul I've had enough of his stepping on my toes."

Emma giggled. "My Colin is a wonderful dancer."

"I never stepped...oh, I understand. It's a metaphor," Deverell said. "Point taken." He bowed his apology.

Josie curtseyed her response.

"So you can see me. Curious."

"Now we'll dance a complete set," Cecily said, saving Josie the necessity of a confirmation.

The *Sir Roger de Coverly* reminded Josie of the *Virginia Reel* from her childhood. They managed from beginning to end with only a few reminders from Cecily, and with blessed silence from Deverell who retreated to watch from the sidelines. They even tried a *straight hey,* which wound up looking more like a game of musical chairs as they marched in and out around the stationary partners.

"Oh my. Perhaps we should take a break." Amelia said, plying her fan with vigor.

Unfortunately, Josie had left her fan in the parlor.

"Are we done?" Vivian asked.

"What's her problem?" Josie whispered to Emma, her *neighbor* in dance terms.

"I don't know. This is more fun than doing the tango with a mop or the electric monkey with a dust cloth."

Josie really needed to get out more. She'd never even heard of the electric monkey.

"I think we could do with some refreshment," Amelia said. "Vivian, would you please fetch us some lemonade?"

Cook scuttled out the door, presumably to prepare her employer's request, but Vivian stood her ground and jerked her head toward the other maid. Emma turned to leave.

"Thank you, Vivian," Amelia said, stopping the second maid mid-step. "Emma will tidy up in here. George, please let in a bit of air," she added with a wave toward the bank of French doors that opened out onto the large stone terrace that had been added to the back of the castle in the late 1700s.

The rain had stopped, and the fresh scent of green countryside wafted in on a cool breeze.

Vivian stomped out of the ballroom, sparing a glare in the other maid's direction.

"Now she's in a snit," Emma said. She moved two chairs back against the wall and returned for the others. "Farewell, Colin." She patted the back of the chair. "You were a good partner."

"Unfortunately, Raoul was a bit stiff."

"Stiff is not always a bad thing in a partner," Emma muttered, but then immediately apologized.

"It's Raoul who deserves my apology," Josie replied with a wink. "The poor stiff," she added over her shoulder as she left to join Amelia and the others.

Cecily was speaking about the waltz. "The Regency version was danced a bit slower than in Victorian times. And, yes, it was considered scandalous. Even that epitome of a Regency bad boy Lord Byron thought it shameful to *embrace* on the dance floor. Lady Jersey did not allow it at Almack's until 1815. She preferred the Quadrille, a French dance of five sections performed by four couples. Much too complicated to learn today."

"Can we have a waltz before tea?"

"I'm sorry, Amelia," Ian said with a shake of his head.

"We can't stay to tea," Cecily added. "It's near an hour back to London, and we have a previous engagement this evening." She looked at her watch. "In fact, we should be leaving soon."

"I'm sorry you can't stay."

"Me, too," Josie added. "Thank you so much for sharing your expertise." She shook hands with both visitors. When Ian excused himself to pack up his equipment, and the women started catching up on mutual acquaintances, Josie slipped away to get some air on the terrace.

The outside temperature was chillier than she'd expected, and for once she wished she had one of those bothersome shawls. Rather than go back inside just yet, she found a seat in a sheltered alcove where she could still enjoy the view.

"Raoul?" Deverell said as he materialized at her side. "That's what you named your dream partner?"

"At least Raoul didn't criticize my every move."

"Critique is not criticism. One cannot improve without knowing what one is doing wrong."

"Again semantics. What were you even doing there? Amelia doesn't want you to be seen or heard."

"Obviously I wasn't. Not by anyone other than you."

"And why is that?"

"I haven't a notion."

"You promised to answer all my questions."

"To the best of my ability."

"Meaning?"

"I have no answer. Always before anyone and every-one could see me to the degree I chose to materialize."

"What do you mean by *degree?*" Josie reached for her notebook, only to realize she must have left her reticule in the parlor with her fan. Didn't Regency women understand the value of pockets?

"Pockets would ruin the line of your dress."

"I thought you couldn't read my mind."

Deverell rolled his eyes. "Your thoughts were transparent to the most casual observer. You reached to your left wrist for something that wasn't there. What would be hanging from your arm other than your reticule with your notebook? Then you patted your side where your usual modern attire of a jacket would have a pocket. A little huff of breath signaled your frustration. The interpretation is obvious."

"Fine," Josie said, stifling her sigh of relief so he wouldn't read anything into it. "Now what about your degree-of-materialization comment?"

"Ah, yes. Back to the research."

"It's the reason I'm here."

He cleared his throat. "As I told you before, everything I do uses energy."

"Of which you have a finite amount."

"Yes. As with many things I have attempted to do, full materialization uses a lot of energy. On a scale of zero to one hundred, I usually spend the majority of time in a five-percent materialization that uses very little energy. To an observer I would appear to be a shadow, or a wisp of smoke, or a stray beam of sunlight. Unremarkable."

"So a person who saw you would dismiss it."

"Correct. But I still maintain a presence and move from room to room as I desire. If I want to be seen, I can partially materialize."

"Does that mean partial like just your head or just a hand? Or like a...a..."

"Ghostly image? Yes."

"Yes, what?"

"Both. Either. The answer to your question is yes."

Josie was sure she'd rather not see just his head or other body parts, and she told him so.

"It does save energy."

"I don't care. It's just too creepy." Then it occurred to her to ask, "What happens if you run out of energy?"

"Zero. Nothingness. Blackness."

When she saw the bleak look in his eyes, she immediately regretted bringing up the topic. "How long does it last?" she asked, knowing he would read her sympathy in her tone of voice.

He shrugged off his distress. "I do try to avoid that particular situation, however it has happened in the past without a discernible pattern of recovery. Five years. Twenty years. What matters a few years when I have eternity?"

Josie shivered, and this time she couldn't blame the weather.

"In anticipation of your next question," Deverell continued, "the last time was when Amelia was a young woman. I blinked out of existence, and when I came to myself again, forty-five years had passed."

"Maybe that wasn't what I would have asked," Josie said even though he was right.

"Liar. Do you know you blink three times after you tell a lie?

"What percent were you manifested when I could see you, but the others could not?"

"The usual. About five percent."

"What did you do differently?"

He barked out a laugh. "Typical woman's response. Why are my actions in question? I should think your ability to see me has more to do with you than with me. What did *you* do differently?"

"Nothing. What could I have done? I don't have the option of appearing or not appearing as the whim strikes me. I was there to learn to dance per your blasted list. Why were you there?"

"As your instructor..."

"Cecily and Ian did just fine without your help. They are the experts."

"Bah! What better expert than one who actually attended the assemblies and danced the dances they cobble together from bits and pieces? Research cannot recreate the excitement of a ball. After weeks of expectation, the evening finally arrives. Everyone dressed in their finest. The ballroom decorated in some theme or other and lit with thousands of candles. The joy of hearing music once again after the long silence of the countryside. The anticipation of meeting that one...."

The faraway look of longing in his eyes told her more about the importance of balls to Regency society than any number of Cecily's lectures could.

"Or so some would say." Deverell brushed an imaginary piece of lint from his sleeve. "Actually, after the first few, balls were nothing more than an interminable evening of ceaseless posturing and gossip. An arcane ritual propagated by matchmaking mammas, whose only goal was to find rich and titled husbands for their daughters, or suitably demure wives for their sons."

"So how come you never married?"

"It wasn't for lack of trying on my mother's part. Even though I had perfectly valid heirs in two younger cousins, she was determined to shackle me to some insipid miss. I did plan to marry eventually. I just never..."

"Expected to die?"

"Don't be ridiculous. Everyone dies. I didn't marry because I never met a woman worth my freedom, that's all."

"From what I've read, it was the woman, not the man, who gave up everything by getting married."

"Easy to say from the perspective of hindsight."

Josie was taken aback. "Are you admitting I'm right?"

"Perish the thought. Although few, there were certain expectations married men met."

"Such as keeping their liaisons discreet rather then flaunting them?"

"A gentleman does not flaunt...anything. I referred to providing for his wife and subsequent family, keeping an appropriate home, hosting and escorting, doing one's duty. Everything designed to limit a man's free time as well as to sap his pocketbook. Resources a single man uses in the pursuit of his pleasure."

"Well, that hasn't changed."

"Nor should it."

"At least now a single woman has the same option."

"And what pleasures do you pursue, Miss Drummond?"

"My work," she answered with only the slightest hesitation.

"Josie? Miss Josie?"

Deverell faded to his aura state just as Emma came around the corner.

"Lady Amelia wondered whether you wanted to say good-bye to the Smythes. They're all packed up and ready to leave."

"Of course." Josie stood and followed the maid.

She hesitated at the door and looked back over her shoulder. Deverell stood near the cozy alcove. From somewhere he'd produced a smoking cheroot and his signature brandy, the picture of a suave gentleman. He raised his glass in salute.

"What a lovely, intriguing liar," he said after she'd gone inside. But he wasn't sure whether she'd been lying to him or to herself. And he wasn't sure why he felt the need to know.

He took a deep gulp of his drink, wishing he could feel its warming effect. If he wasn't careful that woman would—no he couldn't even think that.

Best move up his timetable. Better to get this over with before...before what?

He flicked the tasteless cigar over the stone balustrade.

Before he wasted more energy on useless pursuits.

Five

JOSIE SAT AT THE DESK IN THE LIBRARY, MAKING a list of the questions she wanted to ask Deverell. Although it would be easy to blame him for the limited information she'd gathered so far, she knew the blame belonged squarely on her own shoulders. She had allowed him to sidetrack her. She'd allowed herself to be distracted by his smile, the amused twinkle in his eyes when he baited her into another argument.

She would have to fight that little thrill of excitement she felt in his presence, that curl of warmth when he appeared. She could easily become addicted to that tingle, and then where would she be? When the week was over and his grand plan failed, she would return to her life never to see him again. There was no future in being attracted to a ghost.

Not that she was attracted to him or anything like that. She was just flattered that he seemed to be interested in her thoughts, her feelings. That's all.

She would stick to her research. No more tangents. She looked at her list of questions and crossed off those that pertained to his life before death. She was interested in the now. How did he renew his depleted energy? Did he sleep?

"Where is that butler? I rang for tea at least five minutes ago." Amelia set aside her gardening magazine and stood. Rather than use the bellpull again, she picked up the phone. She paused before pushing the button to call downstairs. "What's his name? Higgins? Hiddens?"

"Higdon," Deverell provided as he appeared in his leather chair. "He will be along soon."

Amelia set down the receiver. "I'm afraid he isn't working out."

"Give the lad a chance."

"But he doesn't know his job."

"He'll learn. If fact, I've written out instructions." He pulled several sheets of paper from his breast pocket, and Josie could not suppress a groan of empathy for the younger man.

Amelia did not take the papers. "Perhaps we should get a replacement from the employment agency..."

"I did not hire him through an employment agency," Deverell muttered.

A sudden horrifying thought occurred to Josie. "Did you transport..."

"No, I did not transport him from another time or place."

Josie sagged back into her chair in relief—as if she'd needed further proof that Deverell could not do what he said he could.

"Then where did you find him?" Amelia asked. Deverell shifted in his chair as if uncomfortable having to explain his methods. "I did call an agency that specifically handles butlers and was told, quite rudely as a matter of fact, they do not take temporary assignments. After I thought about it, though, it made sense. Since we only needed someone for a week, I was forced to think creatively."

"So where did you find him?" Amelia asked again.

"Through a theatrical agency."

"An actor?"

"For a young man he has quite an impressive resume."

"You hired an actor to play the part of our butler? Oh, my. The cost must..."

"I am not unmindful of your pocketbook, my dear. Higdon is doing it for room and board. He is, and I quote, up for a major part in a film. According to our phone interview, he thinks on-the-job training will help him nail the motivation. Though it is beyond me why anyone would make a film about a butler named Jeeves..."

Amelia coughed. "Obviously you haven't gotten to the *W*s in the library. Jeeves is..."

"A gentleman's gentleman. Yes, I am aware of that and also quite aware of the difference between that and a butler, hence the extensive list I've provided for his edification."

Josie was about to ask Deverell about the differences when there was a knock on the door. When Amelia called permission to enter, he went into his aura state where other people couldn't see him, though for some reason she still could.

"You rang?" Higdon said in a sonorous voice reminiscent of Lurch, the butler on *The Addams Family*.

"We'll have our tea now," Amelia said.

"Very good." He bowed and reached for the handle as he backed out the door.

"Before you go, here's a list of some things you may need to know." Amelia held out the papers Deverell had prepared.

Higdon stepped forward. "Thank you." He scanned the pages. "Oh, wow! This is way cool," he said dropping his formal persona.

"Perhaps you can study those in private," Amelia suggested, not unkindly. "After serving tea?"

"Yes, of course." He stuffed the pages into his pocket. "My apologies. I'll be back in a jiff. I mean, very good, madam." He backed out the door in a proper fashion, although he could not entirely erase the smile from his face.

"That was very nice of you," Josie said to Deverell.

"Thank you," Amelia answered.

Deverell nodded his head in recognition of her compliment, and Josie thought she detected a slight blush as he rematerialized so that Amelia could see him, too.

"Now that we've taken care of that, we can get back to the important issues," he said.

Josie picked up her list of questions and joined Amelia on the sofa. "Exactly what I was going to say. First question. How do you..."

"Before you start another Inquisition," Deverell interrupted.

Josie bit her tongue to keep from responding to his

verbal bait and going off on some religious tangent.

"After tea, I've arranged for the carriage to be brought around at four forty-five. We're going for a drive."

"Oh, dear," Amelia said. "I have the contractor coming to look at the south wing and give a repair estimate."

"We can go for a drive some other time," Josie said. Like maybe never, she thought. She had not been near a horse since her riding accident, and she didn't intend to start now.

"The horses are in need of exercise. Miss Drummond and I will have to manage without your company."

Josie was in the middle of framing her decline using the old standby headache for a reason when Amelia spoke up with a better excuse.

"In the spirit of the Regency, it is highly inappropriate for her to go for a drive alone with a man."

Josie could see where the whole chaperone bit might come in handy when a woman didn't want to do something.

"Not applicable in this case. After all I am a ghost, not a man. I am quite positive Miss Drummond will use the time alone to badger me with questions about my existence just as if you were there, perhaps more so since there will be no distractions."

A knock on the door signaled Higdon's return with tea.

"And no interruptions," Deverell added as he faded to a hazy presence.

Josie glanced down at her list of unanswered

questions. Inside the carriage she would have Deverell's undivided attention. "I'll be ready," she said before she could have second thoughts about whether that was a good thing.

If he weren't still visible to her, Deverell would have rubbed his hands together with satisfaction. Not being able to disappear was quite disconcerting. He'd rather gotten used to being an unseen observer whenever he chose. But that was neither here nor there. The important fact was that the situation was now neatly arranged just as he had planned.

He stood and bowed to her before leaving the library. He had a few final details to attend to.

Miss Drummond would not get the drive she was expecting.

Josie had second thoughts as she stepped outside. The weather had turned nasty and a wicked storm threatened. However, Deverell did not seem concerned as he stood near the horses.

"Step lively," he said. "We want to miss the downpour."

The coachman, oblivious to Deverell's presence, stoically held the carriage door open, fighting the wind that not only threatened to slam the door shut but also tried to rip the bonnet off her head. Although she would've gladly let the darn hat go flying, she hurried into the carriage, only to find one seat piled high with boxes and wrapped bundles. What was Deverell up to now?

Regardless of his plans, she was determined not to miss a moment of this opportunity. She settled onto the rear-facing seat and withdrew her list of questions from her reticule.

Deverell popped onto the seat next to her just as a bolt of lightning sizzled through the air, causing the hair on her arms to rise. The flash was accompanied by an earsplitting clap of thunder. The carriage jerked forward.

"Perfect timing," Deverell said, slapping his knee.

Josie reached for something to hold on to, finding a loop of leather next to the door. The window covering flapped in the wind, not only allowing in the cold rain but also allowing her to see the coachman running after them down the curved driveway.

"Oh my God. There's the driver."

"We'll be fine."

The coach picked up speed, jostling her back and forth. "We're in a runaway coach!"

"Just for another minute or two and then everything will be fine," he assured her.

She held on to the strap with both hands. How could he remain so calm? Their lives were in danger. Or rather hers was. He was already dead. Was that his intention? To have her killed just to avoid a few questions?

The coach picked up speed on the straight stretch of drive leading to the long curve by the gatehouse. Everything vibrated: the seat, the walls. Several packages fell to the floor.

"Do something. Stop this coach."

"What would you have me do, my dear? Climb up top and grab the reins?"

"For starters. Before this contraption flips over or rattles to pieces."

Another flash of lightning and crash of thunder shook the carriage.

"It will hold. I know it will hold," Deverell muttered. "Please hold together," he said, closing his eyes as if in prayer.

She decided that if he wasn't going to do something, she would. She grabbed hold of the windowsill to pull herself up. Just as she started out the window, the coach hit a large bump, throwing her sprawling back onto the seat and smacking the back of her head in the process.

Suddenly the carriage slowed.

Josie sat up and straightened her hat.

The wind no longer howled. The rain had disappeared. The scent of roses drifted in, and the only noise was the sound of the horses' hooves on a gravel driveway as they proceeded at a sedate pace.

"We've arrived," Deverell said with a huge grin.

Josie had the distinct feeling they weren't in Kansas anymore. "Where are we? Oz?"

"We're coming up the drive of my estate. See? There's the castle just ahead."

"But we were going down the driveway a minute ago." Josie looked out the window. The yellow stone of the castle practically glowed in the afternoon sun. A profusion of flowers spilled from raised beds. Cold, rainy, and fall had changed in the blink of an eye to warm, sunny, and summer. She put her hand to her head. "What exactly happened?" Nothing made sense. "What did you do?"

"Simply what I said I would do. Admittedly, I couldn't wait the full week for you to complete your lessons, but I'll be able to smooth over any problems. My mother is actually quite nice. I'm sure the two of you will get along." He sounded almost giddy with excitement.

"Your mother?"

A loud snort from the other seat forestalled his answer. The pile of clothes moved. Josie shrank back into the corner. "What's that?"

"Sshh. Don't wake her just yet. I have a few last-minute instructions, and we have very little time."

"Her?"

"Mrs. Binns. Your chaperone. Now, when you..."

"Whoa." Josie held up her hands. "How did she get into the carriage?"

"The usual way, I imagine."

"You know what I mean. How did she get in the carriage with us? She wasn't here when we started out, was she?"

"Of course not. Technically the question should be, how did we get into the carriage with her? since we joined en route when we traveled back in time."

No. It couldn't have worked. And even if it had, there would have been...something other than a bump in the road to signal it happening. Josie pinched herself on the arm. "Ouch."

"We really are in the year 1815. You can believe it."

"Stop reading my mind."

"I'm not..."

"Well, stop whatever it is you're doing." She knew she was being unreasonable, but how could she be rational at a time like this? She needed a few minutes to wrap her mind around the whole time travel thing. Time travel! Oh my God. Could it be true?

"As I was about to say," Deverell continued in a quelling tone, "Mrs. Binns, a cousin of my mother's, was engaged to act as your chaperone. The letter, ostensibly from your father, was penned by me."

Josie ignored his aggravating royal proclamation tone in favor of her other concern. "Won't Mrs. Binns notice that we...popped in mid-ride?"

"She's quite absentminded. If we tell her she picked you up at the dock straight off the ship from America, she'll believe it. She also tends to fall asleep at the drop of a hat, which makes her perfect for the job. You will be free to complete your investigation unimpeded."

"What investigation?"

"Of the gypsy seer's methods. The reason for coming here."

Oh yeah. The gypsy. Josie had almost forgotten about her. Reasonable since she never expected to make the...trip. "Where's my equipment?"

"We couldn't bring any of your gadgets."

"Then how am I supposed to investigate the claim to contact the spirits of the dead?"

"Surely you have other methods at your disposal?"

"Like what?"

"How should I know? You're the ghost hunter."

"Paranormal investigator," she corrected automatically.

The carriage slowed even more on the final

approach to the house. Mrs. Binns stirred and sat up with a start.

"We're almost here," Josie said gently so as not to startle the woman even more.

Mrs. Binns blinked rapidly.

"I can't thank you enough for meeting my boat and agreeing to be my chaperone."

"Well, yes, of course. Although I did hesitate once I learned Honoria is trying to speak to the dead. She was raised to have more sense. Any reasonable person would be terrified of ghosts. But don't you worry, my dear." Mrs. Binns rummaged among the packages until she found a large red velvet case. She hugged it to her ample bosom. "I've enough anti-spirit potions and charms to protect us all."

The carriage pulled to a halt. The door opened, and Mrs. Binns alighted with more spryness than Josie would have suspected.

"Come along then," she said, waiting for Josie at the bottom of the stairs to the front entrance.

Suddenly the enormity of it all crashed in on Josie. Everything she'd learned fled her brain. She cringed back into the corner. "I can't. I'm not ready. I don't know how to act."

"Nonsense," both Deverell and Mrs. Binns said at the same time. "You'll do fine," she added. "Now come along. You can't stay in the carriage forever."

Josie could not refute that logic, although a few hours would be welcome.

"Let's get through the introductions, and then we'll settle in for a little nap before tea."

Josie convinced herself she could make it if she

could escape to a bit of solitude after the introductions. What choice did she have? She alighted from the carriage, entered the grand front door, and immediately faced Deverell's mother.

Honoria Thornton was the epitome of cool elegance. Not too tall—about Josie's height—and slim, she had medium brown hair highlighted with attractive streaks of gray and twisted into a chignon at the back of her head. Although friendly, she made Josie feel clumsy and disheveled by comparison.

She was led through the double doors to the left and into the parlor, which was decorated in navy and cream toile. The dark wood of the Queen Anne furniture matched the paneling, but the room was saved from being gloomy by the bank of floor-to-ceiling windows along one wall. As Josie entered, she glanced over her shoulder at Deverell. How could he help her if he stayed outside?

Deverell had not been unduly disturbed when Mrs. Binns had not acknowledged him in the carriage. After all, his reputation had preceded him and she would not be the first proper lady to ignore his presence. But just now his own mother had given him the cut direct. Shaking his head, he followed the group into the parlor.

While Mrs. Binns completed the introductions, he cast his mind back on the day he'd chosen for their arrival. What had he done in the weeks prior that would cause his mother to be so upset with him that she couldn't spare a greeting? Admittedly his memory of that time was a bit fuzzy. He'd wanted to get as close as possible to the time of his

death so that he didn't accidentally reveal something that hadn't happened yet.

No despicable deed came to mind—at least
nothing out of the ordinary.

Josie had taken the indicated seat next to Lady
Honoria, but she had a difficult time concentrating
on the conversation as the two cousins caught up
on mutual acquaintances. As they drank tea and
discussed the house party and scheduled ball, Mrs.
Binns seemed especially interested in the men who
were invited.

Deverell lounged with one elbow on the mantel. Whenever Josie looked to her right at Lady
Honoria he was directly in her line of sight, yet
both of the other women ignored Deverell and his
comments.

"Hargrave is still grieving his lost fortune. He'll
be jolly company," he said. "Wingate? Gad, you'd
better hope he keeps a rein on his wife."

No response to his comments.

"You can always count on Barstow to show up
for a free meal. I'm surprised at Caster. He must be
more desperate to marry a large dowry than I'd
thought."

"Hardly the caliber of prospects I'd hoped for,"
Mrs. Binns said. "However, it will allow my charge
to dip her toes in society before the season starts."
Learning that a number of responses for the ball
had not yet been received appeared to placate her.

Then she made a comment about Deverell as if
he wasn't standing right behind her. "I assume Lord
Waite will come up to snuff this weekend and do

his duty as host," Mrs. Binns said, her tone indicating the futility of such lofty expectations. "Miss Drummond is quite anxious to meet him," she added much to Josie's surprise.

"No...I..."

Honoria touched Josie on the arm as she leaned forward and spoke toward the door to their left. "There he is now. Dev, dear, come meet Miss Josephine Drummond from America."

Josie turned. He stood in the doorway, dressed for riding in a dark brown coat, tan buckskins, and knee-high boots. Yet something more than his outfit was different. She automatically looked back to where he'd stood a moment before. How had he done that?

He stepped into the room. "Pleased to meet you, Miss Drummond."

His voice, full and rich, sent shivers down her spine. Mrs. Binns hissed at her and motioned for her to stand. Josie jumped up and managed a creditable curtsy despite her unsteady legs.

"I hope you enjoy your visit." He took her hand. His fingers were warm.

But Deverell—

He grazed his lips across the back of her hand, setting up a vibration inside her like the lowest note on a cello.

Something was wrong.

She jerked her hand away and took a quick step back. Too quick. Her heel snagged on the thick carpet and she lost her footing. He caught her before she landed on the floor.

A person happening upon them at just that moment would have thought he held her bent backward in a lover's embrace, his arms around her, his lips inches from hers. Without conscious decision, her hands slipped up his arms to his shoulders. The vibrations inside her kicked up a notch, adding bass fiddles and maybe a violin or twelve.

"How very nice to meet you," he whispered.

His scent surrounded her, bay rum and faint aromatic tobacco and something else that seemed to shout male animal, something distinctly his own. His warmth created an answering inferno inside her—a feeling she'd never felt before. But it was his eyes that made her certain. They were the same deep blue color, but this Deverell's eyes sparked with vivacity, excitement, and...passion. This was not the ghost of Lord Waite. This was the real man. Familiar and yet...not.

"For goodness sake, Dev. Give the girl room to breathe," his mother said.

As if Josie remembered what breathing was.

Dev set her on her feet and stepped back. She expected him to make some smart comment on her clumsiness, but he looked as stunned as she felt.

He shook his head as if to remove unwanted thoughts. "I...I just stopped by to let you know I have an engagement for the evening. I won't be home for dinner."

"But I've already made plans. Tonight is the"— Honoria paused to look at Mrs. Binns—"the you-know-what."

"I'll be home by midnight." Dev kissed his

mother on the forehead and left. He paused at the door for a glance back in Josie's direction before he continued on his way with another shake of his head.

"Just as well," Mrs. Binns said. "We're exhausted from our journey and would not be fit company. We'll take dinner in our rooms and won't disturb whatever plans you've made."

Josie figured Honoria must have referred to a séance scheduled for that very night. The fact that Mrs. Binns spoke for her rankled Josie just a bit, but she decided it was best to go along with the program. Once Mrs. Binns was tucked in for the night Josie could sneak downstairs and hopefully wangle an invitation to participate.

Maybe Deverell could help with that. Where was that pesky ghost anyway? He wouldn't have abandoned her in this time, would he?

She looked in every nook and alcove as she followed Mrs. Binns and the housekeeper up a grand staircase and down a long carpeted hall lined with artwork to a lovely suite of rooms. The two bedrooms were connected by a sitting room decorated in sage green and soft gold.

No ghost.

After Mrs. Binns expressed her satisfaction with the accommodations, they were introduced to Dora, their assigned maid, and Nellie, another maid who was helping unpack the trunks that had been delivered while the ladies had tea.

Still, no Deverell. "Materialize, damn you," she whispered under her breath. Nothing. Not an ethereal image. Not even an intangible presence.

As Mrs. Binns dozed in the chair, Nellie worked in the other bedroom and Dora finished unpacking for Josie.

The maid oohed and aahed as she took dress after dress from the trunks designated as Josie's. She was just as awed as the maid because she'd never seen any of the beautiful gowns before.

"I had them made to order and shipped to Mrs. Binn's residence to include with her own luggage," Deverell said as he appeared lounging against the windowsill.

"Don't do that!"

Although Josie had spoken to Deverell, it was the maid who reacted with dismay.

"What? Don't do what?" Dora asked, her eyes wide.

"Don't put that dress in the wardrobe," Josie said to cover her outburst. "I'll wear that one this evening."

"But this is a day dress."

"Well, it doesn't make sense to get all dressed up to have dinner in my room, now does it?"

"I suppose not," Dora said, laying the dress on the bed and brushing it smooth. "It could use a good pressing."

"Fabulous idea. Why don't you do that now and I'll finish the unpacking myself."

"Oh, no. I couldn't..."

"Go on." Josie scooped up the dress and shoved it into the maid's arms. "Take your time. I'll be...resting—that's it. I'll take a nap in the meantime, so don't rush back." She shooed Dora out the door and then spun around to face Deverell.

"Where have you been, Mister I'll-be-there-to-help-you-with-any-difficulties?"

"This isn't working out as I'd planned."

"What was your first clue? Is that why you disappeared when I needed you most?"

"I had no choice."

"Oh really?"

"I—meaning the flesh and blood me—am already here."

"Yes. I met him, I mean you." She didn't want to elaborate on that, still didn't understand her visceral reaction. Nothing of the sort had ever happened to her before. "And you didn't know he, I mean you, would be here at this particular time."

"My memory is a bit foggy where my final weeks alive are concerned. And it was a very long time ago. It's not as if I called on my mother in the country all that often. I much preferred my town-house in London. Most of my visits were short and unremarkable. It's no wonder I didn't remember this particular date."

"Great, so you're both here. What does that mean to your plan?"

"Well, I, meaning the ghost me, apparently cannot be in the same room as myself."

"I'm getting a headache. You can't be in the same room as you?"

"That's about the gist of it."

Josie paced and rubbed her temples. "If you are both in the same room, it would create an anomaly." She looked at him. "What happened to you when he, the other you, walked into the parlor?"

"I was...pushed by...something into another room. Right through the wall as if I had no substance at all. And that's another thing. I can't fully materialize. No matter what I try."

"You look pretty solid right now."

"Only to you. That maid didn't see me at all. My own mother can't see me."

His voice broke a little on that last statement. She hadn't thought about how he would be affected by revisiting his youthful reality. She sat beside him on the windowsill.

"We'll think of something," she promised. She wasn't sure what, but something. "Maybe we should leave and come back later, or earlier?"

"I'm afraid we only have this one chance."

"Why? Can't you remember how you did it? You do know how to get us back, don't you?"

"I can get us back, but the trip will use a great amount of energy. Even if we left right now, I most likely will be out of contact for a number of years, ten or twenty, maybe more."

"That's not so bad," she lied. She could be forty the next time she saw him.

"That will be too late to help Amelia save the castle," he continued.

"No it won't. I'll help her all I can. The Regency-themed inn is actually a great idea. We can invite visiting professors and get certified for guests to earn college credits. We'll have special events for Jane Austen fans. We'll..."

"It won't be enough to save the south wing. I'm afraid even Amelia is unaware of the extent of the damage years of neglect have caused."

"Then when you come back I'll..."

"Stop," he said gently. He hadn't wanted to tell her the rest of the consequences. But she was making plans that would deprive her of the life she was meant to have. A life he couldn't give her. "When Amelia dies without a direct heir, the property will go to a distant cousin. I've never met him, but if he has a lick of sense, he'll tear down the decrepit south wing."

"And you won't be there to stop him."

"More than likely I won't be there to ask him to preserve it. I've always returned to my suite of rooms in the south wing, and when it's gone..."

"Limbo forever?" Josie blinked back tears.

"I'm not sure what will happen."

Josie jumped up. "Then we will have to make this chance successful."

"Without my help, you can't..."

"I've managed so far."

"Two whole hours."

She resumed her pacing. "This might even work out better than having you here...in the flesh, no, in the materialized...oh, you know what I mean. In the way you'd planned. Think about it."

"I am trying not to."

"Stop sulking. Look, since no one else can see you, you can go anywhere. You could snoop out stuff I would never know without my gadgets."

"Do you mean eavesdrop?"

"Oh, don't give me that lemon-sucking face. You'll be doing it in the name of science, or rather in the name of…oh, never mind. Just remember you're doing it for Amelia."

"And myself. Self-service is hardly noble no matter how you phrase it."

"When you protect your family, you protect yourself at the same time. You are a Thornton."

"If I agree, what sort of information do you need?"

Josie grabbed her reticule and pulled out her notebook. Making lists helped her organize her thoughts. "I'll need to know where they'll hold the séance. I can examine the room before it starts to check for hidden wires and trick furniture. Then…"

Six

"To whom are you speaking?" Mrs. Binns asked as she entered Josie's bedroom. "No one. Just myself. Bad habit."

The older woman stopped stock-still in the center of the room. She turned slowly around, sniffing the air. "Do you feel a presence?" she whispered.

"No," Josie lied. Deverell was very much present.

"Don't move," Mrs. Binns said and hurried out.

Josie shrugged at him and went back to her list. Before she had time to think of a step three, Mrs. Binns rushed back in carrying her red velvet box. She set it on the bed, threw open the top, and pulled out a twisted bunch of weeds, which she proceeded to set on fire with a wooden match. After blowing out the flames, she carried the smoking remains to every corner of the room.

"What is that crazy woman doing?" Deverell asked.

"What are you doing?" Josie asked, rephrasing his question.

"Burning sage. Spirits hate the smell."

"It's not that bad," he said. "Actually rather pleasant."

"I don't think that's…"

"Don't you worry, my dear. I'm rather knowledgeable on these matters. I've read all the books. Studied them I have. Consulted with experts. I stay up all night every night keeping vigil, keeping myself and those around me safe."

No wonder the woman fell asleep during the day.

Mrs. Binns dropped the last of the burning rush into the large bowl on the washstand. "I have the best protection money can buy," she said, retuning to the bed. She pulled out a small cloth bundle tied with red string. "Here. Keep this on your person at all times."

"What is it?"

"A charm to ward off evil spirits."

Mrs. Binns put a second bundle tied with a green string under the pillow on Josie's bed. "Guaranteed effective against demon incubi."

"Is she speaking about me? I am not the devil incarnate," Deverell complained.

Then Mrs. Binns stood in the middle of the room, held her arms out at her sides, and, closing her eyes, turned slowly in a circle. When she stopped, she squinted and stared at a spot near Deverell's head—not directly at him but near enough to be uncanny.

"I see this particular spirit is stubborn. I shall have to read up on this. Don't worry. I'll get rid of it."

"We could just change rooms," Josie suggested. It wouldn't get rid of Deverell, but maybe Mrs. Binns would feel better.

"Nonsense, my dear. If you let a specter get the upper hand, it will chase you the width of England. Believe me, I know. Before I joined the Prevention of Interfering Phantoms Society, the ghost of my second husband nearly drove me to distraction. With the help of the other PIPS, I called on the spirit of my fourth husband, the most recently demised, to intercede on my behalf, and I've been nightmare-free ever since. Not that I'm taking any chances. I have my nightly ritual. And now I shall include you in my circle.

"Do you hear that, Mister Spirit?" she added loudly. "You are impotent here."

"Thank you for that reminder," Deverell answered dryly.

"You're safe for now," Mrs. Binns said to Josie as she latched her case. "I'll not rest until I've rid this room of that presence. I promise."

"A simple 'please leave' would suffice," Deverell said.

"Thank you for your concern," Josie said. "I'm sure it's not..."

"Tut, tut. It's my job to keep you and your virginity safe until you're walking down that blessed aisle."

"But, I'm not..."

"Don't say it," Deverell warned. "Your reputation must remain spotless in order for you to be my mother's houseguest."

"...in any hurry to get married," Josie finished lamely.

"Well, you should be. You're practically on the shelf."

Ah, yes. The Regency version of the "your body

clock is ticking" speech. Josie had thought she was going to avoid that.

"You've still got your looks and all your teeth."

"Gee, thanks."

"And with your fortune you'll be getting offers right and left."

"What fortune?" She had exactly seven hundred and thirty-two dollars in her checking account, and that was before her car payment was automatically deducted.

"Your letter of introduction was quite clear, as it should be. My job is to find you the best match possible, and ten thousand pounds per annum makes any woman all that much more attractive. But even an heiress has to stop running if she wants to get caught. You're not getting any younger. Think about that long and hard."

Deverell had led Mrs. Binns to believe that Josie was an heiress looking for a husband?

With a final humph, Mrs. Binns left the room.

Josie turned to confront Deverell.

He had most conveniently disappeared.

"Damn, damn. Double damn," Deverell muttered as he roamed the house looking for information Josie would find useful.

This was not working out at all the way he'd planned. He couldn't fully materialize and take his rightful place—a greater disappointment than he would have thought.

What had he expected? That he could experience life once again if only for a few days? Embrace his mother one last time? Taste, feel, touch, and be touched? That Josie would...

What was it about that particular woman that caused him to bare his soul despite his best intentions to remain indifferent and aloof? Yes, he'd promised to answer her questions, but a man had his limits. A man should be in control.

And he was not in control of...anything. Impotent. That was the word. And he didn't like feeling impotent. Not one iota.

The only thing he did seem to be able to do was keep them in the past, although that was more of a strain than he'd anticipated. He was beginning to wonder if this had been such a good idea. Maybe he should just zap them back to the future and let the south wing be damned. Amelia would live out her life in relative comfort, and he would take his deserved punishment.

Redemption was bloody impossible, the unreachable bait with the barbed hook. He was tempted to throw in the towel. Call it quits.

Except now he'd involved Josie in the matter, and he must consider her welfare. She would take the failure personally.

Already she'd reacted as if she cared for him, just a little. As if she expected to see him again after all this was over. He should have foreseen this happening. She had a penchant for the underdog. Not a position he relished, but apt considering the circumstances.

He must see that she completed this job and as quickly as possible. Before she became more attached to him.

Or should he say before he became more

attached to her?

"Get dressed. Get dressed," Mrs. Binns said, rushing into the sitting room she shared with Josie. "Hurry, hurry."

"I'm dressed," Josie said. She sat curled in the large wingchair by the window. She closed the book in her lap to cover the list she was making of possible tests to disprove the seer's abilities.

"You must dress for dinner. And quickly."

"Aren't we..."

"Change of plans. I've just learned Lord Waite is expected to return..."

"Not interested," Josie lied. More like not ready to face him and the tsunami of sensations he'd caused again.

"...with several of his friends."

Josie faked a yawn.

"You may well turn up your nose at a roomful of handsome, titled men, but I refuse to let that she-devil Estelle and her pet gypsy..."

Josie sat up. "Who?"

The maid rushed in and curtsied. "Yes, mistress?" she asked in a breathless voice.

"What took you so long?"

"Oh, mistress, everything below is at sixes and sevens. Guests arriving a day early. His lordship with his friends. Six extra for dinner. Cook and Mrs. Osman are frantic."

"Exactly why we're in such a hurry. I've a guinea for you if Miss Drummond is dressed before the assembly gong."

The maid ran to the bedroom, and Josie heard

doors and drawers bang open and shut.

"Come, come," Mrs. Binns said, urging Josie along with sweeping hand motions. "I'll talk while you dress."

Josie stood like a mannequin while the maid stripped her down to her corset and chemise.

"Estelle La Foyn," Mrs. Binns said, taking a seat on the bed. "Daughter of our gullible cousin Mabel who married an émigré French count without a penny to his name. After she died in childbirth, LaFoyn, who was not a count at all, but a bootmaker, dumped his infant daughter on Honoria's stoop and hightailed it back to the hole he crawled out of."

Josie turned this way and that way, raising her arm and lowering her arm as Dora dressed her from toes to head. She felt like a...a...what was the name of that doll? It was on the tip of her tongue. How could she forget? Oh yes, Barbie. She felt like a giant Barbie doll.

"Honoria did her best by the girl," Mrs. Binns continued, "but bad blood breeds bad blood, I always say. Estelle ran off with a cavalry lieutenant the day after she turned eighteen, taking the dowry Honoria had given her. Now seven years later she's back. Claims she was married and widowed. But she's using the Countess LaFoyn name again. Bah! Up to no good, she is. Mark my words. And Honoria is proving to be just as gullible as poor Mabel was."

"And the gypsy," Josie prompted. She sat at the dressing table and chose a simple ribbon for Dora to pin in her hair.

"I don't know much about her. Calls herself

Madame X. Allegedly she doesn't use her real name at her royal father's request. But if she's with Estelle...Birds of a feather is all I have to say about that. In my day we wouldn't have allowed a gypsy in the house, much less at the table."

Josie was ready in record time. Mrs. Binns, who had previously dressed for dinner as a matter of form, handed Dora the gold coin just as the assembly gong sounded.

Picking up her reticule and fan, Josie was on her way to the parlor without remembering that she'd actually agreed to forgo dinner in her room.

"Slowly," Mrs. Binns said. "You don't want to appear eager."

Josie hadn't realized that she'd been rushing to get to the stairs. She couldn't possibly be impatient to see...the gypsy. She matched her steps to Mrs. Binns's tortoise pace, and it seemed to take forever to navigate the long hall, including three stops for Josie to hear about paintings of absolutely no interest to her.

At the top of the stairs, she spied Lord Waite chatting with three other young men in the wide foyer. The event had been called a simple evening of casual entertainment, yet each man wore a high starched collar and elaborately tied cravat. Although more subdued than the others, Dev's charcoal coat covered a colorfully embroidered vest. He looked up at her. *Déjà vu.* She felt the same thrill at his admiring expression, but this time she took a firm grip on the banister before starting down the stairs.

"Good evening, Mrs. Binns. Miss Drummond," Dev

said, bowing over first one hand and then the other.

A very formal salute. No actual hand kissing, much to Josie's relief. Even through both gloves, his and hers, the warmth of his hand was enough to set up the vibrations within her.

A tall thin blond man moved forward and said, "So this is the American heiress we've heard about."

"Not from me," Dev muttered.

The young bucks shouldered one another aside in their attempt to present themselves in front of each other.

"You never said she was a beauty, Waite, old sod."

"You've been holding out. Thought we was pals."

"Introduce us, Waite. You can't keep her all to yourself."

"All in good time, gentlemen," Mrs. Binns said. "All in good time." Taking Josie's arm, she led her charge into the parlor. "An excellent beginning," she whispered, obviously pleased.

Josie glanced back over her shoulder.

The men lost their stunned expressions and scrambled after her like puppies tumbling over each other to get to a saucer of cream. Dev followed with a bemused smile.

In the parlor everything was pleasantly formal. However, Josie detected undercurrents as Honoria introduced her to the other guests.

Barstow, curate at the local vicarage, stammered and blushed his way through Honoria's attention and then scooped candied almonds into his pockets when he thought no one was watching.

Hargrave was as solemn as Deverell had warned,

and Caster went into a long tirade regarding horse breeding. It would have gone on even longer if Honoria had not gently cut him short and moved the conversation on.

Lady Wingate's trilling laugh followed from one conversation group to another. When she was finally introduced to Josie, the vivacious woman said, "How very nice you could join us. Had you remained upstairs, the Countess and I would have been simply swamped with eligible men. Like handsome Galway, here," Lady Wingate said, turning to the tall blond man in such a way that her breast grazed his arm, which sent her off into another eruption of giggles.

Josie understood why her husband sulked in the corner, nursing a drink and glaring at the other men.

Estelle had latched onto Dev as soon as he entered, and she hadn't let him out of arm's reach since. Madame X flanked his other side. The gypsy, a head taller than Josie and twice as wide, was dressed in voluminous layers of heavy fabrics woven with mysterious designs. A golden Egyptian circlet with a rearing cobra topped a large headpiece that covered her forehead, hair, and shoulders, and her scowl warned off all comers. Mrs. Binns was not deterred.

"I hope you are enjoying the evening," Dev said to her as she approached, Josie in tow.

"Yes, thank you." Mrs. Binns performed the necessary introductions.

Estelle looked at Josie as though she was something disgusting stuck to the bottom of her shoe.

"How fortunate that you could come all this way to get some social polish. Sometime you really must tell us about growing up in the wilds of the colonies," she said, her tone indicating that the twelfth of never would be too soon. "Just now Dev and I were reliving some memories. I'm sure such tales would be of no interest to anyone who didn't grow up here." She turned her body toward Dev, effectively cutting off Mrs. Binns and signaling her to move on.

Mrs. Binns sidestepped Estelle's machinations. "Oh, la. Young people shouldn't be looking backward. That's for us old folks on a cold winter's night."

"It is rather chilly in here," Estelle said. "Don't you think so, Mrs. Binns?"

"Not at all. I'm quite comfortable. Thank you."

After a moment of silence, Dev picked up the conversational lag. "Did you get to see much of London, Miss Drummond?"

Josie felt the force of his attention. A hot blush spread from her stomach upward to her ears and downward to the tips of her toes. "No...I...uh...came directly here," she stammered. She couldn't have felt more conspicuous if she'd been standing there naked.

Mrs. Binns came to her rescue. "I was just telling Miss Drummond about your grandfather's portrait. Miss Drummond has quite an interest in artwork, and I'm sure she would enjoy viewing the Gainsborough. I was hoping you would take a moment and show it to her."

Josie blinked at the spate of lies rolling off her

chaperone's tongue with sincere ease.

"We'll be going in momentarily," Estelle said, laying her hand on Dev's arm, staking her claim as the highest-ranking female to the host's escort.

Not that Josie had any big-time craving to see the painting, but she hated to see some upshot fake countess consistently put down dear Mrs. Binns.

Josie glanced up at the clock on the mantel, just beyond Dev's shoulder. "Oh no," she said, pasting on an innocent expression. "Dinner won't be announced for at least another twenty minutes."

"Crown me if the chit ain't right," Galway said from behind Josie.

Did he just call her a chit? What the hell was a chit?

"Aren't you going to do your duty as host and show her your paintings?" Galway asked.

Dev turned to look at the clock, thus breaking Estelle's possessive hold. "I suppose..."

"And while you're gone, I'll entertain the delectable Estelle with my latest ode to her beauty." Galway insinuated his tall lanky body into Dev's former spot.

Mrs. Binns placed her hand on Dev's arm, flashing a triumphant grin. "Come along, Miss Drummond. Lord Waite is taking us into his private study."

Of course, Josie wouldn't be allowed to be alone with him. She breathed a sigh. Not only did she not trust him. She didn't trust herself even more. She'd met handsome men before, met men who turned her on in bed, but she'd never had such a potent reaction to simply being in a man's presence. Thank goodness she could depend on her chaperone to keep her safe.

When Mrs. Binns gave her a wink, Josie realized her relief may have been premature.

Seven

As she trailed Dev and Mrs. Binns down the hall, Josie tried to bring her riotous libido under control. A modern, educated woman of her age should not react like a...like a horny college student. The man had done little more than look at her and touch her hand.

Once in Dev's private study, Mrs. Binns collapsed on a sofa and plied her fan vigorously. "My, my. I'll sit here for a bit. Go on, go on," she said, motioning Josie forward with her free hand. "There it is. Dev will tell you about it."

Josie took a spot next to him, carefully maintaining two feet of space between them. She clasped her hands behind her back and gazed up at the painting over the fireplace.

"Tradition dictates that each earl or heir to the earldom have his portrait painted on his thirtieth birthday. As you can see, this is not a typically posed portrait. Great-grandfather requested that he be painted in what he considered his element."

The large painting, a full eight feet in length and

reaching far up into the fourteen-foot ceiling, depicted an autumn landscape with the castle on a far hill. In the left foreground a man resembling Dev except for the lighter color of his hair sat on a bench under a spreading oak in a casual pose, coat off, hat carelessly held between his fingers.

While Dev explained the details—a monogrammed handkerchief, a skin flask, a half-eaten loaf of bread and a hunk of cheese—Josie tried to stay focused. His whiskey-smooth voice and nearness intoxicated her, raising her body temperature.

The picture before her faded, replaced by one of a tropical beach. Sun-warmed sand and exotic flowers. A man, looking suspiciously like Dev only nearly naked and smiling, lounged beside a stand of palm trees. The large screen of her imagination played and he rose and beckoned her closer. Her breath came in little gasps.

For the first time in years, Dev struggled to maintain control of his traitorous body. He had acceded to the transparent request to view the painting as a convenient escape from Estelle, who had become blatantly possessive. A hasty decision he was beginning to question.

"You will note the artist's expert use of light," he said, keeping up the one-sided conversation while his private thoughts whirled in another direction.

He had assumed himself capable of handling Mrs. Binns's innocuous ploy with the ease of long practice dealing with marriage-minded mothers and chaperones. Perhaps he had been overconfident.

Miss Drummond was the problem. She was

different from the other women of his acquaintance, an intriguing mix of uncertainty and straightforwardness. She had the mien of a timid miss, and yet there was intelligence in her eyes. When he had held her close that afternoon, her gaze had seemed to pierce directly into his soul. A ridiculous thought. However, he had been loath to let her go, and the immediate rush of blood to his loins had nearly robbed him of his common sense. The desire to kiss her luscious lips had been overwhelming.

Lust he was familiar with and knew how to handle. But not in his mother's parlor in front of witnesses.

"Gainsborough had originally sketched out the painting to represent spring; however, great-grandfather nixed the frolicking lambs and overwhelming green in favor of the vivid colors you see."

If he was going to nip the problem of Miss Drummond in the bud, he could not just stand there and spout artistic nonsense while he grew more physically uncomfortable by the minute.

"Although the south wing, the area in which we are currently standing, was still under construction at the time of the painting, the artist used the architectural drawings to show it complete."

Dev needed to act and swiftly, either that or get as far away from her as possible. The prospect of London and its myriad distractions held great appeal at that moment, but since he had promised his mother to attend her silly séance, he could not leave. That left the choices of either scaring her into running away from him or slaking his desire and thus causing it to dissipate.

A passionate kiss would accomplish both.

He glanced over his shoulder at her chaperone to confirm that the gentle snoring he'd heard meant Mrs. Binns had nodded off.

Dev sidled nearer to Josephine and slipped an arm around her shoulder to turn her into his embrace. She did not act surprised or resist, but raised her arms to his shoulders and stepped closer. As he leaned forward, she closed her eyes and tipped her head back.

Josie wasn't sure exactly when she realized her dream had become reality. When her hands touched fabric rather than flesh? When his lips attacked hers? His kiss wasn't one she would have fantasized. His kiss was hard, relentless, demanding. She pulled away, a whimper of disappointment escaping her throat. She pushed against his shoulder, her strength no match for his. He didn't let her go.

She ducked her head and braced herself to knee him in the groin when he said, "Let me try that again."

She shook her head without looking up.

He loosened his hold enough to lift her chin with one hand. Before she could seize the chance to spin away, he said, "Please," in a deep throaty whisper. Then he flashed her a charming smile, and that damned appealing dimple winked.

Any woman would have agreed to another kiss, Josie rationalized even as she nodded.

His embrace gentled, caressing rather than hold-ing. He leaned closer slowly, so slowly, until his lips barely touched hers, exploring their shape, expectant, as if patiently waiting for her to make the next move.

She breathed in his scent, relaxed in the warm cocoon of his arms, and leaned into his chest. He increased the pressure of his lips slightly and, still exploring, kissed the corner of her mouth, her chin, along her jawline, that spot just below her ear before retuning.

Which was all very nice, but she was no simpering Regency miss. Josie was ready, more than ready for some heat. She responded by grasping handfuls of his coat to lift herself up and pull him closer. She deepened the kiss and parted her lips.

When Dev tasted her lips with a tentative flick, she sucked his tongue in deeper and slid her hand up to the back of his neck. He gathered her tightly, one hand supporting her head, the other sliding down to cup her derriere. As he pressed her closer she ground her hips against the hard length pushing against her stomach.

A particularly loud snore brought Dev to his senses like a splash of cold water. He disengaged himself and set Josephine at arm's length with his hands gentling her shoulders.

"My sincere apologies," he said, keeping his voice low. "I meant no insult to you."

"The insult is in stopping," she whispered back. "In leaving me wanting...more."

He raised an eyebrow at her response. "Although I am more than willing to oblige, now is neither the time nor the place," he said with a significant nod toward her chaperone.

She folded her arms and bit her tongue to keep from asking, where and when, then?

Mrs. Binns dropped her fan and it clattered to the floor. She sat up with a start. "What was that?" She looked around the room with an accusing glare.

Josie picked up the offending object and handed the fan back to the older woman.

"Thank you, dearie. My, oh my, is it time for dinner? I'm fair starved."

"We should be getting back," Dev said.

His words seemed prophetic to Josie. She should be getting back, to her own time. She soon would be getting back to her life in the future. What was she thinking?

That was the problem. When she was close to Dev, her brain melted to mush. She couldn't let that happen again. She needed to do the job she'd been hired to do and then get the hell out of Dodge. Before she did something stupid.

Thanks to Amelia's training, Josie managed the intricacies of Regency dining without problems. When in doubt, she simply watched Honoria and copied her actions. As the lowest-ranking woman, Josie was seated near the middle of the long table between the curate Barstow, who concentrated on his meal, and the morose Hargrave, who barely spoke at all, resulting in long silences. She caught bits of conversations, but as far as she could tell nothing was said about the séance planned for later that evening. Near the end of the two-hour meal, she heard Dev speak to Lady Wingate, who was sitting on the other side of Hargrave.

"I have recently discovered a fascination with artwork," Dev said.

Was Josie imagining it or had he raised his voice slightly to make sure she could hear?

"I find the simple activity of viewing a fine painting to be...stimulating." He glanced at Josie and caught her looking at him. "Don't you, Lady Wingate?"

"I would find your artwork fascinating," she responded, leaning toward him to display her ample bosom.

Josie stifled a snort of disgust.

"Are you an artist?" Lady Wingate asked. "I dabble in watercolors, myself."

Dev raised his glass. He rubbed the rim across his lips before taking a sip. "My talents lie in...other activities."

Even though he wasn't speaking to her, Josie felt a hot blush creep up her neck.

"Lavinia Satterly raved about your garden statuary," Lady Wingate said, obviously fishing for an invitation to view his artwork firsthand.

"We should plan a picnic," Estelle said from his other side, laying her fingertips on Dev's forearm. "Then all of our...I mean your guests may enjoy the gardens." Her self-correction was accompanied by a fluttering of eyelashes.

Dev turned his head but did not shift in his chair to face her. "You can certainly make that suggestion to my mother. She may even agree with you. To my mind she has already planned too many activities for her guests."

Estelle snatched back her hand as if burned.

"As for my guests," Dev continued as if he hadn't noticed, "the lads were speaking earlier of hunting. I would enjoy an invigorating diversion. However, tomorrow I'll remain at home and pursue...other pleasures."

When he said the last words, he looked directly at Josie. Was he making a threat or a promise? Either way she was in trouble.

Honoria chose that moment to stand, the signal for the women to withdraw and leave the men to their port and cigars. Josie left the dining room determined to use the opportunity to wrangle an invitation to the séance. In the parlor, Deverell waited.

"Whatever took so long?" the ghost demanded, ignored by all except Josie, who was forced to pretend she didn't hear him either. "Can you get away? We need to talk."

Josie turned to Mrs. Binns, who had already settled herself on the sofa and pulled out her embroidery. She not only wielded her needle with amazing speed but also did it while wearing gloves.

"Can I get you anything? Your shawl? Your..."

"No, thank you. I am quite content, though I do hope they hurry up with the tea. Sit down. I'm sure the gentlemen won't be long. Not with such lovely company so close at hand."

"I think I'll step into the library and choose a book for later. In case I can't sleep."

"That's a good idea," Mrs. Binns said with a sigh. She started to put away her needlework.

"Oh, you don't need to come with me."

Mrs. Binns hesitated.

"I hardly need protection since all the men are safely ensconced in the dining room. And I'll just be a few minutes."

"I suppose..."

Before her chaperone could change her mind, Josie headed for the door, only to be stopped by Estelle.

"And where is our little American guest off to so soon?" she asked in a snide tone.

Josie was short on time, so she simply answered, "I'm going to the library for a book."

"In such a hurry? My, my. Are you running off to an assignation?"

"Why? Were you planning on using the library?"

"What?" Estelle blinked, but she recovered quickly. "No, of course not. I can't imagine why you should even think such a thing."

"You brought it up." Josie tried to step around the taller woman, but Estelle again blocked the way.

"I wanted to have a word with you, Miss Drummond, to clarify a matter about which you seem to be confused."

Josie had had just about enough of the woman. "I can't imagine what you could possibly elucidate that would have eluded my comprehension."

Estelle's brow furrowed.

"Now if you'll excuse me?" Josie stepped to the other side and around the other woman.

"It's about Dev," Estelle blurted out.

Josie hesitated and turned around.

Estelle smiled a superior smile. "I wanted you to know Dev and I have an understanding. We are practically engaged."

Not only had Deverell never mentioned the fact, but Dev certainly hadn't behaved as if he was *practically engaged*. He had acted more as though he only tolerated the woman for his mother's sake.

"We've had an understanding since we were children together. Our union has always been his mother's fondest wish. And, of course, my own." Estelle ducked her head in a shy schoolgirl move that wouldn't have fooled an imbecile.

"Too bad that wasn't your fondest wish seven years ago."

Estelle sucked in her breath and narrowed her eyes.

Josie could have kicked herself. She should have kept her mouth shut. No sense making an enemy over the issue, especially when she knew Deverell had never married.

"Let's get something straight. I'm not interested in Dev, okay? I'm not setting my cap for him, or any of those other cute little euphemisms you have for husband hunting. In fact, if I were to stay in this...country, which I'm not, I'd seriously consider becoming a spinster so I could retain control of my property, my purse, and my person."

"Good God. You're a bluestocking," Estelle said with a laugh. "Wait until Dev hears about this." She turned and walked away, obviously no longer worried.

Josie found Deverell in the library, seated in his favorite leather chair, holding a brandy.

"I find waiting quite tedious."

"Yeah, well, your fiancée wouldn't let me leave."

"Who?"

"You could have told me you and Estelle are practically engaged."

"Hah! According to her, no doubt."

"You didn't…"

"Never."

"Then why did she say…"

"Because she's delusional."

"She said your mother's fondest…"

"My mother wanted me to marry and get an heir. She would have heartily endorsed *any* woman's attempt to shackle me."

"But Estelle…"

"Forget Estelle. We have work to do. It takes considerable energy to keep us here, and I am not inexhaustible."

Now that he mentioned it, he did look a little pale. As a peace offering she reached for his brandy glass and warmed it between her palms. "What did you find out?" She took a seat across from him.

"They've canceled the séance for tonight."

"If that's the case, what can we do?"

"You'll have to convince Honoria to proceed."

"How?"

"I'm sure you'll think of something. In the meantime, you can work on the gypsy's methods. They've held three séances already. Right here in the library. Supposedly Madame X contacted her spirit guide, named Amanu, who promised to seek out Sir Robert and report back."

"So your mother is looking for the emeralds?"

She handed him back the brandy snifter.

"According to Madame X's journal..."

"You actually read her diary?"

Deverell bristled. "I have no interest in stooping that low. I read her spiritual journal, which she makes available to potential clients as proof of her abilities, so it's probably full of lies."

"But?"

"She wrote an account of the séances. She also noted that my mother is trying to contact my father, her parents, her brother who was killed in France, my sister Caroline, who died before I was born, and someone named Mabel."

"Estelle's mother."

Deverell raised an eyebrow.

"I haven't been idle either."

"That I already knew."

Something in his tone prickled. "What's that supposed to mean?"

"I was enjoying a few moments of quiet relaxation in my private study when I was rudely pushed out by Dev's entrance with you and Mrs. Binns."

"Oh." What else did he know? Josie rose and walked around the room, peeking under tables and knocking on the surfaces.

"What are you doing?"

"Checking for false bottoms or places to hide wires and such. Is this the furniture that's always been in here?"

"Yes. I saw you..."

"Did the journal describe any effects? Eerie lights? Moving objects? Mysterious sounds?"

"Nothing like that." He took a sip of his brandy. "I saw you kissing him."

Josie stopped and faced the ghost. She folded her arms. "What exactly do you remember?"

Deverell considered how much to tell her. "My memories remain unchanged." More the pity. "I suspect that will only alter after we return."

"But you said..."

"I said I saw you. I observed you."

"You spied on me?"

"Now you know how it feels. The shoe's on the other foot, eh?"

"How? Is this something new? You couldn't make yourself invisible to me before."

"Although I loathe admitting it, I simply peered through the window like a common Peeping Tom. If you had bothered to look, I'm sure you would have seen me. As a matter of interest you might remember in the future, anyone strolling along the veranda could have seen you."

"Just how long did you *observe* me? Exactly what did you see?"

"I saw you kissing him."

"He kissed me."

"And you kissed him back."

"Okay. Yes, I kissed him...you, no him." Josie threw up her hands. "This is so awkward. He is you, I mean you are him, but you're not...not really the same. I mean he's a very physical presence and you're, well, not."

A condition he felt more keenly with each passing hour. Deverell cleared his throat. "I must warn you he'll break your heart if you let him."

"I won't." She tipped her head to one side. "That advice seems a bit odd, coming from you."

"I may only be a ghost, but I'm not heartless."

"Still." Deep in thought, she wandered over to a bookshelf and ran her finger along the book spines.

"Miss Drummond?"

Josie started and turned at the sound. An unfamiliar maid curtsied in the doorway. "Mrs. Binns sent me to ask if I can be of any assistance."

"No, thank you." Josie reached out and grabbed a book. "Tell her I'll be along in a minute."

"Yes, miss." The maid curtsied again and left.

"I guess I should go," she said, not looking at Deverell.

"Perhaps that would be..."

"Hey. This is an original *Pride and Prejudice*. And a personal note to your mother on the inside cover is signed. Is this authentic?"

"Of course it is," Deverell said, his tone saying she need not have bothered to ask. "We met years before she published anything."

"*You* met Jane Austen?"

"Before she achieved her bit of notoriety. The Austen family lived in Bath for a time and regularly attended the Lower Ballroom. I was quite fond of dancing at the time, as were Jane and her sister, Cassandra." He chuckled. "My mother quite got her hopes up."

"Do you realize if this book is still on the shelf in our time, it could sell for thousands of dollars, er...pounds?" She looked up and down the floor-to-ceiling shelves. "There's probably a fortune here. Amelia could fix..."

"Yes, yes, the paintings are valuable, too. The furniture is valuable. The tableware. The silver. The point of coming here was to save the castle without selling off the family..."

"Possessions are just things, and things aren't..."

"These *things* are more than sticks of wood, daubs of paint on a canvas, and bits of paper. They are my family's heritage. My father sat in that chair. My uncle wielded that sword in battle. That painting over the mantel is Sir Robert, the second..."

"Sir Robert with the emeralds?" Josie asked, looking up at the scowling pirate.

Deverell rolled his eyes. "Why is every woman so fascinated with the emeralds?" As far as he was concerned, the legend was a family myth and not worth any consideration.

"Because it's a romantic story."

"A mistress disappearing with a handful of jewels is romantic?"

"A man having the jewelry made as a bride gift to present to his beloved to convince her to marry him is romantic."

"I see Amelia filled you in on the details."

"The spurned mistress steals the jewels. The countryside turns out to search for her to no avail. No bride gift. But then the girl is so touched by his efforts she marries him anyway. That is definitely romantic."

"Bah! I don't believe the emeralds ever existed. It was an elaborate ploy by Robert to get the fair

Rowena to wed him. Believe me, a man will do just about anything to get the woman he desires into his bed. A fact you should remember, my dear. Although I seriously doubt Dev will go so far as to promise you emeralds."

Josie stared at him for a moment as if his words had stung. Then she turned and left without a word.

Hurting her felt like a mule kick in the gut.

Bloody hell. He was acting like a jealous suitor. And the real jolt was that he was jealous of himself. Deverell produced yet another brandy and sipped. Bah! One of his last pleasures spoiled because she was not there to warm it properly. He threw the snifter across the room.

Eight

BY THE TIME JOSIE REENTERED THE PARLOR her mood had progressed beyond her instant pique to a thoughtful retrospection. Thankfully the other women were occupied and no one questioned her absence. Lady Wingate plucked away one-handed on the harpsichord, her chin resting on the palm of her other hand. Honoria, Estelle, and Madame X sat at a table in the corner playing a card game that appeared to require intense concentration. Josie took a seat on the small sofa across from Mrs. Binns so as not to disturb her snoozing and poured herself a cup of tea.

Deverell had surprised Josie once again. Not only had he shown sentimental attachment to the family heirlooms, but he had appeared concerned about her welfare. Oh, sure, he'd covered his anxiety with gruff tones, but he couldn't hide the genuine affection in his eyes.

Josie shook off her fanciful musing. Reading anything heartfelt into that ghost's expression was asking for trouble. As weird as his self-disparaging advice was, she would do well to heed it. Deverell the man was as much a danger as the ghost. Neither one offered anything but heartache.

As if her thoughts had summoned him, deep voices in the hall signaled the imminent arrival of Dev and the other gentlemen. Even without warning she would have known when he entered the room. His presence seemed to electrify all her senses. The candlelight seemed rosier, the tea more flavorful.

She wasn't the only one who perked up at the entrance of the men. A smiling Lady Wingate broke into a sparkling tune. The card game was shuffled aside. Estelle rose to greet Dev at the door.

"We were just talking about what we should do with the rest of the evening," she said, taking his arm. "My vote is for practicing the waltz. That is, if we can prevail on Lady Wingate to play for us a bit longer."

"Actually..." Dev paused when Lady Wingate stopped mid-tune and jumped up from her seat.

"I'm sure someone else would like to take a turn," she said with a simpering smile. "Far be it from me to monopolize the spotlight. Perhaps Miss Drummond would honor us."

All eyes turned to Josie. "I don't play the harpsichord."

Estelle gave her a superior smile. "Hardly unexpected from someone with a colonial..."

"I have the feeling," Dev interrupted, "that Miss Drummond is quite skilled at playing other...instruments."

Josie wished he'd stop his innuendos so she could stop blushing.

"Ignore her," Hargrave whispered as he took the seat next to Josie. "Estelle is a snob. Personally, I'm fascinated by the fact that you're an American."

The sofa was small and Hargrave much too close for Josie's comfort. Frequent bathing was not in fashion during the Regency period, and Hargrave obviously had not bucked the trend. Either the overwhelming food scents of the dining room had masked his odor, or he'd ripened in the meantime.

"My cousin fought at the Battle of New Orleans last January, and he wrote that American women were quite forward compared to our English lasses and..."

He faltered when she turned to glare at him.

"And lively," he finished lamely. He cleared his throat. "I hear there are great opportunities in America for a man with a bit of capital to invest."

"There are always opportunities for anyone willing to work hard."

Hargrave made a face. "A gentleman does not toil like a common drudge." He put an arm across the back of the sofa. "Surely your father does not labor in the fields."

Since her father had been a computer genius who had made his fortune in the dot-com heyday, she could hardly say he labored, even though he had been a workaholic. After his death her mother had sold off his shares before the collapse and had parlayed her nest egg into a jet-set lifestyle and a series of wealthy husbands. Not only was her family history none of his business, but he would never understand the facts. "My father owned several businesses. He was never idle."

"I see," he said with a sage nod. "Do you have brothers and sisters?"

"No."

"And your mother? Will she be joining you here?"

"Why the sudden interest in my family?" What little he'd said during dinner had been about the deplorable condition of his manor house and the potential of his racing stable if he could bring it up to snuff.

"I'm just making small talk. Trying to get to know you."

"My mother will not be joining me," Josie answered, leaving out that dear Mom was currently at a California spa getting her semiannual Botox. Except for the Spring Sale at Harrods in London there was little her mother found of interest in England. Plus she didn't have a ghost to bring her back in time. "She prefers warmer climates."

"Very good."

What was that supposed to mean? Very good?

But she had little time to puzzle on it. The temperature in the room seemed to climb as Dev moved closer. He assumed his customary position near the fireplace only a few feet from Josie. She tried to ignore him and asked Hargrave about his horses.

"Pandora's Gift shows a lot of promise. I can trace her lineage back to Grafton's Prunella."

As he continued with a list of this-horse-begat-that-one, Josie fought to remain focused when her eyes wanted to glaze over. She was all too aware of Dev observing her even though he pretended to be listening to Estelle's whispers. Under the heat of his gaze, Josie pulled out her fan and tried to cool her warm cheeks.

Dev stepped forward. "Hate to dash your plans, Estelle, but I already promised to meet up with Shermont at Cracklebury's. Ready to go, chaps?"

"But we just left there this morning," Lady Wingate cried. She whipped around to face her husband. "You didn't tell me you'd made plans."

"Sorry, my dear," Wingate said as he stood. "You and the other ladies will have to entertain yourselves. One does not stand up Shermont, you know."

"Really, Dev," Honoria said. "It's already past ten. You can't..."

"Shank of the evening," Dev said, crossing the room to kiss the top of her head. "Shermont never plays cards before midnight."

"More gambling?" A frown wrinkled her forehead.

"Never fear, Mother dear. Shermont is simply trying to win back what he lost to me last week."

"Unlikely," Hargrave said with a snort. He made no move to rise. "I believe I'll keep the ladies company."

Dev raised an eyebrow.

"I've just begun to get to know Miss Drummond," Hargrave explained.

"Please don't stay on my account," Josie said.

"Yes, it has been a long day," Mrs. Binns said with a fake yawn as if she'd been pretending to doze all along. "We will not presume on Lord Hargrave's good intentions when they would be for naught..."

Hargrave sat back as if slapped.

"And we shall seek our repose shortly," Mrs. Binns continued without missing a beat.

Josie was confused. What had she missed?

Hargrave stood and bowed stiffly before marching out of the room.

The other gentlemen left, and after a few good-nights Josie followed her chaperone upstairs.

"Really, my dear," Mrs. Binns said as soon as they were out of earshot of the others, "you should not have encouraged Lord Hargrave. He is totally unsuitable for you."

"I didn't encourage him. I barely spoke to him."

"Your fan, my dear. The language of the fan? Rapid movement indicates you are very interested in the other person."

"I needed some air when it suddenly became overly warm in there."

Mrs. Binns shook her head with a sympathetic tut-tut.

"Sometimes a fan is just a fan."

"A woman with your desirable fortune must be extremely careful."

"What does that have..."

"You noticed the change in Hargrave's behavior? Why do you think he suddenly became so attentive? I'll tell you. Because when the gentlemen were alone the subject of your fortune came up. Hargrave sees in you a convenient solution to his financial woes."

Josie wasn't sure she liked being talked about over port and cigars.

"And then you handily gave him the information that you are the sole heir and have no interfering parent nearby. He was practically salivating
until I let him know in no uncertain terms that his
intentions are not welcome."

Josie had missed that. More of that Regency
subtext to normal conversation. "I never meant...I
didn't know..."

"Of course you didn't. That's why you have me
to guide you through the treacherous matrimonial
waters. I see everything. Even when you don't
know I'm looking." Mrs. Binns swept through their
sitting room. She paused at the door to her bedroom and turned. "I suggest you get right to sleep.
Tomorrow will be another busy day."

"Good-night," Josie called to the closing door.
Once within her own room she realized she could
not reach the fastenings on her dress. Fortunately,
Dora scratched on the door and entered with a tray
containing a cup of hot milk and two thin diges-
tive biscuits. She set the tray on the small table by
the window and lit the lamp. Then she helped Josie
change into a voluminous white cotton nightgown
and light blue brocade robe.

"Will there be anything else, miss? Something
else to drink? Another pillow?"

"No, thank you, Dora. That will be all."

The maid wished her a good night and backed
out of the room.

Josie settled into the comfortable chair by the
window and picked up the book she'd brought
upstairs.

Almost immediately there was another scratching on the door.

"Come in," she called, thinking the maid must have meant to take the tray with her.

Deverell entered.

"I'm amazed you bothered to knock," she said to cover her surprise at seeing him. They had not parted on the best of terms.

"A gentleman never enters a woman's bedchamber without an invitation."

He made it sound as if they had some sort of assignation, and that made her uncomfortable. Unable to think of a response, she reached for the cup of hot milk. Avoiding his gaze, she pretended to be concentrating on her drink and took a sip.

"Yuck." She hadn't had hot milk in ages and had forgotten how much she disliked the taste. She set the cup back on the saucer.

"It will help you sleep," he said, taking the seat on the other side of the small round table.

"I'd rather have a...a..." She couldn't think of the name. "I can see it in my mind. Cold...silver can..." She curved her hand as if holding a..."Diet Coke," she finished triumphantly. "That's what I want. A Diet Coke. I don't know why I couldn't remember that."

"I noticed earlier you seem to be having intermittent memory problems," Deverell said.

She had noticed it too but refused to admit it to him. "There is nothing wrong with..."

"I think your memories of the future are fading—the longer you stay in this past, the more you forget what hasn't happened yet."

That gave her a moment's hesitation. Would she get those memories back when she returned? Not that there weren't a few bad memories she could do without, but her experiences were what made her...well, her. "If that's true..."

"Just one more reason to get this matter done quickly."

"Easier said than done when the séance has been canceled."

"I know. It seems Honoria..."

"Why don't you call her Mother?"

Deverell heaved a sigh. "It's better I retain some distance."

"Distance? She's your mother and you haven't seen her for hundreds of years and..."

"And it's not like I can walk up and give her a hug or kiss her cheek."

Josie heard the frustration in his voice. "Have you tried?"

He looked off into the corner of the ceiling. "What's the point? She can't see me or hear me."

"You should do it anyway. Not only for yourself, but I think she will know...in her heart. Even if she doesn't understand the why of it, she will feel your love."

"Humph." Deverell stood and paced the room. "Getting back to the matter of the séance. I've learned the session was canceled ostensibly because Madame X doesn't want to overburden Honoria...Mother...when she is so busy with all the guests in the house. I personally think the gypsy doesn't want additional people to attend.

After all, it's easier to fool a few rather than many."

"If Madame X refuses..." She paused when he gave her that know-it-all look she hated. "What?"

"I'm sure you would reach the same conclusion if you had the time to ponder the situation such as I have had."

"Don't patronize me."

"I was complimenting your intelligence."

Sure didn't feel like it to her. "Yeah, right. Go on."

"Since we know Madame X is doing this in order to extract money, the logical incentive to get her to perform is to threaten to remove the financial reward. By intimating another spiritualist can be hired in her place, she will jump at the chance to prevent that from happening and hold the séance." He bowed as if she were applauding his plan.

"Just one hitch in your giddyap. How am I supposed to convince Honoria to threaten Madame X with replacement?"

"You can't."

"Then the whole plan fails..."

"Dev can."

"Dev? You? I mean him? I mean...Never mind. I don't know what I mean."

"Mother was always after me to participate in one of the séances. I always refused. However, if you convince Dev to attend, I'm sure she would do whatever it takes to make a séance happen, including manipulating Madame X into agreement."

"You told me to stay away from Dev. You said he was dangerous. How am I supposed to convince him to do something we know he doesn't want to do?"

"Use your feminine wiles."

"My what? Never mind; I heard you. I just can't believe you actually said that. You want me to seduce Dev in order to..."

"Not seduce. Entice. Beguile. Charm."

"I can't."

"Of course you can."

"I don't know how to...do those things." Although, the thought of seduction held certain appeal. Warmth smoldered in the pit of her stomach.

Deverell chuckled. "Every woman has an allure uniquely her own. It's simply a matter of using it effectively."

"Yeah. Well, if I ever had any, I never learned to use it."

Should he tell her that one of her most charming attributes was her lack of artifice? Her blushes captivated him and enticed him to make them appear more often. His fingers itched to touch her skin and tangle in her bouncy curls. He fantasized about connecting her freckles with lines of kisses. Would that make her feel better or only serve to relieve his own need to share his feelings?

"Simply be yourself," he advised. "Dev already finds you enchanting."

"How can you be sure?"

Trust Josie to pick up on his slip. He couldn't tell her the truth. "Because he finds every woman fascinating."

A light knock preceded the door opening. Mrs. Binns stuck her head into the room.

"So, you are awake," she said and entered.

She wore a similar voluminous nightgown, a green silk robe, and a ruffled bed cap with ribbons tied under her chin. In addition she had a long red sash draped around her neck. Numerous trinkets and charms had been tied onto the sash with different-colored ribbons, and they clanked and jingled as she walked.

"I thought I heard voices," Mrs. Binns said.

"I was...reading aloud," Josie said, indicating the book that had sat untouched in her lap.

"I heard a male voice," Mrs. Binns said as she opened the wardrobe. She looked behind the curtains and under the table.

"Just me."

Mrs. Binns scratched her temple. "I was so sure I..." She shook her head.

"I'm sorry if I woke you."

"Nonsense. I never sleep in the dark. Too dangerous, if you know what I mean." She dug into her bulging pocket and pulled out a calico cloth bundle tied with red yarn. "Here, this will help you sleep."

Josie identified the scent of lavender but couldn't name the other spicy aromas.

"Off to bed. You don't want dark circles under your eyes tomorrow." Mrs. Binns blew out the lamp on the table.

Josie removed her robe and slippers and crawled beneath the covers, feeling like a child as Mrs. Binns tucked her in. After wishing her a good night and pulling the bed curtains shut, the chaperone left, closing the door with a soft click.

"Deverell?" Josie whispered. She couldn't see him in the dark but felt he was still in the room. "Where are you?"

He was closer than she knew.

Nine

DEVERELL LOUNGED AT THE FOOT OF HER large bed. The dark did not affect his vision, and he watched as she snuggled into the deep feather pillows. She closed her eyes and gave a tiny sigh of contentment. The day had been long, and she must be more tired than she would ever admit. He decided not to continue their conversation. After all, hadn't everything been said that could, should be said?

"Where are you?" she mumbled in a drowsy voice.

"Sweet dreams," he whispered, his voice as light as a breeze.

The corners of her mouth lifted in a smile as her breathing deepened in sleep.

Certainly he had never found watching a woman sleep mesmerizing before. Had never wondered about her dreams. When he began wondering what she would look like if he held her in his arms, he knew he needed to leave. Immediately.

Josie woke with a start, having slept better than ever. She stretched in the luxurious feather bed, vowing to get one when she returned home no matter what the cost. Usually an early riser, she welcomed the morning sunbeam that found its way through a crack in the bed curtains. Today she needed to seek out Dev and persuade him to convince his mother to hold a séance...hopefully that very evening.

A little shiver shook her insides, but whether it was the thought of seeing him again or attending the séance or just plain ordinary hunger she refused to analyze. Instead she jumped out of bed, eager to get started.

She was soon stymied by her inability to dress herself in the fashions of the day. After considering whether she could get away with skipping the dreaded corset, she rang for Dora to help. When the maid arrived with a large pitcher of hot water, Josie had already chosen her clothes for the day and laid the multiple pieces out on the bed.

"Yes, miss? Oh, my! What are you doing?"

"Getting dressed, of course."

"But it's so early. You haven't even had your hot chocolate and toast. I'll get that right..."

"Never mind that. I need your help getting dressed so I can go downstairs for a proper breakfast. I'm starving and I need protein."

The maid looked confused.

"Eggs," Josie explained. "Bacon. Sausage."

"L...ladies don't usually eat breakfast."

"I don't see why not. It's my favorite meal."

"They don't usually rise until after ten o'clock."

"Waste of the best part of the day."

"But you can't eat in the dining room with the men. That wouldn't be proper."

Josie bit her bottom lip. Talking about breakfast had made her hungrier than ever, and she was more than ready to leave the room, which suddenly seemed confining. "Fine. I'll have my breakfast on the terrace. You can bring me a tray."

"Outside?"

"Of course."

"But...but..."

"I know, it's not proper," Josie guessed, rolling her eyes. "Surely picnics are proper."

"Well, yes."

"Fine. We'll call it a breakfast picnic."

"I suppose I could ask one of the footmen to move a small table from the parlor to the terrace."

"Excellent. You do that and I'll meet you down-stairs as soon as Mrs. Binns is ready."

"Oh, she's sound asleep in her chair. Poor thing didn't sleep a wink before dawn. I know because she rang for tea several times during the night."

Josie decided to let the other woman sleep, but she wasn't ready to give up on her idea. "Nellie can let us know when she wakes, and until then you can have breakfast with me."

"Oh no, miss. That would..."

"Not be proper," Josie finished.

"Staff had the morning meal hours ago."

"Fine. I have no problem eating alone." Heaven knew she'd done it many times before. On the road. At home in front of the television. The trick to dining solo in a restaurant was to bring something to read. "You run along and get things started. I'll meet you downstairs. And don't be skimpy on the portions. I'm starving."

"But miss..."

"No more arguments. My mind is made up."

Dora left muttering about crazy foreigners, which only made Josie smile. If only the girl knew how very far she'd really come to get there.

After grabbing her book and a thick shawl, Josie tiptoed across the sitting room and let herself out as quietly as possible so as not to disturb Mrs. Binns. Her soft leather shoes made little noise on the plush Persian carpet as she walked down the hall. She slowed when she heard angry voices ahead.

Suddenly an unfamiliar maid came barreling around the corner. The young girl sobbed into her apron as she rushed past and disappeared through the door to the servants' passage at the end of the hall.

Ready to confront whoever had made the girl cry, Josie turned back toward the low voices and marched to the turn in the hall that led to the grand stairway. She pulled to a stop when she recognized Dev and one of the men she'd met the night before.

"Aw, come off it, Waite," Galway said, his words slurred as if he was still drunk from the night before. He was barely dressed in a loose paisley robe that appeared to have been hastily donned. "We've been whoring together many a time. You're not averse to a little slap and tickle in the morning. Why the fuss?"

Dev, meticulously attired for his morning ride

and with his hat tucked under one arm, tapped his crop against his booted shin. "This is not a whorehouse, you imbecile," he said in a tight voice. "You're a guest in my mother's home—my home."

"One bed is as good as another, I always say. And you've agreed with me."

"Perhaps. However, I do draw a distinct line between seduction and rape. Forcing an unwilling female is beyond the pale."

"She led me on. Flaunted herself in front of me. Shaking that sweet rounded..."

Dev made a disgusted noise. "She was cleaning the banister. Fortunately I spotted you dragging her toward your room on my way out or..."

"Or she and I would have enjoyed a mutually satisfying morning interlude."

"Hardly. Since you do not seem to understand the error of your ways, and do not seem willing to conform to the standards I expect of my houseguests, perhaps you should repair to London where..."

"The company is more convivial?"

"Where your perverted brand of entertainment is treated with a blind eye. A footman to help you pack and your carriage will be waiting." Dev turned and started down the stairs.

Galway followed a few steps after him, stumbling and grabbing the banister for balance. "You're a bloody hypocrite, Waite," he hollered.

Dev paused and turned slowly to face the other man. "I prefer to think of myself as discerning. In my selection of women and in my choice of friends. I no longer count you among the latter."

Galway straightened and pulled the sash of his robe tighter. "I shall be leaving within the hour. Good day to you, sir." He turned and spotted Josie. "What have we here? If it isn't Lord Waite's little American heiress. Keeping you for himself is he?"

Josie looked down her nose at him, which wasn't easy considering his height. "Congratulations on your ability to display bad manners, ignorance, and stupidity all at the same time," she said in her best imitation of a high-and-mighty duchess.

As he pondered her words with a confused look, she swept by him only to meet Dev as he rushed back up the stairs.

"Miss Drummond. May I escort you somewhere, anywhere?"

"Yes, thank you, Lord Waite. I was on my way to the terrace when so rudely interrupted. Fresh air has even more appeal now. The foul stench at this location is quite disagreeable."

He offered his arm. "My apologies. The matter will soon be remedied and will not offend you again."

They walked down the stairs in silence. Even though she wore gloves she felt the warmth of his arm through his sleeve, and a slow heat resonated within her.

As they walked through the entrance hall to the gallery he said, "Please accept my apologies. You should not have had to witness such unpleasantness."

"Not necessary. My fault entirely. If I'd been in my room like a good little girl, I wouldn't have seen a thing."

He looked at her with a raised eyebrow. "You

have an interesting way of putting things."

"Will the maid be all right? Last I saw of her she seemed very upset."

"She was not harmed, only distressed."

"Could you make sure?"

"The housekeeper will deal with the matter. Mrs. Osman is highly regarded by my mother. I'm sure if there is anything further that I can do, one of them will let me know."

Josie was forced to drop the issue. Obviously it would be inappropriate for the lord of the castle to inquire about a maid's state of mind. As they walked along the gallery that ran parallel to the ballroom, she realized she was wasting a perfect opportunity to accomplish her goal.

"Although I hadn't expected to see you this morning, I'm glad I ran into you."

"Ran into me?"

"I can see you were on your way out," she said with a nod toward his riding hat and crop. "But if you could spare a few minutes, I'd like to speak with you on a matter of some importance to me."

"Would you like to accompany me? I'm quite proud of my stables, and I would gladly wait for you to change. Of course, a groom would come along as a chaperone."

She shuddered at the thought of getting on a horse. "No thank you."

At the end of the gallery he opened the French doors that led outdoors and stepped aside for her to precede him.

Dora and a footman waited on the terrace. In the

short time available she'd accomplished a minor miracle. Not only had a table been moved to the location, but it had been set with dishes and a silver coffee service on a snowy floor-length tablecloth.

"It's lovely," Josie said, clasping her hands together. She sniffed in appreciation. "You even remembered I prefer coffee in the morning. Thank you. Thank you both," she said to the servants, who returned her smile although the footman quickly masked his as he held out her chair.

"Breakfast alfresco. What a novel idea," Dev said.

"Nothing better for the appetite than fresh air, sunshine, and a beautiful view," she said, gazing out over the gardens as Dora poured her coffee. Josie turned back to face him. "Won't you join me, Lord Waite?"

He nodded to the footman, who rushed off.

"I broke my fast earlier, but I will take a cup of tea while we talk," he said.

The footman returned with a chair, and Dev sat across from her. Dora placed a plate piled high with thick ham slices and fried potatoes and a dish of buttery shirred eggs in front of Josie. Dev raised an eyebrow, and it inched higher with each dish the maid added. Half a pound of crispy bacon and several sausages. Four large biscuits. A pot of jam and another of honey. An oval salver with an artful arrangement of fruit slices. Josie shook her head at the offer of kippers but nodded to the small bowl of creamy butter.

"I think you need a larger table and a few more chairs to seat the army you must be expecting to join you," he said.

Josie was forced to make a choice. She could nibble delicately as any Regency lass would do and leave the table hungry, as she'd done the previous evening, or she could really enjoy the meal. She shrugged as she placed her napkin in her lap.

"What can I say? I have a healthy appetite," she said. Even though she remembered her table manners, she wasn't shy. "Are you sure you won't join me? These eggs are fantastic."

Dev raised his cup in salute. "My pleasure is in watching you enjoy yourself." And to his surprise he meant it. What was it about this woman that made mundane matters seem fresh, exciting, and appealing? He shook his head to clear his thoughts. "What was it you wanted to talk to me about?"

"Mmmm." She gulped a swallow of coffee. "I heard Madame X is here to hold séances, but your mother canceled the one planned for tonight because..."

"You heard? You should know better than to listen to servants' gossip," he said with a scowl.

"Oh, no, the servants haven't said anything. I've always been fascinated by spiritualists, and I specifically came here to attend a séance by Madame X. I'm quite anxious to contact my deceased father."

Dev rolled his eyes. "My mother has been after me to attend one of those silly things, but I managed to escape involvement so far. You don't seriously believe that hogwash?"

"I've never been to a séance that actually contacted..."

"Of course not."

"But the possibility..."

"There is none."

"You can't know that for sure. Strange things happen every day that can't be explained by ordinary logic." Like time travel.

"Ha! If logic fails to explain something, that simply means salient facts are missing."

"Well, I think it's worth a try."

"If you have already made up your mind, why come to me?"

Josie took a deep breath. "Because Madame X doesn't want to add any guests to the séance, but if you say you will attend and want to include me, then they will," she said in a rush. "Include me, that is."

"That's all?"

"Yes. No. Could we do it tonight? Please?"

"You want me to promise to attend so Mother will convince Madame X to hold the séance..."

"Tonight."

"Why?"

"I told you. My father..."

"Why tonight?"

"Because...because today is the anniversary of his death and it is an auspicious time to contact him."

Dev knew she was lying. Rather than being put off, which was the usual case when he was confronted with liars, he was more intrigued than ever. She probably didn't lie often since she did it so poorly. That left the question of what she felt the need to conceal—and why.

"If I do this favor for you, I shall expect something in return."

She crossed her arms and narrowed her eyes. "It's a very small favor."

"You're asking me to rearrange my schedule, forgo a potentially lucrative card game to attend a silly..."

"Okay, okay. What favor..."

"*O-kay?*"

"It means all right, fine, yes. Now, what do you want in return?"

"Simple. The pleasure of your company. Walk with me after the séance. The rose garden is especially lovely by moonlight."

Josie was tempted. The heady scent of roses, sparkling stars in a midnight velvet sky, and Dev, a dangerous combination even in her imagination. Not to mention she would need to talk to Deverell right after the séance to plan the revelation of Madame X as a fraud. She couldn't talk to him if he was around. She shook her head. If she thought too hard about differentiating between the ghost and the man, she would get a splitting headache.

Would Dev agree without her promise? "Tomorrow afternoon," she said, offering a safe alternative. If all went as planned, she would be long gone by then.

"I have an appointment in the afternoon I can't cancel again. Some unpleasant business I must settle once and for all."

She shrugged.

"Tomorrow morning," he counter-offered. "Breakfast together right here and a walk in the garden."

She raised an eyebrow to signal she understood he'd raised the stakes. Agreeing to meet him in the

morning would be a gamble, but if the ghost coop-
erated, they could still be out of there in time. She
nodded and forced a smile.

He did not return her expression.

She dismissed an uneasy feeling that he knew
she had no intention of keeping the bargain.

"Excuse me, miss," Dora said with a curtsy. "Nellie says Mrs. Binns is awake and asking for you."

"Thank you, Dora." Josie stood. "I must see to
Mrs. Binns. I thank you, Lord Waite, for doing me
this small favor. If you'll excuse me?"

He'd also stood. "I wish you a pleasant rest of the
morning."

After Josie left, Dev wandered to the edge of the
terrace. He lit a cheroot and gazed over the
grounds. A surge of pride surprised him. From the
time he'd severed the leading strings, he'd spent little time in the country, preferring the stimulation
of the city. And yet on this visit he hadn't felt the
crushing press of boredom after three days, the itch
to move, the hankering for excitement.

Miss Drummond presented an interesting puzzle. At times he could read her as easily as if she sat
across the gaming table from him. He knew when
she thought she held a winning hand and when she
was considering folding. At other times she was a
complete and utter mystery. Fortunately he knew
the cure for such fascination.

He turned to the footman, who was clearing the
breakfast area. "Joseph, please tell the groom I will
not be riding this morning."

"Yes, milord."

"And let Lady Honoria's maid know I will call on my mother in her boudoir shortly."

Dev left the terrace with a light step, eager to change his clothes and set the wheels in motion. He had a few surprises planned for Miss Josie Drummond.

"If you've come to say good-bye, I refuse to wish you a smooth journey."

"Good morning to you, too, Mother."

Dev took a lounging position on the chaise that flanked his mother's dressing table. He crossed his legs at the ankles and tucked his hands behind his head.

"Stop fussing," she said to her maid. "Go, go." Honoria waited for the nosy maid to slowly place the hairbrush on the vanity and unhurriedly make her way out of the room before she turned to her son. "Whatever excuse you have to offer, I will not accept it. The ball is tomorrow night, and I expect you to..."

"What makes you think I'm here to say good-bye?"

"Let me see. You have been here four days. You are not out riding wildly across the countryside." She counted the reasons on her fingers. "You are visiting me in my rooms rather than waiting until a civil hour when I will be available downstairs." She threw her hands in the air. "I am not a fool."

"Am I that transparent?"

She patted his arm. "Only to me, dear. Remember, I have been your mother all your life."

"Remind me never to play cards against you."

"Who do you think taught you to play?"

"The head groomsman."

"Bah!" She shook her head, but at least she was smiling. "So," she said, placing her hands on her knees and giving him an intense stare. "If you are not here to say good-bye, what is it you want?"

"Can't I simply visit my dear mother to..." He paused when she gave him the don't-pull-the-wool-over-my-eyes look. "Very well. I have come to speak to you about a séance."

"We've had this discussion before, and I will not let you talk me out of this matter. I am determined..."

"Can you hold one tonight?"

"...to contact your father and uncle...What did you say?"

"If you can arrange a séance tonight, I would like to attend."

"Are you feeling all right?" She placed her hand on his forehead. "Should I prepare a tisane with feverweed?"

"Stop," he said, swiping away her pretended concern with a chuckle. "I simply feel it a wise move to get to know my enemy, so to speak."

"Madame X is not your enemy. She is a gifted spiritualist and quite sensitive to negativity."

"I promise not to call her a charlatan to her face."

"Dev."

He swung his legs around and sat up. "Then it's all settled. In the library at midnight. I presume that is the appropriate time for such mysterious doings."

"Madame X has canceled the séance for tonight. There are so many guests arriving for the ball tomorrow she was concerned I would have too many other duties."

"And do you?"

"Actually no. The planning was detailed and the staff is very capable. Other than acting as hostess, I don't anticipate..."

"Then you can hold the séance as originally scheduled."

"Only if Madame X feels..."

"Are you paying her to hold these séances?"

"Of course I am. Even a gifted spiritualist has to make a living."

"Then she can either hold the séance when you want or you can find someone who will. From what I hear, there is one on every London street corner now that talking to the dead is considered fashionable."

"Mediums of her caliber..."

"Are tuppence a dozen. I could have six here before midnight, all more than willing to earn what they consider a living wage."

"Madame X..."

"Fine. I understand." Just as when he bargained over the price of a horse and the seller had to be convinced that he was willing to walk away, he stood before tossing out his final offer. "I was willing to attend tonight, but if she refuses..." He paused for effect and shrugged. "I wonder if Shermont..."

"I'll convince her."

"Oh? Do you think you can?"

"Don't give me that wide-eyed innocent look you outgrew at age six. Of course I can."

He kissed her on the forehead and headed for the door. He paused with his hand on the doorknob and turned. "Oh, yes. Miss Drummond would also like to attend," he said as if it was an afterthought.

"Really?"

"She said something about contacting her deceased father."

"Really?"

"No need to use that tone. She asked me as a favor."

"Really?"

"If you say that again, I'll not speak to you for the rest of the day."

"This sounds interesting." Honoria rubbed her chin. "If I include Miss Drummond in the séance, and I'm not saying I can, but if I do...then I want your word you will stay for the ball."

"So you can parade the entire eligible female population of the district under my nose?"

"And the neighboring districts if necessary."

"I promise to stay. But you can get that matchmaker's gleam out of your eye. I have no intention of marrying before I'm too old to totter around the salons of London, if then." He opened the door.

"Your father said the same thing," she mumbled as he stepped over the threshold.

He pretended not to hear.

Now to the rest of his arrangements.

Ten

"OH, LOOK, LOOK," MRS. BINNS SAID, ALTHOUGH she neither surrendered her spyglass nor moved from her place at the window. "That's Lord Dumbries. Widower. Handsome as the day is long if I do say so myself. And arriving the day before the ball. Must be out of mourning and in the market for a new wife."

Josie made appropriate agreeing noises although she was listening with only half an ear.

"Unless you are inordinately fond of children, I would advise giving him a wide berth. Nine children in eleven years. Probably what killed his wife. You would think she would have figured it out and banished him from her..."

Josie looked up from her book.

"Never mind," Mrs. Binns said.

"I do know what happens between a man and a woman."

"For heaven's sake, don't let anyone else hear you say that."

The noise of another carriage coming down the

crushed-shell drive distracted the older woman, and Josie returned her attention to Elizabeth Bennet and Mr. Darcy. The story had additional depth now that she'd witnessed some of the mannerisms portrayed by the characters. The book had been her salvation through the long, boring day spent incarcerated with Mrs. Binns and her embroidery threads.

The chaperone was convinced Josie would appear too eager if she met the new guests before the evening assembly. In truth Mrs. Binns impatiently anticipated dinner while Josie dreaded another long evening before getting to the séance.

If there was even going to be a séance. Josie hadn't heard from Dev, and the ghost had not put in an appearance all day. Though she hated to admit it, she missed them both.

"There's trouble times two." Mrs. Binns turned and gave Josie an arch look. "The Cracklebury sisters are known to put themselves forward."

Something about the comment rang a bell, and Josie struggled to put her finger on it. Her formerly dependable memory kept playing games with her. "Does one of them play the harpsichord?"

"At the drop of a hat."

Relief flooded Josie. At least she hadn't lost all her marbles. Not yet.

"Oh, my. Shermont is with them. Honoria won't like that."

"Why did she invite him then?"

"One should always invite those of similar rank when they are in the vicinity even if they are not of the most desirable character. One just doesn't expect the devil incarnate to show up."

Out of idle curiosity rather than real interest, Josie put down her book and rose to peer over Mrs. Binns's shoulder. "What does the devil look like?" From her angle all she could see was the top of his hat.

"Handsome as sin and twice as...Never you mind, my dear. You'll not be meeting the likes of him. Not if I can help it. Honoria will have her hands full keeping him separated from Lord Wingate."

Mrs. Binns was on a roll. "You weren't here for last year's scandal of the season. Gossip went wild. Not that anyone could prove anything, but it was said Lady Wingate and Shermont were caught..."

"Were caught doing what?"

"Never you mind. Suffice it to say there's bad blood between Wingate and Shermont. Waite will probably embroil Shermont in a card game to keep him occupied."

Josie remembered Dev's comment from the previous evening that Shermont never played cards before midnight. "What will happen if Lord Waite can't play cards with Shermont?"

"And why would he not?"

Realizing her mistake, Josie tried to think of a reason. The clock ticked away while Mrs. Binns waited, her suspicions obvious.

"You haven't agreed to do anything stupid like meet him in the garden at midnight, have you?"

"No." Without any believable lies coming to mind, Josie was forced to tell the truth.

"A séance? Why would anyone in their right mind *want* spirits to appear? Oh, dear. Oh, dear. I simply must have a talk with Honoria."

"I doubt you can talk her out of it. Dev...Lord Waite has agreed to attend."

"Then I shall come with you."

Josie's deal with Dev had not included Mrs. Binns. "That's not necessary."

"It most certainly is."

What would Dev say to the chaperone tagging along? What would she have to promise him in return? A shiver raced up her spine, but she refused to call it anticipation.

"Not to worry," Mrs. Binns said. "I will prepare adequate protection. It's a good thing I restocked my case just before leaving London. 'Be prepared' is my motto. One never knows when spiritual defenses will be needed."

"I'm sure I'll be fine without..."

"Honoria and that rascal son of hers have no idea what powers they are conjuring. I'm the expert, and I'll brook no further argument. If you insist on going, then I will be there to protect you," Mrs. Binns said. The fierce lioness guarding her young.

Another carriage coming down the drive distracted Mrs. Binns, and she resumed her position in the window seat with her spyglass.

Whether the older woman thought the presence of spirits at the séance or the participation of Lord Waite was the more dangerous she hadn't said. Josie knew which one posed the greater threat.

Dinner seemed interminable to Josie. With the

presence of more than double the number of guests at the table, all of whom seemed to know each other from other such parties, she was practically ignored—which was fine with her. If fact she would have been happier if everyone had treated her as if she were invisible.

She had come to expect her sensitivity to Dev's presence, but the intensity of his lingering glances unnerved her. At times he seemed to read her mind.

Every time Estelle glanced her way, which was way too often, she clenched her hands as if she wanted to meet Josie in the boxing ring. Madame X stared at her with narrowed eyes. Mrs. Binns silently encouraged Josie to smile, smile, smile. And Hargrave, apparently still resentful of her chaperone's setdown the previous evening, shot daggered looks Josie's way.

Everyone else seated at the table seemed oblivious to the charged undercurrents except for Honoria, who watched it all with intense interest.

If the absence of the Wingates and Lord Shermont was noted, no one commented on it. At least not that Josie heard.

When everyone mingled around the table and the servants deftly dodged the guests to clear and reset for the next course, Josie noticed Dev pull Hargrave aside for a moment's private chat. After that the disgruntled suitor pointedly ignored her.

Between the second and third courses, Dev paused behind her and leaned over long enough to whisper for her ears alone, "Midnight in the library."

She was so distracted by the warmth of his breath

on the back of her neck, he'd already moved away by the time she realized he'd told her the séance was on.

Wanting to be alert later that evening, Josie refrained from drinking any more wine, and she noticed Mrs. Binns did the same. No one else seemed inclined to moderation. When Honoria stood to signal the women it was time to retire to the parlor and leave the men to their port and cigars, Josie was the first to follow her lead.

The ladies' talk centered on the latest fashions, fresh gossip from town, and the ball to be held the following evening. Several women practiced a new step while another played the pianoforte. After sitting next to Josie on the sofa, Mrs. Binns handed her a small piece of embroidery. Josie had enough time to twist the thread into a knot, untangle it, and snarl it up again three times before the men entered the parlor.

As on the previous evening, Josie garnered more male attention after the men had had a chance to speak alone. This time she knew the reason and deferred to her chaperone when they asked personal questions about her family and future plans. The effect was the opposite of what she'd intended. The men were impressed with her demure attitude and vied for the most outrageous expression of their admiration. Dev appeared amused, but she wasn't sure if it was at their posturing or hers.

Thankfully, Honoria deftly squashed any of the guests' proposed plans to extend the evening, and by eleven-thirty Josie and her chaperone were back in their suite of rooms.

Mrs. Binns immediately fetched her red case and brought it back to the sitting room. She pulled out the decorated sash she wore at night and wrapped it around her neck. She produced another sash for Josie. Charms and medals and more of the little calico bundles had been sewn to a length of red fabric.

"If you're still intent on this foolishness..."

"I am," Josie said.

"Then you must wear something to protect you."

Josie eyed the red sash with trepidation, but she allowed the older woman to wrap it over her shoulders. "What is that smell?" she asked, wrinkling her nose.

"Fresh garlic," Mrs. Binns answered.

"I don't think we'll be encountering any vampires," Josie said with a grin.

"Don't mock these safeguards, child." Mrs. Binns scowled. "Spiritualism is a serious matter. You never know what you will release when someone rips open the veil that separates the beyond."

"But surely..."

"Tut-tut. Remember my motto."

"Be prepared." Josie stifled the urge to salute.

"Exactly." Mrs. Binns lit a dried bundle of sage. After it burned for a few seconds she blew out the flames, producing a smoking rush. "Now hold out your arms."

Josie complied and the other woman circled her, waving the sage rush so the smoke covered her from head to toe.

"I have thought of everything. Demon, imp, sprite..." She touched each protective bit as she named off the creature it would ward against. "Incubus, succubus, banshee, ghoul, poltergeist, goblin, gremlin, fairy, and…"

"I'd like to meet a fairy," Josie said, blinking away smoke-induced tears.

"No, you wouldn't. Spiteful, nasty little creatures. They like to pinch you when you aren't looking."

"Tinkerbell wouldn't do that."

"Who?" Mrs. Binns asked as she threw the rush into the water pitcher on the washstand.

"Never mind." Josie wasn't going to argue, but she also wasn't going to change her mind about them. "Besides, fairies aren't spiritual; they're magical."

Mrs. Binns raised one finger. "Be prepared."

"Next you'll be telling me you have something against leprechauns."

"Tricksters. Twist you around until you don't know which way is up. Not to worry. This emblem protects us." She patted an elaborate circular brooch encrusted with a variety of stones. "The witch who made it for me is half elf herself and very powerful. We won't be seeing any magical creatures tonight."

At least Josie agreed with that.

Josie and Mrs. Binns arrived at the library five minutes early. Dev waited at the door.

"Are you sure you want to go through with this?" he asked.

Of course, she did. The séance was her ticket home. For some reason her throat tightened, blocking her voice. She swallowed and nodded.

"I'm surprised to find you are a party to this perilous undertaking," Mrs. Binns said to him. "I would have thought a man of your position would have more sense."

Dev raised an eyebrow. "I expect the event will be mildly amusing."

"Humph!" Mrs. Binns sailed past him. "Let's get this over with."

"What is that smell?" Dev asked, wrinkling his nose.

"Don't ask," Josie said. She pointed to the red sash around her neck. "Believe me, you don't want to know. By the way, thanks for arranging the séance," Josie said.

"My pleasure," he said, offering his arm. "Or rather my pleasure will come tomorrow," he whispered under his breath as he escorted her into the room.

She couldn't respond due to the presence of the other participants, but she also couldn't stop her rosy blush.

Madame X dominated the room. She was dressed in a lavish turban of deep blue silk patterned with stars and moons and mystical runes. The headpiece extended past her shoulders and wrapped under her chin. The padding supported an elaborate crown, and a golden mask hid her features. "Please take a seat," she said with a wave of her hand. She wore purple gloves with large ornate rings on every finger.

Five armless chairs had been arranged around one side of a round table. On the other side Madame X seated herself on a large carved wooden throne. She sat stone-still while the others took their places, Dev in the middle, flanked by

Honoria and Estelle on his right and Mrs. Binns and Josie on his left. From across the table Estelle glowered at her.

Even though Dev had held the chair next to his for her, Josie had urged Mrs. Binns to take it. Josie wanted to be as close to the gypsy as possible.

"You may light the Candle of Omniscience," Madame X said in a solemn tone. Rather than muffle her voice, the golden mask seemed to make it reverberate.

Honoria jumped up and took another candle from a waiting footman and eagerly performed the honor. The footman extinguished the lamps and exited, closing the doors with a firm click. Honoria locked the door behind him and laid the key on the table in front of Madame X.

"Your instructions have been fulfilled to the letter," Honoria said as she resumed her seat.

Several minutes of silence followed.

"I would have expected a Candle of Omniscience to shed a bit more light," Dev said.

Josie stifled a giggle.

"Shush," Honoria said. "Madame is concentrating."

"Everyone put your hands on the table," Madame X said, doing so herself. They all did the same.

"Shouldn't we be holding hands?" Mrs. Binns asked.

"No," Madame nearly shouted.

"Madame cannot be touched while in a trance. For her safety and everyone else's," Estelle explained.

From under her voluminous robes the gypsy brought out a brass bowl, set it on the table near the middle, and laid several pieces of folded paper in it.

"Those are the names of the people we want to contact," Estelle said, leaning forward to look at Dev.

"Silence," Madame X said, her voice booming. She held one of the papers to the candle and then used it to light the others in the dish. As the paper flared up, the aroma of spicy incense filled the air.

Madame adjusted her robes and settled into a comfortable position. She placed her hands on the table. "We begin."

During the few minutes of dead silence, Josie looked around in the dim light. Estelle sat with her eyes closed, apparently in a trance of her own. Honoria eagerly watched the gypsy. Dev tapped his fingers on the tabletop. Mrs. Binns's fearful gaze darted around the room. Madame X began to moan and rock from side to side. She chanted in a foreign tongue.

Suddenly, she stopped and called out, "Hear me, Amanu. Spirit guide, I command you to do my bidding. Come forward."

The candle sparked and flared and then settled to a glow that was even dimmer than before.

"Amanu, can you hear me?"

"Yes, my queen," a distinctively male voice answered.

Madame tipped her head to the right and turned slightly as if listening to a person standing to her left.

Josie looked around but could not see anyone.

"Have you established contact with the designated spirits?"

"Yes, my queen," the disembodied voice said.

"Very good. I command you to appear and answer my questions."

"You risk much. Disbelievers have tainted the sacred ritual."

"It is my command."

"Yes, my queen." After an audible sigh, he continued, "When you speak the beckoning enchantment, I will appear."

Madame mumbled something and fell forward onto the table.

Dev started to rise but stopped when Estelle hissed, "Nobody move."

The table shook and the candle flared once more.

Suddenly an extremely tall man rose up behind Madame's chair. He was dressed in a simple monk's robe that looked to be made of grayish green silk shot with silver threads. The cowl was raised, hiding most of his head, and what Josie could see of his face glowed greenish in the dim light.

He placed luminescent hands on the back of her chair. "I will answer no questions for the unbelievers." With a wide sweeping motion, he dismissed three-fifths of the table. "For you, dear lady," he said to Honoria, "Daniel sends the message that he is at peace, and he reminds you to wear the ruby necklace as a reminder of his regard."

"My wedding present," Honoria said with tears in her eyes. "Only Daniel would know how special that necklace is to me."

Dev coughed and Josie knew he used it to cover a laugh.

"Tell me more. Has Daniel reconciled with his father?"

The man hesitated as if listening. "He will say only that he is at peace."

Honoria looked disappointed.

"Daniel says he will persevere."

"Good. Send him my love."

The man slowly nodded. "It is done."

"What about Percy? Have you spoken to Percy?"

"Your brother says to tell you he is whole and happy."

"Thank you." By now the tears ran unchecked down Honoria's cheeks. "I have been so worried he would miss his leg that was left at Waterloo."

"Physical limbs are not needed in the spiritual world."

"I know, but it's good to hear it directly from him."

"So to speak," Josie mumbled beneath her breath.

"You!" The specter swung his long arm and pointed directly at her. "You do not belong here. You should return to where you came from, or else you will pay the consequences."

"What about Mabel?" Honoria asked. She laid her hand over Estelle's. "Please tell her that her darling daughter and her dearest friend want to know she has found her ease at last."

The figure nodded. "Mabel says she is happy. And she reminds you of your girlhood promise."

"What promise is that?" Estelle asked with patently false innocence.

"We always said our children would marry so

we could share our grandchildren," Honoria said.

Josie figured Estelle had arranged the self-serving reminder with the gypsy in advance.

"Ha!" Dev said. "If I refuse to listen to my living flesh and blood, why should I heed the word of a..."

"You should heed this," the so-called spirit boomed as he pointed his long bony finger at Dev. "Change your dissolute ways, or you will soon find a bad end."

"Now *that* sounds like my father."

The specter folded his arms and bowed his head. Then he slowly sank away from sight behind the gypsy's chair. Madame X moaned and the table shook. The candle sputtered, and then it flared once again. Madame sat up and pulled her limp hands from the table.

"That is all," she said. "You may blow out the candle and light the lamps."

Honoria did the first and Dev accomplished the latter. Only when the room was again well lit did Josie notice that Mrs. Binns had fainted. While Josie dug in her reticule for the tiny vial of smelling salts, Estelle rushed to the head of the table to help Madame X stand. Dev moved to help, but she waved him away.

"Madame will be disoriented and feeling vulnerable for the next few hours. She is used to me, so I must be the one to help her back to her room."

"My things," Madame said, her voice a weak imitation of her usual commanding attitude. She slumped against her friend's shoulder.

Estelle motioned and Honoria gathered up the

candle and bowl. "Please unlock the door," Estelle said to Dev.

Josie knelt beside her chaperone's chair and waved the uncapped vial under her nose. Mrs. Binns jerked her head away from the sharp acrid odor.

"What? What happened?" she said, bolting up to a ramrod-straight position and clutching the large cross she wore around her neck.

"You fainted," Josie said.

"Nonsense. I never faint."

"Are you all right?" Honoria asked as she appropriated the chair next to her friend.

"Of course. I'm fine."

Josie took the opportunity to surreptitiously check under the table. The single center post appeared to be made of solid wood, and the bottom of the tabletop was smooth and unmarred.

"Did you hear? Wasn't it wonderful?" Honoria gushed like a schoolgirl. "Before we only heard Amanu's voice, but to actually have him make an appearance made it so much more real and exciting. We are so lucky."

"Humph. Hogwash. Nothing but hogwash," Mrs. Binns said.

"I agree," Dev said, coming to stand behind his mother.

She twisted around to look up at him. "How can you say that after witnessing Amanu's appearance with your own eyes?"

"I have seen spirits before, and that man was as alive as you or me," Mrs. Binns said.

Honoria whipped around. "How could a man

have come in? The door was locked, and we were all mere feet away."

"I don't know how it was done, but there's a trick involved. I'm sure of it."

"Then why did you faint?" Honoria asked, folding her arms and giving her friend a superior stare. "Mmm?"

"I did not faint. Last I remember all was dark and quiet. I might have dozed for a moment," Mrs. Binns finally admitted.

Honoria looked to the ceiling as if appealing for divine help in understanding and shook her head. "I can't believe you slept through the most momentous..."

"That's putting a bit of gilding on it, don't you think?" Mrs. Binns said.

"Amanu revealing secrets from the other side of the veil *is* momentous."

"He revealed nothing you didn't already know."

"Well, I am satisfied with the results, and next time..."

"Not another one," Dev said with a groan.

"Josie didn't get to speak to her father," Honoria reminded him.

"You do not know the powers you are conjuring," Mrs. Binns said.

Josie rose from her position on the floor wedged between the chairs. As the older women continued to argue, Dev stepped around them, moved the empty chair, and offered Josie his hand.

As he pulled her to her feet, she realized he'd cleverly arranged the furniture so she had to either step away from her chaperone and thus toward him or trip over the chair. With another deft move he guided her to a position where his body blocked off the rest of the room.

"My offer still stands," he whispered. "The garden is lovely in moonlight."

"What was that you said?" Mrs. Binns asked his back.

Josie smiled as she sidestepped him and took the long route around the table. "He said, it must be late considering we started at midnight."

"I am quite exhausted by all the excitement," Honoria said as she stood.

"We shall bid you good-night." Mrs. Binns also rose.

"Until the morrow," Dev said. His gaze did not leave Josie's eyes even as he bowed formally.

His look promised...

Upstairs, Josie found the ghost waiting in the sitting room.

"What happened?" he asked immediately.

She noticed he seemed paler than usual, but she could not ask him about his manifestation without giving his presence away.

"You must tell me everything I missed," Mrs. Binns said. She settled on the brocade sofa and indicated the nearest chair.

Rather than sit in Deverell's lap, Josie took the straight-backed chair by the small writing desk. "I'd like to take a few notes," she said in explanation, taking out a sheet of paper and a stub of pencil. "While it's still fresh in my mind." She described the séance in detail, ending with her admittance that she didn't know how it had been done.

"A green glow, you say?" Mrs. Binns said, tapping her finger on her chin. "Probably some form of phosphorus rubbed into the skin."

"Not only is that extremely dangerous," Josie said. "It leaves the problem of how a green-glowing man wearing a monk's robe got through a locked door and into the library without being noticed."

"A secret passageway," Mrs. Binns guessed.

Josie glanced at Deverell.

"Not in the library," he said. "There once was a priest hole connected to the fireplace, but Father had it bricked over after a maid got stuck in there. Why she was there I never heard, but her howling sounded as if all the banshees of Ireland had come to Castle Waite to roost."

"These old castles always have secret panels and hidden hallways," Mrs. Binns mused.

"There are some," Deverell said to Josie. "We used to play in them as children despite strict instructions to the contrary. Most go from one bedroom to another. None lead to the library. Was the door locked?"

"Did you feel any air movement or a draft?" Mrs. Binns asked.

"Yes. No," Josie answered. She was getting confused listening to two conversations at the same time. "No drafts."

"We'll have to ask Honoria about the secret passages tomorrow, or rather later today." She slapped her hands on her knees and stood. "We'd best call for help getting undressed so the maids can get some rest."

Deverell waited until Dora had finished and exited before scratching on Josie's door. She called for him to enter from her position propped up on a mound of pillows, her book in her lap, and a lone lamp burning on the nightstand.

"I told Dora I must read for a bit before I can fall asleep."

"I will not stay long," he said, taking a seat by the window. He nearly faded into the tapestry fabric of the chair.

She was worried about him. The longer they stayed, the weaker he became. She leaned forward. "Are you okay?"

"I must conserve my energy."

"I'm sorry," she said. "I've failed."

He shrugged. "The gypsy is smarter than we gave her credit for. You shall have to try again. Tomorrow night if possible."

"The ball..."

"I am not inexhaustible. I risk fading into nothingness so you can dance the night away with..." He paused when Josie recoiled at his sharp tone.

"I only mentioned the ball because it will make arranging a séance for tomorrow difficult if not impossible," she said, blinking rapidly.

"My apologies," he said with a formal slant of his head. "I should not have taken my annoyance out on you. I know you're doing the best you can."

She sniffled.

He rose to give her a handkerchief from the

dresser. "I did not intend to make you cry."

To his surprise she shook her head and chuckled. "These tears aren't due to anything you said. These are tears of frustration. I'm not used to being outsmarted."

He sat on the edge of the bed, his presence barely making a dent in the fluffy feather comforter.

"You will succeed next time," he said. "If you can convince Honoria to hold the séance without Dev, I can be there to help."

"Arranging another one on short notice will be difficult enough even if I ask Dev to talk to his mother for me." Heaven only knew what she would have to promise him this time.

Which reminded her, because she'd failed and therefore would not be leaving, she would have to meet Dev in the morning.

"Every cloud has a silver lining," Deverell said.

Luckily he could not read her thoughts because she doubted he would see her walking in the garden with Dev as a bonus. Did she? What would it be like? Would he kiss her again? One of those smoldering, consuming kisses that had made her want to climb up his chest and wrap her legs around his waist.

"You can enlist him to help you."

"What? Who? Sorry, my mind must have drifted off there for a minute." Off to fantasy land.

Deverell stood. "I will let you get your rest."

"No, no. I'm not tired. What did you say?"

"If you confide in Dev that you do not believe

the gypsy is a true medium, he can help you discover how she produces the apparition."

"Good idea."

"Perhaps you can think of some ways to set up traps that will reveal what she does."

"That sounds good, too. What did you have in mind?" She sighed. "I miss my equipment."

And long hot showers. And deodorant, toothpaste, peanut butter, her computer, her iPod, tissues, chocolate-chip-cookie-dough ice cream…

"We'll think of something after you have had a chance to rest. Now go to sleep. You will need to be alert tomorrow."

Wasn't that the truth! She would be meeting Dev.

Deverell faded away, and she knew when his presence left the room.

But she could not sleep. She needed to think about ways to trap the gypsy. First, she would check for secret panels. Even if Deverell said there were none, that would be the most logical explanation for the fake apparition's appearance. Perhaps she could use some of Mrs. Binns's finest silk thread to string across the floor. Broken threads would identify direction of movement.

She gathered a few things she might find useful and tied them into the handkerchief. What else? Of course she would examine the furniture for places large enough to conceal a man taller than Dev.

Which brought her back to thoughts of meeting him in the morning.

When she did finally drift into slumber, her erotic dreams seemed to carry dire warnings. She woke at dawn more exhausted than before she'd slept, the covers twisted and tossed.

She dragged herself out of bed and rang for Dora. Breakfast, and Dev, awaited.

Eleven

JOSIE WAS GRATEFUL WHEN DORA ARRIVED NOT only with hot water but also with a pot of strong aromatic coffee. The maid fairly danced around the room, humming as she opened the drapes and laid out Josie's clothes for the day.

"You're quite chipper this morning," Josie grumbled, jealous of her energy. The maid couldn't have gotten any more sleep than she had.

"Big doings today. More guests arriving." She giggled. "And other things."

"Like what?"

"Oh, this and that," she said, being evasive, and then she giggled again.

"What is making you so happy this morning?" Josie asked as she stepped behind the screen to wash. She could stand to hear a bit of good news for a change. "Tell me."

"For one, I no longer have to help Sadie see to Lady Wingate. And is she miffed at being moved. Oops, I shouldn't be gossiping. Mrs. Osman will have my head."

"Nonsense. I asked a direct question and there-fore you should answer. Why would Lady Wingate have to move?"

"It's the numbers. With all the new arrivals expected, guests have to share their suites. Lady Wingate has been moved in with her husband. And the Cracklebury sisters are now in her old room. Poor Sadie will be run ragged. She has to do for them and Countess LaFoyn and Madame X."

Josie donned her chemise and then took a seat at the dressing table to put on her stockings and soft leather shoes, which felt more like slippers. Giving Dora permission to speak freely was like opening the floodgates.

"But don't you worry, miss. You won't have to move. His lordship gave specific instructions you were not to be disturbed and..." Dora covered her mouth as if to keep a secret from escaping.

"And?" What was Dev up to? It was not like him to interfere with the running of the house.

"Just...other things."

"Dora?" Josie let her voice carry an implied and totally false warning.

"Well...he told Mrs. Osman I shouldn't have so many extra duties that your wishes are neglected," Dora said as she cinched up Josie's corset. "You are my first pri...pri..."

"Priority?"

"That's it."

When Dora did not elaborate, Josie asked her directly, "What else?"

"Oh, miss. Don't make me spoil the surprise."

"Isn't your duty to see I'm properly prepared for every activity?"

"Yes…" There was a bit of hesitation in the maid's voice as if she already knew she would lose this argument.

Dora had chosen a white muslin dress embroidered with sprigs of tiny lavender flowers and mint leaves. She slipped it over Josie's head, fastened the back, and puffed up the tiny sleeves.

Josie checked her image in the cheval mirror and was satisfied to see she didn't look as exhausted as she felt. "And isn't part of being prepared knowing what is scheduled to happen?"

"Yes." Dora wrapped a narrow dark green ribbon sash around Josie just under her bustline and tied it in a bow at the back.

"Then how can you send me out that door totally ignorant of what Lord Waite has planned?"

"But it is sooo beautiful. I'm sure you'll like it."

Josie sat at the dressing table and picked up her brush. "I'm sure I will. But I would like it *better* if I had an idea of what was coming."

The maid's shoulders slumped. "Instead of breakfast on the terrace, I'm to bring you to the folly."

"What's a folly?"

"The building in the garden. Halfway down the drive there's a path that leads through the grove. Oh, miss, his lordship wanted to surprise you. Don't tell him I told you."

Josie didn't see what the big deal was. "All right."

"We've all been up since the wee hours to make everything perfect. Cook has prepared special dishes and the gardener picked dozens of his most fragrant blooms to decorate the folly like a rose bower, and the footmen moved furniture, the table and chairs and the chaise, and lots of pillows and..."

"Whoa!" Josie jumped up. Sounded more like Dev was planning a seduction rather than breakfast. As far as she was concerned, *walk in the garden* was not a euphemism for sex. She spun around and marched toward the door. "Come along, Dora. His lordship is going to get a piece of my mind."

"But, miss! Your bonnet? Your gloves?"

"Whatever. Bring them along if you must, but hurry." Josie wanted to confront Dev before her indignation cooled. She left the maid scurrying around the room in a panic.

"Wait, miss. Your shawl," Dora called as she followed down the hall.

Josie marched down the main stairs. How dare that man make such a big deal out of a simple breakfast meeting. Did everyone in the castle have to know about it? Did everyone think she and Dev were going to *walk in the garden*?

She passed the surprised butler and didn't pause for him to open the door. The heavy portal moved easily on oiled hinges and smacked the side of the house as she sailed through. The crushed shells on the drive crunched under her feet. "Ouch." She moved to the side of the road and into the soft grass. The morning dew quickly soaked her shoes, but she did not slow down.

"Please, miss," Dora called. "Wait for me. I have your parasol."

Josie did not bother to turn even though Dora sounded farther away than before. At the clip-clop and jangle of approaching harness horses, she moved another few feet into the lawn to give them wide berth. When the carriage stopped a few feet behind her, she glanced over her shoulder to see Hargrave leap down. She picked up her pace, hoping he would take the hint and leave her alone. She wasn't in the mood for more of his inane conversation.

"Miss Drummond?"

She knew he followed her but didn't slack off her pace. She was beginning to feel like a drum major leading a parade. "Not now, Mr. Hargrave. I'm late for an appointment."

Suddenly, a strong arm wrapped around her waist, pulling her back off her feet. She heard a scream but knew it wasn't hers because a hand covered her mouth, cutting off her air. Her shoes slipped in the slick grass as she struggled to stand. She clawed at the hand covering half her face, but the thick fingers would not budge.

"Eager for your little tête-à-tête with Waite, are you?" Hargrave hissed in her ear. "Just like a bitch in heat."

He lurched to the side, pulling her with him.

"Let her go, you beast," Dora cried from nearby.

She must have jumped on his back, because Josie caught glimpses of a folded parasol swinging wildly overhead.

"Let..." *Crack*. "Her..." *Crack*. "Go!" *Crack*.

"Get this lunatic off me," Hargrave shouted.

Seconds later he spun Josie around. The coachman

dragged an inert Dora into the nearby stand of trees. Blood seeped from her nose and stained the front of her apron. Josie said a quick prayer that the maid would be all right. Then she added her own name to that very short list.

"Hurry up," Hargrave said to the coachman. "And pick up all those things she dropped on your way back. I don't want to leave anything to sound the alarm."

While the hulking coachman did his bidding, Josie continued to struggle. Hargrave may have been only inches taller than she, but he was built like a barrel and had a grip of iron.

"Get her feet," Hargrave said when the coachman returned moments later.

Josie kicked and kicked with all her might, catching the villain on the chin at least once, but to no avail. The two men lifted her and shoved her into the carriage. She scrambled to the other side, shook the door handle, and pounded on the panel, but it would not open.

Hargrave leaped inside behind her, and the carriage jerked into motion. He lurched onto the seat across from her and then straightened his lapels and smoothed back his hair. "You may as well make yourself comfortable. I assume you're smart enough not to jump from a moving carriage, and it's a long drive to Gretna Green."

She scooted as far away from him as she could and crossed her arms. "Why are you doing this? What could you possibly hope to gain?"

He laughed. "Everything. Once we are married,

your inheritance will buy me back my life, the life I was born to lead."

"You can't actually expect me to marry you after...this?"

"With your reputation in shreds, you will have no choice."

"Read my lips. I will never marry you."

"And if you don't agree to cooperate..."

"Killing me would defeat your purpose."

"Nothing so barbaric." He withdrew a tiny vial from his breast pocket. "One dose of this drug and you will agree to do anything I say. I've found it quite handy." He returned the bottle and patted his coat into place. "Now if you will excuse me," he said, slouching into the corner and propping his boots on the seat next to her. "It's been a long night, and a man should look his best for his wedding."

"There will be no wedding."

He grinned and then tipped his hat down over his eyes. Within minutes his snores rattled louder than the wheels.

Josie could not have slept even if she wanted to. How long would it be until she was missed? How long before Dora regained consciousness? If she regained consciousness. If she didn't, how would anyone know what had happened? How long would Dev wait for her in the folly before he came looking for her? That is, *if* he even bothered to look for her.

Stop it! No use worrying about that. She had better concentrate on her current predicament.

As long as the carriage was in motion, especially at this clip, she dared not jump. But it would have to slow down sometime. Stop to rest the horses or even change to another team. How long could the poor beasts keep up the present pace?

Dev paced the folly. He didn't bother to check his watch yet again. The sun had climbed well above the horizon, the coffee had cooled, and the egg soufflé had collapsed into a disgusting lump. Josie was not coming.

Not that it mattered. A bit of wasted effort, that's all. Insignificant. He picked up the bouquet of deep red roses that he'd personally selected.

And threw them across the room.

Damn. That aggravating woman had reduced him to childish temper tantrums.

Taking a deep breath, he straightened his cravat. A moment of foolishness, that's all.

He grabbed the no-longer-quite-so-chilled champagne and poured a generous portion. Brandy would have been preferable, but the bubbling wine was the acceptable choice for breakfast. He drained the glass and took up the bottle again. Rather than refill the glass, he tossed it after the roses and took a long swig straight.

Josie deserved a proper setdown for her rudeness. And he was just the one to do it. He spun on his heel and descended the four steps down from the folly in two long strides. As he strode along the path through the trees, he whipped up his indignation to cover his disappointment.

Just before he stepped onto the lawn a strange noise gave him pause. He listened. What sounded like a painful moan came from deep in the brambles. Josie? Could she have been hurt?

He bullied his way through the underbrush and discovered one of the maids lying facedown beneath a tree. He knelt, gently turned her over, and propped her head on his arm.

"Dora? Are you all right? What happened?"

She appeared to be breathing normally if a bit noisily. Using his free hand he awkwardly withdrew his handkerchief, poured a bit of the champagne on it, and wiped her face. Her eyelids flickered open. "Oh, your lordship. It's you again. Are you going to sing to me some more?" Her eyelids drifted shut.

The woman had obviously suffered a head injury. "Drink," he commanded, holding the bottle to her lips.

She took a healthy swig. She reached out to touch his arm, and her eyes widened to saucers. "Oh, my, you're real," she cried and sat up. "Oh, my." She grabbed her head with her hands and swayed. "Oh."

"Slowly," he said. "Can you tell me what happened?"

She seized his arm. "You've got to help her."

"Who?"

"My miss. That horrible man took her."

As hard as it was to keep his voice calm when his gut was churning, he knew he would get more information if Dora did not slip further into hysteria. "Do you mean Josie?"

"Yes, yes. You've got to find her."

"Take another drink," he said, handing her the bottle. "Now take a deep breath and tell me what happened."

"We were on our way to the folly," she began and managed to relate the incident with only a few tears. "Why would anyone want to hurt my miss?"

He had a pretty good idea of Hargrave's motivation. Dev could kick himself. He'd seen the determined look in that villain's eye the night before. When he'd told Hargrave to back away from Josie, the man had looked like a gambler who thought he held a winning hand and was too desperate to fold when the stakes were raised above his purse. Dev should have insisted the man leave the premises.

He stood. "I will find her," he promised. He looked down at the poor maid, still seated and hugging the bottle of champagne to her breast. She sniffed and wiped her tears and nose with her bloody apron.

"Do you trust me?"

She nodded.

"I want you to go to the folly, finish that bottle, and then take a nice long nap. When you wake, clean yourself up and go back to the house as if nothing had happened. If anyone asks about the stains on your apron, say you walked into a door and got a bloody nose."

"You're not going to raise a hue and cry? Rouse the servants and neighbors to help you look?"

"Your mistress will be better served if no one knows Hargrave took her off. Wait in her rooms for her return. She'll want a hot bath and a long rest. Don't worry. I think I know where they've gone.

I'll bring her back safe and sound."

If he'd guessed the right destination.

If he picked the same road.

If he was in time.

❋　　　❋　　　❋　　　❋

Josie fought the drowsiness caused by the swaying coach, monotonous view, and boring company. By her reckoning three hours had passed and the horses had not slowed significantly at any point. If she was going to have a chance to escape, she would have to make it happen.

"Hey, Hargrave," she said. When he continued to snore, she poked his foot a couple of times with the parasol that had been thrown in behind her along with her bonnet and shawl. "Hargrave."

He raised his hat and glared at her. "What?"

"Is there an inn on this godforsaken road? I'm starving."

He sat up, put his feet on the floor, and twisted in his seat to open a panel behind his head, revealing a small storage compartment. He took out a half loaf of bread and a chunk of cheese and threw them on the seat next to her. Right where his dirty boots had been.

She wrinkled her nose.

"Have you ever seen Shakespeare's *Taming of the Shrew?* Yes? Then you should take the bard's advice to heart." He again tipped his hat over his eyes.

He'd obviously missed the whole point of the play and the fact that it was supposed to be a comedy, not a blueprint of admirable behavior. He was no Petruchio, and she was no Katharina, but she was willing to play the part of a shrew.

"Hargrave."

"What?" He didn't bother to remove his hat.

"Do you also have a chamber pot in there? I have to pee."

He sat up. "My, my. Such a fine example of delicate womanhood. After we're married I expect you to watch your language."

She bit her tongue.

He knocked on the panel behind him, and immediately the carriage began to slow. If she'd known that was all it took, she would've done it hours ago.

"I could do with a bit of leg stretching myself," he said.

The carriage stopped at the side of a deserted road, the coachman opened the door, and Hargrave alighted first. He stepped away, waving his arms and doing knee lifts. Josie was left to clamber down as best she could. As she sidled around the back of the carriage, she noted the coachman was already busy seeing to the horses. If she could just get out of sight in the woods, she could take off. Surely she would come across some sign of civilization sooner or later.

"Stay with the horses," Hargrave said to the coachman. "And keep your eyes to yourself. We have private business."

She glanced back and saw her captor unwinding a length of rope.

"Can't have you going too far away," he said to her.

She ran. But the hours seated in the carriage had not been kind, and her leg muscles protested the sudden activity. An imminent cramp burned down the back of her leg. She continued to hobble as fast as she could.

Hargrave grabbed her. Even though she stomped on his toes and kicked his shins, her dainty shoes had little effect on his thick, knee-high boots. He soon had her immobile, her right arm wedged against his side and his left arm wrapped over her shoulders. His left hand gripped her just above the elbow and pinned her other arm.

With his hand he reached for the vial of drugs. "You'll be sorry you caused me so much trouble." He flipped out the cork with his thumb and raised the nasty-smelling bottle to her lips.

She twisted her head away.

He was forced to turn her toward him, and when he did, she resisted until he pulled harder. Then she reversed her bearing and used the impetus of his uncontrolled reaction to add extra impact as she bent her leg. She kneed him in the groin.

Hargrave immediately released her and fell into the dirt with a pained groan.

Her self-defense teacher would have been so proud.

He moaned and whined like a baby. Okay, a foul-mouthed baby. His words were indistinct, muttered between his gritted teeth, but she caught the drift.

Pleased with herself, she grabbed the rope and tied Hargrave up while he was still incapacitated. She was concentrating so hard on tying him securely, she failed to notice a horse and rider galloping down the road until they were practically on top of her. She dove out of the way, cursed the careless rider under her breath, and continued her task.

As she secured his legs, she remembered the coachman and glanced up to check on him. He was out of sight in front of the carriage about eighty yards down the road.

Was that all the distance she'd managed to run? She really was going to have to get serious about going to the gym regularly.

As she secured Hargrave's wrists, the sound of a single horse walking toward her caused her to look up.

Dev pulled the beast to a stop. He crooked one leg over the pommel and propped his elbow on his knee. "I'd offer my services, but you seem to be doing rather well."

Josie stood up and dusted off her hands. After smoothing her dress, she retrieved the stuff she'd dropped when Hargrave had tackled her. She draped the shawl over her arm and plopped the bonnet on her head, not bothering to tie the ribbons. Her first inclination was to leave the parasol, but then she thought of a good use for the silly thing.

She poked Hargrave with the pointy end. "Let that be a lesson to you."

Another string of invectives spewed out of his mouth.

She turned to Dev. "May I have your handkerchief?"

He held it out to her. His mount shied at the white flag flapping in the breeze.

"Easy, Galahad."

Even though Dev kept the enormous horse under control, the beast's withers twitched and he pawed the road with his front hooves in apparent annoyance with the sudden inactivity after the freedom of a long gallop.

"Toss it to me," she requested, not wanting to get any closer to Dev's stallion than necessary. After catching the large square of linen, she stuffed it into Hargrave's mouth and secured it by wrapping the last of the long rope around his head.

Suddenly she remembered. "Ohmigod. I forgot the coachman." She spun around.

"He should wake up in a few hours with a pounding headache," Dev said.

"Good."

"Vengeful little wench, aren't you?"

"You don't know the half of what I've been through."

"Well, it hasn't been much of a rescue..."

"I really do appreciate your help."

"But if you will return to the carriage, I shall be honored to drive..."

"I'm not getting back in there. Not ever." She turned and headed away from the coach.

Dev followed along, keeping his horse to a sedate walk beside her. She moved further to the side of the road, but there was no soft green lawn to cushion her steps. Only rocks and twigs and sticks and more rocks.

"Would you like to ride? Galahad can handle double..."

"No, thank you." She did not slow her pace, but she couldn't keep from wincing as her feet and leg muscles protested. "Ouch. It's not that I'm, ouch, ungrateful for your help. I'm not fond of riding."

They walked along for a few minutes, the silence broken only by her involuntary complaints.

"It's a long way back," Dev said.

"I'll, ouch, make it."

"No food. No water." Dev looked up at the sun overhead. "You ought to get there about midnight."

"I'll...ouch." Josie hopped on one foot after stepping on a particularly sharp stone. "Damn rocks."

Dev leaned over and swooped her up to sit in front of him.

"What are you doing?" She struggled against his hold, and in the process one or the other of them knocked off her bonnet.

The horse, spooked by the bonnet fluttering to the ground, reared and then danced away from it.

Josie twisted toward Dev and wrapped her arms around him. The parasol flew and the shawl slithered away. The horse reared again. She clutched Dev tight.

Dev struggled to hold on to Josie and manage the reins. "Easy. Easy. Settle down," he said, his voice smooth yet commanding.

Both the horse and Josie obeyed.

She relaxed, but she did not remove her arms from around his neck. Looking up she gazed deep into his gray eyes, and for a moment it was as if she saw directly into his soul. Despite his flaws she felt...safe. She saw...respect. Oh, he might laugh at some of her outrageous ideas, but not in a disparaging way. He would never belittle her or demean her. His eyes promised to cherish her.

This could not be. She let her arms slip away as she untwisted her torso so she sat sideways on the horse.

"I thought I'd lost you," he said, his voice husky and thick. The words were appropriate for that moment, but he knew he was referring to earlier that day. When he'd found out she'd been taken, it had seemed as if the rest of his life had been ripped away, as if without her he would have no future. When he'd heard she was in danger, he'd felt soul-deep fear for the first time.

The fact that he'd come to care for her so deeply in so short a time terrified him. Somehow they had a connection that transcended their brief acquaintance.

Would she think he was crazy if he told her? He forced himself to relax his hold around her waist.

"So, what are we to do now?" she asked.

She was probably talking about the ride home, but that was the least of his worries. As far as everything else went, well, it was a damn good question.

Twelve

EV GRITTED HIS TEETH. JOSIE'S NEARNESS was arousing enough without her wiggling and twisting to find a comfortable position. She seemed to be trying to get as far away from him as possible. Every step of their mount threatened her precarious perch.

"Lean against me," he suggested.

"No, thank you. I'll be fine as soon..." Her breath left in a whoosh as he pulled her back against his chest.

"If you fall and break your neck..."

Josie stilled.

"My efforts to rescue you will have been wasted," he finished.

Her back remained stiff. He knew from experience she needed a bit of time before she could relax after a fight. The walking should have helped. She crossed her arms under her breasts as if to keep his arm that remained around her waist from sliding upward. Fine with him. Her action made his view all the more interesting, but if she didn't relax, the ride would seem even longer than necessary, for both of them.

"Where did you learn to fight?" he asked. "I was quite surprised when you used that trick with your knee. But not as shocked as Hargrave," he added with a chuckle.

"Every woman should know self-defense," she answered without giving him any particulars.

Her nearness warmed him better than a roaring fire on a winter's night and was more intoxicating than the best Napoleon brandy. When she relaxed a bit against his chest, he was careful not to tighten his hold as his baser impulses prodded him to do. Her needs were more important than his.

"Quite a blow to my self-esteem," he said, keeping his tone light. "Rather than rescue a damsel in distress, I simply watched her save herself. Not good form, you know."

"You took care of the coachman."

"Clobbering an unsuspecting henchman over the head with the butt of my pistol is not the same as defeating a nefarious villain," he said, acting annoyed. "My shining armor is intolerably tarnished."

"I'll never understand men," she said, but she also leaned her head back against his shoulder. "And you are saving me from a long walk back," she added.

"A pittance," he said with a sniff.

"I imagine my feet would not think so if you hadn't overruled me on the matter. Again I owe you my thanks."

"You are quite welcome. In truth you saved me

from what promised to be an uncomfortable if not downright unpleasant meeting. I doubt we'll be back before one o'clock." He chuckled to himself. "She won't be happy when I fail to appear at the appointed rendezvous."

"She? Meaning Estelle, who is convinced you will marry her if for no other reason than the spirit guide Amanu says so?"

"No. I will have to deal with Estelle at another time. I was supposed to meet Lady Wingate in the rose garden."

Josie stretched her neck to look over her shoulder at him. "You have a romantic assignation with that featherbrained, giggling..."

"An appointment. At her insistence. No romance. My mother may despair of my morals, but I do draw the line at pursuing married women, especially wives of my friends."

"So you agreed to meet her to tell her to leave you alone?"

"I might not have put it in those exact words, but basically yes. If she does not cease her outrageous flirtations, I'll have no choice but to cut both her and Timothy from my social circle."

"I'm glad you missed your appointment. Take my advice. Never meet that woman alone. You'll...stay healthier."

He wasn't sure what she meant or why the discussion of the Wingates made Josie finally relax, but he was grateful all the same. She breathed a deep sigh, her eyelids drifted closed, and she snuggled into his arms, the inevitable exhaustion overtaking her as the last of the fight drained away.

Cradling her gently, he urged Galahad to a smooth mile-eating gallop and allowed him his head, knowing the horse would take them home. Dev did not expect Josie to sleep long, and by the time she woke he wanted to have a plan for salvaging her reputation ready to put into motion.

In her dreams Josie relived the kidnapping, only somehow her worry about the ghost and the need to set up another séance got mixed into the ordeal. Hargrave became seven feet tall and glowed green like the spirit guide Amanu. He mocked her puny attempts to escape with bone-chilling laughter. Deverell rode past her on a menacing ghost horse and kept on going into the black void he dreaded. She jerked awake with a gasp.

As soon as she recognized where she was and that she'd been dreaming, she slumped against Dev's warmth, just for a minute, just to allow her heartbeat to slow to normal.

He pulled the horse to a sedate walk, and she realized her anxiety about riding had not returned. She had too many other things to worry about, she rationalized.

"I'm glad to see you are finally conscious," he said. "We are close and we need to discuss..."

"Another séance," she said, sitting up and twisting so she could see his face.

"What?"

"Tonight. Can you arrange another séance tonight?"

"There are more important matters to..."

"Not until you give your word as a gentleman that you..."

"The ball is tonight."

"I don't care about that."

"My mother does, and she will be busy with her hostess duties."

"You can convince her to do it. I know you can. I can't explain why this is so important, but I'll promise you anything you want..."

He raised an eyebrow.

"Within reasonable limits, of course."

"You still owe me a walk in the garden from the last séance."

"You're right, but it's not my fault Hargrave interfered." Now was not the time to bring up that she'd been on her way to give him a piece of her mind rather than enjoy the planned walk.

He stared at the road ahead as if deep in thought.

"Please," she added in a wheedling tone for good measure.

When he looked down at her the corners of his mouth twitched. "If I somehow manage to convince Mother to schedule a séance in the middle of a ball, then you will..."

"Walk with you in the garden right after the séance," she supplied in a rush, hoping his previous first choice of rewards would still be valid.

"No chaperone. No maid," he bargained.

After a moment's hesitation she said, "Agreed." As much as she'd fantasized about kisses in the moonlight, she intended to hold him to the letter of the agreement. A walk. That's all.

"Then we have a deal," he said.

She didn't trust that sparkle in his eye. A tiny frisson of anticipation shivered up her spine. Dev might be dangerous, but her physical reaction to him was an even bigger problem.

"Whoa," Dev said, accompanied by a gentle tug on the reins. Galahad halted with a snort. "Easy, fella." Dev patted the horse on the neck. "I know you're anxious to get home," he added as he dismounted.

"Why are we stopping here? If we're that close..."

Dev lifted her down. "We've been on the estate proper for some time now, but we can't just ride up to the front door. Your reputation..."

"But *I* didn't do anything wrong."

"I agree, but others may not see it that way."

"That's their problem." The roadbed was a bit smoother than before, but her feet were still tender. Taking gingerly steps she tottered to the side, where thankfully there was now a strip of mown grass.

"As a gentleman and your host I am responsible for safeguarding your good name."

"That's ridiculous."

"That's reality. Unless you wish to be shunned by all..."

Josie thought of sweet Honoria and dear Mrs. Binns. Surely they wouldn't think the worst of her, would they?

"...and bring disgrace upon both my mother and your chaperone, then you will do as I say."

"Okay."

"Don't argue with..." He hesitated. "Oh, I remember that means you agree. In that case here's the plan. We will use the private entrance to my rooms. You can clean up, and when the coast is clear you can slip down the hall to your..."

"That's your grand plan to salvage my ruined reputation?" She put her hands on her hips. "Sneak me into your bedroom? What if someone sees us?"

"They won't."

"Are you kidding? That place is crawling with servants."

He blinked as if the possibility of being seen by servants had never occurred to him as important.

"And if you think servants don't gossip, boy, are you in for a rude awakening. Just this morning Dora...ohmigod, Dora? What happened to Dora? Is she..."

"She's...okay. Maybe a bit of a headache." He chuckled.

"Not funny. She'd tried to help me and that man...that evil coachman dragged her off unconscious and...and..."

"I found her and she seemed fine except for a bloody nose. I gave her a bottle of champagne..."

"Champagne?"

"It was handy. Don't ask why. I told her to finish the bottle, hence the headache. I instructed her to take a long nap and then wait for you in your room. I specifically requested she not tell a soul what had happened. If anyone notes your failure to appear at the folly as planned, the story will be that you got lost in the woods."

"Servants have eyes and ears."

"My valet is the soul of discretion."

She shook her head. "I don't know. Doesn't sound like a good plan to me."

"And you have a better one?"

Perhaps if she had more time, but she could hardly stand on the side of the road until inspiration hit. "No," she admitted.

"Then we will proceed as I had planned." He bowed and held out his arm. They walked along the road.

"Where is this private entrance of yours?"

"We access it from the folly."

She raised her eyebrows, and he had the grace to blush.

"My grandfather had it built," he explained. "So he didn't disturb the household on returning from his late-night card games."

"I'll bet he did."

"I've used it myself for the same reason."

"I'll bet you have."

"Now who's thinking the worst without regard to the facts?" He turned to the right and onto a path she would have missed if he hadn't known where it was. The narrowness forced them to walk closer together, and they automatically matched their steps.

"My apologies," she said. "I'm sure you've never used the secret entrance to further your own means."

"Well..." He swallowed deeply, and with his free hand he adjusted his cravat. "Perhaps a time or two."

"Aha!" she grinned.

"I see you enjoy being right."

"Don't you?"

"Well, yes, but..."

"But you're a man and lord of the castle; therefore being right is your prerogative."

"That's not what I was going to say."

"But it is what you meant."

"Not exactly. I was merely going to comment that most women would agree with me—or any man, for that matter—simply to seem...agreeable."

"And the men of this...land...find meaningless conformity attractive?" Whew. She'd almost slipped and said *of this time*. "Agreeableness is a virtue?"

"I used to think so. Now I'm not so sure."

"Good. The differences between men and women are more than just physical and contribute to a full and interesting relationship."

"You are quite bold, Miss Drummond. I don't believe I've ever met anyone quite like you."

"And you probably never will again." Not unless time travel became as common as taking the red-eye to New York. Flight 753 to the Regency now loading at gate H15. She giggled and then realized he was looking at her strangely.

"Sometimes I have absolutely no idea what you are thinking," he said. "I find you...intriguing."

"I'll take that as a compliment."

"I meant it so." He shook his head. "At least I think I do. Here we are."

The folly had been built to resemble an open Roman temple, with fluted columns at each corner of the eight-sided structure. She went up the steps with a bit of trepidation but found no remnant of the earlier planned assignation. Other than a few carved stone benches there was no furniture at all.

Dev strode across the floor without the slightest hesitation or sign of surprise at the emptiness.

Could Dora have been mistaken about his intentions? He'd been nothing less than a true gentleman so far.

"This way," he said.

She followed him down the steps at the far side of the folly and directly into a tunnel made by a long arbor covered with fragrant white roses.

"At the far end is the moon garden. Although visible from a few select windows, it is quite private. All the plants were chosen for their fragrance and the way their blooms reflect the moonlight."

"Sounds lovely."

"If all goes well, you will have a chance to experience it yourself later tonight," he said with a mischievous grin.

She turned her head away to keep from returning his smile—and nearly bumped into him when he stopped in the middle of the tunnel. He moved aside some of the profuse greenery and, using a key attached to his watch fob, unlocked a low door that had been invisible moments before.

"Wow. You weren't kidding about a secret entrance."

"What do goats have to do with it?" he asked, his brow furrowed.

"Huh?"

"Goats. Kidding?"

"Oh. No, that means joking, not serious."

"Sometimes I think we do not speak the same

language. Aren't the colonies still speaking English despite two wars?"

"Certainly." Because she didn't know much about either the Revolutionary War or the War of 1812 she decided it was a good time to change the subject. She stepped through the door. "Into the lion's den, as they say."

"Hardly."

Although she wasn't sure what she'd expected, it wasn't a neat storeroom approximately eight feet by fifteen feet.

Dev ducked through the door and stepped around her to lead the way. "The staircase is back here. This is where I keep my private stock and...other items. Only Carson, my valet, and I have a key."

"Like what?" she asked, craning her neck as she passed, but everything was in closed and locked storage.

"Nothing you would find of interest."

"You never know. Come on. What's in the..."

"Have you never heard that curiosity killed the cat?"

"Yes. And a cat has nine lives."

"May we speak of something else?"

"No."

He sighed in resignation. "In addition to my stock of brandy, other potables, and cigars, which takes up most of the space, there is gambling para-phernalia and items certain gentlemen guests find interesting."

"Do you mean pornography?" If Regency men found the sight of a woman's ankles titillating, what really cranked their tractors? Knees? Bare legs? Or was she confusing them with Victorian men? "Can I see?"

"Absolutely not," he said, clearly horrified by her suggestion. He turned her by the shoulders and pushed her toward the back of the room, where a winding iron staircase led upward.

Disappointed, but distracted, she looked up. The stairwell was an odd crescent shape. "That's a lot of steps." She began her ascent. The going was steep and she gripped the railing.

He followed. "This stairway goes to the top of the east tower, but we'll stop at the second landing. Grandfather designed the windows to mimic those on the original tower that became the inner wall. While the work was being done, scaffolding hid the true goal of the construction and everyone was simply told the tower needed repair. Remarkably, when it was finished, no one seemed to notice the difference."

"People see what they expect to see."

"I suppose so. The stones were from the same quarry as the original and were treated to look weathered."

While he continued his tourist guide spiel, Josie's mind went off on a tangent. Had she seen what she'd expected to see at the séance? Had the specter really been seven feet tall, or had she assumed so based on the other visual clues in the room such as the height of the chairback? He could have been shorter and standing on something. He could have been on mini stilts. He could have been raised to that height by the use of wires and pulleys. She determined then and there not to let her preconceived notions color her observations at the next séance.

"The stairway was forged to Grandfather's specifications at the Sirhowy Ironworks as a special favor."

How could he continue talking and climbing without so much as a pause? Tall ceilings were beautiful, but they made for a lot of steps between floors. She was already out of breath. One more reminder she'd skipped her last workout session at the gym to...what? Why couldn't she remember? Oh yeah. She'd just bought the DVD of *Buffy the Vampire Slayer* season three, the best one because it had Faith and Oz in it, and she had spent the evening with the vampire hunters and a bag of extra-buttery microwave popcorn.

When they reached the landing, Dev again took out his key, but the door opened before he had a chance to use it.

"Good afternoon, milord. Miss Drummond," the valet said as he bowed and stepped aside simultaneously.

"Good heavens, Carson. You quite startled me."

"My job is to anticipate your needs." The valet grinned. He was of a height with Josie and bowlegged. His short gray hair stuck out in all directions and was a direct contradiction to his impeccable formal attire.

"I swear you must have the second sight," Dev said, guiding Josie into the short hallway and then handing his hat and leather riding gloves to the valet.

"I was having a cup of tea with the head groom when Galahad returned," Carson said. He shut the door behind them. "I simply assumed you would not be far behind."

"Miss Drummond has had a slight mishap," Dev said.

That was an understatement if she'd ever heard one.

The valet tipped his head to the side as if he hadn't previously noticed her disheveled appearance.

"I would like you to go, unnoticed, to her suite of rooms, where her maid is waiting. Bring Dora back with an appropriate change of clothing for her mistress. Also unnoticed, of course."

"Certainly, milord. I have laid out light refreshments in the reception room."

"Thank you, Carson. We will serve ourselves."

The valet bowed again and scurried away down the hall.

"Shall we?" Dev said and offered his arm.

Josie placed her fingertips on his arm. Until that moment she hadn't really considered how she would feel entering his private domain. She decided to play it cool.

That lasted about five seconds.

The room was bigger than her entire apartment, including her prized parking space. Two sofas and half a dozen chairs, upholstered in shades of deep blue with various subtle gold patterns, were arranged in casual groupings on a huge Persian carpet. A variety of landscapes and portraits in heavy gold frames hung on rich royal blue walls, and golden curtains framed each of six tall windows.

Here and there were bits of green and yellow, a vase, a pillow, but most of the accessories were gold, lots of gold.

"Does the king live here?" she asked.

"It is a bit much, isn't it? This room was meant to impress. In the past the lord received his important visitors in his private rooms rather than downstairs. I inherited the room, but not Grandfather's fondness for the grandiose."

"Why haven't you changed it?"

Dev shrugged. "I spend so little time in the country. My townhouse in London is furnished in a much simpler style."

Overwhelmed by the grandeur, she wandered around the room, focusing on individual items. A golden cat statue looked as if it had come from an Egyptian tomb, and probably had. A large mosaic bowl made of lapis stones held three golden apples. A scale replica of a Roman chariot including horses was so intricate the tiny driver wore armor and carried weapons.

"That model has wheels cleverly hidden beneath the horses' hooves. I used to race it up and down the table and drive my grandfather to fits."

"It's like a trip around the world," she said, gently spinning the antique glass globe. "What in here is yours? I mean, what did you bring into the room when you moved in?"

"Are you referring to personal mementos?"

"Yes. You can really tell a lot about a person by their stuff. You know, their things, their possessions. Their stuff."

"Well, I keep my...stuff in the...in another room."

"Can I see?"

"Absolutely not."

"Please? Why? Is it your bedroom?"

"Miss Drummond! Are you trying to shock me?"

"No, but you must remember I'm from a different...place." And in her place and time a woman could tour a man's bedroom without everyone assuming sex would follow. Of course, if she wanted to have sex with him...

Josie realized she did. Want to have sex with him. The entire day of polite dancing around each other had been a form of restrained foreplay, so subtle she hadn't realized the efficient way it had worked on her until now.

Now they weren't perched on an anxiety-producing beast or out in the stone-studded wilderness, neither of which were particularly conducive to making love. Now they were only a short walk away from one of the castle's sinfully comfortable feather beds. And she wanted him. In his bedroom or right there on the plush carpet.

If he was shocked before, what would he say if she told him she wanted to see his real stuff? Was he ready to get down and boogie?

Was she?

Josie wandered to the windows and looked down into a garden surrounded by a high ivy-covered wall.

Was she ready? Physically? No question about it. She had that fluttery feeling low in her stomach, and the slightest movement of her light muslin dress against her skin caused a delicious tingle. Mentally? That was another matter.

Not to say she hadn't ever been with a man before. She'd just never thought of herself as the one-night-stand kind of woman. Her experience was limited to three relationships. After her last breakup she'd buried herself in her work and lined up a number of investigations in England for a change of scene. She hadn't been with a man for...ohmigod had it been a year since...what was his name? Oh yeah, Richard, a.k.a. Dick the Deceitful. Him she could forget without regret.

An amber paperweight caught her interest. She held it up to the light and felt a strange kinship with the hapless insects trapped in its tawny depths. Far away from their natural place, years away from the time in which they'd lived. Caught in a moment by what was once sticky tree sap. Snared by a single bad decision. She put the stone down so quickly she nearly dropped it.

"Please have a seat, Miss Drummond. You'll feel better after a cup of tea." Instantly he wanted to kick himself. He could hardly believe the prudish words had come from his mouth. Here he had a beautiful woman alone in his rooms and he was serving tea like his grandmother.

True, he'd refrained from bringing his amorous liaisons to his ancestral home. At least he had once he was past his impetuous youth and since moving from his old rooms in what was still called the bachelor wing. This suite had been his sanctuary away from his mother's matchmaking activities, which always coincided with his visits home. And yet bringing Josie here had seemed natural, imperative. Not only was she different from any other woman he'd ever known, but his response to her was most unusual.

As she traced bits of his family history with her fingers, his soul responded as if she was reaching across time and space to touch him.

He shook off the ridiculous thought.

He'd been enamored with women before. And even if this felt somewhat different, he was sure the same cure would work. Once conquered, and bedded, her encompassing allure would fizzle to simple controllable attraction. With that purpose in mind, he strode to her side.

She watched him stalk her with wide eyes.

"If not tea...perhaps..." He ran his fingers down the smooth skin of her arm and lifted her hand. He turned her hand over, peeled back the edge of her glove, and kissed the inside of her wrist. "Can I interest you in something stronger?" he said, letting his breath warm her exposed skin before looking up.

She shook her head and then nodded. She swallowed and licked her dry lips. "Sure," she croaked out. After clearing her throat she said, "I'm sure you have brandy handy."

He stepped away. As he opened a nearby cabinet and poured two generous servings, he heard her blow out a breath. He suppressed a smile.

"A toast?" he asked as he handed her a snifter. He leaned closer and gave her his most charming smile. "To mutual enjoyment of pleasant diversions."

She took a hasty gulp of her drink. "Is that the Regency version of a pickup line?"

"I beg your pardon?"

"Never mind." She finished the potent brandy. "It works." Of course the way her blood was pumping, a simplistic *You woman, me man* might have had the same effect. She looked around for a place to put her empty glass but could not in good conscience set it on the priceless antique furniture.

Dev took the crystal snifter from her and pitched it over his shoulder and into the fireplace, where it shattered against the marble. He drained his drink and followed suit with his glass.

"Why did you..."

"To ensure the truth of the toast."

"Oh."

Again he took her hand, only this time he slowly removed her glove and tucked it in his breast pocket. "So now you have an obligation..."

She shot him a questioning look.

"...to enjoy this pleasant diversion." He kissed each finger and the palm of her hand. "I know what I like, but what do you find enjoyable?"

"This is a good start," she said, holding out her other hand.

He chuckled and removed the second glove. He dropped it but didn't bother to take the time to retrieve it from the floor. Again he kissed each finger, lips warm and smooth. He licked a streak across her palm and blew on the dampness, sending electric shivers up her arm.

"In chiromancy, or palm reading, this is your mound of Venus," he said, grazing the skin at the base of her thumb with his teeth. "Mmmm. Firm and prominent."

"What is that supposed to mean? Not that I believe..."

"You have great capacity for...sensual pleasure."

Josie stifled a laugh. What a line.

"These prominent horizontal lines indicate a person of great charm, but the ones that crisscross your love mound mean your feelings are complex. Complications are inevitable."

Okay, maybe *that* was true, but still..."You don't really believe..."

"That your hands foretell your fate? Not really, but I do find palmistry coincidentally truthful and therefore interesting."

And useful for picking up women, she added to herself.

She flipped the positions of their hands and turned his palm up. "What does this mean?" she asked, tracing a line.

"That's considered the life line."

His seemed rather short. Not wanting to discuss that, she looked for another line, any other line. She picked a crescent-shaped one that curved across his mound of Venus. "And this one?"

He smiled. "It means I'm trying to seduce you and apparently not doing a very good job of it if you're more interested in my palm than..."

"I'm not," she said, and dropped his hand.

For a moment he just looked at her, the intensity

of his gaze unnerving.

"Is something wrong?" Suddenly she remembered she wasn't exactly looking her best. She patted her unruly curls. A quick peek at her dress confirmed her worst suspicions. She looked as if she'd been in a knock-down, drag-out fight and rolled around in the road.

"I want to remember this moment. You make such a lovely picture, standing there with the afternoon sun glinting off your auburn hair. The pink on your cheeks from going without your bonnet. The..."

"Enough already." She had to give it to him. The guy was good, but quite frankly the mood had been destroyed once she remembered what she must look like. Added to the fact she hadn't had a decent bath in days.

"Do you doubt my sincerity?"

"Rather than question your eyesight?"

He chuckled. "Actually I find your imperfections..."

"That's one way to say filthy dirty, mussed..."

"Genuine and unpretentious."

"Yes, well, I'd rather be that *and* clean *and* smell good all at the same time."

"You are such a..." He didn't finish his sentence but leaned over and kissed the tip of her nose instead.

He hesitated for a moment with his lips inches above hers. Just for a second, a tenth of a second, but to her amazement, that's all it took for Josie's blood to go from chilled to boiling. Without conscious decision she lifted her chin so her lips met his.

Thirteen

THOSE FEW INCHES BETWEEN THEIR LIPS SIG-
nified a huge gulf of time, if not space, yet
Josie crossed it without hesitation. Dev
waited on the other side. The resulting kiss burned
away all her concerns in a flash of igniting passion.
She raised her arms to his shoulders as he wrapped
his around her waist. He deepened the kiss and she
opened her mouth, welcoming his tongue, tasting,
exploring, demanding more.

She slipped her hand to the back of his neck
and buried her fingers in his hair. He tightened
his embrace and she leaned into him, molding her
body against his. She wanted to rip off his clothes,
her clothes. She wanted to feel his molten hot
skin against hers.

His erection pulsed high against her stomach,
and she raised herself up on her toes to settle it
between her hips. Not close enough, she pulled on
his shoulders to lift herself higher. He reached
down and cupped her derriere, lifting her to her
tiptoes and pulling her against him with a groan.

The doorknob rattled and his senses returned. He felt like a boxer splashed with cold water after an unexpected knockout punch. Fortunately he retained enough wits to set Josie aside and take a step away from her. For a moment they stared at each other with equally stunned expressions.

When Carson entered the room, they stood a respectable distance apart even if Dev had chosen to stand behind a chair and Josie held on to the back of another for balance. The bandy valet turned around and pulled Dora into the room behind him. The poor maid looked much the worse for her run-in with the coachman. Her nose was swollen, and both eyes had begun to develop major shiners.

"Oh, Dora," Josie said. She rushed forward and put her arm around the other woman's shoulder. "You were so brave to try to help me. I'm afraid you got the worst end of it."

"I'b all bight, biss," the maid answered, her speech hindered by swollen lips. "I'b just glab you're all bight." She clutched the bundle of clothes to her breast, and her gaze darted around the room as if she feared a bogeyman would jump out at any moment.

"You're safe now," Josie assured her. "Lord Waite took care of those villains for us." She ignored Dev's snort of disagreement.

"Hab you seen id?" Dora whispered.

"What?" Josie whispered back, expecting the maid to say a ghost haunted these rooms.

"Da jower. Sabie seen ib last spring and she said ib was monsberous. Big brass arms waibing do grab you."

"Huh?"

"Da jower." The maid stomped her foot when Josie shook her head to signal she still didn't understand. "Lorb Waib's jower."

"I think she means my shower," Dev interjected. "I had it installed last spring..."

"You have a shower?" Josie asked, spinning around to face him. "Why didn't you say so?"

"When I built my modern house in town I became aware of the latest advances in construction, and since I quite enjoyed both the convenience and the luxury, I decided to have the same..."

"Where is it? Can I use it? I've been dying for a hot shower." She looked around the room as if he'd hidden it like an Easter egg.

Carson rushed to a door in the far corner and blocked the passage with his body, his arms outstretched.

"Aha." Josie strode across the room and stood before him. "Out of my way," she commanded in her most imperious voice.

He shook his head and gripped the jambs on either side of the door.

She pasted a sweet smile on her face. "If you don't move," she said in a sugary tone, "I'll wrestle you to the floor and climb over you."

The valet blanched, but he stood firm, bravely protecting his master's inner sanctum.

Josie didn't really want to hurt the valet, but she so wanted a shower. She turned a pleading look toward Dev.

"It's all right, Carson," Dev said with a chuckle.

"Miss Drummond is welcome to use any...amenities of this house she desires."

The valet sidled aside with alacrity and collapsed onto the nearest chair.

Josie had noted the twinkle in Dev's eye, but she couldn't wait to give him a witty reply. The man had a shower. She eagerly opened the door only to have it reveal a hall running parallel to the main one outside the suite and three more closed doors.

"First one on the left," Dev prompted, and she nodded to show she'd spotted the door about halfway down the hall.

"Come along, Dora," Josie said.

"Bud biss..."

"If you refuse to attend me, I shall be forced to ask Carson to help with my stays."

The valet, who had since regained his feet, sank back into the chair, this time with his hand over his heart. He closed his eyes and moaned.

"Would you like me to show you how it works?" Dev called after her as she marched down the hall.

"No, thank you," Josie answered. "I'll figure it out."

Although when she entered the bathing chamber, she wasn't so sure. In addition to a claw-foot tub large enough for two, the room held a dressing table, a barber chair, and several items she couldn't identify. That almost included the shower, which was half hidden behind a screen, and didn't resemble any shower she'd ever seen.

She examined the contraption. Four long copper pipes sprang out on each side of a central post and curved around, encircling two-thirds of the area above a circular stone platform approximately five feet in diameter. The arms, as the maid had called them, were pierced with holes along the inner surface, and Josie deduced the water would spray out in an all-over body wash. Overhead a more familiar looking showerhead promised clean hair, but she couldn't find any faucets or other mechanism to turn the thing on.

"Perhaps, we'd better ask Lord Waite..."

"Did I hear my name," he asked. He leaned against the doorjamb, another brandy in his hand. "May I be of service?"

Dora rushed over to block his way and simultaneously tried to shut the door.

"We need his help," Josie admitted.

Dev gave a superior smirk and sauntered into the room. "There is a tank on the roof that holds water pumped from a nearby spring. The pipes run through this fireplace, where the water is heated. Thankfully Carson thought to stoke the flames; getting the temperature just right is a bit tricky."

"All I really need to know is how to turn it on."

Dev stepped to the fireplace and slid open a panel above the mantel. He turned a handle, and after a few gurgles and spurts water beautifully cascaded out of each opening in the awkward contraption.

Josie watched it for a minute, entranced by the fountainlike quality. But her desire to jump in soon overrode, and she pushed Dev toward the door. "Thank you, thank you. Time for you to go."

"Must I?" he teased.

Dora sucked in an indignant breath.

"I suppose I must," he said with a dramatic sigh.

Josie giggled. She was going to have a real shower, and at that moment nothing else mattered. She began to disrobe almost before Dora closed the door behind Dev and turned the key with a flourish.

With Dora's help, Josie adjusted the screen for privacy. Despite the maid's insistence that a lady didn't remove her chemise to bathe, she stripped off the wet garment as soon as she was safely ensconced within the water jets and out of the maid's censuring glare. Dora, assuming Josie would want to wash in a basin, had brought a sliver of soap. Hah. No miserly bit of tepid water in a bowl today.

Josie enjoyed washing away the grime of the road, lathering the lavender-scented soap even into her hair. She hummed as she got clean, even vocalizing a few bars of "Singing in the Rain," which seemed appropriate even though she couldn't remember all the words. Hot water spraying from all sides soothed her aching muscles from her shoulders down to her abused toes. She lacked only decent shampoo and a razor for her legs in order to feel normal again.

She stepped out of the water and wrapped herself in a towel, a bit on the thin side as far as fluffy went, but as large as a bedsheet.

She wasn't sure how long she'd been in the shower, but the maid had seated herself in the corner and dozed with her head against the wall. Josie dried herself and tiptoed over to put on the clean chemise and as much clothing as she could by herself. She sat at the dressing table and hesitated a moment before picking up Dev's comb to untangle her curls. Such an act seemed so...intimate, even more so than using his bathing chamber.

"Ob, biss, I hab your cobb id by bokgeb," Dora said.

After a moment's thought, Josie understood the maid meant she had a comb in her pocket, and smiled her thanks. The rest of her toilet was completed efficiently.

Carson waited in the reception room and acted as if nothing out of the ordinary had taken place. He handed Dora Josie's shawl, neatly folded, with one glove on the top. "His lordship has left to call on Lady Honoria," the valet announced with a slight bow. "He said you would know what it concerned."

Josie hoped Dev was able to schedule a séance for that evening.

"His lordship also said you could wait for him here. However, the hallway is clear if you wish to return to your suite immediately."

Josie was sure that last bit was Carson's own idea, but she happened to agree with him. No good would come of her hanging around in Dev's rooms.

"Hey, where's her obber glub?"

Josie knew full well where her other *glub* was, and she didn't want Dora to make a big deal out of it. "I'm sure it will turn up later," she said, turning the maid by the shoulders toward the door. "Thank his lordship for his hospitality," she said over her shoulder to Carson as she pushed Dora out the door in front of her.

They returned to her suite without incident. Dora tried to explain several things to Josie, but her speech was getting worse and Josie understood very little of what she said.

Josie had no idea how to help the poor girl. "I think you'd better go downstairs and let Mrs. Osman put something cool on your mouth," she said, insisting when the maid demurred. "Yes, I understand, you'll be back to dress me for the ball, but that's really not necessary. Someone else can...okay, okay, I won't ask for anyone else. Now go and let the housekeeper help you."

After Dora finally consented to seek treatment, and a quick peek into the other bedroom to ensure that she'd understood correctly and Mrs. Binns was indeed absent, Josie went to her own room intending to take a short nap.

"Where the hell have you been?"

Josie was startled, not only by the ghost's presence but also by his wan and disheveled appearance and the virulence of his tone. "Excuse me," she said, placing one fist on her hip and shaking one finger of her free hand in his direction. "Where the hell were *you* when I was kidnapped by Hargrave this morning?"

Deverell ran his hand through his hair as he paced back and forth in front of the windows. "Don't point. It's rude."

"I'll give you rude. How about when you didn't..."

"Before you get wound up with your righteous indignation, allow me the chance to explain."

Josie crossed her arms, but she remained silent.

"Because you intended to meet with Dev, against my advice I might add, I didn't accompany you since I knew I would only be bounced out of the way. When I realized you were in danger, I could not materialize a strong enough presence to be of any assistance. Once you'd left the grounds of the estate, I could not follow."

"Because you can't leave," Josie said softly, remembering that he'd said something to that effect when they'd first met. Gads, so much had happened since then, it seemed ages ago.

"I hated feeling so useless. All I could do was watch over Dora and keep her semiconscious until Dev could find her and learn what had transpired. Then I had to trust him to rescue you."

"He did. Well, sort of."

"And how was I to know? I waited here for hours with that drunken maid snoring her brains out. Even after Carson woke her and fetched her with fresh clothes for you, I couldn't be sure. I couldn't see for myself that you were unharmed."

"Because I was with him."

"For hours," the ghost said, and stuck out his bottom lip. "Hours," he reiterated. "And why does your hair look damp?"

"Does it?" She ran her fingers through her curls to fluff them up. Her short hair usually air-dried quickly. She tucked several loose strands behind her ears to stall for time but realized she would have to answer him or he'd magnify the matter into an issue. "No big deal," she mumbled, shrugging one shoulder. "I took a shower."

"With him?"

"No!" Her imagination immediately conjured up

some interesting possibilities for two people using the unusually constructed shower. Handholds. Footrests.

"There is currently only one shower in the entire castle."

"*His* shower does not mean *he* was in it."

Deverell pinched his chin and furrowed his brow. "Something is wrong with this picture."

"What do you mean? Wrong?"

"I can't see me, him, standing idly by while a beautiful woman clad only her chemise..."

"Naked." She immediately regretted correcting him.

"Pardon?

"Nothing."

"You said something. What?"

"Um, I said I was naked."

"Oh, thank you for that added worry. What I want to know is, why didn't he try to seduce you? I don't understand."

She decided not to share any more of what had happened with him. If he found out from altered memories after they returned to the future, so be it. She would deal with it then. "Maybe I'm not his type."

He flashed her a look of disbelief.

Time to change the subject. "I do have a bit of good news,' she said. "Because Dev was busy rescuing me, he wasn't able to keep his appointment with Lady Wingate."

Deverell made a face.

"And that means Lord Wingate didn't find them together, and so he can't demand satisfaction, and there won't be a duel. It was Wingate who shot you, wasn't it? Well, now he won't. Isn't that good news?"

The ghost shook his head. "It won't make any difference."

"Of course it will. You'll die eventually, of course, but at least not..."

"I can still feel the presence of the bullet in my heart."

"But if there isn't a duel, then you won't be shot." She fought back unexpected tears. "It's that altered memory thing. You'll remember when we get..."

"You can't change history."

"Then why are we here? Aren't we supposed to change what happens by debunking the gypsy seer?"

"Maybe I was wrong to think we could alter the future." Deverell sat in the chair and turned away from her to stare out the window. "Maybe that's why we can't figure out how she..."

"No! I refuse to believe that," she said, rushing to his side and sinking to her knees. She wanted to reach out to touch him, but she gripped the chair arm instead. "We can do it. I know we can. I refuse to leave until..."

"We may not have a choice." He turned sad eyes to her. "I thought we would have more time, but my strength is flagging."

That was obvious, although she didn't say so. He not only was paler but also looked...grayer, indistinct around the edges. "Then save your energy. Stop materializing. Stop...whatever."

"I don't think it will make a great difference. I will hold out as long as possible." But he must reserve enough energy to get her home. That he could not, would not, put at risk. He dematerialized and withdrew his presence. At the last second he glanced back. Josie dropped her head onto her hands.

She wasn't ready to leave. Was it simply her usual dog-with-a-bone attitude toward completing any given project, or did it have more to do with Dev and the unfinished business between them? She had little time to analyze her strong desire to stay before a knock on the door interrupted her thoughts.

"Come in," she called as she jumped up. She slid into the chair and grabbed her book off the table.

Honoria entered. "Oh, I am so glad to see you are none the worse for your ordeal," she whispered.

Josie blinked. What had Dev told his mother? And why was she whispering?

"The coast is clear," Mrs. Binns said from the doorway in a normal voice. "Come. Come. Nellie laid out a lovely tea before she left, and I always say everything looks brighter after a cup of the healing brew."

"So traumatic," Honoria said, reaching out to help Josie stand as if she were some sort of invalid.

"Really, I'm fine."

"Of course you are," Mrs. Binns assured her. "And you are not to worry. Honoria and I have let it be known, subtly of course, that you were regrettably confined to your bed with the headache."

At least the prosaic and mundane excuse was more believable than Dev's proposed lost-in-the-woods story. In order to get lost off a well-marked path a person would have to be practically brainless. Not an adjective she aspired to have connected to her name.

The women settled into the sitting room, Honoria next to Josie on the sofa. Mrs. Binns took the nearby side chair and poured.

"Do I smell mint?" Josie asked.

"I added a pinch as a general pick-me-up. I also added verbena as a restorative for your nerves."

"Your reputation is safe with us," Honoria said, patting Josie's hand.

"Lord Waite was quite self-effacing," Mrs. Binns said. "He said you rescued yourself and he just provided transportation. However did you get away from Hargrave?"

"I kneed him in the groin."

Honoria blanched, but Mrs. Binns leaned forward. "Tell me more."

"That's all there is to tell. It's a self-defense technique that can be used if a male assailant is facing you."

"Show me. Show me."

Josie dutifully stood by the side of her chair and demonstrated the move as she'd been taught, adding her own refinement of lifting her skirt for more knee room. "One good whack and it'll down any man immediately."

"I think I'll remember that."

"More tea," Honoria asked, her voice strained.

Josie took the hint and changed the subject. "I'm concerned about Dora. Her poor face. How is she doing?"

"She's under Mrs. Osman's care," Honoria said.

"I tried to persuade Dora to take a few days off to rest, but she refused. I admit I'm relieved because of all the extra work necessary for the ball. I must be a terrible person to even..."

"Nonsense. You are only being practical," Mrs. Binns said. "Don't worry yourself. I gave Mrs. Osman some herbs to make a poultice that works absolute wonders. Now, now, I'm sure Mrs. Osman is quite competent, but I never travel without my remedies. One never knows when a tisane or tonic will be needed."

"How did Dora explain her injuries?" Josie asked.

"She walked into a door," Honoria said.

"Who would believe..."

"No, she really did walk into a door," Mrs. Binns said. "Apparently on her return from the folly, a bit tipsy some say, teary-eyed others insist, she was directly in front of a door when a footman kicked it open. He carried several heavy crates of food destined for storage in the icehouse until later tonight.

"The door hit her, and she screamed and stumbled, tripping and falling onto her back. He twisted around to see what had happened, and a platter of stuffed capons slid out of the overfilled top box. Whether she was hit in the face yet again by the plate or by flying poultry no one could say, because the hunting pack arrived at the same time as the other servants. One of the dogs knocked over the footman, who then dropped the other crates, spilling out sweetmeats, puddings, and, to my complete dismay, all of the salmon tarts."

Horrified by her reaction to the story, Josie covered her mouth to hold back a giggle. Poor Dora.

"Dogs snatching capons, footmen grabbing at dogs, maids waving their aprons and dishcloths to shoo them away but succeeding only in contributing to the chaos, shouting and falling all over the animals and each other, elbows and knees flying. Everyone running around higgledy-piggledy. Everyone except Cook, who fainted."

"Oh my."

"Oh my, indeed," Honoria said with a sigh. "I fear my reputation as a hostess is in dire jeopardy. A ball without a supper is an affront to decency."

"Cook is recovered and talented," Mrs. Binns said. "I'm sure your supper will pass muster, albeit without salmon tarts. Now drink your tea. We can all use a bit of relaxation."

"I may need more than verbena before the evening's over," Honoria lamented. "The ruined supper, the Wingates leaving in a huff..."

Josie stifled a cheer.

"Limping footmen," Honoria continued. "Bruised and bandaged maids, holding a séance during the ball, and..."

"A séance?" Josie perked up. So Dev had made good on his promise. Now she owed him that walk in the moon garden.

"Let me go on record as saying I heartily disapprove," Mrs. Binns said.

"Noted," Josie said, hoping to cut her verbose chaperone short and get to the details. She twisted in her seat to face Honoria. "Midnight? In the library?"

"Actually, we'll have to meet at eleven. Supper was already scheduled for midnight, and I haven't the heart to ask Cook to change the schedule after all she has been through. Oh, no, what if she..."

"Drink up. Everything will be fine," Mrs. Binns said. "Cook will..."

"Not Cook. What if Madame X cannot contact Amanu if it's not midnight?"

"Did she express any doubts?" Josie asked. If the séance was a bust, how would she get her evidence?

"Not exactly," Honoria said. "But she didn't seem pleased with the idea of another séance tonight. I had to stand firm. Even so, it took both Estelle and me to convince her."

"And Lord Waite," Josie added.

Honoria looked confused.

"He suggested another séance tonight?" Josie prompted.

"Noooo. That was my idea. I was so disappointed that we failed to contact your father. I know what a comfort it can be to know your loved ones are happy."

"But Lord Waite helped you convince Madame X?"

"Did he?" Honoria furrowed her brow. "No, he couldn't have. Dev left the library right after you. I stopped by Estelle's rooms to make sure Madame was recovering and to see if they needed anything. That's when the subject came up. Dev most definitely was not there."

"Then how..."

"I immediately sent notes to everyone. Didn't you..."

"Ours were waiting for us early this morning," Mrs. Binns said. "As Josie would have seen if she had not rushed out willy-nilly without checking the salver on the desk. Several gentlemen we met last night sent 'round calling cards," she added with a satisfied nod. "And more came today. I'll get them so we can talk about prospects for your dancing partners tonight at the ball."

Josie wasn't interested in dancing or other men. She wanted to know more about how and when Dev had found out about the séance. "You sent a note to Lord Waite? And he would have read it this morning?"

"Most likely last night. My maid was instructed to tell Carson the missive was important, and he is quite efficient at making sure Dev reads my notes in a timely manner."

"Why you would want to have another séance on the night of your ball is a mystery to me," Mrs. Binns said over her shoulder. "Oh, just look at these notes."

"It is quite strange. As I walked down the hall, I kept hearing this faint voice saying over and over, 'Séance tomorrow. Séance tomorrow.' You don't think I'm channeling Amanu, do you? Wouldn't that be exciting? Or perhaps terrifying—I'm not sure."

Josie bit her lip to keep from assuring Honoria the ghost she heard was probably her son from the future. Go Deverell. He must be thrilled to have finally gotten through to his mother.

"You're not channeling anything but a little bird,"

Mrs. Binns said. She returned to her seat carrying a shallow silver plate about the size of a shoebox lid. "Oh my, Lord Chalmsey left his card." She held the card to her breast. "Such a handsome man. He would be the catch of the season."

"After my son," Honoria said.

"Of course. But he is still a confirmed bachelor." Mrs. Binns set the salver on the table between them, and she and Honoria went through the formal cards, notes, three poems, and a nosegay of dried violets.

Josie sat back and listened to their comments on the assorted gentlemen who had "called." Phones might be more efficient, but she'd never received a poem on her voice mail. All the verses were written by the same man and were ridiculous enough to cause giggles when read aloud. She thought the ode to her eyebrows had a nice meter, and to give the writer his due it wasn't easy to find a word that rhymed with *arched*. Both older women deemed the penniless poet unsuitable.

Josie tuned out the discussion of titles, habits, and incomes, although she did maintain an expression of mild interest and remembered to nod now and then.

So Dev had known that another séance was already scheduled when he made the deal with her. The dirty rat. If he thought she would keep her end of a bargain made under false pretenses, he had a surprise coming.

Her first inclination was to confront him with his perfidy, but fortunately he wasn't handy and she had a chance to rethink her position. He didn't know she knew. That gave her an ace in the hole. Now the trick would be how to play her advantage to the best effect.

"Don't you think so, Josie?" Honoria asked.

"An excellent idea," Mrs. Binns said.

"Josie?"

"Ah...sure."

"Then it's settled," Honoria said. "While you two are napping, I will arrange for trays to be brought up later."

"This will work out just fine," Mrs. Binns said, rubbing her hands together. "Her absence at dinner will create a bit of anticipation, and then Josie can make a grand entrance fashionably late."

"But not too late," Honoria added. "The dancing will start at nine and you don't want to miss a minute of that."

"I don't know how..."

"What girl doesn't love to dance?" Mrs. Binns asked.

"I..."

"Estelle planned the musical program and insisted we have several waltzes. She says it's all the rage on the Continent," Honoria said, neither woman giving Josie a chance to talk.

"A bit risqué, don't you think?"

"Perhaps for a public assembly, but perfectly acceptable for a private ball. The young people are quite eager to display their new skills."

"I'm sure they are," Mrs. Binns said with a sniff. "I think Josie will stay with the traditional quadrilles and country dances."

Josie didn't remember any of her one dancing lesson with...whoever that was that came to tea with Amelia. "I don't..."

"She can waltz if she wants to. I might even have a try at it myself."

"Honoria! I'm shocked."

"I am not an old fuddy-duddy yet."

"If you're insinuating I..."

"Whoa! Time-out." Josie made the *T* with her hands and even though the other women couldn't possibly have any idea what it meant, they did stop talking. "There's no sense arguing. I won't be dancing, because I don't know any of the steps. No, my education wasn't lacking—okay, maybe a little as far as the quadrille is concerned—but I'm sure I'll enjoy watching everyone else."

"Oh, I wish I'd known," Honoria said with a commiserating expression. "I could have arranged for a dancing master to come in yesterday or earlier today."

"We certainly will engage one before heading to town for the Season," Mrs. Binns said.

"I'll give you Master DuPree's card. He is the very best."

"Thank you. Hasn't he written a book?"

"We have a copy in the library. I'll have Nellie bring it up for you. You and Josie will just adore his wit. Who are you going to have do her wardrobe?"

"I was thinking of Solange of La Petite Salon."

"Excellent choice. But you must have Mrs. Smithson do her millinery. Fabulous featherwork.

The proper headpiece can take an outfit from ordinary to amazing."

"I agree. So important. And she will need new gloves, boots..."

Friends again, the two women were off planning Josie's future. A future she couldn't afford, monetarily or time-wise.

"Speaking of the library," Josie said to no one in particular. "I think I'll go down and pick out a book. I've nearly finished mine." It was a lie, but she needed an excuse to inspect the library before the séance and put her pitifully few traps in place.

"I'll come with you and get Master DuPree's book," Honoria said.

"If you don't mind keeping an eye on Josie for me..."

"I don't need a chaperone to get a book."

"Yes, you do," both women said simultaneously.

"Remember your reputation," Mrs. Binns added. "Right now is an especially precarious time. Considering your...adventure this morning."

"I'll see her safely to the library and back," Honoria promised.

"Thank you. I'll have a bit of a lie-down," Mrs. Binns said. She turned to Josie. "And you should too, my dear. It will be a late night."

"I will. Later," Josie promised. "I'll be right with you," she said to Honoria.

Josie went into her room and grabbed the small bundle of potentially useful items she'd prepared the night before. It was too big to fit into her teensy-weensy reticule, so she tied a loop into the large handkerchief, stuck her arm through the makeshift handle, and then draped her shawl in such a way as to cover the entire package.

She wasn't sure how she was going to get rid of her substitute chaperone, but she'd think of something. She would need to be alone to set her traps before the séance. And then she would decide what to do about Lord Waite and his scheming.

Fourteen

GETTING RID OF HONORIA WAS EASIER THAN Josie had anticipated. After only two minutes in the library, a servant rushed in with a potential disaster that required her immediate attention or else the supper for the ball would be utterly ruined.

"Oh, dear. I really must see to Cook immediately," Honoria said.

"No problem. I'll wait right here for you to return."

"The last time she locked herself in her room with a bottle of schnapps, it took Mrs. Osman and me three hours to talk her out. She was hungover for two days. Cook, not Mrs. Osman."

"Then you should go right away."

"I could call for Dora or..."

"Don't bother poor Dora. Hopefully she's resting."

"Mrs. Binns..."

"Already asleep, I'm sure. Go on. She'll never know the difference."

"Oh, dear. Oh, dear. I don't know what to do."

"Really, I'll be fine. Look on the bright side. You'll probably take care of the emergency in a few minutes. But if it looks like you'll be tied up for hours, you can send me word and I'll go back to my room like a good little girl and take my nap."

"You are a sweet child," Honoria said, thanking Josie several times before rushing off.

"Well, that was easy," Deverell said as he popped into the room.

"Did you have something to do with that?"

"If you mean did I lock Cook in her room, then the answer is no. If you mean did I open the cabinet door and move the schnapps bottle a few inches to where Cook could see it...?"

"You didn't? That was a terrible thing to do. Poor Cook has had such an awful day, and now you cause your poor mother additional worries."

"She will cope magnificently. She always does. And *someone* had to help you. Would you rather have spent the afternoon discussing the relative merits of your many suitors?"

"You were eavesdropping."

"I was waiting for you to do what we came here to do. Did you devise any traps?"

"Yes, as a matter of fact, I did." Josie plopped her bundle on the table and crossed her arms.

"Well, don't just stand there. We only have about twenty minutes."

Suddenly suspicious, she asked, "And how do you know that? Did this exact incident happen before? I mean, do you have a memory of it? Or are you 'remembering' the revised version? Or..."

"Don't get your garters in a knot. I simply know Mrs. Osman had a duplicate of Cook's key made after she locked herself in with a bottle..."

"Your mother told me about that. But that means we only have a few minutes." She removed a twist of Mrs. Binns's finest silk thread and began to position five- to six-foot lengths across sections of the wood paneling and bookshelves. She kept the thread near the floor, and the brown color blended perfectly. If someone used a secret door, he or she would inadvertently break the silk. "You could give me a hand with this."

"I'm conserving energy. You have time. The housekeeper will have to find the key first."

His self-satisfied grin prompted her to ask, "Did you take it?"

"No, but I did move it to a spot behind a foot-locker. I don't know why you're doing that. I've told you there aren't any secret passageways into this room."

"Look for the simplest solution first. It's usually the right one." She stood back to admire her handiwork. Unless you knew the threads were there, they would go unnoticed. She returned to the table to set her next trap. She removed the box of rice face powder and fluffy applicator from her bundle and then crawled under the table.

"What are you doing now?"

"I'm dusting the area with a fine film of powder. If she touches the underside of the table, or the legs, it will leave a trail."

"I don't see how that will help. If we are going

to figure out how..."

"Before we can deduce *how*, we have to find out *what* she does." Josie stood up and dusted off her hands. "And I don't see you coming up with any brilliant ideas."

"Isn't that why I brought *you*?"

"Then stop second-guessing everything I do." She removed a small vial and a plain handkerchief from her bundle. "Before you ask, I'm applying a thin coating of oil to the top of the chair where Madame sits. Hopefully, the so-called spirit will place his hands on the chairback again and leave a residue of whatever it is that glows in the dark."

"Is that oil of cloves? Makes me think of a toothache."

"I borrowed it from Mrs. Binns's medical kit."

"Won't the smell be a bit obvious? Won't someone question why..."

"Not likely with all the other odors emanating from those protective charms she'll insist we wear to the séance."

"What else have you got in that bundle?"

"Only these tiny beads I'm going to put on the window sashes to indicate if they are opened." She took out the tiny glass vial with the cork stopper that she'd borrowed from her chaperone's sewing basket. "That's all I could think of. Hopefully it will be adequate."

"How do you expect to use the information you gather to reveal the charade?"

"Sometimes evidence of foul play is enough to cause doubt."

"But is doubt sufficient to convince Honoria to cease having these séances?"

Josie shrugged. "You know her better than I do." She carefully placed the tiny glass beads on the sides of the window sash, not that anyone coming or going that way in the dark would notice a few red and blue bugle beads.

"I suppose it will depend on how the gypsy defends herself," Deverell said. "Damn, I hate that the future we want hinges on uncertain odds."

"So now you're back to thinking we can change history."

"After reviewing the relevant facts, I realized my original reasoning was correct."

Heaven forbid he should admit to being wrong.

Deverell continued, "I have concluded we can change this particular piece of history because we are rectifying a wrong, serving justice. Madame X preys on emotional vulnerability for monetary gain and deserves to be stopped."

"But you don't deserve to have your history changed?" she asked over her shoulder as she knelt to place more beads.

"I am not looking for redemption. I must be content with carrying out the task I accepted as my penance. I can only..."

At the sudden silence, Josie stood and spun around. He'd disappeared mid-sentence. "Deverell?"

A surge of panic seized her. Had he blinked into oblivion and left her alone and stranded? Despite knowing he was no longer there, her gaze darted from one corner to another. "Yoo-hoo, Deverell?

Lord Waite?"

Then she realized his disappearance must mean Dev was near. She quickly returned to the table and tossed her shawl over the unexplainable supplies just as the door opened.

"I thought I heard your voice," Dev said. Actually he'd been headed to the stables when he'd thought he heard his name called. Spending time with her had more appeal than a ride. Because she was alone in the library, he left the door open for propriety's sake. He also motioned to the footman. "Please fetch Miss Drummond's chaperone."

"No," Josie said. "Don't disturb her. She's resting. Your mother said she'd be right back."

Dev signaled the footman. "Please inform Lady Honoria her presence is requested."

The footman scurried to do his bidding.

"That wasn't necessary."

"I see you did not attend the picnic luncheon with the other guests. Do you not enjoy picnics?"

"Don't change the subject. I find this obsession with chaperones a great inconvenience." She scooped up her shawl in an awkward manner. "I shall return to my room now."

"One moment, if you please."

"I'd rather not."

She stopped a few steps away, her expression indicating she was impatient for him to move out of the doorway. He didn't budge. Every time he saw her, she intrigued him all the more. What was she hiding under that shawl she held clasped so tightly to her lovely breasts?

He stifled a smile at the sound of her foot tapping impatiently. "I am delighted to see the shower had such a restorative effect."

"You're keeping me here to discuss your plumbing?"

Her blush and rapid shallow breathing revealed more than her bold words.

"I would rather discuss our mutual..." He paused when the voices in the hallway behind him became louder.

"I told you she is not receiving," the butler said.

"Step aside, old man. I will see Miss Drummond."

"Wait here," Dev said to Josie. He stepped into the hallway and closed the library door behind himself. "Thank you, Carleton," he said to the butler. "I will deal with Lord Hargrave."

"Very good, milord."

He waited until the servant was out of earshot before speaking to the piece of filth before him. "If you leave immediately, I will not..."

"I'm here to do my duty toward Miss Drummond," Hargrave said, raising his chin. "I offer her my name in order to salvage her reputation."

"You what?" Josie screeched.

Dev spun around. "I asked you to wait..."

"Why? So you could politely..."

"Miss Drummond." Hargrave pushed past Dev and rushed toward Josie.

Dev reached for the man's arm and missed. Josie automatically backed away from the oncoming villain.

"Miss Drummond, you must forgive my precipitous actions of this morning. I was driven mad by your beauty. Wild by the need to be with..."

"Oh, shut up," Josie said.

Dev had to give her credit. Once she'd recovered from her surprise, she stood her ground. He came up behind his former friend. "Har..."

"You stay out of this," she said, rounding on Dev.

He raised his hands in submission and backed off. But not too far.

Josie turned back to Hargrave. "I can't believe you had the balls to show up here. You're lower than low. You're..."

"I am here to restore your good name by giving you mine."

"What?"

"Once we're married..."

"Listen, you thick-skulled cretin, I told you before but I tell you again. I will never marry you. Never. After what you did to..."

Hargrave fell to his knees and groveled. "Please, forgive me, Miss Drummond. Your beauty drove me to it." He grabbed her foot and tried to kiss it.

In her futile effort to escape his grasp, she fell backward. She dropped her bundle and scrambled to retrieve an odd assortment of objects even as she shook her leg to dislodge Hargrave's desperate grip. He held on like a dog with a bone.

Dev had started moving the instant the other man's hands had reached for her. He didn't understand the fury deep in his gut, but he knew for certain the villain would never touch Josie again.

"Let go of me," she said, grabbing the nearby chair for leverage and kicking her captor in the face with her free foot.

"Enough," Dev said. He leaned over, grabbed two fistfuls of coat, and lifted Hargrave to his feet. "Time for you to leave."

"The bitch bloodied my nose," Hargrave complained as he was half carried, half pushed out the door. "This is not over," he called back over his shoulder.

Dev stopped short of throwing the despicable man down the front steps—not out of any consideration for Hargrave, but because the guests were returning across the lawn from their picnic. Any comment caused by his actions would come to roost on Josie's head.

Hargrave straightened his coat and dabbed at his nose with his handkerchief.

"You are no longer welcome in my home." Dev turned away without the courtesy of a bow.

"You won't be so high-and-mighty once word of your precious guest's activities..."

Dev spun back to face the bounder. "I demand satisfaction."

"Which I gladly give. The woman as the prize, eh?"

"My second will call on your second," he said, refusing to validate that last comment with a reply. He spun on his heel and reentered the house.

"I'll be at the inn in the village," Hargrave called through the closed door.

Dev dismissed the matter from his mind and

anxiously returned to Josie. He wasn't sure what he'd find when he reopened the library door, surely not her on the sofa in a faint, but possibly she would be in need of comfort. He scoffed at his own thinking. She was more likely stomping around the room in a towering rage at his interference. He certainly never expected to find her sitting cross-legged on the floor examining the back of a chair.

"What the hell?" Josie had sensed his presence and for a nanosecond couldn't tell if it was the ghost or the man. When his deep voice sent an electric thrill down her spine, she knew Dev was still keeping Deverell away. She was torn. On the one hand she wanted to share her find with the ghost, and yet she wanted to be near the man. Considering her position, she had no choice but to offer an explanation.

"Look what I found. This chair has a secret compartment. I must have knocked the release with my elbow when I fell."

Dev went down on one knee next to her. "Are you hurt?"

She dismissed his concern with a wave. "Did you know this was here? Don't you find this fascinating?"

"No, and no. In this old place secret compartments are as common as dirt. Is anything in there?"

"Empty," she said with a sigh.

"What? Did you expect to find the mythical emeralds?"

Now he was making fun of her. "Actually, I find the access to the compartment the most interesting part. Very cleverly hidden. See, this lion's head moves to the right, that releases this catch, and the door flops down."

"Absolutely enchanting," Dev said, but he was looking at her, not the chair.

"See how the door folds out and then a second level flips open? I'd bet it's strong enough to stand on."

"Library chairs that incorporate steps are not all that uncommon. What is all this?" Dev asked, indicating the near-empty vial of beads, powder container, and other stuff.

When she'd spotted the secret compartment, Josie had totally forgotten the remainders of her supplies that had spilled from her shawl when she fell. Caught red-handed and unable to think of another reasonable—or even far-fetched—explanation, she told him the truth. During her account he helped her to rise and to pick up the leftover bits of her traps.

"So you are more interested in debunking the séance than in contacting your father? Why? What harm can the gypsy's little charade do? If it gives my mother some comfort..."

He'd never believe the whole truth. "Because it's wrong." She paraphrased the ghost's earlier words. "The gypsy is preying on Honoria's emotional vulnerability for the sole purpose of monetary gain and deserves to be exposed as a fraud." Josie realized she'd moved closer to Dev in her fervor. "Before it's too late," she added, stepping back.

Dev raised an eyebrow. "I wonder..." He closed the distance between them and took her cheek in his hand. He rubbed his thumb over her lips. "Do you bring such passion to everything you do?"

The picnicking guests returned, but neither Dev nor Josie responded to the sounds of revelry filtering through the closed door as the others entered the foyer and then left to find amusements elsewhere. But the break was enough to bring Josie to her senses. She stepped away from him.

"If you're not going to help me, at least promise you won't give away my intentions. I wouldn't want the séance canceled because I..."

"A gentleman never betrays a confidence. Besides which, I have a vested interest in tonight's event. You have not forgotten our deal, have you?"

How could she? Not forgotten and not forgiven. However, intuition told her now wasn't the most advantageous time to confront him with what he'd done. "Of course, I remember," she said in a sweet voice.

He gave her a mistrustful look, but his mother's entrance spoiled any chance for further discussion of that matter. For now.

"Thank goodness. Another disaster averted." Honoria stopped short. "Oh, Dev. What are you doing here?"

"I live here. At least occasionally."

Honoria shook her finger at him. "Don't be smart with me, young man."

"Didn't the footman tell you I awaited you in the library?"

"What footman? Why?"

"Nothing more than that I saw Miss Drummond alone. As host I am responsible for safeguarding her reputation, as are you."

"I appreciate your concern for our guest," Honoria said, taking the slight rebuke with good grace. "I mistakenly assumed everyone else had left the house. In fact, I thought you went riding."

"I was just on my way." He bowed and took his leave, pausing a moment with his back to his mother to wink at Josie and put his finger over his lips.

Honoria's thoughtful gaze followed him out the door before she turned to Josie. "My son appears to be very concerned for your welfare." She tapped the tip of her index finger on her chin.

Josie wasn't sure where Honoria was going with that. "He is a considerate host."

"Yes. Yes, he is."

Honoria sounded somewhat surprised.

"The other guests have returned," Josie said to change the subject.

"I suppose that means I should make sure everyone has everything they need in their rooms," Honoria said. "As much as I love entertaining, I fear I am getting too old for all this work." She sighed dramatically. "I would gladly turn the office of hostess over to a younger woman." She looked sideways at Josie for a reaction to her statement.

Assuming the other woman was fishing for signs of interest in the position, Josie kept her expression bland.

"Well, my dear," Honoria continued, her tone disappointed and yet at the same time hopeful. "Let's get you safely back to your room so you can rest and then dress. The ball tonight is bound to be most exciting."

Honoria left Josie at the door to her suite and rushed off to contain another disaster. Apparently a ball gown had been singed during pressing.

Josie let herself into the suite quietly although it was unlikely Mrs. Binns could have heard the noise of a parade over her own snoring. The woman sounded like a diesel truck in stop-and-go rush hour traffic.

In her room the drapes had been pulled to block out the late-afternoon sun, but Josie was not tired nor did she think she could sleep fully clothed. Not being able to undress oneself was inconvenient and aggravating. As she reached to pull open the heavy velvet window covering, a voice came out of the murky shadows.

"Please leave them closed!"

"Deverell? Why?"

"I have not fully materialized to save energy, and I'm afraid you may find my appearance...disturbing."

"Don't be ridiculous," she said, flipping the drapes aside. She had expected a transparent image, but instead his head and hands seemed to float in midair. She instantly turned away, swallowed, and composed her expression as she busied herself opening the other half. "There we are." She turned to face him and crossed her arms. "Well, I can't exactly say you're looking well."

"What happened in the library?" he asked, getting right to the point. "I know Dev was there. It had to be his presence that knocked me clear to the dining room."

Josie related the incident with Hargrave.

"Good for Dev," the ghost said. "Although I would have taken a punch or two at the bounder."

"Which would have served no purpose."

"Would have made me feel better." He grinned.

"Fine." She changed the subject and told him about the library chair and Dev's agreement not to rat her out.

"And what did that cost you?"

"Nothing. Why do you have such a negative opinion of Dev? He's not that bad."

"Ha! You forget I know him better than anyone."

But he had not been there when she'd looked deep into Dev's eyes, or when he'd touched her cheek so tenderly.

"But that's not important," Deverell said. "You've set the traps, and by midnight we should know how the gypsy does it."

A twinge of regret surfaced unbidden.

"We could be home for breakfast," he said.

She turned away from the sight of his disembodied hands rubbing together. Even though she had no intention of meeting Dev in the garden, even though she knew they had no future together, the thought of never seeing him again left a gaping emptiness inside her.

"What's wrong?"

She didn't want him to see the tears in her eyes. "Nothing." Fortunately her voice did not betray her emotions.

"Then why are you showing me your back?"

Thinking fast, she reached behind and untied

her ribbon sash. Then she lifted her dress over her head and tossed it on the nearby chair. She still wore several layers of underclothing. "I need you to undo my stays so I can take a nap."

"You're joking."

The few moments' respite and his shocked tone restored her equilibrium. She peeked over her shoulder at him. "Surely you remember how to undo a woman's corset."

Deverell raised his chin. "A gentleman does not brag of his amorous experience."

Josie rolled her eyes and shook her head. "Just untie this thing so I don't have to call Dora."

He did, although he took longer to complete the task than the maid ever had. Did his hands tremble, or was that simply an effect caused by the partial materialization?

Josie held the corset in place until she retired behind the screen, where she stripped down to her chemise and donned the blue brocade dressing gown. When she returned to the main part of the room, the ghost had disappeared.

Knowing it would be a late night, and with nothing else to occupy her for the next couple of hours, she decided she would try to nap. She closed the drapes and crawled beneath the covers. Unexpectedly, she fell asleep almost immediately.

Deverell sat on the edge of her bed. Even totally dematerialized he still retained a sense of himself. As if to prove it, he ran his hand through his hair. Although he leaned back against the headboard, he would not totally relax until he returned Josie to her time. When had watching over her become as important as his assigned task?

Deverell placed a kiss on her forehead. He denied his feelings for her as anything other than duty. She was his responsibility and nothing more. After all, he was old enough to be her father, several times over.

He lifted a lock of her hair, his gut constricting when it curled around his finger, as easily and as unconsciously as she had curled around his heart.

Although anxious to have this adventure safely done, he knew that once it was completed he would never see her again. The double-edged sword cut to the bone no matter which way it sliced.

Exhaustion was his persistent companion and constant worry. He stretched out next to her, not touching her, but close enough to inhale her scent. Propping his elbow on the edge of her pillow, he rested his head in his hand. And closed his eyes. Just for a moment.

When a scratching on the door woke him, he was astounded to learn that not only was he fully materialized, but he also held Josie in his arms, her head resting on his chest. Even if the maid couldn't see him, it would appear very strange for Josie's head to be resting several inches above the bed. Horrified at the thought of being caught, he quickly dematerialized and moved away.

Josie woke with a start from a nightmare of falling.

"Miss Drummond?" Dora called in a soft voice

as she lit the lamps with her taper. "Time to get dressed for the ball."

Josie sat up. "I'm awake. You sound much improved." She stood and stretched. "Your face looks much better, too."

Dora brought in a tray with coffee service. "Mrs. Binns's poultice really did work wonders. And Sadie lent me a bit of her precious face powder to lighten the bruising."

"I'm glad you're better. Is Mrs. Binns awake?" Josie sipped her coffee, hoping the caffeine would help clear the persistent dream that continued to haunt her. Not the nightmare of falling that woke her, but the prior one that had both Dev and Deverell in it, together, separate and yet one and the same.

Dora bustled around the room, straightening the bedcovers and laying out fresh undergarments and silk stockings. "Yes, Mrs. Binns is awake. Nadine is doing her hair. Once you are dressed except for your gown, you'll have a bit of supper in the sitting room."

Josie donned her silk stockings and tied them in place with ribbon garters. The dancing shoes were thin leather slippers so supple it didn't matter that there was no right or left. More ribbons fastened them on her feet.

Dora combed Josie's hair and lightly dusted her face with rice powder. Josie declined the use of the red papers that were the forerunners of blusher, a cosmetic she had never needed thanks to natural and all-too-frequent blushing of her own. Dora also offered to darken Josie's lashes with kohl, but since neither woman knew what it was really made of, she declined that too.

"Do I hear an orchestra?" she asked the maid. After days without a radio, her iPod, or even elevator music, the sounds seemed so strange.

"The Countess LaFoyn insisted the band play during dinner." Dora made a face when she said Estelle's name. "How's a body supposed to listen to music and converse politely and eat all at the same time?"

"I don't know," Josie agreed, hiding a smile. Wouldn't Dora be shocked to learn that in the future lots of people worked and played with earphones constantly pumping out their favorite tunes?

With Dora's efficient help, Josie was quickly ready except for her gown. Wrapped in her dressing gown, she joined Mrs. Binns for supper.

"Ah, yes, just as I requested," Mrs. Binns said as they sat down to the makeshift dining table. "Cream of potato soup, bread, and rice pudding."

"Yum," Josie said, but wasn't able to inject any enthusiasm into her voice.

"Don't complain. There is nothing here to cause indigestion, gas, or bad breath. You'll thank me later."

"If not now," she mumbled under her breath.

"I've also prepared a special tea. Mint Party Brew I call it. A little tonic to start the evening."

Josie sniffed the cup containing a strong infusion with a slightly green tinge. "What's in it?"

"In addition to my favorite blend of leaves, I've added mint, Saint-John's-wort, and a pinch or two of several secret ingredients to put us in a party mood."

Josie set the cup aside. She'd read that the use of opiates, sometimes unknowingly, was rampant in the Regency, and she was afraid to try any secret ingredients. As she ate her bland soup, Mrs. Binns went down a litany of dos and don'ts. Mostly don'ts.

"Don't dance more than two sets with any one gentleman; it would show you favored him."

Josie would have reminded her chaperone that she had no intention of dancing, but by the time she swallowed the bit of plain bread, Mrs. Binns had moved on.

"Don't leave the ballroom with a gentleman. You can step out on the terrace, but only if you stay in the area lit by the ballroom windows.

"Don't sit down unless your feet are in excruciating pain. You don't want to put lap wrinkles in your dress. Plus, a gentleman is more likely to ask a standing woman to dance.

"Don't drink any alcoholic beverages. We don't want you stumbling around the dance floor. There will be orgeat or lemonade for the ladies..."

"What the hell is *ohr-zhat*?"

"And don't curse. I can't believe you don't have orgeat in the colonies. It's a sweet almond syrup with a little orange water added that's used to make a somewhat palatable milky punch. My advice? Stay with the lemonade."

That Josie would definitely remember.

"There probably won't be a receiving line or majordomo to announce entrances because at a country ball most of the attendees are already known to the other guests. Don't speak to any man until you have been formally introduced. And by that I mean by someone you know and trust not to make your acquaintance to someone unworthy or unprincipled. Unknown gentlemen introducing each other is not acceptable.

"Don't think I haven't noticed your tendency to remove your gloves and bonnet. You won't have a hat tonight..."

Josie breathed a sigh of relief.

"But do not remove your gloves for any reason."

Josie would have mentioned that Amelia had taught her how to adjust her gloves in order to eat, but the chance passed. Mrs. Binns was on a roll and continued along the same vein until Josie had finished the last bite of her rice pudding.

"And finally, do have fun. Don't worry; you'll do fine. Now go finish getting dressed."

Josie thanked her chaperone for all the good advice and returned to her room. Dora had laid out the ball gown, stuffed with tissue paper to keep it from creasing, on the bed.

"Isn't it the most beautiful dress you've ever seen?"

Actually it looked rather like a headless corpse at the moment. A very nicely dressed corpse, she had to admit. She had never worn a gown half as fine.

Dora had put on white cotton gloves to handle the delicate material, and with her painstaking help Josie donned the dress and then looked in the mirror. The empire-waist silk gown was a shade lighter than her eyes, making them appear darker blue.

Silver threads gave the fabric a shimmer that was echoed along the bottom third of the skirt by three rows of sparkling silver and crystal beaded fringe, each a full six inches in length. Extra material gathered onto the back of the bodice gave room to move without spoiling the straight lines of the gown.

Dora puffed up the tiny sleeves accented with a row of brilliant crystal beads. Josie pulled up on the low-cut bodice, but Dora slapped her hands away.

"It's perfect just as it is," the maid said.

"I'm not comfortable displaying half my boobs, er, breasts. If I twist around too quickly, they'll pop right out."

"Then don't twist around. Turn your entire body."

Now even Dora sounded like Mrs. Binns. Josie rolled her eyes and yanked upward on the bodice again.

"Here," Dora said. She tucked a tiny bouquet of a few violets and a bit of lace into Josie's cleavage. "This tussy-mussy should do the trick."

Josie looked down to view the effect. At least her cleavage was covered. "Better."

Dora added elbow-length gloves, a circlet of blue flowers made from beads and ribbons on Josie's head, and sapphire earbobs. "Lady Honoria insisted on lending you these when she saw your dress."

"I will remember to thank her."

Dora looped over Josie's wrist the ribbon handles of a dark blue fan and a small beaded reticule just large enough to hold a lace-trimmed handkerchief and the inevitable vial of smelling salts.

"You probably won't be needing this," Dora

said, laying the shawl made of white silk embroidered with blue flowers over Josie's arm. "But it completes the *ensemble*. I learned that word from Lady Griffin's French maid."

"Don't I need a necklace, maybe a ribbon?" Josie suggested since she had no jewelry of her own.

"Oh, no. You want a smooth, uninterrupted expanse of skin to attract the gentlemen."

Josie shook her head. Women who wouldn't dare show their ankles would parade around a ballroom nearly naked from the boobs up. She turned toward the mirror again and was amazed by the image there. She had to admit the ensemble was stunning.

"You look like a princess," Dora said.

The funny thing was, Josie *felt* like a princess.

But was she ready to go downstairs and face a roomful of strangers and Dev? Would he think she was beautiful? Would he ask her to dance?

Josie shook those thoughts out of her head. Beautiful clothes should not affect the person she was inside. No dancing. Detached observation was the researcher's credo. At the stroke of midnight she would change from princess back to scientist, and there would be no glass slipper for her.

She'd best remember that.

"Mrs. Osman told us we can watch from the balcony when we're not needed," Dora said. "I'll be so proud to point out my miss to that snooty French maid."

Mrs. Binns called out that it was time to leave if they wanted to arrive before the dancing started. "Are you ready, my dear?"

"One moment."

Josie thanked Dora for her help and left her room to attend her first, and last, Regency ball.

Fifteen

B Y THE TIME JOSIE AND MRS. BINNS descended the stairs, only the butler, a footman, and two maids waited in the main foyer to help any late arrivals with their wraps and hats. With a formal bow, the butler indicated the entry to the parlor on Josie's right. To her surprise, the far wall, which she'd thought was simply wood paneling, was in actuality floor-to-ceiling doors that folded back. The parlor furniture had been rearranged, and the room made a grand antechamber to the ballroom.

Josie paused just inside the doorway. She'd seen the ballroom before, but nothing had prepared her for the glittering spectacle of a thousand candles, mountains of fresh flowers, and hundreds of guests in silks and satins. She descended the wide marble steps she'd originally thought was the stage for the musicians. Mrs. Binns stayed a step behind to allow Josie a dramatic entrance.

A number of guests turned her way, but Josie figured curiosity drove their actions. The musicians struck up a tune, and Mrs. Binns guided Josie to the sidelines. Without conscious thought her gaze sought out Dev. She located him quite easily. He was the center of attention as he led his mother out onto the empty dance floor to formally open the ball.

After a stately promenade around the dance floor, other dancers joined Dev and Honoria for the rest of the dance. She could not help watching him, fascinated that such a big man, a head above most of the other dancers, could move with such grace. He made the complicated steps look effortless. As each turn caused him to face her, he found her gaze and smiled.

She could have watched him all night, but Mrs. Binns had another agenda.

"Don't get your hopes up, my dear," the chaperone whispered behind her fan. "Lord Waite will be occupied for some time with his obligatory dances. Honored guests and the highest-ranking females are in line in front of you. Though I'd bet my best whalebone stays he'll save the supper dance for you."

"I told you I didn't intend..."

"Ah, there she is. Lady Jersey. The queen arbiter of London society. Quite the coup for Honoria to have her accept her invitation. Don't stare at her as if she were an exotic animal in the zoo. Act nonchalant," Mrs. Binns said, even though she herself appeared as excited as a game show contestant. "I must present you to her. You simply must have entrée to Almack's or your London Season will be a disaster."

"If you say so." Josie's laid-back attitude was real. She wouldn't be there for the Season and would never set foot in Almack's.

"We'll work our way over to her, but not directly. We don't want to appear too keen. Deferential, yes, but not eager. I recommend you not accept any invitations to dance until after you meet Lady Jersey."

"Fine with me."

Mrs. Binns stopped to introduce Josie to several nearby ladies. After a few insipid comments on the weather, the decorations, and the music, they moved on to the next group. And repeated the process. Mrs. Binns cleverly fended off any young men who might have a dance invitation in mind.

Josie quickly got the hang of the chitchat and was able to act her small role in the conversation and still keep an eye on the dance floor. Dev looked more than yummy in his formal clothes. Only a man secure in his masculinity could carry off a sapphire blue waistcoat, an embroidered vest, and white satin knee breeches with such panache. His smiles in her direction seemed to indicate he wanted to seek her out.

By the time they'd worked their way down the length of the room, Josie realized she truly missed air-conditioning. Even though the glitterati of the Regency ballroom were beautiful, most of them used heavy perfume in a futile attempt to mask body odor. The room was overly warm, and the air was so thick with scents that Josie's head pounded.

"Here we are," Mrs. Binns said as they approached the corner where Lady Jersey held court. "Mind your p's and q's."

The introduction went pretty much like all the others until Lady Jersey asked Josie, "Are you related to Mrs. Drummond Burrell?"

"Um...I don't think so."

"She is also a patroness of Almack's," Mrs. Binns whispered.

"Everyone knows that," Lady Jersey said with a flip of her fingers. "I do believe her father, James Drummond, Lord Perth, had some distant cousin who went to the colonies. What was the name of that place? Boston, if I'm not mistaken."

"She rarely is," Mrs. Binns whispered.

Lady Jersey ignored her. "Do you have relatives there?"

"My family is from Baltimore," Josie said truthfully.

"That's the town I was thinking of. I don't know what made me say Boston. Sadly I admit my knowledge of your geography is somewhat limited. We must chat further on this when you are in town next. I'll have Mrs. Drummond Burnell and a few others who have friends and acquaintances in the colonies to tea. I'm sure we'll find we know some of the same people."

Josie didn't think the six-degrees-of-separation theory applied across the centuries, but without any way to explain her disagreement she simply smiled and nodded. She let Mrs. Binns and Lady Jersey carry the rest of the conversation and walked away feeling like a bobble-head figurine. And it didn't do much for her headache, either.

"That went well," Mrs. Binns said with a cat-got-the-cream smile as they resumed their circuit around the ballroom. "Now let's find you a dance partner." She watched the dancers parade past them as if she was the judge at a dog show. "Hmmm. No. No. Definitely not him. Oh, there. Lord Fennimothy is perfect for starters. Leave everything to me."

Josie opened her mouth to remind her chaperone she couldn't dance, but Mrs. Binns had been momentarily distracted from her duties by an old friend. Josie seized the opportunity and escaped into the gallery. The long hallway was deserted and cooler than the ballroom. She immediately felt better.

"You look especially fetching tonight."

Josie spun around to face Deverell. Despite his semitransparent manifestation, the ghost was perfectly dressed for the occasion in dove gray knee breeches and a charcoal waistcoat.

She curtseyed properly and thanked him. Then she grinned. "You don't look so bad yourself."

He bent at the waist, making a leg as they called the formal bow. "Miss Drummond, may I have the honor of this dance?"

To her surprise she wanted to, but she shook her head. "I can't."

"Come, come. If you can walk to the beat of the music, you can do this step. Just follow my lead."

Remembering his pithy comments during her first and only dance lesson, she said, "Only if you promise not to criticize."

He held out his arm and she placed her gloved hand on it. Or technically above his arm because she couldn't actually touch him since he wasn't fully materialized.

At first the steps were simple. He gradually added twists and turns, skips and hops as they danced the length of the gallery and back again. By the time they reached their starting point she was breathless.

"I knew you would prove to be a good dancer simply by the way you carry yourself," he said. "You have an innate sense of rhythm and body movement."

"Thank you," she said. "Of course if helps when you can step *through* your partners toes," she added with a giggle.

"You did not. I would have noticed if you had."

"Well, it wasn't for lack of trying."

"Why do you keep putting yourself down, as your generation would say?"

Josie shrugged. The music changed to a waltz and she stepped back.

"Our set is not over," he said. "When you agree to partner, it is for two dances." He must have realized her problem because he showed her a simple box step and let her practice a few times before holding out his arms.

Her anxiety was for her feet and not proximity to him. She moved into the circle of his arms without hesitation.

After a making a few boxes together, he said, "Close your eyes and feel the music. Now we'll try moving. No, keep your eyes closed so you can't look at your feet."

"No criticism."

"Right-o. Please keep your eyes closed and allow me to guide you. When I want you to move backward, I'll push with my left hand, thusly."

Josie kept making the box with her feet and smoothly transitioned to moving backward.

"And when I want you to dance forward, I will apply light pressure on your back with my right hand. Do you feel that?"

"Yes."

"That is how I would conduct you around obstacles such as other dancers and how I lead you through the steps."

"Like steering a bus."

"If I can't criticize you, then you can't criticize yourself. Promise? Thank you. Now for the turn. Step, slide, and close. That's the way."

Before she knew it they were making wide sweeping turns around the room. Waltzing was pure joy, like floating down a lazy river in slow eddying circles. She could not help but smile.

Suddenly, Deverell was gone. She stumbled to a halt and looked around for the elusive ghost. Instead Dev approached from the far end of the gallery. There was no way she could escape facing him.

"Why do you dance alone when I so eagerly sought to partner you?" Dev asked as he came near.

"I...I was practicing. I don't really know how to dance."

"Your waltzing is as beautiful as you are. You

have an innate sense of rhythm. I knew by the way you carry yourself that you would prove to be a wonderful dancer."

Déjà vu. Josie blinked. He...his ghost had said almost those exact words.

"Miss Drummond, may I have the honor of this dance?"

Danger, danger, the voice in her head screeched. She ignored the warning, raised her arms to the dance position, and stepped into Dev's embrace.

But her recent lessons with Deverell had not prepared her for the amazing sensation of dancing with Dev. Although he held her at a proper distance and they both wore gloves, she felt the warmth of his hand cupping hers, his light touch on her bare back, and the firmness of his bicep beneath the silky fabric of his waistcoat.

Her body temperature ratcheted up a notch due to his nearness. He smelled of soap, bay rum aftershave, and that exotic scent that was his alone. She could have stood just so and listened to the lovely music, but he started the steps of the dance and she followed his lead. Simply at first, almost dancing in place as they synched their body's movements to the tempo, and to each other.

His mischievous grin gave her a moment's warning before he swept her into grand circles as they glided across the floor. Their bodies moved apart and came back together as he swung her out to arm's length and then curled her back into his embrace. More than floating, they were flying in tandem. His smile of pleasure resonated to her toes.

He gathered her close and spun her in a tight, fast turn as the music rose to a crescendo. Joy bubbled up and she threw her head back with laughter.

Then the music stopped.

Yet he did not release her.

Dev stared at the woman in his arms and realized Josie affected him as no one else ever had. A vision of her lying naked on his bed invaded his head and was more intoxicating than the finest brandy. Addicting. Could his light-headedness mean he was falling in love? Breathing became difficult. He felt as if a high-tempered steed had kicked him in the chest. If this was love, he wanted none of it.

He could not deny he wanted this woman as he had no other. But that was merely lust, and that he understood.

Lust was controllable and would prove his salvation. She had played with his passion for long enough. In his experience a display of unrestrained ardor would result in a young miss scurrying for the protection of her chaperone. She would have to leave him because he knew he had not the strength to send her away, even to save himself.

He tightened his embrace and kissed her with the fierce need burning his soul.

But Josie was not the usual Regency miss. She responded with equal ardor, kissing him back, pulling him closer still. Flame meeting fire. She folded her arms around his neck and moaned into his mouth. He slid his hand lower and cupped her derriere. She ground her hips against his rock hard erection.

Breathless, he lifted his head. They could not make love in the middle of the gallery. He looked around and forced his brain to function. Where was the nearest place of privacy?

A new vision wormed its way into his head. Josie with a babe at her breast. The instantaneous surge of pride was the scariest thing he had ever experienced, including his first duel. His body, however, responded to the image with intensified desire.

Josie drew in a deep breath, the extra oxygen helping to clear her senses. She couldn't possibly be falling in love with a man from the past, could she?

Damn ghost and his crazy scheme had brought her to an impossible situation. Taking the first step backward, away from Dev, was the hardest thing she had ever done, but she knew that if she stayed, she would sob out her love and despair.

"I have to go," she croaked out. The stark truth in more ways than one. She turned away. As she hurried back to the ballroom and the relative safety of the crowd, she refused to allow herself a final look back.

Dev watched her scurry away and forced himself not to follow as instinct prodded him to do. He credited frustrated lust as the cause of the impulse, refusing to entertain the other outrageous notion that persistently tried to surface. He, too, left the gallery, but not to return to the dancing. Not yet. Not with his desire still obvious. He needed a few moments to collect his thoughts. And a cold shower to calm his raging libido.

Josie looked for her chaperone, intending to tell her she had a headache and wanted to retire to her room. Why torture herself by watching Dev waltz with other women, hold them in his arms? She would have to return downstairs in time for the séance, of course, and she would see him there. She stifled a sob. If she was lucky, Dev would be having so much fun dancing he wouldn't bother to come. Either way, pain was inevitable.

She just wanted to go home.

Unfortunately, she ran into Estelle before she could find Mrs. Binns.

"Well, well, well. If it isn't the belle of the ball."

Josie looked over her shoulder, but no one else seemed near.

"No need to play coy with me," Estelle said with a snide smile. She played with the handle of her punch cup. "It appears I underestimated you."

"I doubt it will keep you awake at night."

"Your name is on everyone's lips. They are already calling you an original. Mrs. Binns is *in alt*."

Josie had never heard the term *in alt* before, but she refused to ask Estelle for a definition and assumed by her usage and displeased expression she meant Mrs. Binns was thrilled.

"Lady Jersey has all but guaranteed you will be at the first assembly of the season at Almack's," Estelle said with a scowl.

Josie snorted. She didn't have time to discuss theoretical impossibilities with the malicious bitch. "Whatever. Have you seen Mrs. Binns? No? Fine." She started to walk on by, but Estelle blocked her path.

"Our conversation is not over."

Josie crossed her arms. She decided not to knock the other woman into the middle of next week, but only because she wasn't worth the effort.

"I wanted to wish you enjoyment of your brief success," Estelle said.

"Really?"

"Yes." Estelle heaved a dramatic sigh. "Adoration is brief among the *ton*. Once everyone learns you are the cause of a duel, your fleeting fame will fade into infamy."

"Impressive alliteration, but you have the facts wrong. There will be no...what do you mean I'm the cause?"

"Lord Waite challenged Lord Hargrave to a duel over some unspecified insult to you. Pistols at dawn."

"What?" She hadn't changed history after all. That's why Deverell still felt the bullet in his heart.

Estelle continued speaking even though Josie paid her little heed. "Without specific details, wild stories will abound and word will pass like wildfire. Soon everyone will know. Tonight, most likely."

With Estelle's help, no doubt. "Don't be so quick to spread tales or you may be named a gossipy fool," Josie warned the other woman. "There will be no duel, especially not one over me." She wasn't sure how she would stop it, but she would.

Mrs. Binns came up to them, positively glowing and with a wide smile. "Such a wonderful party."

"Have you seen Lord Waite?" Josie asked her.

"Why, no. Oddly enough, I..."

"I need to speak to him immediately. Hey!" She jumped back too late. Estelle emptied her cup of punch down the front of Josie's dress.

"Oh my, I am so sorry."

"You did that on purpose."

"Such a terrible accident," Estelle continued, ignoring Josie's accusation. "Someone must have bumped my arm. You should put some cold water on that stain before your gown is ruined."

Josie curled her fingers into a fist.

Fortunately for Estelle's nose, Mrs. Binns took Josie's arm and steered her toward the door.

Dora met them at the bottom of the stairs. "I saw everything," she said. "That...that witch did it on purpose."

"I know," Josie said.

"Don't you worry. I'll have it cleaned up in no time," the maid assured her.

As she started up the steps, Josie turned to Mrs. Binns. "No need for you to miss any of the ball."

"That's all right."

"No. I insist you go back and enjoy yourself."

"Well, I did want to speak to Lady Georgina, and she usually retires before the supper."

"Fine. You do that and I'll join you later," Josie said even though she had no intention of coming back to the ball before the séance. Inspiration had hit her during the short walk. She had a plan for stopping the duel, but she needed to think it through first. "We'll be back in no time. Isn't that right, Dora?"

The maid nodded, glancing warily at her mistress. Mrs. Binns, however, accepted the ruse and returned to the ballroom.

"What are you up to?" Dora asked, as they walked up the stairs.

"Nothing. Nothing at all," Josie lied.

Dora left the room with the damaged ball gown. Josie tied the belt of her dressing gown and stepped from behind the screen. Deverell sat in the chair by the window.

"Did you hear what Estelle said?" she asked. "Dev has challenged Hargrave to a duel."

"One cannot simply let an insult pass without..."

"But the insult was to me, not him."

"So you intend to challenge him to a duel yourself? A fencing match with knitting needles? Fisticuffs in petticoats?"

"Don't be patronizing. I don't want there to be any duel at all. And if I choose not to retaliate, that should be the end of the matter. Insult to me equals my decision to act or not. Get it?"

"Dev is the master of the house where you are a guest, and therefore he is responsible for your well-being and safety."

"I'm safe. I'm well. An insult is not worthy of a duel. He could be shot. You could be shot. Because of some overblown sense of responsibility?"

Deverell shrugged. "I hate to say I told you so."

"No, you don't. You relish saying it. Well, in this case I won't let you be right. I will stop this ridiculous duel."

"How?"

"Dueling is illegal. I'll get the cops or whatever you call them from the nearest town to stop it."

"A blind eye is turned to matters of honor. And Dev owns the nearest town. The sheriff works for him."

"Then I'll talk Dev out of it."

"Not bloody likely. The challenge has been given. If he backed out now, he would never be able to show his face in society again."

"A fate worse than death?"

"There are such universal truths, you know. There are fates worse than death." With that cryptic comment, he disappeared.

Sinking into the chair he'd vacated, she put her chin in her hands. Her plan was to meet Dev after the séance according to the terms of the deal and talk him out of the duel. She would still try, but if he was anything like the ghost there was little hope of changing his mind. She needed a plan B.

What else could she do? How far was she willing to go?

Her gown had been saved thanks to the housekeeper's secret cleansing formula, but Josie didn't return downstairs until minutes before the séance was scheduled to begin. Wearing the simplest dress Dora deemed appropriate for evening, Josie paused at the head of the stairs. Her mind was made up and she was committed to her plan, but she would need strength to pull it off.

"I don't like this," Dora said. "Not one bit."

"But you'll do as I asked?"

The maid hesitated before she nodded. "Oh, miss. Be careful."

Josie ran down the stairs and paused to raise her chin and paste a smile on her face before entering the library.

"There you are, my dear." Mrs. Binns rushed over and draped the sash of charms around Josie's neck.

"I heard about your gown," Honoria said. "I am so sorry your evening was ruined."

"Such a terrible accident," Estelle added, her pitying expression unable to mask the malevolent glee in her eyes.

Josie shrugged, refusing to give Estelle the satisfaction of knowing just how much she'd upset her. Not with the attempt to ruin the ball gown, but with the news of the duel. "No sense crying over spilled punch. Shall we start the séance?"

"We're waiting for Dev," Estelle said.

"What about me?" Dev asked as he entered the library at the stroke of the hour.

Estelle looped her arm through his and drew him into the room. "Only that we would not start without you."

"I was afraid you had decided not to attend," Honoria said.

"What? And miss out on such a promising event?" He took a folded slip of paper from his vest pocket. "In fact, I have a question regarding a deal I recently made. I want to know if the party involved will hold up the other end of the bargain."

Josie rolled her eyes at his not-so-subtle reminder.

"I am sure Amanu will be happy to help with your business decisions, won't he, Madame?"

"Of course he will," Estelle answered for her friend.

As before, the gypsy was dressed in her voluminous robes and lavish turban that revealed only the golden mask. She sat on the thronelike chair. "We can begin."

Dev seated each woman in turn, surreptitiously passing Josie a note in the process. She opened it in her lap and glanced down at the bold handwriting.

The door at the end of the gallery opens onto the garden path.

Innocuous words to anyone else.

"You may light the Candle of Omniscience," Madame intoned.

Repeating the procedure of the previous séance, the footman put out the lamps and left the room. Josie put her hands on the table as directed, and when the slips of paper were placed in the brass bowl and set afire, she added Dev's note.

The lone candle sputtered and flared. Madame X chanted in tongues and moaned and rocked. "Hear me, Amanu. I command you to come forward and do my bidding."

"Yes, my queen," the spirit guide answered. "Speak the beckoning enchantment and I will appear."

Madame mumbled and fell forward onto the table in a trance. In a few moments the glowing specter rose behind her chair.

Josie watched closely and saw a slight hitch in his rising as the man stepped up onto the door of the chair's secret cabinet. Funny how you saw things differently once you knew how they were done. At least she knew he wasn't seven feet tall. She hoped her traps would provide additional information about how the man got into the locked room.

"There is great unrest among the spirits you seek," Amanu said. "They are angry because you do not listen to their advice."

"Daniel is upset with me?" Honoria asked in a shaky voice. "Tell him not to be angry. Tell him..."

"The spirits are not your servants. I am not your servant. If you do not intend to heed the spirits' advice, I will not bother to come again."

"No, please," Honoria cried. "I will. I will. Please tell Daniel I will do everything he wants me to do."

"Now, Mother, I think..."

"Hush, Dev. I cannot lose this last link with your father."

"You must not allow the unbelievers into my presence again," Amanu said. "The spirits are hurt by skepticism."

"I won't. I promise. Is Percy there, too?"

"That is all I can say for now." The specter folded his arms, bowed his head, and sank away from sight. The candle sputtered and the table shook. They waited.

Moments later Madame X sat up. "You may blow out the candle and light the lamps," she said in a weak voice.

"He was a bit bold for a spirit, don't you think?" Mrs. Binns said.

Estelle shot her a disgusted glare and rushed to help her friend. "This session has been especially hard on Madame. I must get her to our room immediately."

After they left, Dev said to his mother, "These séances are getting out of hand. You must see..."

"What I see," Honoria said, turning to her son with tears in her eyes, "is that you are one of the unbelievers. I cannot ban you from any function in your house, but I would appreciate it if you would refrain from hurting your father's spirit again."

"Madame X is..."

"Perhaps we will continue this discussion another time. Right now I have duties that require my immediate attention. As do you."

Dev bowed his acquiescence.

"The supper dance will be called soon," she reminded him. With that, Honoria left.

"May I escort you back to the ball?" Dev said, offering his arm to the elder of the two.

"Yes, thank you," Mrs. Binns said, laying her fingertips on his forearm.

"No, thank you," Josie said. "Dora is waiting with my repaired ball gown," she explained to Mrs. Binns. The truth, if not the whole truth. "You go on. Dora will take care of me."

As if he understood her plan, Dev placed his hand over Mrs. Binns's to prevent her from pulling away. "Then I will see you later," he said.

"You can count on it," Josie answered.

Sixteen

EV PACED THE GARDEN, SECOND-GUESSING his decision to keep his appointment with Josie. She disturbed his equilibrium, made him think about things he had long ago decided were not for him. Marriage. Children. His plan did not include becoming leg-shackled to one woman so early in his life.

Especially that woman. She challenged his preconceived notions of the perfect female. Josie was neither meek nor mild, and definitely not demure or unassuming, sedate, modest, or even proper. She had none of the expected talents. Couldn't paint or play the pianoforte. Although he must admit she danced beautifully.

What was dancing when the woman was too intelligent, argumentative, aggravating, and outspoken? She was also passionate and endlessly fascinating. He should be going to London instead of subjecting himself to self-torture.

But she was trying to prove Madame X was a fraud, and he had just witnessed the control the gypsy had over his mother. If he didn't do something, there was no telling where that would lead. And Josie, for some unknown reason, seemed to have a plan for accomplishing exactly what he needed to do.

He would just have to maintain a distance from her. No romance in the garden as he'd originally planned. No moonlit kisses. Definitely, no kissing. One touch of her lips and he would be lost. Just get the information from her and then get the hell out of there.

Josie approached the moon garden with trepidation. If she couldn't talk Dev out of the duel, was she willing to proceed with the rest of the plan?

Willing? Ha! Eager *was a better word.*

Okay, she admitted she'd had her dreams of meeting him in the garden and making love. But she'd always been able to distinguish fact from fiction and maintain a certain amount of personal dignity. However, she'd recently stumbled on one of those universal truths, one Deverell had never mentioned. *When the right man beckons, any woman is a one-night-stand kind of girl.*

And if in the process of living out her fantasy she happened to keep him from attending his dawn appointment, so much the better. Even if her motivation wasn't noble, the end would be. At least she would return home knowing she'd saved his life.

Her steps faltered. Home. How would she live the rest of her life without him? Wouldn't she be better off not making love? Shouldn't she protect her heart? No. If all she had was this one night, then she would make enough memories to last her a lifetime.

She opened the door at the end of the gallery and stepped into the darkness with firm resolve. The occasional shuttered lantern barely illuminated the rose arbor. Her eyes adjusted to the dim light as she followed the path to her right. One foot in front of the other.

When she reached the end of the darkened tunnel, the garden itself seemed brilliant. All the white flowers glowed in the moonlight, giving the enclosed area a fairy-tale ambience. Dev waited in the far corner, seated on a white marble bench near a seashell fountain. She ran the rest of the way.

He stood as soon as he saw her. "Thank you for being on time. Promptness is often underrated, but I consider it a virtue."

Josie skidded to a halt. Not exactly the welcome she'd anticipated. Perhaps her fantasy was just that after all. "Uh, sure."

"Please have a seat."

"I think I'd rather stand."

"Would you care for a tour? I shall endeavor to answer any of your questions. In a moon garden the plants are specifically chosen for white-colored blooms that remain open at night and for their scent."

What was wrong with him? She hadn't come to the garden for a freaking tour. Could he have meant literally a walk in the garden? Had she misunderstood his intent? No, something had changed. Perhaps he was thinking about the duel and regretting his rash action. "Dev," she said, reaching for his arm.

As if he did not see her hand, he turned and pointed to a flowering bush. "These roses are not particularly attractive, but the scent is heavenly." He stepped to his left, putting the bench between them, before indicating another plant. "This..."

"I don't care about the flowers. We need to talk."

He faced her with a solemn expression. "I agree."

"I was quite disturbed earlier this evening." That was a bit of an understatement. She'd been devastated when she'd heard about the duel. She would try to talk him out of it, but if that didn't work... "Very disturbed," she added for good measure.

"As was I."

"It must be stopped. I can't allow..."

"I am in absolute agreement."

Well, that was easy enough. Josie suppressed a sigh of disappointment.

"Things have gone beyond what is reasonable," Dev continued. "The problem is, how do I stop it? I was hoping you..."

"Me? I should think you would know more about this than I!"

"You're the one with all the strings and...things."

"What in the world are you talking about?"

"Your trap...things." He paused and gave her a quizzical look. "Why? What are you talking about?"

"The duel. I came to talk you out of..."

"Oh, that." He waved off her concern in a motion the ghost had used many times. "Closed issue. I will not discuss it further."

At least that was the response she'd expected. "Then what were you...the traps. You were talking about the séances."

"Of course."

"And for some reason you no longer believe they are a harmless diversion and you want them stopped."

"Were you not there when that so-called spirit guide manipulated my mother? Now I'm essentially banned from any future proceedings, so I won't even know what that...that..."

"Person. An ordinary man. Actually, a rather short ordinary man."

"Be that as it may, I won't know what that person is telling Mother to do and therefore will not be able to defend against it...him."

"Hopefully my traps will give us enough information..."

"Let's go check them now." He reached for her hand but quickly pulled back.

"What is wrong? That's twice you jumped away rather than touch me. Am I suddenly a leper?"

Dev ran his finger around his collar. "I am doing my best to maintain a respectful distance."

"Why?"

He looked at her as if she was crazy. "Because you are a guest in..."

"Oh, don't treat me like a fool. Why now? You haven't been *respectful* from the moment we met."

The corners of his mouth twitched. "I've seen the error of my ways."

"Try again."

"Because I've realized you are deserving of my respect."

She knew that wasn't the reason either, but if she called it bullshit, she'd be admitting de facto she wasn't worthy. Score one for Dev in the verbal battle. She nodded her defeat, but one skirmish did not win the war. "If you want the information on the séance, it will cost you."

He raised an eyebrow.

"I'm here because we made a deal. I have another to propose."

"I can tell you the answer before I hear the terms. Since you have an interest in exposing the gypsy as a fraud, I need only wait until you do so and I will have what I want. At no cost."

Rats. He was right again.

She sat on the nearby bench. If she wanted to keep him occupied past dawn, she would have to try another tack. Never having done anything like this before was a distinct disadvantage. What was it women of his time did? Pretend to faint and fall into his arms? Sprain an ankle so he would have to carry her inside? She doubted she could pull off either convincingly. Better to approach the problem head-on.

"I came here expecting you to try to take advantage of me. Which would have made matters so much easier since I have no idea how to seduce you."

"You what?"

"I want you, and I thought you wanted me."

"I do, but..."

"Then what's the problem?"

"It's just not done. We cannot simply..."

"Hop into bed together? Of course we can. Look, I'll be leaving soon, probably tomorrow and..."

"Why are you leaving?"

Josie took a deep breath and decided not to tell the truth. "I've had word that my father is ill..."

"I thought you father was dead?"

Oops. What did she expect? She was making the story up on the fly. "I meant to say my stepfather is ill and I must return home immediately. Therefore tonight is the only chance I'll have to be with you. No strings attached. No expectations of the future. Purely enjoying the pleasure of each other's company. How's that for a deal, Lord Waite?"

"If something sounds too good to be true, it usually is." He paused. "However, I must admit I am intrigued."

"Since we're discussing this like two modern adults, I do need to make sure you don't have any sexually transmitted diseases. I hear syphilis and..."

"I assure you I am disease free."

"Well, that's my only concern." She slapped her knees and stood. "How do we start?" She stepped toward him.

"Whoa." He held up his hand. "Aren't you concerned at all about your virginity?"

"I'm not a virgin," she admitted. At his shocked expression she explained, "Where I live, virginity is not prized as it is here."

"Ah! You are a freethinker, a follower of the free love doctrine. I have read William Blake, and also

Percy Bysshe Shelley's *Queen Mab*. His recent *On Love* was quite interesting, although I can't say I agree with his views." But it did allow him to see her in a different light.

"If we're going to discuss philosophy all night, I vote for a comfortable chair and a bottle of your best brandy."

Dev chuckled. "Perhaps another time. Oh, right, there will be no other time."

"It's now or never."

And he'd be crazy to let a stray, impossible vision rob him of the pleasure she promised. "I'm intrigued. How did you intend to seduce me?"

Josie shrugged. "I guess I was just going to play it by ear."

"No, no, no. A proper seduction takes thought and planning."

"Really. How would you do it?"

"First you must choose a romantic setting."

"A moonlit garden."

"Music provides a relaxing atmosphere."

She cocked her head to listen to the soft echoes from the ballroom. "Done."

"I would provide wine and foods with aphro-disiac properties. I would select the choicest bits and hand-feed them to you, my fingertips lingering on your lips."

"We'll have to skip that part."

"Too bad. It can be quite sensual."

She shook out her fan and cooled the blush on her cheeks. "What would you do next? In this hypothetical seduction."

"Hmmm. That would depend on how receptive you...the woman is to my attentions. Possibly a dance would follow. A waltz, of course. A private waltz can be...erotic."

Josie cleared her throat. "We've...a...done that."

"Not this way." He removed his gloves, tossed them on the bench, and stretched out his hand. "May I have the pleasure of this dance?"

She followed suit, rolling down her elbow-length gloves and awkwardly yanking them off. She stepped into the circle of his arms. "I can't see what difference...oh." If his hands were warm before, now they were hot, hot, hot.

"The trick is to remember to keep your feet moving." He led her into the simple box step. Instead of holding her at arm's length, he pulled her close.

He leaned back to look at her face. "You are not wearing a corset."

"I don't care for them."

"Too bad. I rather enjoy taking off a woman's corset. Sort of like unwrapping a Christmas present."

"This way is quicker."

"My sweet little adventuress." He leaned over to whisper in her ear. "I never said I was interested in quick."

He kissed the spot behind her ear, and she wrapped her arm around his neck. He slid his right hand down her back, branding her with his fingers. Her thighs tingled. He sucked in her earlobe, and she let go of his other hand to run her fingers through his hair. She tipped her head to the side and leaned back to allow him better access as he nibbled, and licked, and nipped the line of her jaw.

His lips seared hers with a fiery kiss. Her knees buckled, but he held her in place with one arm around her back and the other hand cupping her derriere.

"I can't dance when you do that," she said. The words came out in a breathy whisper.

He untangled their bodies, set her on her feet at arm's length, and cupped her face in his hands. "Are you sure you want to continue?"

She returned his intense gaze. "I want to make love with you. Show me," she said, although even she wasn't exactly sure what she meant.

Still he did not move. "Whatever has gone before, for either one of us, is not important. This is our first time because it is our first time together."

"Do you say that to all..."

"No. Only you." He dropped his hands and turned away. "Forget it. Silly thing to say."

She walked round him, and when he would not look her in the eye, she took his face in her hands. "I think it was the perfect thing to say." She tipped her head to the side and smiled shyly up at him. "Good Sir, it is my first time. Please forgive my mistakes."

He gathered her into a gentle hug and kissed her forehead. "There is nothing to forgive. The mistake is mine. My pride is at fault. I wanted you to forget any other man as I have forgotten all other women."

"Done."

He released her and stepped back. "That easily?"

"Well, there weren't that many, and all were

unremarkable." She already knew she would never forget him. "I expect you will be quite different."

"Is that a challenge to make this a memorable night?"

"If you wish to take it that way." She grinned. "So far it's been pretty good."

"Pretty good? I see I shall have to try harder. No pun intended."

She raised her eyebrows. "I'm game."

"I presume that means you are ready to begin again."

"It means I'm ready for anything."

He ran a finger from her ear down her shoulder and under her puffed sleeve. "I think the first step in this new dance is to be rid of some excess clothing."

"Out here in the open?" she squeaked out, looking up at the bank of windows above them.

"This is a very private garden. Only visible from my suite."

She counted the windows but could not remember how many she'd observed in his rooms. She would have to trust him. Easier said than done. She looked deep into his eyes. And reached behind her back to untie the sash of her dress, letting the loose silk hang free. She had specifically chosen the style for its generous cut.

When she flipped the ribbon away, his eyes widened and appeared to darken to a slate gray. Emboldened by his appreciative gaze, she slowly raised the skirt of her gown, finally pulling it over her head and throwing it over her shoulder with a flourish. His charcoal gaze never left hers.

She lifted her knee to untie a garter but decided against balancing on one leg like a flamingo. She turned toward the bench. Dev ripped off his coat and spread it over the marble. "It's about time you took something off," she said as she sat. She crossed her legs and leaned back on her hands. "Please continue."

He tore off his vest and clawed at his elaborately knotted cravat, cursing Carson under his breath.

"Come here." She sat up and patted the bench next to her. "Let me help you."

She worked at the series of knots, hampered by him kissing her wrist, her arm, her shoulder, her neck. Finally she took his chin and pointed it over her head. "Unless you want to wear this all night, you'll sit still."

"You are asking the impossible."

"Only for a moment." She freed the linen and started undoing his shirt, fumbling with the fancy studs.

"I've got that," he said. He stood and ripped the soft lawn fabric apart, golden studs popping apart and flying in all directions. After discarding his shirt, he knelt beside the bench. Slowly he slid the hem of her chemise up her thigh, revealing the tops of her silk stockings tied with red ribbon garters. "Ah, yes," he said, pulling the bow undone. "Merry Christmas."

She leaned back on her hands again and straightened one leg. Holding her ankle up with one hand, he used the other hand and his teeth to untie the ribbon. He rolled down the silk, kissing each inch of her skin as it was bared. Although she liked watching him, the strain on her neck proved too much and she let her head fall back. Somehow that intensified the sensations, and she closed her eyes. By the time he repeated the slow process on her other leg, her breathing was shallow. When he did not release her foot, she struggled to a sitting position.

"No one has ever kissed my feet before," she panted.

He grinned up at her. "One of the wonders of a woman's body is that every part can be responsive to stimulation if treated properly." He massaged her foot while kissing her toes, and she groaned in pleasure.

"Is a man so different?"

"We are simple creatures. Easily aroused."

She pulled her foot free and slid to her knees in front of him. "Show me how to please you."

"Everything about you pleases me."

The sincerity in his voice gave her a warm glow. She ran her hands up his arms, feeling the muscles quiver under her touch. "Then tell me what gives you pleasure."

"Pleasing you gives me pleasure."

She blew out a breath and sat back on her heels. "Lovely sentiment but not very helpful. I'm looking for some direction here."

"You want me to tell you what to do?"

"Why not? To sort of get the ball rolling."

"I rather thought we were rolling along quite nicely."

"Oh, I'm not criticizing, believe me. But I'd like to participate, not just lie back passively enjoying your attention. Although that was very nice."

"What if I enjoy lavishing attention on you?"

"Come on. This is a getting-to-know-you phase. It'll be fun. You ask me to do something to you, and then I'll ask you to do something to me. You're not into anything kinky, are you?"

"Kinky?"

"You know, whips and chains, that sort of thing."

He shook his head. "I am not *into* inflicting pain if that is what you mean." He chuckled. "I do have a few toys we both may find pleasurable."

"Hmmm. Maybe later. Let's keep it simple for now." She laid her hands on her knees. "Okay, you go first. What do you want me to do?"

"If you are determined to play this game... Very well, I want you to take off your chemise."

She rose up on her knees and pulled the sliplike undergarment over her head. She wore nothing else.

Dev sucked in his breath. He clenched his fists on his knees, leaned his head back, and closed his eyes. "I don't think I can do this."

"Oh, no you don't. You can't quit when it's my turn." She debated with herself for a moment. Her nipples had puckered in the cool night air, begging for his attention. But it was hours until dawn, and she wanted to draw this out as long as possible. "I want... to see you naked."

After a moment, he stood. He watched her watching him as he kicked off his dancing shoes, undid the knee buckles of his breeches, and peeled off his stockings. He hesitated with his hands on the waist ties, his erection bulging the flap of his trousers.

"I have never done this before," he said. "I mean not like this. As if I were on a stage and you the audience. It's a bit disconcerting." He took a deep breath, undid the ties, dropped his pants, and kicked them aside. When he dared look at her, her smile of appreciation appeased his anxiety. She was not appalled by his size.

"You are like the statue of a Greek god...only bigger." And right in front of her face. She licked her suddenly dry lips. Size might not matter but...ohmigod. Dampness pooled between her thighs. She reached out but stopped herself. "Your turn."

"Touch me. Please."

Josie ran her fingers along the length of his penis from base to tip and back, reveling in the feel of silk over steel, but more so enjoying his reaction to her touch. She wrapped both hands around his shaft and an idea occurred to her. She kept her hands moving while she turned it over in her mind.

She'd given only one blow job before, and it had been a disaster involving lots of gagging and spitting. But as she fondled him so close to her face, she truly wanted to take him into her mouth. When she kissed and licked the tip, he moaned and called her name. When she took it in her mouth, his thighs quivered and he locked his knees to remain standing. He ran his fingers through her hair but thankfully didn't push on her head or shove himself in deeper. She found the small opening on his penis with her tongue and tasted his salty essence.

He started to back away and she grabbed his balls to hold him in place.

"You must stop, Josie-love, or I will lose myself."

She paused her ministrations long enough to mutter, "Go ahead." She both increased and varied the pressure and speed of her hand up and down his shaft, tickled his balls, and swirled her tongue over and around the tip. When she sucked him hard to draw him in, he suddenly reached down and pulled her up into his arms.

He buried his face in her neck and muttered her name over and over as his entire body shook with his release. His penis throbbed between them, and her stomach was quickly bathed in spurts of warm liquid. She held him tight and felt, surprisingly, powerful.

Dev released her only to cup her face in his hands. "What can I say other than thank you?"

She grinned up at him. "The word *wow* comes to mind."

"Wow!" he shouted to the sky. Then he kissed her, long and slow, his lips gentle. "Your turn," he whispered against her lips.

She opened her eyes and drew her head back. "No. Yours. If you recall, I'm the one who told you to go ahead. So it's your turn again."

"Hmmm."

"I told you this would be fun. What do you want me to do?"

"Something you said earlier gave me an idea."

"Not the whips and chains?"

"No. I would never want to hurt you or mar your beautiful skin. I'm thinking more along the lines of Greek statues."

He picked her up and she squealed in surprise.

He kicked his coat out of the way and stood her on the marble bench. "You are now a stone goddess and must hold the pose as long as you can, no matter what I do."

Josie did not feel really comfortable as he watched her try out several poses. "Don't I need an urn or something?"

"You are perfect as you are."

She crossed her arms and stuck out her bottom lip.

"Can I be of assistance?"

"Where *does* a goddess put her hands?"

With gentle pressure he posed her, left hand palm out at the small of her back and her right hand reaching over her head to the back of her neck. He stepped back to admire his work and then returned to tip her head down a bit and lift her left knee a few inches so she balanced that foot on her toes. "Are you comfortable?"

"Yeah, sure. Not exactly natural. Who stands like this? Give me a long-handled brush and a bar of soap and I could be titled Goddess Washes Her Back."

He snapped his fingers and moved out of her sight. She heard splashing in the corner fountain.

"What are you doing?"

"Don't move. I'll be right back."

She sighed. Her right arm was already feeling the strain. "Please hurry."

He returned with his shirt, now soaking wet, held against his chest. "I'm afraid this will be quite cool despite me trying to warm it up." He used the material to wash off her stomach, causing her muscles to clench and her nipples to pucker. He pitched the sodden shirt into the bushes. "Now you are perfect."

He circled the bench to view her from all angles. She really was perfect, and his hands itched to touch her. He started at her left elbow, where she could see his hands and not be startled. From there he molded his hands down her back to her knees and back to the other arm. "If I were a sculptor, I would make you just as you are."

"Didn't Pygmalion come to a bad end?"

"No. Aphrodite took pity on him and brought the ivory statue to life as Galatea. They married and had a son."

He moved around to face her and cupped her breasts. He rubbed his thumbs over the distended nipples, and it took all her willpower to ignore the electricity tingling to her toes.

She swallowed. "I heard of a guy who practiced his technique on the breasts of a statue so much that when he touched a real woman he was horrified by the squishiness." She wasn't sixteen anymore and hoped her breasts had not succumbed too much to the effects of gravity. Without the corset, she no longer had cleavage.

"Your breasts are lovely," he said as he fondled them. "See how they fit my hands perfectly." He leaned forward and ran the tip of his tongue around one nipple and then the other. "And so responsive."

She could not hold back a little mewl of enjoyment. Her entire body shivered with her effort to stay still.

Stepping to one side, he wrapped one arm around her back, resting his hand on her hip. He took one breast into his mouth and at the same time ran his free hand down her stomach; he combed through the curls between her legs, his finger finding her clit.

She cried out at the intense bolt of pleasure. As much as she didn't want him to stop, her legs would no longer support her. He did not let her fall, using his body to brace her stance, but neither did he stop the manipulations of his hand.

Slowly and gently he lowered her until she lay on the bench. The cool marble against her back was a stark contrast to the heat between her legs. He knelt beside her.

Tracing her aureole with his tongue, he asked, "Do you like this?" his breath against her wet nipple yet another pleasurable sensation.

"Yes. You know I do." She threaded her fingers through his hair and braced herself with her other hand on the edge of the bench.

He chuckled and slid a finger inside her, leaving his thumb to circle her clit. She raised her knees higher and shifted her hips in response.

"And does this give you pleasure?" he asked.

"Yes," she panted out, near to losing all rational thought. She closed her eyes. Her hips followed the rhythm of his hand. "Yes, yes, yes," she chanted, unable to find any other words to encourage him, to demand more.

He trailed a line of kisses down her stomach, circled her belly button with his tongue, and then drifted lower and lower.

She was barely aware of him shifting position until his head moved out of reach of her hand. He paused in his ministrations long enough to slide her bottom down to the end of the bench and raise her legs up over his shoulders. She made an extreme effort and curled up on her elbows to look at him.

"I want you inside me."

"Not yet, Josie-love. My turn. And I want to send you to the stars."

"Dev, I…"

"My turn," he reminded her as he lowered his head.

His hands and his lips and his oh-so-talented tongue sent her soaring. She cried out his name as she left the earth.

When she came back to herself, she sat cuddled in his lap. She put her arms around his neck and kissed him. "Thank you," she whispered.

"I was hoping for a wow."

"I believe you got that when I screamed your name."

"Is that what that was?" he asked, looking pleased with himself. "Are you recovered?"

"I feel fantastic."

"Good. Because it's your turn."

"Hmmm. I want to see your bed. I heard it's monstrous."

Seventeen

D EV STOOD IN THE MIDDLE OF THE MOON garden, holding Josie in his arms. When he'd started thinking about the process needed to get her to his bedroom, other thoughts intruded despite the naked woman in his arms. The key to the secret door was in the pocket of his coat, the one he'd kicked aside earlier and had no idea where it landed. Plus they would have to use the rose arbor walkway, usually private, but he'd left the entrance from the gallery unlocked for Josie to use.

He'd hate to meet a stray guest. Not that he had any concern for himself, but Josie would be mortified.

"Um, my dear, as much as I would like to carry you off to my lair..."

"I'm quite heavy, I..."

"You are light as a feather. However, before we leave the garden, perhaps clothing would be a wise precaution." He slid her to her feet. "Much to my dismay."

"Last one dressed is a rotten egg."

"First one gets an extra turn."

Like giggling children at an Easter egg hunt, they scrambled around gathering the bits of their ensembles that had been flung hither and yon. The process was complicated by their competitive natures, which meant if one grabbed a piece belonging to the other, it got tossed even farther away.

She found and slipped on her chemise. She picked up his cravat, now simply a long length of linen. "You're not putting this thing back on. Too hard to undo." She wrapped it around herself like a shawl.

She found her dress and her gloves, which were now wadded-up balls. She found one shoe under the fragrant climbing rosebush and the other near the fountain. Her red ribbon garters were both next to the bench, somewhat trampled, but still usable. One stocking, however, was missing.

When she turned to Dev he had donned most of his clothes. Shoes without stockings. His white satin breeches were stark against his bare legs. His vest covered his flat stomach but, of course, he wore no shirt because it was soaking wet. His waistcoat was rumpled, and he had tied one of her stockings around his neck as a cravat.

"That's cheating," she said.

"Isn't that a bit of the pot chiding the kettle," he said with a significant glance at his cravat draped over her arms.

"I had the best intentions. I didn't want to..."

"Not relevant."

Frustrated by her lack of a retort, and because she hated to lose, she threw her balled-up gloves at him.

He easily caught the gloves and pocketed them. "I declare myself winner by default."

"Fine. After I get to see your bed, you have two turns."

He bowed formally and offered his arm.

Instead she handed him her sash and presented her back. "I can't tie it myself."

He wrapped it around her, taking the opportunity to bestow kisses along her shoulder and the back of her neck.

"What is taking so long?"

"I have had more practice at undressing a woman than I have had acting the lady's maid. I would not want to create a knot that is impossible to undo. Ah, finished."

She turned and he again offered his arm.

They left the garden at a regal pace totally at odds with their ragtag appearance.

"If I had won," she said as she climbed the winding stairway, "I would have chosen a long hot shower as my turn."

"I will take that suggestion under consideration; however, the operative word *hot* depends on whether Carson banked the coals properly before leaving."

She stopped and leaned over the curved railing to look down at him. "You gave him the night off? Quite sure of yourself, weren't you? What if I'd not kept the bargain?"

"Then I would have spent a lonely vigil in a beautiful garden."

"Ha!" She continued climbing. "You would

have been back on the dance floor within twenty minutes."

"You wound me. I would have waited at least an hour for you."

"Sure." She reached the landing and paused at the locked door to his suite.

"Of course, knowing what I know now," he said as he caught up with her. He gathered her in his arms for a heady kiss. "I would have waited all night."

He pushed the door open and escorted her through the opulent receiving room to the long hall. "The bedroom is straight ahead. I'll check on the hot water."

She continued down the hall. Visible through the opening was a fireplace flanked by two comfortable-looking chairs. The table between them had been set with a platter of assorted fruit and cheeses, and another of fancy sweets. A crystal decanter and two glasses sat ready.

The blue of the receiving room was echoed but softened several shades and used as an accent against a soothing slate and white color scheme. Where gold had been overused in the other room, in the bedroom judicious touches of silver added shimmer and reflected both the firelight and the low-flame night lamps.

As she stepped into the room the bulk of the area to her left came into her line of sight. The huge bed dominated the large space. Massive posters anchored the corners of a mattress that had to be fifteen feet across and ten feet long. Steps provided access to the surface a full four feet off the floor. Dozens of pillows softened the elaborately carved headboard. Slate and silver damask bed curtains hung ready to make the bed a private sanctuary or block out the light coming from the wall of windows that had surprisingly been left bare of the usual complicated window dressings of the time.

She wandered to the windows and saw that this room also had a view of the moon garden.

"I like to wake to the morning light," he said.

She turned to face him. This was the same handsome man she'd played with in the garden, but in this setting she recognized the wide gulf between them. He lived every day on a scale she could only imagine. What was plain old Josie Drummond doing in a place like this? She swallowed. "I think it's lovely."

Sensing her unease, he leaned against the doorjamb, giving her plenty of space and time to adjust. "A glass of wine?"

"Ah, sure."

He took his time pouring and crossing the room to hand her the glass. "What shall we drink to?" When she didn't respond, he added, "I think the traditional *long life* is a bit prosaic for the situation, don't you? Shall we instead drink to a long night?"

His inadvertent reminder of why she had come in the first place was the kick in the pants she needed. If she was going to keep him past his dawn appointment, she couldn't just stand there like a ninny. She touched her glass to his and took a healthy gulp of wine. "I do believe it's your turn."

"Ah, yes, the game. You have seen my bed."

"Hard to miss. Sort of like the five-hundred-pound gorilla in the middle of the room."

"It was built at the same time the room was constructed. I would have to cut it into pieces or take down walls to move it out. Do you think it monstrous?"

"I can honestly say I've never seen one that big. Where do you get sheets for it?"

He chuckled. "I would have to ask Mrs. Osman to be sure." Josie relaxed visibly as they chatted, so he kept talking. "I care little for the chore of going over the household accounts, but Mother occasionally insists on the formality. Usually when she is in a high temper over one or another of my misdeeds. Upshot, I seem to recall a bill from Ireland for specially made linens of an appropriate size, so that would be my best guess."

She drained her glass and set it on the windowsill. "Have you decided?"

He raised an eyebrow. "After consideration of the many possibilities, and making sure there is plenty of hot water, I choose your suggestion of a shower first."

With a curt nod she headed for the bathing chamber. He drained his own glass and slowly followed, more confused than before. Why did he feel as if she were checking off items on her agenda?

Josie was already in the shower when he entered the steamy bathing chamber, water sluicing down her smooth skin. Venus protected by the copper arms of the shower apparatus. Protected? Or a goddess temporarily caged?

She wiped her face and smiled provocatively. "Aren't you going to join me?"

He steeled his willpower. "Of course." He stripped and mounted the dais, pausing at the opening, blocking her escape.

"Are you a gambler?" he asked.

"No. What does..."

"The most important part of being a successful gambler, which I am by the way, is the ability to read the other players, to know when they are bluffing or holding back. You, Josie-love, are holding aces and betting low to draw me in. What I want for my bonus turn is the truth. Why are you doing this?"

"I told you. I'm in the pursuit of pleasure. And although the water is nice, I'm sure we can think of other..."

"My definition includes the whole truth." He crossed his arms and waited, not an easy task when the sight of her was so intoxicating. He might not be able to hide his physical response, but he was not an untested youth. He could choose not to act.

Josie let the water rain over her head, hoping it would wash some sense into her brain. How was she supposed to think clearly when he was so close? And frowning. Was there anything more disconcerting than a scowling naked man? As if she could tell him the whole truth. Would he be put off with less?

"Fine." She slicked her hair back. "Naked truth."

Dev sucked in a breath. Did she have to use that word? He was having a difficult enough time maintaining his stance without the blatant reminder of their circumstances.

"When I heard you challenged Hargrave to a duel for the insult to me, I had a very strong premonition you would be killed. A shot to the heart even though he aimed...elsewhere. I could not let you die for some overblown, outdated, ridiculous sense of responsibility. I figured if I could keep you occupied past dawn, then you wouldn't..."

"There is no duel."

"...die and I could return...what?"

"No duel."

"But Estelle said..."

"There was a challenge, which I do not regret and would willingly meet. However, when Shermont, my second, went to the village inn earlier to make the arrangements with Hargrave's second, the coward had skipped town. Headed for India, I hear. So, no duel. You have sacrificed yourself on the altar of..."

With two running steps she launched herself into his arms and he caught her by reflex. She wrapped her arms around his neck and her legs around his waist.

"That's wonderful," she said, raining kisses all over his face.

"That was not..." He forgot what he was going to say. With his arms full of naked Josie, her skin slick and slippery, all the blood in his brain rushed to where his penis was knocking at Heaven's gate.

She leaned back in his arms. "Don't you see? Without a duel to worry about, I can truly be here because...because I truly want to be here. Come on." She smiled. "I'll wash your back."

"Maybe later," he said, his voice a low rumble. He raised her hips and was rewarded by her widening eyes as he slowly entered the tight sheath of her body. He paused, supporting her weight with his hands under her derriere, and waited for her vagina to accommodate him before entering her fully. He stepped to the left to brace himself against the shower apparatus. Warm water bathed his back and the few places their bodies did not touch.

Josie eyed the bars on either side of his head and shoulders. "Will these hold my weight?" she asked, grabbing one and giving it a shake. The one-and-a-half- to two-inch bar, though necessarily hollow, seemed strong enough.

"Made of the finest steel, coated with copper inside and out." He leaned his head back. "I can't believe we are discussing metallurgy."

"A simple yes would have sufficed. Give me a sec." She grabbed the bar over his head with both hands and braced her feet on either side of his hips. She smiled. "Now you can move."

He tentatively released her and let her hold herself with her arms. She flexed her knees a bit, resulting in movement up and down his shaft. She was as slick inside as out.

"And so can I." She lowered herself further, taking more of him inside. "Ohmigod, that feels good."

Now that his hands were free, he cupped her breasts, manipulating the nipples between his thumbs and forefingers. She moaned and pumped with her legs. Her movements goaded him, urging to match her downward strokes with thrusts of his hips slamming their bodies together with a wet *slap, slap, slap.*

He found her mouth with his lips and drove his tongue into her moist softness at the same time he shoved forward with his hips, seating himself inside her as deep as he could. Again and again, the tip of his penis banged against her womb.

He noted a change in her breathing as the muscles of her vagina rippled, stroking him, milking him. The sounds she made in the back of her throat were sweet music to his ears.

Josie was so close, so fast. The intensity built like a raging inferno.

"I'm sorry, Josie-love. I can't...hold back...any longer."

She threw her head back and screamed his name, along with garbled animal noises that sounded something like, "Yes, go, yes."

Her vagina clenched him so tightly he could not move, as if they were fused into one. She felt it. He felt it.

His howl of release joined hers.

He slumped back against the cage, her feet slid to the floor, and her body draped limply on top of his. He wrapped his arms around her.

"Let go of the pipe now, Josie-love."

"I don't think I can."

He helped her loosen her fingers, and with an arm around her shoulders he guided her under the overhead flow of warm water, which was not quite as warm as earlier. He grabbed a soapy sponge and washed both bodies down with efficient swipes.

She gave a snort of laughter. "I'm supposed to be the one energized and you're supposed to be ready to collapse."

He picked her up and carried her out of the shower, setting her on an armless chair near the fireplace. He rubbed her dry with a large soft towel. "I don't know about your reactions, but I have about fifteen minutes before that exhaustion sets in."

"Time enough to get dressed and out of the lady's bedroom?"

"I refuse to answer that," he said. He threw a towel over her head and rubbed her scalp. "What did you say?" He lifted one corner and she peered up at him.

"I forgot to say wow."

He smiled and bent to kiss her nose. "You didn't forget."

After wrapping a towel around his waist, he picked her up, towels and all, and carried her to the bedroom. He stood her on her feet long enough to pull back the huge goose-down duvet.

"No wet towels in the bed," he said.

She stripped hers off without hesitation, and then she pulled his towel off as well.

"Feeling better, I see." He picked her up again, and then he walked up the steps and right out onto the middle of the massive bed.

"What can you do in five minutes?" she asked.

He dropped her onto the feather softness and

then lay down beside her, pulling the duvet over them both.

She hit his shoulder with her fist. "That was rotten."

"No. It was expedient." He adjusted a pillow under his head. "Give me about fifteen minutes and I'll be good as new." He gathered her into his arms and closed his eyes.

Placing her arm on his chest, she propped up her chin. "Is that time frame estimate also based on experience?"

A slight snore was her only answer.

She snuggled into a comfortable position to wait. And promptly fell asleep.

Josie stretched and tried to wipe the satisfied grin off her face. Then she realized she was no longer in Dev's bed and she sat up with a start. They had made love several times during the night using every square inch of the huge bed. The last thing she remembered was making slow, sweet love with Dev as the sunrise tinged the wall of windows pink and gold. Now she was back in her own room.

As she swung her legs over the edge of the bed, she noticed the note leaning against the lamp on the table. She grabbed her dressing gown from the end of the bed, padded barefoot over to the table, and settled into the chair. She tucked her feet up before unsealing the folded sheet of paper and reading Dev's flamboyant handwriting.

My dear Josie-love,

I have an errand this morning and you are sleeping too peacefully to disturb. (And too soundly to wake.) I

*will return at approximately noon. Please have luncheon
with me in the folly.*

    Yours,

    Dev

P.S. Wow, wow, and WOW.

Josie checked the clock on the mantel. Two
hours until she saw him again. She hummed a little tune as she rang for Dora and retreated behind
the screen to wash.

While dressing, she realized she hadn't heard
from Deverell for a while. She hadn't had a chance
to discuss the séance with the ghost and missed his
acute observations. She also missed his appreciative
smile when she returned his repartee.

Perhaps he would be waiting in the library to
help her check her traps. Eager to see him, she
ran down the stairs. The entry and library were
empty.

Josie set about checking her traps. To her disappointment, none of the threads or beads had been
disturbed, so no one had entered or left the room.
Confused, she peered under the table. Definite
activity there. She checked the back of the chair
Madame used. Traces of green fingerprints were
preserved in the sticky oil.

"Aha." Specters did not leave fingerprints. She'd
bet her entire CD collection that those prints
would glow in the dark. She wondered if she could
preserve them and match them to someone in the
house. She let down the secret panel in the back of
the chair to see if any green dust was present there.
When the library doors opened she spun around,

expecting Deverell. She instantly realized her mistake. The ghost never bothered to use doors.

Madame X entered, closing the doors behind her.

"So, it was you."

Josie crossed her arms. Even though she still didn't know how the gypsy did it, she had enough proof to discredit her. "You are a fraud, and I will expose you and your accomplice to Lady Honoria."

"Quite the little detective, aren't you?" Madame moved closer. "And becoming quite a nuisance."

"You'd better go pack your bags. I'm sure Lord Waite will be asking you to leave soon."

"I think not." Madame lunged for Josie.

She turned to run but smacked her shin on the secret door. The momentary delay gave Madame enough time to grab her from behind. The older woman was amazingly strong, and her hand covered Josie's mouth with a firm grip. She fought back, but she managed only to grab scarf after scarf.

Madame dragged her to a chair by the fireplace and threw her into it. Before Josie could rise, the other woman pulled out a pistol and pointed it at her.

"Scream and you die."

Estelle entered the library, and with a sense of relief Josie waited for her to raise the alarm. Instead Estelle turned and locked the door. She sauntered across the room and sneered at Josie, "I knew you were trouble the moment I laid eyes on you."

"What are we going to do with her?" Madame asked.

Josie realized Estelle was also Madame's

accomplice. Then who was the man helping them? "Let me go and you…"

"Tie her up," Estelle ordered.

"…can still get away scot…"

"And gag her."

Madame X handed Estelle the pistol and followed her orders, using the scarves Josie had pulled from the gypsy's head during the struggle. The close position and lack of covering on Madame's neck revealed *an Adam's apple*. Suddenly Josie knew how she, rather he, had done it. There was not another accomplice. The man who played Amanu was in reality Madame X.

"Now what?" he asked.

Estelle stepped to the fireplace and opened a small door. She pulled a lever, and a section of the wall swung open. Josie was vindicated. She'd been sure there had to be a secret panel.

"Time for her to magically disappear. Take her down to the dungeon."

X picked her up and slung her over his shoulder. She wiggled and tried to get free despite her bonds.

"Gads, she's a handful."

Josie felt a sudden pain on the back of her head and then only blackness.

She woke sometime later. X's shoulder still dug into her stomach, so she figured she hadn't been out long. Her hands hung over her head. All she could see in the dim light of the lamp he carried was the rickety wooden steps they descended.

"Hurry up, Xavier," Estelle hissed from somewhere far above them, her voice echoing against the stone walls. "Someone is knocking on the library door."

Xavier stopped, and by the change in the light, Josie deduced that he had set the lamp on the step. He slipped her off his shoulder and sat her on a step, her back against the cold stone wall.

"Stall them," Xavier hollered. He looked down at Josie, no pity in his dead black eyes. "Much as I've enjoyed the feel of your sweet bum, you'll have to make the rest of the trip alone."

With that, he kicked her shoulder. Not hard, but enough to send her tumbling sideways into dark nothingness. Unable to reach out with her arms or legs to stop her motion, she ducked her head and covered it with her arms as she tucked into a ball.

Josie woke curled in the fetal position, her head resting on a large rock. And to absolute darkness. So black was the air around her, she raised her hands to her face to make sure her eyelids were open.

Her body was bruised and hurt like hell, but she didn't think anything was broken. She pushed herself to a sitting position and rested a moment until a dizzy spell passed. She clawed away the gag and breathed in several deep gulps of the musty air.

"Help! Help! Can anybody hear me?"

Her words echoed back, and she deduced that she was in a large chamber. Judging from the dirt beneath her, she was on the lowest level of the cave or dungeon or whatever it was.

Using her teeth and twisting her hands back and forth, she finally freed her hands. Then she made short work of the bonds around her knees and ankles. Something warm ran down her temple, and her fingers found what could only be blood. She used one of the scarves to dab it away and discovered crusted blood underneath. That meant she must have been lying there for some time. She tied the scarf around her head.

With determined thoroughness, she examined the rest of her body with her fingers. She used other scarves to bind up two bleeding gashes on her legs and to cover a burning scrape on her left arm. Satisfied that she'd done everything she could, she stood up slowly, testing for dizziness. She kept the large rock she'd used as a pillow beside her right foot as an anchor in the darkness.

Stretching her arms out, she reached for the wall and felt nothing in any direction. Panic reared its ugly head.

Stay calm. Stay calm.

"Help! Help! Help!"

"There's no use wasting your energy yelling. No one can hear you."

"Deverell!" Her relief at not being alone was so great, she sat on the rock. "Where are you? Your voice echoes and I can't see a damn thing."

"Exactly why I haven't wasted energy manifesting myself."

"Couldn't you at least appear as a glowing apparition? Even Amanu could do that."

"Very funny."

"I'm serious."

"No, I cannot. Since I never needed that skill, I didn't bother to practice it."

"Great. Could you try? Please?"

"I will think of something. In the meantime, you might consider getting out of here."

She stood up. "Fine. You can talk me out. Which way do I go? Left? Right? Straight? Hello?"

"Uh, I don't know the way out."

Stay calm. "But you are here. Which way did you come?"

"I didn't come a *way*. I'm not exactly sure how it worked, but I sort of *heard* your distress inside my head, like a scream. I focused on your unique energy, and here I am. Do you mind telling me *why* you are in the dungeon?"

She gave him the short version of the Xavier and Estelle show.

"Are you injured?"

"Bruises, abrasions, and one hell of a headache, but other than that I'm fine. And anxious to see a little sunshine. It's your dungeon. Surely, you've been down here before."

"In my youth. However, I didn't care for exploring the narrow tunnels and secret staircases the way Estelle did. Believe me, I would help you if I could. I don't like being down here either."

He wouldn't leave her, would he? He kept her panic at bay even if he had no better idea of what to do than she did. "I appreciate you staying with me."

There was no point running around blind. Josie sat down with a sigh. "Tell me what you do know."

Eighteen

EVERELL KEPT HIS VOICE LOW AND SMOOTH even though he wanted to shout out his frustration at not being able to help Josie escape the dungeon. No need for her to feel his panic. Despite the fact that he didn't see how his small store of useless information would be of service, she had asked and he would comply.

"It has always been called the dungeon, and undoubtedly held prisoners at one time or another. There is evidence that leg and arm shackles had once been attached to the walls. However, since several of the secret passages in the castle proper lead down here and one tunnel supposedly leads to an exit near the lake..."

"Supposedly?"

"I never heard of anyone actually using it, and some evidence in period diaries suggests it collapsed many years ago under the weight of newer construction. The foundations of the east wing caused particular problems for my ancestors."

"How many passages lead down here?"

"Three that I know of."

"But you didn't know about the passageway from the library. That makes four."

"Which lends credence to the theory the passages were meant as escape routes. Possibly added during Jacobean times, although there are no records. Understandable, if that were the case. There is also a theory that Robert, often referred to as 'that old pirate,' actually was a pirate and used this area to store his smuggled and stolen goods until he could bury his booty somewhere on the estate. Totally unproven. And again, there are no written records..."

"Naturally."

"Except for Robert's journals, which are written in code. I tried to decipher one of them when I was about fifteen, but after weeks of absolutely no progress I tired of the effort."

"Anything else?"

"Not really."

"That means there is something else. What?"

"It is not relevant. And you won't like it."

"I insist you tell me."

"Very well. Rumor has it that several times over the years servants had come down here for whatever reason and never returned. It is said their ghosts haunt the dungeon. Probably just a scare tactic to keep the staff out for their own good."

"Can you feel the presence of other ghosts?"

"No."

"Too bad. You could have asked them the way out."

"If they'd known the way out, they wouldn't have died down here."

"I think it's time to leave." Josie slapped her hands on her knees and stood. "Any suggestions?"

"The best way out of a maze is to trail your right hand against the greenery and never take any route that causes you to lose contact. Therefore, I expect the best action to take is to find a wall and follow it to an opening."

"Exactly what I was thinking. Since my head was pointed this way when I landed..." She turned so that the rock was against her left foot. "This should be the direction I came down."

"Illogical. You said you blacked out during your descent. Your body could have tumbled any which way and come to a halt facing an entirely different direction."

"Thank you, Mr. Spock. Do you have a better idea?"

Silence was her answer.

She instantly regretted her testiness. The absolute darkness was agonizing enough. Adding silence made it unbearable. "Okay, this way it is," she said, making her tone cheerful if only for her own benefit.

Waving her arms back and forth in front of her, she began walking. Slowly at first, but her confidence soon matched her determination and eagerness. And caused her to trip and fall.

"Ow, ow, ow." She tried to grab her sore elbow, which had landed on a rock, and her twisted ankle at the same time.

"Are you all right?"

"No, I am not all right. I'm bruised, and tired, and hungry, and thirsty, undoubtedly filthy from rolling around in God knows what on the ground, and...and..." Josie sucked in a deep breath and blinked her eyes to keep from crying. If she once gave in to panic and tears, she would be lost.

She rolled to a sitting position. She pulled a rock the size of a golf ball from beneath her hip. "Damn rocks." She threw it as hard as she could.

"Perhaps, you should..."

"Be quiet." She scooped up a handful of rocks and stood. Her ankle gave only a twinge of pain. She threw another stone and listened to the sounds it made as it came to a halt. She turned her body a few degrees and threw another one, repeating the process until she ran out of rocks.

"What are you doing?"

"Finding the nearest wall," she said. She knelt and ran her hands along the ground to find stones of the right golf ball size. Using her skirt as a makeshift pouch, she gathered the eight rocks she would need to quarter the four cardinal directions. She explained her plan to Deverell as she worked.

"Very scientific," he said.

Josie smiled at his compliment. She stood and hefted the first stone in her hand. "How big would you say this room is?"

"My best estimate, based on absolutely nothing but a vague memory, is approximately one-hundred-and-twenty feet in diameter."

"That's room for a lot of pirate booty." Josie made some quick calculations in her head. If the distance from the pitcher's mound to home plate in women's fast-pitch softball was forty feet, she could conservatively estimate throwing the uneven rough-surfaced rock half that distance. If she didn't hit a wall on the first go-round, she would take twenty steps and try again.

She set her feet, wound up, and let the rock fly. Low on the inside corner. Her form was a little rusty, not having played since college. But the noise of the stone rolling to a stop provided the information she sought, if not the result.

Josie used the distance between her chin and her shoulder as her forty-five-degree angle template and turned to her left until her nose was halfway between her imaginary lines. Nothing different happened on the next stone or any of the subsequent six. She counted out twenty steps, using a sliding motion similar to that employed by a beginning ice-skater so she didn't trip again.

Repeating the gathering, throwing, and turning process, her second throw yielded a satisfying thwack.

She wanted to jump up and down and cheer, but because she was afraid she'd lose her direction, she settled for a fist pump and a shout of, "Strike!"

"I'm presuming that has something to do with your unfortunate baseball phase." Deverell sounded bored.

"Softball. And don't knock it—I found the wall." She counted her steps as she ice-skated to the wall. "Approximately thirty-two feet. Not bad."

"You must be so proud."

Josie ignored his sarcasm. "Left or right?"

"Six of one and half dozen of another."

"Okay. I'm holding up my fingers. Pick a number, one or two."

"Two."

"Right hand. So we go left." She turned and started walking.

"Why left if I picked your right hand? What is that supposed to mean?"

"Nothing. Just a silly method for choosing a direction. Like flipping a coin."

"If I had said 'left' to your first question, would you have gone right?"

"Probably."

"Why?"

"I don't know. Now I've lost count of my steps. How far until we find a passageway?"

The ghost was silent.

She started counting over. At forty steps she paused. "Stop pouting. Shouldn't we have hit a passage by now?"

"I am not sulking. I am working on producing a light. Can you see anything yet?"

"No." She continued walking. Suddenly, her hand moved into thin air, surprising her so that she stumbled to her knees. She felt around with her hands, almost afraid to believe. "Steps! Uneven, rough-hewn real stone steps." She blinked away tears and stifled the urge to rush up them. "We did it. We found a passage."

"Where do you suppose it goes?"

"Like I care?" She climbed, careful with her footing and keeping her hand on the wall for balance. No way did she want to repeat her earlier tumble down the steps. "It's not the passage to the library, because those steps were made of wood. These are very uneven and feel like solid rock."

The passage suddenly narrowed. "Something's different. This wall doesn't feel like stone. Plaster maybe. Why would anyone build..."

"By Jove, I think I've got it!"

She automatically turned toward his voice. After the stygian darkness, the tiny pinprick of light Deverell produced blinded Josie like the sun. She quickly raised her arm to cover her squinting eyes and stepped back. Her foot slipped.

Terrified of falling again, she shoved her back up against the wall. The old plaster and lathe construction disintegrated under her weight. Leaving her sitting in an alcove. Next to a skeleton. The gruesome bones were clad in a dingy white wig and the tattered shreds of what was once a green brocade gown.

Josie screamed and struggled to stand, but her knees were draped over the remains of the wall. In her attempt to get away, she elbowed the skeleton in the ribs and the skull fell into her lap. With another scream, she batted it aside and crawled out of the alcove. She scrambled on hands and knees to the other side of the passage. Shaking too much to run, she pulled her legs up, covered her face, and cowered against the other wall.

"Would you look at that."

"No."

"But you must. It must be Robert's mistress. Look."

"No. I don't want to."

"Or for heaven's sake, it's just old bones. Where's that scientific bravado?"

Past her first shock, her breathing retuned almost to normal. She peeked through her fingers. "Ohmigod." She dropped her hands and stared. The now headless skeleton wore an elaborate necklace, a huge square-cut emerald surrounded by diamonds hung between the rib bones. Smaller emeralds, similarly set and linked together, looped up and around the top of the backbone. The unfortunate mistress also wore the matching bracelet and ring—a bit dusty, but still obviously a fortune.

"No wonder they never found her," Deverell said. "Do you suppose Robert killed her and then put her there, or did he wall her up alive?"

"Don't be macabre."

"I'm a ghost. It comes naturally."

Josie stood and tentatively crossed the width of the passage. "Can you give me a little more light? Look at her leg. That's a nasty break."

Josie examined the inside of what was left of the wall. "No bloodstains on the wood or plaster. And her fingernails aren't broken as they probably would be if she'd been walled up alive and tried to claw her way out."

"Oh." He sounded disappointed.

"I'm no detective, but logically, it appears she fell down the stairs and broke her leg." Josie was doubly thankful for her own good luck. "If that shattered bone broke through her skin or punctured a major vein, she probably bled to death while crawling up the stairs to get help."

"What about the wall?"

"I'd say Robert found her body sometime later and interred her remains. Say he was already married to the fair Rowena. He would hardly want to produce his mistress, even dead."

"But why leave the emeralds?"

"Since everyone knew she'd stolen them, if he produced the distinctive jewelry, it would be the same as producing the mistress. He was willing to give up the emeralds to save his marriage. Sort of romantic."

"Only a woman could twist a mistress walled up in the dungeon into something romantic."

Josie stepped back. "We don't even know her name."

A knocking sound came from the head of the stairs far above them. "Hello? Is anybody there?" a voice called, faint but understandable.

"Dev." Josie turned and ran up three steps before Deverell called for her to stop.

"Take the emeralds," he commanded. "They will save Amelia."

"Ohhh." Josie returned and whispered an apology to the hapless mistress. With a squeamish wince, she gingerly lifted off the necklace and removed the bracelet and ring without actually touching the skeleton. The earrings had fallen to the floor and were easy to pick up. Josie hiked up her skirt and knotted everything into a makeshift pouch.

"Don't forget the tiara," Dev said, as she made to ascend the stairs. "It's probably still attached to the wig."

Josie shook her hands, not wanting to pick up the skull. "Why didn't the wig disintegrate like her hair?"

"Probably made of horsehair. More durable."

She made a face and picked up the skull. After disentangling the tiara, she started to drop the skull, but something stopped her. Josie had had a small taste of what the mistress had gone through in the dungeon, and the other woman had not even had the comfort of a ghostly presence.

Josie plopped the tiara on her head to have both hands free. She leaned over the remaining wall and placed the skull gently on the floor next to the hip-bone, facing outward. More knocking from above urged her up the stairs. "I'm sorry about taking your emeralds, but at least you'll get a proper burial now."

Josie turned away and climbed steadily toward Dev, the going made easier by Deverell's light.

At the top of the stairs, Josie encountered a solid wall, no door, no handle. "Dev! Open the secret panel."

"Josie? What are you..."

"Never mind that now. Just get me out." She ran her fingers over the surface and around the edges, searching for a button or a dial or a loose board or anything to indicate an opening device. "There must be a way to open the panel."

"What panel? Where's the release?"

"Look around. There should be a hidden lever or some such mechanism."

"Don't worry, Josie-love. I'll get you out," he promised.

And she knew he would. Relief engulfed her. The stress of the morning overwhelmed her, and she sank, shivering and shaking, to the floor of the small landing.

On the other side of the wall, Dev searched desperately for the mechanism to open the unknown secret panel. How had she got behind the door? First, he'd been told by Estelle that Josie had gone into town with a relative. That in itself should have tipped him off to a problem because he hadn't passed her on the road, but he'd been too occupied setting up his big surprise for their luncheon meeting.

When she hadn't arrived on time, he'd gone to her room only to be told that Dora hadn't seen Josie since that morning and had assumed she was with him. Dora had been worried, but Dev had been angered by Josie's disregard of other people's feelings. He should have known better.

He'd left Josie's sitting room and encountered Sadie in the hall. Literally. She'd run into him upon exiting the guest suite she'd been cleaning, sobbing that she'd heard the dungeon's ghosts screaming and howling and threatening to drag her down to the depths if she didn't reform her sinful ways.

To calm her fears and stifle any wild rumors among the staff at the source, he insisted she return with him to the room. Several nearby footmen, who had avidly listened to her outrageous tale, were drafted to *help* her along.

They had all heard strange noises. Dev's first assumption was that a hapless servant had somehow managed to get caught in one of the secret passages. Despite being forbidden for safety reasons, the convenient shortcuts between certain rooms had occasionally been used by the lazy, soon to be former servant. Dev had not been aware of this particular passage, but then he'd never liked the confined, steep stairs and narrow hallways of the passages.

While Sadie cowered in the corner mumbling her childhood catechism, Dev and the footmen knocked on the walls until they found one in the bedroom that returned a hollow sound. Soon after that he'd heard Josie's voice.

Frustrated with his inability to find the release, Dev leaned his weight against the panel, testing its thickness. When it showed no sign of giving, he turned to his helpers. "A guinea to the first man to bring me an ax."

Both footmen scrambled out the door.

"Just a little longer," Dev called to Josie.

On the other side of the wall, she leaned her head back and closed her eyes.

"I expect we only have a few minutes until Dev rescues you," Deverell said.

A tired smile teased the corners of her lips. And tore at his heart.

"Josie, we have to talk." Now, before he was transported away to who knew where. He would not likely have another chance. If he knew Dev, the man wouldn't let Josie out of his sight for a good long while.

She looked up at him. So lovely despite the dirty smudges and ridiculous ensemble. Deverell cursed the villains who had hurt her, and wanted desperately to soothe her cuts and bruises. He was sorely tempted to tell her what he'd figured out, that his energy level was not fading based on time. His strength was directly and inversely linked to Dev's feelings for her. The more the man cared, the weaker the ghost became.

"I am weakening more rapidly than anticipated," he said.

He was aware of where she'd spent the night; he had felt the enormous drain on his energy and the stab of unreasoning jealousy. Bloody hell. How could a man be jealous of himself?

"We must leave by six o'clock tonight," he said.

"So soon? Can't we stay a little longer?"

Like one more night? Not her words, but he sensed her thoughts. "Absolutely not," he said, his voice gruffer than he'd expected.

She ducked her head.

"The return is not without risk." He'd softened his tone. "I must have enough energy to take us all the way back or you could wind up...in some time other than your own."

"And you?"

He was headed for the bleakness of limbo regardless. "I will always be with you," he promised. If only in his dreams.

"Josie?" Dev called through the wooden panel. "Stand back. I'm breaking through the wall."

With a loud thwack, the tip of an ax head

broke through the wall. The resulting stream of light put Deverell's tiny pinprick to shame. Splinters flew as Dev attacked the wood that separated them with desperate fury. Josie curled into a ball and covered her head.

"Six o'clock," Deverell said. "Not a minute later."

And then he was gone.

As soon as the hole in the wall was large enough, Dev reached through and lifted Josie out. The light nearly blinded her, and she rested her head on his shoulder as he turned away from the dungeon exit.

He'd only taken two steps when Sadie screamed.

"Oh God. It's the pirate's mistress," she cried, awe and terror in her eyes before she fainted.

Dev turned to the nearby footmen, both standing at attention, expressions professionally impassive. "Not a word of this to a soul," he demanded in his most lordly voice.

"Yes, milord," they answered in unison.

He glanced significantly toward the slumped maid, and the senior footman nodded in silent understanding and assurance.

"I guess I must really look a sight," Josie said as Dev spun and carried her out of the room with long strides. She raised her head to look at her filthy dress and her bruised and scraped arms and legs.

"You never looked lovelier," he said, his throat almost too dry to get the words out. He tightened his hold on her.

She wiped away a tear and wrapped her arms around his neck.

"Come on. I look like a Halloween ghoul. I frightened Sadie into a faint."

He understood that she was making light of the situation in order to cope with the trauma she'd undoubtedly suffered. Although he might have shown his concern in a different manner, he followed her lead. "Probably caused by the bloody scarves." His gut clenched. "Although the tiara is a nice touch."

She laughed as she raised her hand and removed the emerald crown. "I'd forgotten about this." As he carried her down the long halls and to his suite, she told him about finding the skeleton and the lost jewelry. She fumbled with the knots she'd tied in her skirt. Fortunately, he didn't question her ability to see in the darkness.

"I don't give a tinker's damn about the emeralds," he said, kicking his own door open. "Fetch her maid," he said to Carson, who exhibited momentary surprise before assuming a bland expression. "Use discretion. And tell Mrs. Osman to bring her medical kit." He didn't bother to slow down either to offer an explanation or to see if the valet carried out his orders.

"I don't need medical attention," Josie said. "I'm fine. Okay, maybe a few cuts and bruises, but I don't need..."

"Your head is bleeding again."

Dev walked directly to the bathing chamber and straight into the shower, where he finally set her down. While he turned on the tap, she gladly stripped off her filthy dress. It hit the floor with a thunk. She tossed the tiara in the same direction.

"Hot water?" She raised one eyebrow.

"I...uh...requested Carson to...in case we..." He gently removed the bandage from her head. "It doesn't look too bad."

"Head wounds always bleed a lot. I keep telling you I'm fine."

He kissed her forehead near the wound.

"And feeling better by the minute," she added. She wrapped her arms around his waist and pulled him close. She lifted her face for a kiss and tried not to think about leaving him.

Their building passion was interrupted by the entrance of Mrs. Osman and Dora.

"Here now, here now. None of that," Mrs. Osman said. "At least not until we're sure she's all right," she added with a wink.

Dev backed out of the shower, pausing to whisper, "Later," before turning to face the intruders. "I give her over to your tender care. I will wait in the receiving room." He executed an elegant leg, quite a feat to pull off with aplomb when he was soaked to the skin. He left a trail of wet boot prints.

Josie peeled off the rest of her wet clothes and washed with brisk efficiency. She had yet to tell Dev about Xavier and Estelle, and she didn't want the villains to get word of her survival and escape.

Wrapped in a sheet, she sat at the dressing table. Mrs. Osman insisted that Josie drink a cup of fortifying broth while the older woman applied salves and ointments and gauze bandages. Josie was relieved to learn she'd been correct in her assessment of her injuries. Then Dora dressed her in the clean clothes she'd brought at Carson's request. Neither woman asked about her misadventure, and Josie didn't volunteer any information. She asked for a moment alone, and the servants reluctantly left.

Josie found a large box of shirt studs on the dresser and dumped the contents. She found her soiled dress on the shower floor under a pile of wet and filthy scarves. The emeralds and diamonds glittered in the afternoon sunlight streaming in the high windows. She threw all the pieces into the box, closed the lid, and carried it out to Dev.

Dev sat in the chair by the window, an untouched snifter of brandy at his elbow. He'd poured the drink after changing into a brocade robe, yet his desire for the soothing warmth had cooled along with the blood rush of rescuing Josie. After knowing she was safe, he'd had plenty of time to think. Maybe too much time.

Josie entered the reception room with a broad grin. She presented him with the emeralds.

"I believe these rightly belong to you," she said.

He took the box but, knowing what it contained, set it unopened on the table. He picked up his drink. "They rightly belong to my mother. The family jewels pass to the lady of the house."

"Then let's go give them to her."

He leaned back in his chair and sipped his brandy.

"Dev?"

"Do you want to tell me what you were doing

in the secret passages? Were you searching for the emeralds? Why did you..."

"Whoa." She was taken aback. "Why the inquisition?"

"You must admit your actions lead to certain logical..."

"My actions?" She leaned over until her face was inches from his. "Let me tell you something, mister." She poked her finger in his chest and related what had happened with Xavier and Estelle. By the time she finished the story, she was seated in his lap and he'd said, "I'm sorry" several times, each apology accompanied by a kiss.

"I'll send one of the footmen for the constable and..."

"You'll have to tell your mother. Unfortunately, she really believed Amanu talked to your father."

"Perhaps it would be best if the truth were revealed during one of those fake séances. Then she could see for herself. I'll send her a note immediately..."

"Later," Josie whispered, trailing her hand along the neck of his robe and then under the silk lapel to the smooth, warm, firm surface below. "I think you owe me another...apology."

After a passionate kiss, she stood and pulled him to his feet. "I'm wearing a corset," she taunted him with a seductive smile.

"I do love Christmas."

Dev tried to take it slow, but she was wild, demanding.

Josie was all too aware of the clock ticking, her

time with him running inexorably out. He didn't know it but she was making memories, saying good-bye. Only four hours left.

The second time Dev insisted on slow, gloriously slow.

During a brief rest period, Josie traced her initials on his chest and tried to keep him awake by asking, "How did you find me?"

"Huh? Oh, Sadie heard mysterious screams coming through the wall of a guest suite she was cleaning." He chuckled. "She thought the hounds of hell were..."

A frisson of alarm caused Josie to sit up. "Whose room?"

"I don't know."

She crawled over him and to the edge of the massive bed. "Get up. Get dressed," she called back over her shoulder.

"Hey? What..."

"Suddenly it makes sense. That had to be Estelle and Xavier's suite of rooms. Sadie was assigned to them, and Estelle was familiar with the passages. The séances were a ruse. They were looking for the emeralds."

"Josie-love, come back to bed."

She looked back at him. A beautiful naked man in the middle of a majestic bed. He held out his hand. So tempting. She hesitated. Maybe...

"We can deal with that later," he said.

His words were like cold water. She didn't have the luxury of time. "Hurry. Call Carson."

"I will not. You're not decent."

Josie threw her chemise over her head, tossed the corset aside, and donned the green muslin dress. "Now call him."

"Would this be the point where you're feeling energetic?" he grumbled as he climbed off the bed. He paused with his hand on the bell pull because she sat and hiked up her skirt to pull on her stockings. "We can schedule the séance for tonight and..."

"Not if Estelle or Xavier returns to their suite and just happens to notice the big hole in the bedroom wall. I think they'll figure out the jig is up and escape before the constable gets here. If they haven't already."

"Easily remedied. I'll have several footmen detain them..."

"Where? How many more passages are there that you don't know about? No, I think you're right about confronting them in front of your mother, but I don't think we can wait until tonight for a séance."

Josie certainly couldn't. "I have a plan. Hurry. We have lots to do." And she had only two-and-a-half hours left.

Nineteen

"THIS IS NOT A PROPER KNOT," DEV SAID, glancing in the mirror at the floppy bow under his chin.

Because Josie had sent Carson on an errand, she'd tied Dev's cravat as best she could. She tucked the ends under his vest. "Think of it as a new style."

"I'd prefer being properly dressed before going downstairs."

She stood on her toes and kissed his chin. He wrapped his arms around her and gave her a kiss that left her breathless.

"Although there are certain advantages to having you play valet," he said. He roamed his hands over her body. Without her corset, every curve and her pebbled nipples were palpable beneath the delicate muslin. "And definite advantages to you not being properly dressed."

Before he distracted her beyond her ability to resist, she pushed away and stepped back. "Think of it this way. It will be easier to undress later." She forced a promise into her voice that she knew she couldn't keep.

He looked deep into her eyes.

"What's wrong, Josie-love? Tell me."

"Nothing," she said with a laugh she hoped didn't sound as false as it felt. She took his hand and pulled him from the room. "Let's get this denouement over with."

Dev entered the library alone, leaving the door open several inches so Josie could hear the proceedings and enter on cue. He carried a large jewelry case under his arm. His mother, Estelle, and Madame X were already in the room.

At his first sight of the villains, he regretted agreeing to Josie's plan, which did not include beating Xavier to a bloody pulp. Dev's willpower was sorely tested, but he managed to place a smile on his face.

"Thank you for coming as I requested," he said.

"I am always at your service," Estelle simpered. "Whatever you require or...want."

"What are you doing with my ruby...good heavens, Dev," Honoria said. "What is wrong with your cravat?"

"It's the latest style. And this is only the case for your ruby parure. I borrowed it for this." He flipped open the lid and presented it to his mother.

"Oh, my," she breathed.

The emerald jewelry sparkled against the black velvet lining, drawing Estelle like a magnet.

Honoria looked up at Dev with a furrowed brow.

"Yes. Lord Robert's emeralds. They were behind a wall in one of the secret passages." He related

Josie's theory, leaving out certain facts about how the jewels had been found. "Apparently the mistress fatally injured herself while trying to escape through the dungeon tunnels and died crawling back up one of the stairways. At some later time, Robert must have found her body, and rather than present the tangible reminder of his past to his beloved wife, he walled up both the mistress and the emeralds she so coveted."

"Sort of romantic," Honoria said.

Dev rolled his eyes. "Only a woman would think a dead mistress walled up with a fortune in emeralds was romantic."

"Not that part. Robert gave up a fortune for love."

"I knew they were more than a myth," Estelle said, sliding onto the sofa next to Honoria and reaching out to touch them with one finger.

Dev snapped the case shut. "Really? And how did you know that?"

Estelle jumped back but quickly recovered her poise. "I always believed the legend, ever since I was a child."

"Is that why you wanted to see Robert's journals?" Honoria asked innocently.

Dev sat on the opposite sofa, setting the box next to him. He had not been aware that his mother had allowed Estelle access to the notebooks. "Yes. Do tell us. Did you decode the journals?"

She licked her lips. "Only one of the later ones. And that was years and years ago. Dev gave me the idea when he worked on them. I've made no progress on the other journals. Each one has an entirely different code."

"You never told me that," Honoria said. "What did it say?"

Estelle waved away any interest. "Nothing but boring reports of estate business, dull details of horse breeding, and pages and pages of how much he adored the fair Rowena." As she talked, her gaze kept darting to the case of jewels.

"Did he mention the emeralds?" Honoria asked.

"Not in so many words. There was a veiled reference when the crops failed for the second year in a row. 'I long to see my fields emerald green, my wife in a new emerald green gown. I am sorely tempted but fear the monetary relief readily available but a few steps below would not be worth destroying my true jewels, my wife and family.' Then he lapses into more romantic drivel and his plans for smuggling to avoid the duty on brandy."

The fact that she'd memorized the words was more telling than the passage itself.

"From that you concluded the emeralds were real and buried somewhere in the castle?" Honoria asked.

"Beneath the older part of the castle," Dev amended.

"And I was right," Estelle said with a satisfied smile.

"Ah, yes," Dev said. "But you were not first. I wonder, if you had found the emeralds yourself, would you have turned them over to Mother?"

"Of course I would have," Estelle said.

And if he hadn't known better, Dev might have

even believed her righteous indignation.

"Really, Dev," Honoria said. "You are acting quite strange."

Estelle turned and beckoned her gypsy friend closer. "Madame, did you get a chance to see the emeralds?"

Dev laid his hand on the case. "That reminds me of the other issue I wanted to talk to you about, these séances."

"There is nothing to discuss," Honoria said. "You know my feelings. I am determined to follow Amanu's directions to the letter, and he has specifically requested you not be included."

Dev glanced at Madame X and noted the avarice in her—correction—in his eyes. Dev could well imagine the unscrupulous Amanu convincing his gullible mother that the emeralds were cursed and that she must rebury them at some specific spot where Estelle and the so-called Madame X could later dig them up. "And I know why he doesn't want me there."

"Because you are a nonbeliever," Honoria said. "You know how important this is to me."

Dev leaned forward and took his mother's hands in his. "I know you find comfort in believing you're speaking to Father."

"Don't treat me like a silly old woman. I know..."

"But it's a sham, a charade."

"No, it can't be. Your father..."

"Madame X is a fraud, and we can prove it."

Josie entered right on cue, followed by Carson and a footman carrying the séance paraphernalia.

"How did you...," Estelle started to say as she jumped up from the seat. Then she switched tracks. "Honoria, you can't believe a word this woman says. She's a stranger, a nobody. She lied about being related to the Duke of Landemere. And she has no fortune, no income from the funds, no..."

"Sit down, Estelle," Dev said, indisputable command in his voice.

Estelle sat with a thump.

"Josie, what in the world happened to you?" Honoria asked.

"I'll explain later." Josie had hoped the face powder would hide most of the bruises, and her clothes hid most of the bandages, but apparently it was not enough. Fortunately, her muscles had not stiffened up, thanks to the hot shower and Dev's attentive...massage. Tomorrow would likely be a different story, but by then she would be home and it wouldn't matter.

Josie directed the servants to put the stuff on the table. They bowed themselves out and closed the door. She turned to face Honoria's confused expression. "Estelle is right."

"See, I told you. Now..."

"Shut up, Estelle," Dev said.

"Dev! There is no need to be rude to our guest."

"Please continue," Dev said to Josie through gritted teeth.

"Thank you. Lady Honoria, I entered your home under false pretenses, and I apologize for that. I am a stranger to you and a nobody. I have no fortune and no funds. But a certain shading of the truth was necessary."

Dev raised an eyebrow.

Josie had not told him that part and his reaction was disconcerting, but she forged ahead. "I came here specifically to investigate the séances and expose Madame X as a fraud. To that end, I set certain traps before the last séance to reveal her method of producing the fake spirit guide."

"Fake?"

"Yes, milady. I'm sorry. I truly wish it was otherwise."

"But how?"

"That's why I had these items brought down, so we can examine them in broad daylight."

Madame X edged toward the door. Dev stood and blocked the way. "I really think you should stay to hear this," he said to the so-called gypsy in an almost pleasant tone. "Miss Drummond?"

His sudden formality stabbed at her heart. Was learning she was not an heiress such a big deal? *It doesn't matter. You're leaving soon.* Perhaps it would be better if Dev started distancing himself now. She concentrated on her task.

"First, I will light the Candle of Omniscience," she said, her hand trembling as she stuck the lucifer match and touched it to the wick. She blew out the match and positioned herself so she could see the mantel clock as she talked. "You will note during the rest of the demonstration that the candle sparks, flares, and dims in a repeating and predetermined pattern. The wick burns at a consistent rate and was pretreated at specific spots with chemicals that cause the desired effect. With a bit of practice, one can time appropriate pronouncements with those effects. For instance, now." She turned and pointed to the candle, and it flared and sputtered.

"That proves nothing," Estelle said in a dismissive tone. She turned to the woman on her left. "Honoria, please stop this ridiculous exhibition by an admitted liar who..."

"Shut up, Estelle," Honoria said.

Dev grinned. And nodded to Josie.

"The candle was the easy part, quite elementary. The appearance of Amanu was a bit trickier. At first I was sure there must be a secret entrance to the library."

Estelle stiffened, but Josie ignored her.

"My traps revealed that no one entered by any method other than the usual. The only logical conclusion was that the man playing Amanu had to have been in the room all along. But where would a seven-foot-tall green fellow hide? We'll leave that puzzle for a moment and talk about the spirit guide.

"He glowed because he was coated with a phosphorescent powder. Quite dangerous. Phosphorous is highly flammable, hence its use on such items as the lucifer match I used earlier. Even in a more stable form it can cause serious injury and is potentially deadly if exposure is prolonged."

Xavier did not flinch, so Josie knew he had been aware of the danger and deemed the potential reward worthwhile.

"We know he did this despite the risk," Josie continued, "because I painted the top edge of the chair Madame X used with a sticky substance, and Amanu left powder residue there in the form of fingerprints."

She wasn't sure whether the science of individual fingerprints had been invented yet, so she'd decided not to pursue that line beyond what anyone of the period might have seen on silver plates or waxed furniture. She'd also decided to avoid the issue of whether a true spirit would actually leave fingerprints.

Josie pulled the chair to the center of the room and stood behind it. "As to him being seven feet tall..." She leaned down, popped the latch of the secret compartment, and climbed up on the door. "I realize I'm not quite seven feet, but that indicates the man is taller than me to begin with." She stepped down, closed the door, and said, "And the evidence disappears and no one is the wiser."

A commotion outside the door interrupted her train of thought. The door burst open and Mrs. Binns marched in.

"What is going on? If my charge is involved..."

"My apologies, milord," the footman said. "She would not take no for an answer and just barreled by me."

"How can I be expected to do my duty," Mrs. Binns said, "when my charge disappears for hours on end, fails to let me know..."

"Miss Drummond is exposing Madame X as a fraud," Dev said.

"Josie? What happened to you? Where did you get those bruises?"

"I'll explain later."

Dev stepped in front of Mrs. Binns. "You may stay and hear the rest of the evidence if..."

"How did..."

"...*if* you can sit quietly and ask no questions. You have missed certain explanations and can be filled in on those items later."

"But how did..."

"Sshh." He held up a finger, and Mrs. Binns closed her mouth and meekly sat down. Dev took the precaution of locking the door before resuming his position next to the sofa where his mother and Estelle were seated.

"That brings us back to the man hiding in the room," Josie continued at his nod. "But where? There are no closets, no cabinets large enough to conceal a man. I was stumped until I got a little help. The answer is he was hiding in plain sight. Madame X is no lady."

"You may remove your headgear," Dev said to him.

Xavier pulled off the scarves and turban he wore. "At least that's a relief." He also stripped off Madame's signature purple gloves and several layers of heavily padded clothes to reveal a slim gentleman dressed in a white shirt and fawn knee breeches. "Those rags are bloody hot."

"Count LeFoyn, I presume," Dev said.

Xavier clicked his heels and bowed.

Josie was impressed. She hadn't figured out that connection.

"But if he was Madame X, how could he also be

Amanu?" Honoria asked. "A person can't be in two places at once."

"I had an idea how he did it," Josie said. "Based on the disruption of the powder I placed beneath the table before the séance. Carson's discovery of this box in their rooms..."

"An unpardonable invasion of privacy." Estelle sniffed and raised her nose even higher in the air.

Josie unbuckled the leather straps that bound the large wooden box, opened the lid, and took out the golden mask Madame wore during the séance. "I'm sure you recognize this."

Honoria nodded.

Then Josie removed a cagelike apparatus and clicked the mask onto the appropriate hooks. She set the cage over her head, thankful she'd remembered to ask Carson to wash the mask.

"Now if you will imagine this headpiece swathed in scarves and me in a long loose robe," she said as she moved the chair Madame always used to the side of the table so Honoria would have the proper view.

"So, Madame sits down thus." Josie began moaning and chanting in imitation of the gypsy seer and then suddenly stopped. "Sorry, I forgot the hands."

She jumped up and reached into the box. She pulled out wooden replicas of Madame's arms, correct down to the purple gloves and fancy rings. Josie draped the leather strap connecting them around her neck and hooked it under a clip at the back of the cagelike apparatus over her head. When she sat again in the chair, the dummy arms hung at her sides.

"I ask you again to imagine I'm wearing volu-minous robes. The séance is proceeding, yada yada yada." She waved and gestured as she talked, and the candle flared as if on cue. Josie smiled. She placed her hands in her lap.

"Then comes time for the trance." She placed her hands on the table and mimicked Madame's moaning and groaning routine, except this time she substituted the wooden hands for her own. She fell forward facedown on the table with a loud thunk.

"Ouch. I suppose that takes a bit of practice." Almost immediately she slid her butt forward on the chair, snaked out of the cage, and went to her knees under the table. She crawled around the legs of the chair, not an easy feat in a long dress, but she finally managed by hiking her skirt above her knees.

"Josie!" Mrs. Binns exclaimed.

"Remember, it's dark and no one can see me." She again unlatched the secret panel and stood on the door. Spreading her arms, she looked over her shoulder and said, "Voila. The specter appears."

"Amazing," Honoria said. She shook her head, deep in thought, the logical part of her brain visi-bly at odds with her need to believe.

"The so-called spirit guide uses knowledge gained by ordinary methods to convince everyone of the authenticity of the connection to the spirit world. Often the attendees themselves will reveal the necessary information during pre-séance con-versations. Did Madame ever ask who you wanted to contact and why?"

"I don't remember," Honoria said, but she ducked her head and would not look Josie in the eye.

"If providing false comfort were the only aim, exposure would seem unnecessary and even cruel. However, once the ruse is accepted as real, the spirit can subtly and cryptically *guide* any believers to the behavior desired, usually involving parting with large sums of money or jewels."

Honoria's sudden upward glance told Josie all she needed to know.

"Amanu's disappearance," Josie concluded, stepping down and closing the panel in the back of the chair, "was simply a reverse process. A bit more physically demanding and tricky to do without moving the headpiece, but possible with a bit of practice."

Xavier applauded. When all eyes turned to him, he said, "Bravo, mademoiselle. You are quite astute." He bowed and motioned in her direction.

When everyone's attention turned back to Josie, Xavier bolted for the window.

But Dev had been waiting for just such a move. He hadn't realized how eagerly he'd waited until he tackled the villain and pulled him to his feet. Dev's fist connected to the other man's jaw with a satisfying sound and spurt of blood.

Honoria and Mrs. Binns screamed.

"Fight back, you son of a bitch," Dev muttered. "Or do you only hit women half your size?"

Josie grabbed a nearby statuette and stepped toward the fighters.

"Stop it this instant," Estelle yelled. "Or I'll shoot her."

Twenty

DEV PAUSED WITH HIS FIST IN MIDAIR AND glanced back. On the other side of the library, Estelle held a pistol aimed at his mother. He could kick himself for not thinking of the possibility. Along with the passageways, she had always been fascinated with firearms and insisted on learning to shoot.

"If anyone screams or calls for help, I'll shoot her."

Honoria whimpered and hid her face in her friend's ample shoulder.

Mrs. Binns tried to comfort her. "She would not really shoot you, my dear."

With a sly smile, Estelle moved her arm and pointed the tip of the muzzle at Josie.

"Let him go," Estelle directed Dev.

He hesitated, quickly judging the distance, calculating whether he could grab the weapon or knock it from her hand before she could fire. He dared not look at Josie, for the terror in her eyes would unnerve him.

"Don't try it," Estelle said, reading his eye

movements as if she easily read his thoughts. "I can hardly miss at this distance."

Dev released his hold on Xavier.

"Tie them up," Estelle directed her partner.

Xavier scooped up one of Madame's discarded scarves and dabbed at his bloody mouth. "The blighter loosened a tooth. My lip is cut. My..."

"Don't be such a coward. We haven't got all day. Him first," Estelle said, indicating Dev with her chin.

Xavier gathered the rest of the scarves.

"Sit over there," Estelle said to Dev.

He bypassed the heavy chair she indicated, choosing instead a contemporary chair his mother had recently purchased against his advice. While Xavier tied his arms and legs to the chair, Dev tensed his muscles so the bonds would loosen on relaxation. Any little bit might help.

"Now the old busy-body," Estelle said.

Mrs. Binns sucked in her breath, but she sat in the chair as she was told.

"I have no more scarves," Xavier complained. "I told you we should have gone back to the room to change..."

"Rip up the gypsy dress. You won't be needing it again."

Xavier mumbled his gratitude for small favors as he tore several long strips off the skirt.

Dev could not resist a quick glance at Josie. She stood with her arms at her side. Rather than appearing terrified, she seemed quite calm. Her unexpected demeanor confused him. Then she caught his eye and he realized she was alert, waiting for a chance. He began flexing and twisting his arms every second when no one else was watching. She saw the movement and gave a slight nod.

Xavier went to one knee in front of Mrs. Binns. When he reached for her ankle, she kicked out and caught him in the chest, knocking him over. She stood. He scrambled to his feet and slapped her so hard that she fell back into the chair, cracking her head and knocking herself out.

"Don't move," Estelle said to Josie, who had taken a step forward.

"Was that really necessary?" Josie asked.

"Bitch hurt me," Xavier said, rubbing his chest. He spit on Mrs. Binns. She did not stir.

"Enough of this," Estelle said. She backed to the fireplace and with her free hand fumbled blindly until she found the latch that opened the panel leading to the secret passageway.

Honoria gasped and sat on the sofa.

"Do you have your knife?" Estelle asked Xavier.

He slapped his boot. "*Ma petite dent* is ready and hungry for blood."

"Good. Get the equipment," Estelle said to Xavier.

"We don't need..."

"We'll take it with us." Estelle laughed at some wicked thought, which she declined to share with her partner.

Xavier shrugged and packed Madame's equipment into the large wooden box. He pulled the leather straps over his shoulder, positioning the heavy box like a backpack, thus leaving his hands free.

"What about her?" Xavier asked, jerking his head toward Honoria.

"We'll take her with us as a hostage." She turned to Dev. "If anyone follows us, we'll hear and kill her."

"Follow you where?" Honoria asked.

"Into the dungeon," Estelle said with a grin.

"Oh, dear." Honoria raised a limp hand to her forehead.

"Come on. Let's go."

"I don't think I can stand, much less..."

"Get her on her feet," Estelle directed Xavier.

With a frustrated sigh, he clomped over, offered his hand, and pulled her to her feet.

"I feel faint," Honoria whispered.

Raised as a gentleman, Xavier automatically stepped in front of her and held out his hands, ready to catch her no matter which way she fell. She put her hands on his shoulders to steady herself and tried to knee him in the groin.

Honoria jumped back with her hands over her mouth.

"Ha!" Xavier gloated as he bent forward and moved out of the way of her knee.

The door slammed open as if propelled by some mysterious force, the signal for chaos to enter, followed by two bewildered footmen.

Thanking the ghost for the distraction, Josie underhanded the figurine in her hand toward Estelle's nose and then executed a tuck-and-roll forward to help Honoria.

Dev roared to a standing position, the slender arms and legs of the chair splintering under the pressure of his adrenaline-fed strength. He lunged for the pistol in Estelle's hand.

Estelle had ducked and the figurine had shattered against the fireplace. She followed Josie's unorthodox movements with the point of her pistol and fired.

Honoria fainted, quite elegantly, all things considered.

Estelle was knocked to the floor by the weight of Dev's body. He yanked the weapon from her hand.

Xavier, in his dance to escape Honoria's knee, had forgotten the heavy box on his back. When he bent forward, gravity caused the case to slide up his spine and smack him on the back of the head. He fell facedown on the floor.

Dev jumped to his feet.

Estelle cowered against the arm of the sofa. "Forgive me. Forgive me," she sobbed.

"Watch her," he directed the footmen. With Estelle no longer armed, Dev turned his attention to the other villain.

Mrs. Binns, who had only pretended to be unconscious, jumped up and sat on top of the large box that was strapped to Xavier's back, pinning him to the floor. She placed her foot on his head, displaying the very ankle he'd grabbed earlier. "Never touch a woman without her permission."

Only when he was assured both had been subdued did Dev allow himself to seek out Josie. She was seated on the sofa next to his mother, trying to rouse the older woman.

"You're hurt," Dev said to Josie, the blood on her head causing his stomach to clench.

Josie touched her hand to her head. "I must have reopened that cut when I smacked my head on the chair leg. Not as much room in here as I thought. Your mother..."

"You're not shot?"

She shook her head.

Relief flooded him as myriad horrible possibilities drained from his imagination. Estelle must have been rattled, because she was usually a better shot. Thank God it was over. He sank to the sofa.

"Here are my smelling salts," Mrs. Binns called. She tossed the vial to Dev. "Pardon my not getting up to help," she added in a tone that was more cheerful than apologetic.

Honoria roused but she was still a bit dazed. "Oh no. My poor new chair," she cried upon noticing the splintered remains.

Dev laughed, half in relief, half in amusement. "I told you it wasn't well made and wasn't worth the cost."

"But it was so pretty."

Suddenly Josie shot off the sofa.

She'd noticed Estelle crawling for the open secret panel. Once in the passages, she would get away. She might have made it, too. If she hadn't been wearing a long dress to slow her down. If she'd used both hands to move rather than using one to hold the case of emeralds to her breast. And if Josie hadn't seen her.

Josie knocked her to the floor, but Estelle didn't give up easily. They struggled. Josie got in a few satisfying blows, payback for the trip to the dungeon.

Estelle swung the case at Josie's head but missed when Josie ducked. The corner of the case hit the floor, the latch popped open, and the pieces scattered.

"Nooooo." Estelle stopped fighting to gather up the emerald jewelry.

The other woman's greed made it easier for Josie to plant a knee in her opponent's back. She twisted Estelle's arm up and behind her back and forced the other woman to stand.

Dev stood nearby.

"You could have given me a hand," Josie said, a bit breathless.

"And spoil your fun? Do you realize you were smiling? Most unladylike. Most improper."

"Tell her to let me go, Dev," Estelle wheedled. "For the sake of our childhood friendship. For the sake of our feelings for each other. I know you've always loved me."

Josie raised an eyebrow. She resisted the urge to yank upward on her hold to inflict pain.

"Only in your imagination," Dev said to Estelle. "I barely tolerated you, then and now, and only because Mother seemed to enjoy your presence." He signaled to the footmen.

The contrite servants scurried over and stood at attention. "Yes, milord."

"Take Countess LaFoyn to the meat cooler, lock her in, and guard the door until the constable arrives. If she gets away from you..." He paused as a subtle reminder that they had been easily distracted from their duty earlier. "If she gets away, every servant in this house will be dismissed." He said the last word loud enough for the crowd of curious servants gathered at the door to hear. The sound of the gunshot had apparently brought the entire household staff.

"Yes, milord."

As the footmen escorted her out, one holding each arm, the other servants parted like the Red Sea.

"Help me," Estelle pleaded to one after another. "Help me. I have money. Lots of money. Help me."

Each servant, from butler to bootboy, from housekeeper to scullery maid, looked away. She had made no friends with her incessant unreasonable demands and imperious attitude.

"Yoo-hoo," Mrs. Binns called. "Don't forget about me."

Xavier fought to raise himself and buck off the hefty chaperone. She held on to the straps and maintained her seat like any experienced horse-woman would. He plopped back flat on the floor.

"I can't breathe," Xavier complained. "Get that cow off my back."

Mrs. Binns tapped him on the back of the head with the toe of her substantial lace-up boot. "Mind your manners."

Dev folded his arms and cocked his head. "May I be of some assistance, Mrs. Binns?"

"And spoil her fun?" Josie asked.

Mrs. Binns swung her legs to the side and slid off her erstwhile mount. "I believe I could use a glass of something bracing."

Dev signaled to several footmen. Two he directed to lock Xavier in the root cellar. The third he requested to fetch a glass of sherry for Mrs. Binns.

"Claret," she corrected.

"Yes, ma'am."

Before the footmen led Xavier away, he made a disgusted noise and shucked off the large box that had led to his capture. The crate hit the floor corner first and the bottom of the case cracked open, spilling out packets of cash, rolled-up canvases, and several jewel cases.

No one seemed more surprised than Xavier. "A false bottom? I can't believe my very own wife held out on me. That bitch. I'll kill her."

"Apparently she wanted more than just the emeralds."

"That cache represents more than a year's worth of work."

"I shall endeavor to return the items to their rightful owners." Dev jerked his head and the footmen led Xavier away.

Josie touched Dev's arm. She nodded toward his mother. Honoria still sat on the sofa, still appeared dazed.

"Go on," Josie said. "I'm fine."

"I'll take Mother up to her rooms. Wait for me here," he said to Josie, taking her hand in his. "We need to talk about something important." His wonderful gray eyes darkened and promised so much more.

She glanced at the clock. Five thirty. "I should..."

"I will only be a few minutes," he added. "Please."

"I'll be here," Josie promised, her throat tight. But maybe it would be better if he didn't hurry back. If he took her in his arms, she would find leaving all the more difficult.

Dev turned away, responsibility warring with a gut feeling that he shouldn't leave Josie.

"I'll take you up to your rooms," he said to his mother in a gentle tone.

Honoria looked up at him as if startled. "I do not need to be treated like an invalid. I was only..." She glanced around the room. "Perhaps I could use a bit of a lie-down for my nerves."

He helped her to her feet and offered his arm. As they exited the room, the crowd of servants had varying expressions—pride, amusement, but mostly concern.

"May I be of service?" Mrs. Osman asked. She had her medical case under her arm as if she'd expected to treat a gunshot wound.

Honoria paused. "Thank you, no. I presume duties elsewhere are not being neglected." She did not raise her voice, and her tone was pleasant and conversational. Yet she cleared the entrance hall in a matter of moments. Everyone scurried back to work except the housekeeper and the butler, who curtseyed and bowed, and Dora, who was finally able to push her way into the library.

"Well done," Dev said as they mounted the stairs at a regal pace.

"Did you expect a little excitement to rob me of my wits?"

Dev had to smile at her description of the previous

events, and in relief she had apparently recovered. "You did seem a bit dazed."

"I was only deep in thought. I have a few questions and would rather speak to you in private."

When they entered her sitting room, the maid had tea set out and waited with a bland expression as if she had not been in the avid crowd of gawking onlookers outside the library just minutes earlier.

"Thank you," Honoria said to the maid and dismissed her. "Please have a seat," she said to Dev, indicating the chair next to her.

"Perhaps later. If you are settled, I should..."

"I know you are anxious to return downstairs."

"The constable should be arriving momentarily. I sent a note some time ago."

"He will wait. I cannot put my mind at ease until a few questions are answered. Please sit down, dear, and I will be as brief as possible."

Barely able to contain his impatience, Dev sat and accepted a cup of tea.

"The reason I was confused earlier, dazed as you called it, is because the facts do not add up."

"The séance..."

"Not about that. Josie explained everything quite well, and quite to my chagrin. I had been taken in by that...that..."

"You wanted to believe."

"Yes, well, that is a different issue we can discuss at a later time. How did you find the emeralds? Estelle had obviously been searching unbeknownst to us. Yet you produce the prize out of thin air. You have not studied the journals since you were a child. You do not like the passageways. For that matter, you never even believed the legend was true. Add to that the fact that you have never been interested in the séances, and yet you suddenly want to attend and then are party to the exposure of Madame X. These facts do not make sense. And why is Josie bruised and bandaged?"

"Whew! That's a lot to answer."

"Not to mention Mrs. Osman reported that Sadie has decided to join a convent even though she's not Catholic. And there were several axes found next to a large hole in the bedroom wall of one of the guest rooms. At the housekeeper's suggestion I kept those particular guests entertained downstairs until it could be repaired, but as that was Estelle and Xavier, I assume there is a connection. My mother's instinct tells me you know more than you've said."

"It is quite complicated."

"The abridged version will do. For now."

Dev explained, as briefly as possible, that Josie had piqued his interest in the séances and he'd agreed to help her debunk the charlatan. Of course, he left out the deals they had made and any resulting intimacies. Honoria was indignant at his brief description of Xavier's treatment of Josie when he discovered the traps and was appalled to learn that Estelle had directed him to consign Josie to the dungeon.

"The poor girl. That horrible place." Honoria shivered in sympathy. "However did she cope?"

"I'll let her tell you that herself. It's rather amusing the way she tells it."

"I sincerely doubt that."

"Maybe keeping a sense of humor about being stranded down there is one of the ways she is coping with the ordeal."

"I suppose so. How did she escape?"

Dev told her about Sadie hearing the screams, how he got involved, and the hole in the wall. He explained how Josie had figured everything out, how she had planned the denouement, and that he had only assisted her.

"But what about the emeralds? How did you..."

"Actually, Josie is responsible. Now before you say anything, I never claimed to have found them. I merely presented them to you. Perhaps Josie should be the one to explain how..."

"I cannot wait. Out with it."

Dev repeated the story Josie told him about falling through the wall and finding both the skeleton and the jewels.

"But how could she see what she was doing?" Honoria asked with a wrinkled brow. "It's black as pitch down there."

"I never thought of that," Dev said, sitting back. He had been so relieved to finally get her out, he hadn't asked any questions. Josie had not had a candle or lamp. How strange.

"Oh, I know," Honoria said, with a dismissive wave of her hand. "Obviously, there must have been cracks in the wooden panel door that allowed just enough light through."

"A logical conclusion," Dev said, relieved his mother had provided her own answer. Still, perhaps he should ask Josie about that. The thought served as a reminder that she waited for him downstairs. "If that is all..."

"One moment more. I have been meaning to speak to you about Josie. Your regard for her has not gone unnoticed."

"Now, Mother. I've told you before I do not need your matchmaking."

"Actually, you've said you did not want my assistance, that you hated, abhorred, detested my interference, and various other permutations of the same theme. You have never said you did not *need* my help."

"Do not make something out of nothing. A simple word..."

"I noticed your reaction when she admitted to not having a fortune or even any income."

"My reaction, if there was such a thing, was to what she left out. She did not deny being related to the Duke of Landemere."

"Hmmm. Interesting. I have been thinking...since Josie found the emeralds, they rightly belong to her."

"She insists they belong to the family, and thus to you as Lady Waite."

"Perhaps she would accept the emeralds as they were originally intended, as a bride gift." She gave him a knowing smile.

"You are a conniving, conspiring..."

"Observant, caring."

"And much too clever."

"Where do you think you got your brains? Your father was an admirer of that American character

Benjamin Franklin, who advised marrying an intelligent woman if one would have smart sons."

"Didn't he also advise nude air baths? Never
mind. I do not need to know that about my father."

"Are you going to ask her to marry you or not?"

Dev stood and kissed his mother on the forehead. "I am considering the possibility. If I decide
to ask her, you will be the second person to know
her answer."

"And just who will be the first?"

"Why, me, of course."

"Do you doubt she will accept?"

He scratched his jaw. "One of the things I enjoy
most about Josie's company is her unpredictability."

"Not to worry. I have seen the way she looks at
you." Honoria clapped her hands. "A wedding. And
grandbabies."

"Whoa, whoa. Do not get ahead of yourself.
First I must ask her and she must accept."

"Then what are you doing here? Go on. Go."

Dev laughed and shook his head as he left. His
mother had solidified the thoughts that had been
hovering on the edge of his consciousness since the
moment he'd met Josie. But she was unconven-
tional, stubborn, argumentative. Also curious,
smart, and inventive. Life would never be dull with
Josie at his side. And in his bed.

Now he needed to convince her.

Josie bent to pick up the emerald jewelry and put
everything back in the case. "An earring is missing."

"Something rolled under that...that piece of furniture," Mrs. Binns said, waving to a large unit with

doors and shelves with her near-empty glass.

Josie got down on her hands and knees. "I think I see it." But the only way she could reach it was to lie on her back and scoot her left shoulder half underneath the cabinet.

"When one has servants, one does not crawl around the floor retrieving lost emeralds."

She touched it with her fingertips but could not quite get a hold of it. "Arrrgh." She stretched and strained. "Got it."

Dora rushed to her side. "Oh, miss. They said you'd been shot." The maid fell to her knees and wrung her handkerchief between her hands.

"I'm..." Josie attempted to sit, but Dora's weight on the fabric of her dress prevented any movement. "Oops."

"Are you in pain? Just lie still."

"I'm not..."

"You are so brave." Dora dabbed at her eyes.

"But I'm not..."

"Yes, you are, and don't you worry. Sadie promised to learn her rosary so she can keep vigil." Dora spoke really fast as if she thought Josie would expire on the spot.

"I am not..."

"And Cook will make her special salmon tarts for your funeral luncheon."

With a sigh, Josie gave up trying to convince the maid. "Dora, will you do something for me?"

"Oh, yes, miss." She sniffed. "Your dying wish..."

"Hardly that. Would you move off my dress so I can sit up?"

Dora quickly scooted back. "Should you be moving?"

Josie scrambled to her feet. "I'm fine. Not shot. Not dying. See, no blood. Well, that's just a bit from a cut on my head. Not fatal."

"You're not dying? But I heard the gunshot myself."

"Missed me completely."

"I'm going to strangle that Sadie."

"But don't tell Cook," Mrs. Binns called from the corner. "What?" she responded to Josie's glare. "She's making salmon tarts." Her words were starting to slur, and the last came out sounding more like *shaman moosh tarsh*.

Josie could only roll her eyes. Turning her attention back to the maid, she noticed Deverell standing just inside the door. He looked dreadful, weak and thin.

"Dora, I'd like to thank you for all your help."

"Ah, sure."

Josie wanted to talk to Deverell, and she needed an excuse to get rid of Dora. "I'd like to take a walk outside. Would you please fetch my bonnet and shawl?"

"Don't you want to change your clothes?"

"No. After all the excitement, I need the fresh air first."

The maid shook her head as if to say there was no way to understand such an odd request, but she curtseyed and left the room.

"Time to go," Deverell said.

"It's only five forty-five."

"Amazing, isn't it?" Mrs. Binns said. "So much has happened, it feels as if it should be suppertime at least. Oh, yoo-hoo." She wiggled her fingers in Deverell's direction.

He moved a few steps left, and Mrs. Binns's gaze followed him. He moved right; she watched. "I think she can see me," he whispered. "Why can she see me?"

"Now you sound like the scientist. She's always seemed aware of your presence, but the enhanced ability is probably due to a mix of adrenaline and whiskey. I doubt she'll remember any of this."

Deverell waved back. "Feels very strange. Fortunately, it won't be a problem for long. Come now. I have the carriage waiting. We have to go."

Josie realized she still held the earring in her hand, and placed it in the case, closing the lid with a soft click. She knew that once they made the jump forward in time, she wouldn't ever see him again. "We did it, didn't we? Changed history?"

"I won't know for sure until we return, but yes, I think we did. You did. You changed history."

"How does your heart feel?"

He knew what she meant. Unconsciously, he rubbed his chest. He would not burden her with the knowledge that a broken heart caused worse pain than a bullet. She did not deserve to know the agony Dev would feel, the agony he felt at the thought of never seeing her again. "No sign of a duel," he said.

"Good," she said with a relieved smile.

"Time to go. My energy is flagging rapidly."

"Five minutes more," Josie said. "I'd like to say good-bye to Mrs. Binns."

"Yoo-hoo, Lord Waite. I've been wanting to talk to you," Mrs. Binns said. "My, but you look ghostly." She burped. "I mean ghastly."

"I will wait outside for you," he said. "Don't be overlong."

Josie promised and he disappeared.

"Where did he go?" Mrs. Binns asked. "Was it something I said?"

"Not at all. I'm sure when Lord Waite returns he'll act as if nothing happened."

"I did not mean to insult him, you know. But he did..."

"I know." Josie seated herself in a nearby chair. "I wanted to thank you for all your help and guidance. Without you..."

"Don't thank me yet, my dear. I have not completed my job, but it won't be long now." After several tries, she laid her finger aside her nose. "I can smell a marriage proposal, I can. Once you are officially engaged to Lord Waite, then you can thank me."

"I'm sorry. I have to go home now, but I wanted..."

"Home?" Mrs. Binns reared back. "This will be your home. Waite will come up to snuff and soon. I've seen the way he looks at you."

Josie shook her head. "I don't belong here." She stood up. "Please remember what I said, and tell Lord Waite..." What could she say to him? What message could Mrs. Binns pass? "Tell him not to look for me. Tell him I wish him laughter, and music, and dancing. I wish him love."

Josie ran from the room before her tears could fall. She crossed the entrance hall and opened the door.

"Josie? Where are you going?"

She turned for a last look at Dev, his dear brow furrowed with confusion. Her vision blurred.

"Quickly, Josie," Deverell called. "We must go. Now."

She stepped on the threshold.

"Wait," Dev said. Something in her expression told him she was leaving forever, and desperation squeezed his heart. He bounded down the long stairway. "I love you," he shouted. "Wait for me."

"If you do not come now," Deverell said, "I can't guarantee you will get back to the future where you belong."

Josie looked from one to the other. She hesitated. Past and present and future seem to swirl together, making her dizzy.

How could she choose between the man who was and the ghost who is? Or was that the man who is and the ghost who will be? How could she choose between a man and himself?

Twenty-one

"WHERE HAVE YOU BEEN ALL DAY?" Josie asked Deverell as she joined him at the top of the grand stairway.

"Since I spent the day in the tower room reading, as I am *supposed* to be doing, I believe it more apropos to ask where *you* have been."

Josie smiled inwardly at the slight fretfulness of his tone because she knew the cause. The first day of Open House for Charity Week was always difficult for him. "I joined some of the tour groups. The docents are Amelia's students, and they always manage to surprise me with some fact or other they've dug up. Did you know the pair of Sheraton chairs in the parlor are worth over fifteen hundred pounds?"

"Humph. The very idea of people traipsing through our home, gawking at our belongings for a few shillings..."

"Hardly that. Twenty-five pounds a head is nothing to sneeze at. Of course, they do get a lovely tea and our traditional salmon tarts served in the garden." Josie stepped closer, and he automatically opened his arms and wrapped them around her. She hooked her hands behind his waist and leaned back to see his face. "It *is* for charity."

He raised his gaze to the ceiling as if appealing for patience. An act, and she knew it. He was just as interested in giving back as she was.

"Which cause is it this time?" he asked. "Gorillas? Orphans? One-eyed beggars named James?"

She ignored his sarcasm. "Literacy."

"Ah. Speaking of reading..."

"Were we?" She gave him a wide-eyed look.

"We were speaking of my assigned task...you do remember the *act as guardians of the castle until such time as we read every book* deal?"

"Of course I do, but we both know it's impossible."

"Perhaps that is the point. If the task were easy, guardians would change every generation, and what good would that do?"

"What if the assigned task is only a ruse to force a long-term commitment? Eh? Have you thought of that?" she asked.

"Believe me, over the years I have thought of every possibility and permutation."

"And?"

Deverell kissed her on the forehead before releasing his embrace. "Guardianship is not about atonement for sins; it's about family, and ensuring that there is always someone older and, it is to be hoped, wiser available to ask for advice. I have come to the conclusion it's a voluntary choice."

"And the alternative is..."

"Ahh, yes—moving on. That is why it is referred to as the great unknown."

"Not the black void?" Josie shuddered.

"I think not. Perhaps…"

"Sshh! Someone's coming. It's one of the tour groups."

"It's not as if they can hear. I believe you're avoiding the issue of moving on."

"I simply want to listen to his spiel."

"Eavesdroppers never hear good of themselves," he warned her.

"Gather round, everyone. We are now in the grand entrance," said the docent, whose nametag identified him as Jon Higdon. He stood with his back to the door. "On my left is the receiving parlor. We will be going through there in a moment. To my right is the library. You'll be able to take a quick peek inside before we move on. Since today is Thursday, Lord and Lady Waite-Burrows will shortly be having their tea in the library."

"I thought the swells always took tea in their fancy drawing rooms," a tourist in plaid shorts said, elbowing his friend.

"Thank you, sir, that's right on cue," Jon said, handling the heckler with ease. "The parlor or drawing room is the usual location, and outdoors is also popular in good weather. In this case…mind you, I'm not one to spread gossip, but"——he lowered his voice to a stage whisper and looked from right to left in a conspiratorial manner——"I'm sure you won't tell anyone else."

"That boy has had theatrical training," Deverell said.

"Every Thursday, Lord and Lady Waite-Burrows entertain the ghosts of Waite Castle, and *she* says the ghost of Lord Waite prefers *his* tea in the library."

"Ghosts? You mean them?" a young female tourist squeaked and pointed to the top of the grand stairway.

Apparently everyone assumed the child pointed to the life-sized portrait on the landing. "Yes," the docent said. "In this painting, Deverell Thornton is posed casually—despite his formal evening clothes—one elbow on the mantel, a white rose dangling from his long, elegant fingers. In the language of flowers, the white rose symbolizes pure love."

"I always thought that rose was a mistake," Deverell said. "A brandy would have been better, or at least a red rose..."

"Sshh."

The docent continued, "His snowy neckwear is tied in an elaborate knot as if he were about to leave for a dinner engagement, or perhaps the opera. His gray eyes seem to hold merriment and anticipation."

"Impatience and aggravation," Deverell said. "Sitting for a portrait was not my idea of..."

"Sshh."

"His beautiful wife is standing by his side, her dress a perfect match to the fabulous emerald jewelry, a family heirloom rumored to be part of a pirate's booty. The jewels sparkle only a bit more than her eyes, which the artist captured in such a way that they seem to reflect a secret amusement. The artist went on to paint several members of the royal family and seemed destined for greatness, until he supposedly set sail for America and was never heard from again, presumably lost at sea."

"That's it?" Josie said. "That's all he has to say about me? What about the school for girls I founded, my campaign for women's suffrage, the orphanage...?"

"Sshh," Deverell said with a smile.

Josie clamped her lips together in a tight line.

"The ninth Lord Waite and Lady Josephine, as famous for their philanthropy as for their lavish entertainments, died peacefully after thirty-nine years of blissful marriage," the docent said. "There are those who claim to have seen their ghosts walking in the gardens or dancing in the gallery."

"Really?" the young girl whispered, her tone revealing rapt attention. "Will they come to our tea in the garden?"

"Well..." Jon leaned down with his hands on his knees. "They just..."

"Don't fill her head with nonsense," the girl's mother interrupted, stroking her daughter's hair as if to wipe out any imaginative thoughts. "She's at an impressionable age," the woman explained to the crowd.

"But they're right up..."

"There's no such thing as ghosts," the woman said to the child in a stern voice. "And even if there were such a thing, everyone knows ghosts do not take tea."

The docent stood and cleared his throat. "We'll be going into the parlor now." He motioned to his group to move. "Please stay together."

"That girl could see us," Josie said, pulling away from Deverell and standing up straight. Even as she spoke, the child looked back over her shoulder and waved. Josie smiled and wiggled her fingers in return. "How odd. I'm not materialized and neither are you," she said to Deverell. "Why do you think...?"

"Can't you feel the rise in energy?"

Josie cocked her head to the side almost as if she was listening. "No," she said after a minute. "But you're always more sensitive to the fluctuations than I am. What does it mean?"

"I think we will soon have the chance to recruit our replacements. That is why I brought up..."

Josie gasped. "Amelia? Or Charles?"

"You know I can't foretell the future, but from the energy shift, I believe it will be both of them together. Maybe an accident."

"Oh, dear. How soon?"

"Some time yet. But we should make plans, think about asking them..."

"Poor Emma will be devastated. She's so young to assume the responsibilities of the title, and the property. She'll need our help."

"Amelia and Charles would make wonderful guardians."

"Yes, of course they would. But they'll need time to adjust. Death can be quite traumatic, you know."

"They will have each other, just as we did."

"Helpful, but they'll still need to learn what a ghost can and can't do. They won't even know how to materialize. How much information can we pass along? Albert told us practically nothing. What if they overextend and wind up in the void for forty years like we did? Who will help poor Emma then?" Josie shook her head. "No, no. Too chancy. I think we should stay."

"I agree."

"I know you want to...what did you say?"

"I happen to agree with you."

Josie jumped into his arms and placed a searing kiss on his lips.

"What is that for?" he asked without releasing her from his embrace.

"I just love it when you agree with me."

He nuzzled her neck. "One can only wonder why I don't do so more often."

"Because complete agreement would be boring."

Deverell chuckled. "I can honestly say boredom is one thing I haven't suffered from the day I met you."

"I wish I could remember when I first saw you." Josie shook her head and sighed. "Lost with all the memories of my childhood."

"I thought perhaps your memories might return now that we're approaching the date you came from."

Josie looked at him in surprise. "I've read everything I wrote in the journal before I completely lost those memories, but I never thought you believed any of it. Sometimes it was hard for me to believe my own handwriting."

"I admit it was difficult at first, but since you lost those memories within a month of our meeting, the point became moot. Eventually, the evidence made it impossible not to believe. Either you came from this time or you saw accurately into the future."

"Even if I never get those memories back, I'm glad to know you believed me."

"You trusted me with that knowledge. That meant a lot to me."

Josie sniffled and Deverell gave her his handkerchief. She never managed to have one of her own.

She dabbed at her eyes. "How did we get on this subject?"

"I don't know. I was quite content with this..." He kissed her forehead. "And this..." He kissed her eyelids and cheek. "This."

She turned her head to give him better access to the sensitive spot beneath her ear.

He kissed his way down her throat and slid her sleeves off her shoulders, baring the cleavage caused by her corset.

"Mmm," she said. "I hope no one else can see us."

"Josie-love, I have an idea what we can do to stay out of the way of the tourists."

"Oh?" she asked as if she didn't know what he had on his mind.

She ran her fingers through his hair and then lifted his head so she could look him in the eye. "We're expected for tea in less than an hour," she said with a rueful smile.

He swept her off her feet and carried her down the hall with long strides. "We might be fashionably late."

She threw her arms around his neck. Between kisses along his jaw, she said, "You may have mellowed over the years, my love, but you haven't completely reformed. You're still a rake."

She wouldn't have it any other way.

About the Author

Laurie Brown writes because she loves to, because she needs to in order to stay sane, and because it gets her out of housework. By day a mild-mannered accountant, she spends her evenings and weekends writing, following her alpha-heroes and spunky heroines on their madcap adventures to a happy ending. She has taught writing classes at the college level and has presented seminars at conferences all over the country, including the Romance Writers of America National Conference. The author of three published novels, Laurie Brown was twice a Golden Heart finalist and has received the Service Award from the Chicago-North Chapter of RWA. She lives in Glendale Heights, Illinois.